John F Plimmer's

Bloody Retribution

The Richard Rayner Victorian Detective's Casebook series

"Power does not pardon, power punishes."
Amit Kalantri, 'Wealth of Words'

Chapter One

It was that time of year when a seasonal quietness, almost solemn ambience, descended on the busy streets of London, accompanied by falling leaves boasting their captivating reds, golds, and browns that dominated both towns and villages throughout the country. The evenings were drawing in as the temperature began to fall, and the days economised with their daylight working hours in preparation for the oncoming of winter. Each Autumn brought an air of romanticism and those privileged country gentlemen, having not tasted the hard labour experienced in the fields, lanes and hedgerows, often accompanied their wives and lady friends to the cities to shop, or just to wander around, indulging themselves on the bright lights and perpetual urban sounds of excitement. And yet, their counterparts residing in the densely populated municipalities, preferred to frequent the quieter and rustic provinces for rest and solitude, away from that which their fellow country peers craved.

Betty Tinkler and Arnold Grubb had been in love since their childhood days, both young people having been raised in the same village and taught by the same local schoolmaster. It was inevitable they would one day marry and in the Autumn of 1894, following their wedding ceremony, the newlyweds had decided to begin their life together by spending their honeymoon week exploring the adventurous magnetism of London, seeking out bargains and sharing their dreams for the future.

On their first night in the country's capital, Mr. and Mrs. Grubb found the Autumnal air enticing, adding to the enamoured feelings they had for each other. The bride could not conceal her infectious exhilaration and boldly suggested they should take a stroll together along the nearby River Thames, sharing the enthralling environment in which they were now immersed.

Before leaving their lodging house in Lambeth, Betty made specific mention of having an urge to see the newly erected, magnificent Tower Bridge she had read so much about. So, off they went, both mesmerised by a large silvery moon, feeling the adventurous exhilaration, as they made their way towards where their landlady had described the location of the impressive structure.

Arm in arm, the two love birds slowly continued walking, intoxicated by each other's company and enjoying the peaceful solitude surrounding them. Arnold looked down into the sparkling eyes of his bride and feeling a need to imbue his personal feelings on what already existed between them, quietly recited a poem he remembered from their schooldays.

"By thy pale beams I solitary rove, to thee my tender grief confide; serenely sweet you gild the silent grove, my friend, my goddess, and my guide." He spoke quietly and with deliberation, his country accent embellishing the chosen prose.

"That is so beautiful Arnie," she responded, smiling as she whispered, "But are you saying those words to me, or that glorious moon?"

"To you silly, although the original words were intended for the moon."

"I had no idea you were so gifted; so poetically talented."

"I'm not, Mrs. Grubb, it is part of a poem written by Lady Mary Montagu called, 'A Hymn to the Moon'."

"How romantic, and at least you remembered the words, which is more than I could have done. Look there it is." Betty stopped and pointed towards the dark outline of the distant structure, standing proud and linking one side of the river to the other, quickly explaining that she had heard it was the largest and most sophisticated bridge ever built, "In the whole world."

"Do you think we will be able to cross it, Arnie?" his young wife asked.

"I don't see why not, if we have time, but it's getting late now Betty."

"Will we be able to see the bridge rise up into the sky to allow the ships to pass beneath, do you think?"

Her husband chuckled and then suggested that perhaps in the daylight, when one of the big ships comes up the Thames and needs to pass beneath London's most recent phenomenon of Victorian architecture.

As the couple drew nearer to what had been commonly referred to as, 'the seesaw bridge,' a stiff breeze suddenly and unexpectedly came off the water, chilling both visitors to the capital.

Arnold suggested they should turn back, worried that his wife of just a few hours might catch a chill in the evening air, but Betty insisted they continued, enjoying the rose-tinted nostalgia of their night excursion, and not being prepared to wait until the morning to look more closely at the colossal structure.

As they continued, they passed a patrolling policeman, looking extremely dignified and authoritative in his helmet and cape, who tipped his helmet and wished the couple a good night. The constable had only walked a few yards past the visiting newly-weds, when suddenly and totally unexpectedly, he heard a scream coming from the young woman.

Royston Thomas had only been a member of the Metropolitan Police for a few weeks, and this was the first night duty he was required to work on his own. Without hesitation, he ran back to where Arnold and Betty Grubb were standing, with the husband placing his arm tightly around his wife and both looking up towards Tower Bridge.

"What on earth has happened?" he enquired, shining his bullseye lantern on the backs of their heads. And then, having had no response, he followed their eyeline and could see hanging from the lower level of the bridge and silhouetted against the moonlit night sky, a body on the end of a rope, swinging to and fro, hanging just above the water.

Sergeant Henry Bustle had only recently lost his dear wife, Nellie, to a dreaded outbreak of Typhus. Still feeling mournful he was trying hard to adapt to the task of raising his four young children alone. The assistance given by his mother-in-law was a God send and she would often remain overnight, to help with the chores and supervise the youngsters. It was fortuitous she was present when the detective was awakened at midnight by a uniformed Sergeant telling him his presence was required at Tower Bridge, where he was to meet Chief Inspector Rayner.

It mattered not that Bustle hadn't had a wink of sleep, in fact, prolonged respite had avoided him since Nellie's misfortune and by the time he arrived at his destination, Richard Rayner was already there, dressed in his usual immaculate attire, resembling a man who had just left an Aldermen's Annual Dinner.

The Sergeant first noticed his senior detective standing on the bridge crossing, talking to the pathologist, Doctor Albert Critchley. The vague outline of a body could be seen lying prostate on the ground close by; a fully clothed young man with a noose tied around his neck.

"If it was suicide Richard the victim somehow managed to subject himself to a severe blow to the back of the head before jumping off the bridge," the Sergeant overheard the physician remark.

Richard Rayner was a man who never squandered his words and just nodded, seemingly concentrating on that section of railing used to secure the rope used to facilitate the dead man's destiny. When he saw the arrival of his closest friend and confidante, the Chief Inspector explained the circumstances in which the deceased had been found.

"Henry, a young man and woman discovered the corpse, hanging from just over there, and have been taken to Scotland Yard by Constable Thomas who was apparently with them at the time. I need to speak with all three of them, so, I require you to accompany the body to the mortuary with Doctor Critchley."

"Do we know who the victim is sir?"

"No, not as yet, there's nothing in his clothing to identify him, but I've arranged for the bridge to remain closed until we have conducted a proper search once it gets light, but it would appear we have another murder on our hands."

Bustle nodded, accepting the need to keep the ligature around the deceased man's neck in place and recalling his Chief Inspector's preference to leave knots undisturbed. Rayner had always preached that the way a strangler tied their knots could disclose characteristics of the person who had tied them, if scrutinised with care and optimism.

The senior detective left shortly afterwards, seemingly deep in thought, as he always appeared when confronted with an enigma and the Sergeant stood by the pathologist's side, watching the man he admired so much, return to his official carriage.

Richard Rayner was a tall, slim, handsome man, now in his mid-thirties and always immaculately dressed, so much so, he was widely known by colleagues as 'the Dandy of Scotland Yard.' Having been educated at Oxford, he remained to lecture on his subject, following his graduation with a degree in Mathematics.

However, he quickly became restive, finding his position to be tedious and unable to assuage the frustration he was experiencing, desperate for a more varied and adventurous life. Hence the reason he had grasped a more capricious future by joining the Metropolitan Police.

Richard Rayner's analytical way of thinking was quickly recognised by the senior officers in the force, including the unorthodox manner in which he was capable of profiling various criminal minds, resulting in those talents soon endearing him to the Detective Branch at Scotland Yard. Success followed success, many attributed to the most complex and serious crimes on record, guaranteeing a reputation that soon propelled him up the promotion ladder.

The man who had often become the toast of London, never forgot his roots and always remained appreciative of his parents' willingness to ensure their son remained financially independent. After marrying his young wife, Clarice, a researcher at Kings College, the couple took up residence in Richmond, where he could afford to employ domestic staff. The only real surprise in Richard Rayner's life thus far, was the unexpected discovery that he had a son, Matthew, born to a former lover he had known when at university and who now lived with the Rayners, the boy's mother having been brutally killed just prior to the Chief Inspector finding out about the young lad's existence. Although Richard and Clarice did have a child of their own, a young daughter, Rose, who tragically succumbed to cholera, their traumatic experience was eased by the coming of young Matthew, who quickly became the light of both their lives.

In contrast to his Chief Inspector's privileged upbringing, Henry Bustle had been raised in a diametrically opposite environment, in which riots and street fighting were common features of daily life in the complex and impoverished backstreets of Whitechapel. His features gave testimony to an earlier existence where physical confrontations were as common as eating scraps off a neighbour's table. Facial disfigurements consisting of broken noses, missing teeth and scars, all evidenced a harsh upbringing and Bustle boasted one noticeable past injury that ran down the side of his face, earning the respect of other pugilists and villainous characters who survived by using their fists in the many courtyards, alleyways and wasteland of the darker side of London's poorest communities. And yet, even though the Sergeant's background had been one of violence, he had never been partial to watching a human body being cut to pieces, ensuring he stood well back from the slab upon which the pathologist conducted the post-mortem. But, before actually applying the knife to the corpse, Albert Critchley confirmed that the victim had sustained a heavy blow to the back of the head, resulting in a depressed fracture to the skull that had driven a shard of bone into the brain.

"I have little doubt Sergeant, such was the cause of death, but come closer," Doctor Critchley insisted.

Tentatively, Rayner's right-hand man stepped a few steps nearer to the slab, feeling a little unglued and exposed, before the pathologist indicated several bruises and other blemishes around the rib area of the upper body.

"It looks as though he's been in some kind of fight before being topped then, doctor," Bustle suggested.

"Of that Sergeant, I have little doubt, but what is important and for Richard Rayner to know, is that this man was dead before being hanged from Tower Bridge."

Doing his best to think as his Chief Inspector would have done in the circumstances, Bustle then asked if Albert Critchley had any idea of the kind of weapon that might have caused the injury to the back of the victim's head.

"A rounded hammer or similar object," came the reply.

The Sergeant then made good use of his notebook and left to return to Scotland Yard to meet up with Rayner and share what information he had just gleaned.

By the time the Chief Inspector had spoken at some length to all three witnesses, Constable Thomas, Betty and Arnold Grubb, he was satisfied that he had extracted all the information he could, which was very little in the context of identifying the culprit. No one else had been seen on or near to the bridge from which the murdered victim had been dropped at the end of a rope, and Royston Thomas and the two newlyweds were allowed to leave, to get some much-needed rest.

For as long as Richard Rayner had worked with him, Chief Superintendent Frederick Morgan, the Head of the Detective Branch and whose office was on the first floor of Scotland Yard, next to Rayner's, was always the first to arrive at work every morning. However, on this very morning the Welsh born and bred, former Major in the Coldstream Guards, was surprised to find his senior detective already sitting at his desk.

After making some caustic comment about Richard Rayner's early morning presence, he was given a condensed account of what had taken place during the previous night.

"Murdered, you say Rayner, well now my old mucker, the circumstances seem a little strange, topping the man by hanging him. Any idea why he was bumped off?"

"No sir, not yet, but I suspect he was killed before being thrown off the bridge."

It was then that Henry Bustle's appearance interrupted the senior detectives' conversation, having returned from the mortuary and the Sergeant wasted little time in relaying all that the pathologist had discovered during the post-mortem, including confirmation of the Chief Inspector's assumption that they were dealing with a murder and not suicide.

"Bleedin' hell, the thing was only opened a couple of months ago," Morgan pointed out, referring to Tower Bridge, "And now I suppose we'll have every bleedin' nutter in London jumping off, just to make a name for themselves. The newspapers are going to have a field day with this one."

"We need to speak with whoever is now in charge of the bridge," Rayner suggested, "I am somewhat dubious as to why a man should be taken up there already dead, and then thrown off like a rag doll. There must be some connection between the victim and the structure."

"Perhaps it was meant to attract as much publicity as possible," Morgan offered.

"Perhaps, but it might just well be that our victim was employed in some capacity in the construction of the bridge."

"In that case, talk to an old mucker of mine, Dickie Roberts, he's the Assistant Bridge Master and has an office there. He might be a good starting point."

Rayner nodded, appreciating Morgan's suggestion and within a few minutes both he and Henry Bustle were travelling back towards the scene of London's latest murder.

Captain Roberts was a robustly built Welsh gentleman with thick side whiskers that compensated for the loss of hair on top of his head, and after the initial introductions, Richard Rayner appraised him of the Investigation he was conducting and of his suspicion that the victim might have been employed at the time the bridge was constructed.

Of course, Frederick Morgan's friend was already aware of the tragedy that had befallen the structure for which he oversaw and asked how he and his staff could be of assistance.

"We need to identify the deceased sir, and I was wondering if it would be convenient for you to accompany us to St. Mary's Hospital to see if he is known to you."

"I shall do better than that, Mr. Rayner. If your man was involved in the bridge construction, Sidney Fellows was our construction supervisor throughout the building processes and was responsible for hiring and firing the labour. I'm sure that if anyone knew him, Sid would have, so if you wish I can get a message to him to also attend."

"I am obliged sir, but perhaps we could arrange that, provided the victim isn't known to you personally." Rayner suspected the gentleman was an autocrat, but this was his Inquiry and he had every intention of managing it in accordance with his own preferences.

When the two detectives eventually arrived at the mortuary with the Assistant Bridge Master, they found Doctor Critchley to be as accommodating as he always was, asking them to wait outside while he prepared the body for viewing. That small task didn't take long and when the pathologist pulled back the top of the shroud, revealing the victim's face, Richard Roberts stood gazing down at the lifeless features.

"There will be no need to send for Sidney Fellows, Chief Inspector," he declared, "This is Mr. Raymond Carter, one of Mr. Fellows construction engineers."

"You are quite certain of that, sir."

"Oh yes, Carter was with us from the very start of building the bridge and remained in his position for the whole of the eight years it took to construct."

"Are you aware of his domestic circumstances?" the senior detective enquired.

"I believe he was married, but that's all I am aware of."

"Have you an address for him?"

"Sorry, no, but I suspect Sidney Fellows will be able to help you with that."

"Then might I suggest you send that message to arrange for Mr. Fellows to see me at Scotland Yard." At least they no longer had an unidentified victim and that in itself would be of great assistance to the Investigation.

When Richard Rayner arrived back at the police headquarters building, he had every intention of waiting for Mr. Sidney Fellows to meet him there, preferring to speak with the man himself. However, there was another problem to deal with, in the form of Sergeant Jack Robinson, a young thinly built man with a pale face and the beginnings of a goatee beard on his pointed chin. While Bustle was a man of the streets who pursued his detective's career by maintaining contacts throughout the various backstreets of London, the district of Whitechapel in particular, Robinson's strengths lay in his abilities to analyse and approach problems with a much wider perspective. Richard Rayner felt blessed to have both individuals on his team, with totally different approaches to their work and after hanging his hat and coat on a peg near to the door, enquired with the younger Sergeant whether he had had any joy with his enquiries into a number of factory burglaries where large amounts of copper had been stolen.

"I'm afraid not sir," the younger detective confessed, "Except to confirm there have now been almost twenty break-ins and we have been checking with the usual scrap metal dealers but with little joy."

Rayner turned to Henry Bustle and suggested he should make some enquiries with his usual contacts in Whitechapel, to assist Jack Robinson.

"It seems obvious to me that these people must have a regular outlet for the copper they are stealing and with the amount they have taken so far, I would have thought it wouldn't be too difficult Henry, to get hold of somebody who knows something about it."

Bustle nodded and suggested he would get on to it immediately, "Provided you won't require me for a bit on the Tower Bridge murder sir."

Before Rayner could answer, there was a knock on his door and the Desk Sergeant from downstairs appeared.

"Sorry to interrupt, sir," he said, "But there's been a kidnapping of a girl on the Strand, earlier this morning."

"If it doesn't rain, it pours," Henry Bustle quipped.

"Jack, go and see what has happened and let me know," Rayner instructed the younger Sergeant.

"I think you might want to look into this yourself sir," the Desk Sergeant suggested, "The girl in question is Chief Superintendent Morgan's daughter."

Chapter Two

Twenty years previously, Frederick Morgan had been a dashing young officer in the Guards Regiment, when he first met Dorothy Roland and fell in love with the West Indian beauty. At the time their daughter was born, the Welshman with the fiery red hair and dominant character, had moved on from the association, unaware that his lover had become pregnant. Estelle's birth remained a confidence that was never shared until the Head of the Detective Branch at Scotland Yard received a letter written from Dorothy, desperately requesting his help and begging him to travel to Liverpool, where she would meet him.

It was a strange and sensitive reunion, Morgan now being a happily married man and his former mistress having remained a single woman. When he learned for the first time he had a daughter, and that the girl had gone missing from home, his world instantly changed.

Having accepted the task of finding the girl, he succeeded but with some difficulty and managed to return Estelle to her mother, at the same time helping to build bridges between the two females, and of course, the girl finally learned who her father was. Following that personal and emotional assignment, the Chief Superintendent returned to London and shared his news with his wife, Sally-Anne, but instead of receiving the kind of understanding he had been hoping for, the enraged circus owner threw him out of the family home.

It was Clarice Rayner who persuaded Sally-Anne Morgan to accompany her to Liverpool and meet Dorothy Roland and her daughter in person, and when the two travelling women finally met the impecunious mother and daughter and saw the squalid conditions in which they were living, Morgan's wife instantly took pity. Realising that Estelle was in fact, her only relative, if only by marriage, she purchased a far more suitable accommodation for them away from the densely populated centre of Liverpool and all was forgiven, as far as her detective husband was concerned.

Estelle Roland had grown into an attractive girl who, her mother had raised in a disciplined and religious environment, resulting in acquired scruples and ambition. To those who knew her, she was a highly intelligent girl, having qualified at a teaching college in Liverpool, and was fully committed to her recent position at the Ragged School in the Strand. Naturally, she had come to London to stay with her father, only after obtaining her mother's consent and blessing, and after being warmly and lovingly welcomed by Frederick and Sally-Anne Morgan, enjoyed the benefits and respect afforded by her work colleagues. In the short time the girl had been living with the Morgans, preferring to retain her real mother's surname of

Roland, she had become a popular young lady, but now, the news of her recent predicament came as a shock to all that knew her.

According to several witnesses, at nine o'clock that morning, Estelle had been seen arriving at the front gates of the school where she worked and as she was about to enter, was grabbed by two men wearing 'grubby' masks, who forced her into a waiting non-descript carriage that then galloped off, heading for Temple Bar and Fleet Street.

After sharing what little knowledge of the incident he had gleaned, Sergeant Claude Davey stood in the detectives' general office on the ground floor of Scotland Yard, facing Richard Rayner, who appeared to be quite moved and obviously concerned by what he had just been told.

"Has Mr. Morgan been informed about this yet, Claude?" the senior detective finally asked.

"No sir, I thought it best to tell you first."

"Yes, yes you were right to do so. Gather every detective on duty and I shall join you shortly."

Rayner returned to the first floor and as he walked down the corridor towards Frederick Morgan's office, the Chief Inspector wasn't looking forward to the next few minutes, anticipating something similar to a volcanic eruption, once he had told the senior officer of what had taken place. Reluctantly, he entered the smoke-filled office and found the Chief Superintendent sitting at his desk, grasping his lit pipe that resembled a miniature bonfire.

"Don't tell me you've already got hold of the jasper responsible for topping that bloke on Tower Bridge, Rayner," the Chief Superintendent jocularly quipped, shifting uneasily in his chair and grimacing somewhat.

"No sir, there's been an incident." The Chief Inspector then quietly repeated all that he'd been told by Claude Davey, suspecting that he had just torched the fuse to a keg of dynamite.

But there was no explosion and at first, Morgan sat in silence, placing his pipe down on the desktop. At least it allowed the smoke to partially clear and Richard Rayner could see the senior officer's face had been transformed into a paler version.

"I'm going across to the school to obtain some accounts from witnesses, as to what they actually saw, and we have already begun a search of the immediate area so try not to worry, I'm confident we shall soon have her back." The Chief Inspector realised his words were hollow and patronising, but there was nothing more sympathetic he could think of at the time.

Still, an uncontrolled outburst and display of verbal blasphemy remained absent, and Richard Rayner wondered for a moment if Morgan had gone deaf. Then the Welshman whispered, looking like a man in shock, "Why Estelle? I mean, for what purpose? If they lay one finger on my girl, Richard, I shall save the hangman the trouble."

Those last few words sounded more like the old Frederick Morgan, and Rayner could see the man's blood rising, feeling nothing but compassion towards him.

However, he needed to avoid any emotional stirrings and remain objective, if they were to be successful in tracking down the kidnappers and recovering the girl.

"I'll come with you," Morgan then declared, rising from his chair and tapping the ashes from his briar into a litter bin. It was a suggestion Rayner had been anticipating but preferred that the Chief Superintendent agreed to return home and stay well clear of the subsequent Investigation, although knowing Frederick Morgan as he did, he also knew it would be futile at that moment to argue with him.

Rayner led the way, and the two men visited the ground floor office where the assembled detectives were waiting to be addressed. Soon afterwards, both senior detectives were leaving Scotland Yard in an official carriage.

After arriving outside the Ragged School, Richard Rayner's sympathy towards Frederick Morgan increased, when seeing the senior man standing alone with glazed eyes and resembling an individual in mourning. The pain on the Chief Superintendent's face couldn't be concealed and Rayner could only guess at what agonising fears were going through his mind. No delay was brooked in putting officers to work, questioning those individuals claiming to have seen what had taken place, outside the front of the school. Alas, nothing more positive or informative came from the exercise and by the time Big Ben had struck its midday chimes, all of those interviewed had been unable to provide much more than was already known, except for Jack Robinson, who managed to find a witness who gave a better description of the culprits.

The young Sergeant reported that a passing chimney sweep had seen the abduction of the girl from close by.

"According to the sweep, one was a tall, robust looking and scruffy individual, wearing a green cape. The other much smaller with dark clothing. Both men were apparently wearing rags or grubby handkerchiefs across their faces with black woollen hats, similar to what dock workers have."

"What about the carriage, Jack?" Rayner enquired.

"All that people can tell us was that it was black without any markings and was pulled by a single black horse."

"And nothing more than that?"

"No sir, except a Miss Fisher who was walking to work, saw a carriage, similar in appearance to the one used by the kidnappers, go along Fleet Street, and turn right into Salisbury Court. It sounds as though it was the same one and according to the lady, the curtains were drawn across the windows."

By then the traffic along the Strand was busy, making it impossible to try and distinguish any wheel ruts left by the same carriage. So, the Chief Inspector suggested they should make their way to where the suspect carriage had turned off to see if anyone else had seen it. But before leaving the front of the school, Rayner stepped across to speak with Frederick Morgan, who still appeared to be in suspended animation.

"Has Sally-Anne been told yet, sir?" he enquired.

"No."

"Then might I suggest ..."

"I need to stay here, Rayner, for a while in any case because this might have been my fault. You see, I used to take Estelle to work every morning and Sal would arrange to have her collected in the afternoons, but just recently she told me she wanted to make her own way here and I stood for it."

"That's no reason to blame yourself sir," Rayner remarked, "What I strongly suspect is that your daughter has been followed in recent days for the kidnappers to know where she would be at a certain time. I think you should go home and inform your wife as to what has happened. What of the girl's mother, Miss Roland, would you like me to arrange..."

"I'll see to all of that, Rayner, but I'm not going home, not just yet."

"Forgive me, but you need to be there, in case the kidnappers' deliver a ransom note to your house."

Morgan stared at Rayner, accepting he had made a valid point, which he himself had not considered and then conceded that was a necessary step to take.

"But let me know, Richard, if you come up with anything, I shall never forgive myself if anything happens to that girl of mine."

After seeing his senior leave in an official carriage, both Rayner and Robinson made their way on foot along the Strand, until they reached the junction with Salisbury Court on their right. Rayner stopped at a corner tripe shop and enquired if anyone inside had seen a horse and carriage answering the same scant description given by the witnesses, but no one had.

Continuing to walk along Salisbury Court, they came across the opening of a Blacksmith's shed with the owner working just inside on an anvil.

The senior detective sent his Sergeant across the thoroughfare to speak with the man and after a short time, Robinson returned with some positive news.

"It appears, just after the girl was taken, the blacksmith noticed a black carriage with the curtains drawn, swing through those double wooden doors just down on the right there."

"Did he see anything of the driver or the others?"

"No, I asked him, but he was only concentrating on the horse and carriage."

"Very well, let's go and see, Jack."

Both detectives stopped outside the doors mentioned by the smithy, only to find them secured by a padlock and chain.

"I'll see if our friend can lend us a crowbar," Robinson suggested and quickly disappeared.

Rayner noticed the absence of any signwriting on the doors, which boasted green paint that was peeling and forlorn in appearance. He assumed the structure was some kind of storage facility and when Jack Robinson returned with a crowbar, it took just a couple of seconds to prise the padlock open.

Both detectives stepped into the interior, and could see similar doors at the far end, probably secured from the outside, but in the centre of the enclosed space stood a black painted carriage, although the horse that had pulled it was missing.

Rayner stepped up inside the back of the vehicle, but the darkness prevented him from examining the carriage thoroughly. However, there was a noticeable odour that didn't escape his attention and when he stepped back down, he had a look of concern on his face.

"This was without doubt used to transport Miss Estelle away from the school, Jack, and we need to get it back to Scotland Yard."

"Is there any indication that the girl has been inside there then, sir?"

"Only the strong smell of ether."

Robinson nodded, understanding the inference being made.

Surprisingly, the other doors were found to be insecure and after pushing them open, Richard Rayner found himself standing in a narrow muddy lane that ran adjacent to the rear of shops and terraced houses leading back to the Strand. He had little doubt this was the route of escape taken by the kidnappers, but his priority at that time was to arrange for the discovered carriage to be transported to Scotland Yard. So, leaving his young Sergeant with the vehicle, he quickly returned to where Claude Davey and his men were still making enquiries at the Ragged School. After arranging for a couple of detectives to take a horse back to assist Jack Robinson in getting the kidnappers' transport to Scotland Yard, he entered the school to speak to the headmaster.

Rayner's obvious question as to whether any stranger had been seen loitering around the building in recent days, was answered in the negative, so knowing that nothing more would be gained at the scene of the abduction, he eventually made his way back to the police headquarters.

Being blessed by the riches earned from the 'Pratchett and Longfellow Magnificent Circus', located in Bermondsey, both Frederick and Sally-Anne Morgan lived in a palatial residence in Richmond, about a mile from where Richard Rayner and his wife, Clarice, resided. They were fortunate to have domestic staff, and when the distressed master of the house finally arrived home, he was told by their butler, James, that the mistress was in the downstairs drawing room. No matter how devastated Frederick Morgan was feeling when entering the room, he knew only too well that his wife would feel the same, once she received the news.

Sally-Anne was a tall, attractive, elegant lady, with shoulder length fair hair tied back in the nape of her long swallow-like neck, and Morgan found her sitting at a small table, cleaning two silver pistols she used when performing as a sharp-shooter with her business partner, Emily Pratchett. His wife looked concerned and immediately enquired as to the reason for her husband's appearance so early in the day, but the senior detective was at first, reluctant to share his grief with her.

"Well, Frederick, as the cat got your tongue?" she remarked, noticing that something was not quite right with her perplexed partner in marriage.

Slowly and quietly, he shared details of the nightmare situation, describing as sensitively as he could the ordeal his daughter must have been going through. Instantly, the atmosphere inside the Morgan household changed dramatically and within seconds, every member of the domestic staff became aware of what had taken place.

At first, Sally-Anne remained momentarily silent and just looked across at him stone-faced. Although Estelle was not her own daughter, she might just as well have been and her feeling towards the girl were entirely maternal. She had unconditionally grown to love the girl as though she was in fact, her own.

Morgan then stepped across to the drinks cabinet that stood in one corner of the room, shaking his head and was about to pour himself a brandy when she spoke for the first time.

"Is Richard Rayner aware?" she quietly asked, having the highest regard for the most successful detective working at Scotland Yard and confident that if anyone could retrieve the girl, it would be Rayner.

"He's working on it as we speak, dear."

Then came the vitriol; the expected gush of blame sourced from a refusal to accept the seriousness of what had happened.

"It's your fault, Frederick, you should have taken her to work."

"I know that Sal, but how the bleedin' hell was I to know she would be kidnapped?"

"You are supposed to be a detective aren't you? If anything happens to that girl, I shall..."

"I know that Sal, and don't you think I feel guilty enough."

Then came the reality of the gravity of the actual dilemma they were both facing and seeing her husband riddled with self-blame, Sally-Anne quickly subdued her anger. She sat facing her husband, lost for words but no longer prepared to blame anyone except those who had forcibly taken Estelle, confused and fearful for the safety of their beloved girl. Eventually, they found some mutual comfort in each other's arms and cried together like a couple of lost orphans. There were no words that could be spoken, only tears and a sense of frustrating anger that was tormenting the Chief Superintendent.

When Richard Rayner returned to his office, it was time to put his blackboard to good use and he quickly chalked down what he had learned so far about the kidnapping, including his personal thoughts and ideas. It was a habit he had developed over the years and being a methodical kind of man, found that by recording the most pertinent points of any Investigation, helped him to analyse and identify the path to follow. Even when studying Mathematics at Oxford, Rayner had always been meticulous, possessing an organised nature and requiring snippets of data to be placed into systematic order. The driving force behind the Dandy of Scotland Yard had always been his ability to store in chronological order, all clear and fundamental patterns of thought.

His wife, Clarice, was a lecturer and researcher on the subject of facial reconstruction, a science that Richard Rayner had taken advantage of during several previous Investigations, and although, having experienced their own personal traumatic ordeals, were now living a happy life. Ironically, their history, or rather Richard Rayner's, was not too dissimilar to that of Frederick Morgan, in that he had recently discovered he had a twelve-year old son, Matthew, born out of wedlock and from an earlier association. After experiencing such an incredible discovery, his greatest fear was that his son would not be accepted by his wife, but such concerns were quickly dispersed when Clarice took to the boy as if he was her own son, in similar fashion to that of Sally-Anne Morgan's maternalistic feelings towards Estelle Roland.

The only other tantalising problem that dogged Richard Rayner on a daily basis, came from within his own character, often sensing a distinct fear of failure. The famous detective's achievements in bringing the most complex of Investigations to finality, and the widespread highly respected reputation he had unwittingly earned, was difficult to come to terms with. Whenever the Chief Inspector was allocated an Inquiry to complete, it was expected that he would achieve the utmost success, but his own personal nemesis was always present; a constant fear of being defeated that constantly plagued him. And yet, the only person who doubted his abilities, was himself, on occasions to the point of total negativity. But now, such self-analysis had to be shelved. Apart from the victim of what appeared to be an atrocious act of kidnapping, being Frederick Morgan's daughter, she was also a young lady who had been subjected to an horrendous ordeal and could very possibly be in danger of losing her life.

Rayner did not require any reminder that this particular Inquiry would need every slither of his analytical mind to concentrate on finding the girl and bringing those responsible to justice, and time itself was his enemy. There was no way in which he could have concentrated on the Tower Bridge murder, until Estelle Roland had been found and safely returned to her father.

After concentrating his mind on the task that was confronting him, he stood back from the blackboard and stared at the results of his work, desperate for inspiration. This was one case in which there could be no room for failure; no room for doubt, or no room for missed opportunities, no matter how much he doubted his own abilities.

Chapter Three

Estelle's nightmare came to an end when she opened her eyes, having dreamt that she had been abducted by men outside the school gates, only to discover her fantasy had in fact, been a reality. She found herself with both feet and hands tied together by ropes and lying on an old, damp mattress in some sort of small room with one tiny window intruding on a sloping ceiling. It was cold and she began to shiver looking around what appeared to be an attic, in which there wasn't sufficient space to swing a cat. Not knowing why she was there, she could only pray that her prison was of a temporary nature.

The young teacher just lay there for a little while, staring up at the bare walls and space above her head, from which a multitude of spiders' webs hung. Her mind felt stupefied, and she realised she had been drugged, allowing fear and confusion to become dominant in her thinking ability, exacerbated by being subjected to the unknown.

Set against the wall to her right and close to where her feet lay, there was a door and Estelle slowly managed to find her feet before hobbling over to it with both wrists secured around her back. She stumbled a couple of times, the girl's head swimming and the bare floorboards beneath her feet appearing to move like the waves on the sea, creating a sensation of nausea. But she persevered with every effort she made being an ordeal. Eventually, she awkwardly tried to turn the knob but found the door to be locked. Despairingly, she fell back down to her knees and groaned, her discomfort being intensified by a craving thirst. Estelle's mouth was so dry, her tongue kept sticking to her palate. She tried to cry out, but the dryness in her throat made that difficult, so she just knelt there, trying to unsuccessfully come to terms with her tortuous predicament. It was then she heard footsteps approaching from the other side of the door and hurriedly returned to the unwelcoming mattress to listen and wait in anticipation.

The sound of bolts being removed could be heard, and then a man appeared in the open doorway, wearing a scarf around the lower part of his face. He was tall with shoulder-length fair hair and light blue eyes that stared down at her. They were eyes that lacked compassion or any other emotion, causing Estelle to fear even more so for her safety. But she had to be brave and did her best not to disclose any sign of that same fear that was eating away beneath the surface.

"Why am I here?" she hoarsely and nervously enquired, "Who are you?"

"No talking," her captor answered in a gruff, disguised voice, before producing a bottle of water and placing it on the floor at the girl's side.

"How long are you going to keep me here, I beg of you to tell me what all of this is about," she croaked unashamedly.

He just looked down at her and pointed towards a bucket located in one corner of the room, suggesting she could use that whenever she required.

"That depends upon your father's willingness to pay for your release," he continued, now seemingly smiling through those icy, watery eyes.

"But my father isn't a rich man," Estelle lied, "Do you know who he is?"

"Oh, I know very well who he is Miss Morgan, but enough. You need have no fear, provided you don't cause any trouble and from now on you will remain quiet."

Although he was speaking in a strange sounding voice, she got the impression that he was young and educated from the way he addressed her and from his demeanour.

"My name isn't Morgan, it's Roland," she quickly replied.

He just nodded and pulled her by her arms from the bed to her feet. The rope wrapped around Estelle's wrists were cut with a knife and she began to rub them to restore the circulation. She asked if he would do the same with her ankles, but he turned and left the room without speaking another word, locking the door behind him. She called out, but the only response she got was the sound of footsteps walking away.

At first, she poured just a little water down her parched throat and then her thirst demanded more, and half the bottle was consumed very quickly. At least her captor hadn't caused her any physical harm, which meant his only motive was to obtain money from his actions and she stood in deep thought, looking up at the window through which there came the only natural light available. There was a gas mantle hanging from the ceiling but of course she was in no position to light it and acknowledged to herself, that when the darkness of night came visiting, her ordeal would become even more intense.

The untimely murder of a man found hanging from the newly constructed Tower Bridge, London's most recent pride and joy, was sufficient to give the Commissioner, Sir Edward Bradford, more than a little concern, but when, at virtually the same time the daughter of his Head of the Detective Branch had been kidnapped, the most senior officer in the Metropolitan Police began to wonder what he had done in a previous life to deserve all of this. Of course, the priority had to be the safe recovery of Estelle Roland, but sadly, that was not the story being favoured by the newspapers and Sir Edward was now being bombarded by questions not only from reporters, but also from the Home Secretary and other Members of Parliament, their focus remaining on the unusual but callous murder, one that could possibly deter people from using the bridge.

The fact the Commissioner had made his presence known in Richard Rayner's office, rather than summon the Chief Inspector to his own sanctuary on the top floor, was an indication of the depth of apprehension occupying Sir Edward's mind. As soon as he stepped into the Chief Inspector's office, he demanded a full explanation on what course of action had been taken so far, regarding both incidents, beginning with the kidnapping.

"It's early days yet sir," the senior detective told him.

"I am well aware of that Mr. Rayner," the man in charge of the Metropolitan Police snapped back, "I am not asking you for a time schedule sir, I need to know what you have done so far to recover Mr. Morgan's daughter."

Rayner felt well admonished and sheepishly answered, "We believe we have found the carriage used to abduct the girl, and I suspect she is being kept close to where she was taken from." The detective paused to clear his throat, before continuing, "As we speak, Sergeant Davey and his men are making enquiries in that area." He was about to add that he was confident they would quickly recover the victim, but refrained from saying that, not wanting to commit himself unduly, only to later look foolish should he fail.

"I take it that Mr. Morgan is at home," the Commissioner remarked, taking a chair in front of the blazing fire.

"Yes sir, I suspect a ransom note of some sort will be the next move by the kidnappers and until that arrives, if it's money that's behind this atrocious crime, then all that can be done is being done."

The Commissioner paused, seemingly in deep thought and perhaps a little dubious as to whether Richard Rayner was in fact, doing enough. Changing the subject, he then enquired, "And what of this gentleman that was found hanging from Tower Bridge, do we know who he is yet?"

The senior detective then gave an attenuated account of what had been revealed over the past couple of days, including the name of the victim and the address at where he lived.

"Mr. Carter lived with his wife and two children sir, and I intend going to see them as soon as I possibly can."

"Do we have any noticeable reason for the murder?"

"No, not yet sir."

"Very well, then you must treat the girl's disappearance as a priority Mr. Rayner but keep me updated and whatever you require to bring this awful business to a successful conclusion, you shall have."

"Yes, thank you sir." Rayner assumed that the Commissioner would have been pestered by the newspapers and offered to chair a press conference regarding the Tower Bridge affair.

"Leave that with me, I would prefer you concentrated all your efforts on finding the girl and apprehending those responsible for taking her."

Rayner nodded, somewhat relieved.

Shortly after Sir Edward had left, Henry Bustle appeared, looking concerned, having just heard about the kidnapping. The Sergeant asked if Rayner needed him to leave the enquiries he had been making about the spate of burglaries committed in the Whitechapel district, to assist with the ongoing Investigation being conducted by Sergeant Davey.

"No Henry, at present I don't think there is much you could do more than what Claude is already engaged with, so it might be best to continue with what you have already started."

"Have we any idea who might be behind this sir?" Bustle asked, referring to the kidnapping.

Rayner shook his head, explaining as he had done so with the Commissioner, that it was too early to make any identification.

"Anybody who would kidnap a young lady off the streets like that is the lowest of the low in my book," the Sergeant commented.

"The question is Henry, what kind of person would target Scotland Yard's most senior detective to blackmail? It must be some individual who knows him or has been close to him in the past."

"I take it the carriage in the backyard is the one that was used to carry the lady off in, sir."

"I believe so, Henry, and from the smell inside it looks as though they used ether to keep her quiet."

"As I said, lowest of the low, where was it found?"

Rayner told him and explained that he was about to conduct his own examination of the transport.

"Someone then, must have seen them take the girl out of the vehicle. Would you mind if I came with you just to take a look at the inside."

"Of course not, Henry, I would welcome it."

Both detectives then made their way down the stairs to the basement where a door led them to the back of Scotland Yard. Claude Davey had been efficient, and the horseless carriage recovered from Salisbury Court could be seen standing against a far wall. As Rayner and Bustle approached, Jack Robinson stepped down from inside the vehicle and quickly explained he had made a thorough examination of the interior and found nothing.

"It appears to have been cleaned out sir," the young Sergeant told Rayner, "And it looks like the manufacturer's plate has been removed from the side panelling."

The Chief Inspector thanked him, but still took the trouble to peer inside, noticing how the odour of ether had diminished considerably over the past hour or so. He then took a small penknife from his jacket pocket and carefully scraped a coat of the black paint away, revealing the carriage's original colour that was a dark blue.

"It must have been a strong horse to have pulled this," Henry Bustle remarked.

"I agree Henry, it's an old type of Clarence, which does appear to have been renovated, perhaps for the specific purpose for which it was used by the kidnappers. The paintwork appears to be fairly new."

Then turning to Jack Robinson, Rayner directed that he made enquiries with known manufacturers and retailers in the London area.

"I'm not sure that there have been many Clarence transports made in recent years Jack, especially one that was originally painted blue, so we might get lucky."

"I'll get on to it straight away sir."

After the youngest of the two Sergeants had left, the other two detectives made their own extensive inspections of the interior but experienced the same result as Robinson.

"You are thinking that the girl is being kept somewhere close to where this was found," Bustle suggested.

"Yes, unless they had a second vehicle to take them further afield, I'll be interested to know what Claude Davey and his men have found out. I requested them to search through the surrounding vicinity."

"I don't envy them sir, it's like a rabbit warren down there."

The senior detective nodded, intending to make his own enquiries, but without Henry Bustle. He preferred that his most experienced Sergeant remained working on the Whitechapel burglaries, only because he suspected they weren't looking for the usual backstreet villains that would normally fall within his Sergeant's domain. No, Rayner believed the kind of planning that had gone into the kidnapping would be beyond the criminal mind that lurked about the backstreets of Whitechapel.

It was in the late afternoon that Richard Rayner returned to Salisbury Court in his own official carriage driven by his driver of many years, Constable Jacob Studley. Having told his man to wait close to the enclosure where they had earlier discovered the black painted carriage, he made his way to the narrow lane that ran down the backs of the neighbouring houses and shops. It was there that he came across an elderly man tending to a vegetable garden at the rear of the first house in the line. The gardener was wearing an old well-worn pullover and cap and was crouching down at the side of a bed of young cabbages, putting a trowel to good use. From the stains on his unshaven chin, it appeared the old man was chewing on a plug of tobacco.

Rayner introduced himself and complimented the elderly gardener on his display of vegetation, before asking how long he had been working in his garden that day.

"Since the dawn mister, you have to nurse these vegetables constantly until they's right for picking see," the man answered, expectorating a stream of black liquid from his mouth.

The detective then asked if he had seen anyone on horseback coming from the direction of the nearby alleyway earlier that morning, in the company of a young woman.

The elderly gardener looked puzzled and shook his head, responding in a perplexed manner.

"Can't say as I have mister, you don't see many back 'ere, 'cept a few delivery men."

Rayner thanked him and turned to walk away, but then the old man remembered, "There was that ruffian Jimmy McBride and his two mates. They was on horseback and I shouted out, 'Mornin'' to them, but they ignored me, as you would expect; arrogant bastards."

"Did you see a woman with them?"

"No, no woman."

"Did you notice if any of them was carrying a large parcel or something similar across the back of one of the horses?"

The gardener stroked his chin and then confessed, "Now I come to think of it, yes, but it wasn't Jimmy, one of the others was struggling with something wrapped in some kind of sacking across his saddle."

"Could it have been a person inside that sacking? It's most important."

"Well, if it was, he would have only been a small gent."

Rayner's eyes lit up and he lowered his voice when asking if the old man knew the names of Jimmy's associates, but the answer was in the negative.

"Do you know where this McBride fellow lives?"

"He's a bad lot and I'd advise you to stay clear of him, mister, he'd have no hesitation in slitting your throat."

"Do you know where he lives?" Rayner asked, repeating his question.

"Of course, he lives over The Horse and Jockey, up in York Street. There's a few of them young pugilists live up there. The landlord, Blackie Jones, hires out rooms to them."

"Street fighters?"

"That's them, as hard as nails, or that's what they thinks they are."

"Might I ask your name, sir."

"Henry Clements, but most people round here knows me as 'Clem'."

Richard Rayner tipped his hat and once again thanked the old man before leaving, but not to go directly to The Horse and Jockey in York Street, but to return to Scotland Yard. He had instantly regretted not having allowed Henry Bustle to accompany him and was now in need of his most experienced Sergeant's help.

Chapter Four

Richard Rayner was anxious to speak with Henry Bustle, to extract what he knew about The Horse and Jockey public house in York Street, Whitechapel, specifically more about what the old gardener, Henry Clements, had told him regarding young street fighters lodging there. But the senior detective was a patient man and whilst waiting for his older Sergeant to appear, busied himself recording on his blackboard what the old man had told him.

A knock on the door preceded Claude Davey's unexpected appearance, but only to inform Richard Rayner that the search around Salisbury Close hadn't yet revealed anything of interest and that it appeared the kidnappers and their victim, had disappeared into thin air. The Sergeant was an extremely tall man, measuring well over six feet and possessing a build that could have been attributed to an athlete, but Davey, although enthusiastic and reliable, failed to show the same initiative in the art of detection as either Bustle or Robinson.

"Very well, Claude, but keep your men at it until every crook and cranny has been looked at."

Only a few minutes after Sergeant Davey had left, Henry Bustle appeared and was immediately quizzed as to whether he had experienced any success in trying to trace those responsible for the burglaries and larceny of copper wiring.

The Sergeant shook his head and explained that he had been trying to find 'Spotty Finkel', a close informant he often turned to when trying to unravel information in the Whitechapel district but hadn't had much luck so far.

"I suspect the scallywag is lying pissed in some hovel and probably won't come back to life until nightfall comes, but what he doesn't know about what's going on, isn't worth knowing."

"Yes, I agree Henry." The Chief Inspector then repeated what he had learned earlier that day, asking if his Sergeant could enlighten him further regarding the activities at The Horse and Jockey.

"The landlord, Thomas Jones, who is known by the locals as 'Blackie', runs a few fights in his backyard, mostly at weekends and I know he lets some of his fighters' lodge rent free upstairs, above the public house. It's fair to say, he looks after his lads and trains them himself, having been in the business a few years back."

"Was he any good?"

Bustle shook his head and confirmed, "Nah, not from the bumps and scars on his kisser he wasn't, but apart from what he makes from running the public house, Blackie makes a bit extra from betting on the fights he promotes."

"What about this individual, Jimmy McBride, ever heard of him, Henry?"

"No, he doesn't ring a bell, forgive the pun sir, but the clientele at that place consists of some of the hardest men in London, all having an interest in the fight game."

"Very well, but tell me, what kind of individual is this Blackie Jones?"

"Talkative and amicable enough to those within his circle. As I've said, he used to punch his weight in the backstreets for different purses on offer, but that was before he met and married his missus, Ruby; now she's a different kettle of fish altogether. A hard-nosed woman who wouldn't hesitate in sticking a knife in your belly if you spoke to her in the wrong way."

"Would the landlord talk to you, if he was aware of any of his fighters being involved in this kidnapping Henry?"

"He might do sir, if he thought he was in danger of losing his licence. Were you thinking of raiding the place then?"

Rayner sat back in his chair and considered his options. If Estelle Morgan, or rather, Roland, was being kept at those premises, then a raid would be the best way of retrieving her, but from what Bustle had just told him, he doubted that the girl would be kept there against her will. And if she wasn't there and a group of heavy built police officers went charging in, all they would do was to warn the kidnappers they were getting close, which might endanger the girl's life, if she was being kept elsewhere. The Chief Inspector convinced himself, such a move would be too risky and therefore considered another means of finding out more about Jimmy McBride.

"Does the landlord know you personally, Henry?" he finally asked.

Bustle nodded and explained that he had attended some of the fights organised in the backyard in the past and had spoken with Blackie Jones on a number of occasions. He also confirmed that the man was aware he was a detective from Scotland Yard.

"I don't think there would be any problems if I went and had a quiet word with him though," Bustle added.

Now it was Richard Rayner's turn to nod his head.

The Horse and Jockey wasn't exactly teeming with customers when the detective stepped into the bar room. Blackie Jones was a huge, impressive looking man, leaning over the counter and talking to one of his customers, a man with half an ear missing and who looked as if he had been attacked by a group of wild dogs when he was a child. As soon as the landlord saw Henry Bustle, he unfolded and moved towards him.

"What will you be having, Mr. Bustle?" he asked, in a gruff voice, holding an empty glass in one shovel-like hand.

The detective ordered a jug of black ale and waited for the landlord to pour it. Once he had taken his first gulp of the liquid, he asked how the fight game was going.

"So and so, Mr. Bustle, you know how it is, you can't seem to find the youngsters today who can go further than a couple of rounds."

"I've heard that one of your proteges, a Jimmy McBride is promising, Blackie, but you've been keeping him back." Bustle smiled sarcastically, as he spoke, inferring he was jesting.

"Jimmy, nay lad, he's okay but there's not room for much advancement there. Now if I was a betting man, there's a youngster..."

"Has McBride got a room here?"

The landlord looked inquisitively at Bustle and then verified the lad in question shared a room with another young fighter upstairs.

"Is he up there at the moment, only I'd like a word with him."

"What about Mr. Bustle?"

"Is he up there?"

"Aye, he usually is at this time of day. I can get the missus to take you up if you like."

"I'd prefer it if you did, Blackie, if it's not too much trouble."

The landlord nodded and stepped to one side to allow the Scotland Yard man to step behind the bar, he then led the way into a narrow corridor at the back of the public house that led to a flight of stairs. When they reached the first landing, Blackie walked down a small dimly lit passageway, stopping at the third door on his right, which he banged with a heavy fist before waiting, but there was no answer. After knocking a few times, he turned to Bustle and suggested the lad he wanted to speak to was obviously out.

If the kidnapped girl was being kept on the other side of that door, the detective certainly wouldn't have expected Jimmy McBride to have answered the call and decided to open the door the old-fashioned way. It took one kick, before the obstacle flew inwards, hanging on its hinges.

"I wish you'd have told me your intentions Mr. Bustle; I've got a spare key."

Ignoring the landlord, Bustle led the way into the room, where he saw two beds up against separate walls that were both sparsely covered by a single woollen blanket. A great deal of the original plaster on the walls was missing, but the biggest surprise to greet the Sergeant was the body of a young man, lying on his back on top of one of the beds with both lifeless eyes staring up at the cobwebbed ceiling. He was dressed in a grey, open-necked shirt and rumpled woollen trousers. There was an open gash across the victim's throat, the obvious reason for his life being extinct.

"Christ Almighty," Blackie Jones hissed.

"Is this Jimmy McBride?"

"Yes, that's him sure enough, God forbid."

Bustle then asked the landlord the usual questions, including if he knew who had a grudge against the young man laid out on the bed, and had he seen anybody making their way up to the first floor. But no help was forthcoming, and the Sergeant instructed Blackie Jones to fetch a constable off the street.

When Richard Rayner arrived at The Horse and Jockey, the only people he found sitting at the tables in the bar room, were two constables and Henry Bustle conversing with Blackie Jones. The usual customers had been made to leave at the request of the police and as soon as the Sergeant saw his senior officer appear, quickly outlined what had happened. The fact there were no witnesses to the murder surprised the Chief Inspector and he quickly ascertained that Bustle had questioned everyone before clearing the room.

"Nobody saw anything," the Sergeant confirmed, "But I've written a list of who they were before kicking them out."

Rayner then asked about the dead man's rooming mate.

"According to Blackie, his name is Benny Whistler, but he seems to have gone missing at the moment."

"Do we know if this Whistler lad is in employment at present, Henry?" Rayner enquired, feeling a little angry at Bustle having cleared the public house before he had got there, but appreciating that the recent death of the Sergeant's wife might have affected his judgement.

"There's half a dozen youngsters boarding upstairs here, and they are all street fighters, including Master Whistler. What the landlord tells me is that he gives them free board and lodgings in return for them fighting for him at weekends. He says that it's not unusual for one or two of them to go missing from their rooms for a few days, but they always turn up for training and the scheduled fights at the weekends."

"Have we a description of this room-mate?"

Bustle glanced down at his notebook and read from it.

"Short, stocky with a shaven head and flattened nose. Just like the majority of these young scrappers, he has a few scars on his face that's not unusual considering his occupation."

Rayner glanced at the scar running down the side of his Sergeant's face, and was momentarily reminded of Bustle's background, but made no mention of it.

"We need to find this Benny Whistler as soon as possible, as your man got any idea where we might find him?"

"He reckons he sometimes does some casual work at the docks, and I was thinking of nipping down there and asking around."

"I'll come with you; I take it you've searched the lad's room."

Bustle explained that he had but found nothing of interest. He described the room as being sparse with very little in what few drawers and cupboards he'd looked in.

"There's no doubt, if it wasn't for Blackie Jones taking these unfortunates on board and running them through their paces, their only alternative would be to live on the streets and survive by robbing people."

Rayner nodded his acquiescence and followed his Sergeant up to where the victim still lay on the bed. Whilst making his own cursory examination of the body, he asked Bustle if arrangements had been made for the pathologist, Doctor Albert Critchley, to attend from St. Mary's Hospital and was told he was on his way. In fact, the physician who had worked on numerous cases with Richard Rayner previously, arrived soon after that and agreed that it appeared on the surface that the knife wound to the throat was the cause of death. Directions were then given to the constables present to have the body removed to the mortuary for the inevitable post-mortem.

"Have you a time of death, doctor?" the senior detective asked.

"Not more than a couple of hours, I would say, but I shall be in a position to be more accurate once I have him back at the mortuary."

"Would you agree that from the amount of blood on the bed, it seems he was killed where he lay."

"Yes, that does seem to have been the case."

Rayner then turned to Bustle and asked if there were any known relatives of the deceased man and was told that, according to the landlord, McBride had a sister living in Dublin and that he was going to try and contact her.

"Very well." Rayner thanked the doctor and left with Henry Bustle, intent on visiting the nearby docks to see if anyone was aware of the young man, Benny Whistler.

As their carriage took them the short journey to the main London Dock, Bustle asked why, in Rayner's opinion, would anyone murder a young man in his own room, where the likelihood of being seen was extremely high.

"Perhaps Henry, this was an on the spur killing, or the person responsible might have already been well known inside the place, but we need to find the motive before jumping to any conclusions."

Bustle was aware of Rayner's methods, and the way in which the senior detective always made the motive of any heinous crime, top of his agenda. The senior detective had always described a motiveless murder as being the most difficult to detect and it was always his priority when beginning an Investigation.

"My main concern though is that Master McBride was involved in the kidnapping of Estelle Roland, having been seen in the company of two other men this morning by the old gardener, Henry Clements."

"And you are thinking they might have had a fall out over something that resulted in our lad having his throat cut open."

"It's possible Henry, but if that is what actually happened, then I fear we are dealing with brutal men and those same fears extend to the safety of young Estelle."

The room was in complete darkness now and although the water bottle left by her kidnapper was empty, the young lady's intense thirst had returned. It mattered not that she hadn't eaten since breakfast and the last thing she felt any desire for was food, yet strangely, she had never felt so thirsty before. Having managed to untie the bonds around her ankles Estelle could at least move about in what little space there was. Several attempts to reach the small skylight window had failed and a realisation that she would remain a prisoner until her father eventually came for her, was an ever present. At least she was still alive and unharmed.

When she heard the man's footsteps returning, she hoped that he was bringing more water for her. Standing upright, she listened to the sound of the bolts being withdrawn again and heard the lock turning in the door, before noticing a dim light in the background as he stepped into the room. His face was still partially covered, and he immediately ordered her to sit on the bed. Then he handed a small wooden box to the girl, explaining that there were a few biscuits and pieces of bread inside.

She thanked him and began to open the box.

"I shall bring you some more water later," he said, still maintaining that disguised voice.

The room was extremely dark by then, and Estelle didn't see him remove his face covering.

"Lie back," he ordered, in a demanding voice.

She was reluctant and asked the reason why, placing a broken piece of dry biscuit in her mouth.

He repeated his directive, but still she remained sitting on the side of the bed.

He then unexpectedly struck her across the face with an open hand, causing her to yell out and fall backwards. The box containing the morsels of food fell to the floor and without warning, the stranger then leapt on top of her and began to fondle her before tearing the front of her dress. The girl's greatest fears were about to be realised and she tried to fight him off, scratching the side of his neck and causing him to move away from her, nursing his wound.

Estelle was delirious with fear and tried to leave the bed to make for the partially open door, but was struck again, once, twice across the face. She fell silent and he returned to his original position on top of her. Again, she struggled but he was too strong, and his upper body covered her like a heavy blanket, rendering her helpless.

"Oh God," she moaned, feeling him inside her. This was her worst possible nightmare, and at that very moment, she was desperate for death to come calling and take her away in its grasp. She began to cry as her captor took full advantage.

After he had finished with her, he got up off the bed and left the room, leaving his unfortunate victim in a state of shock. Estelle grasped the front of her torn blouse and sobbed, she couldn't stop trembling uncontrollably, but then her overwhelming sensation of fear and self-pity, was replaced by an upsurge of anger. She stood and fled to the far corner of the room and vomited. Now, she was no longer a human being, but just a violated creature without dignity or decency, or so she felt. Her anger continued throughout the remainder of that long and dreadful cold night and the girl's most prominent thought was that whoever this vile individual was, he had just signed his own death warrant. She knew exactly what her father would do to him, if she lived that long to see it.

Chapter Five

It didn't take long for the detectives to track down young Benny Whistler, finding the part-time street fighter loading up crates in one of the warehouses in the London Dock. Their first impression when talking to the lad was that, although unschooled and like so many other young men surviving in the backstreets, slow witted, he appeared on the surface to be an honest and hard-working individual, trying to make his way in the world as best he could. When Richard Rayner disclosed the recent demise of Whistler's fellow lodger, he initially seemed to be genuinely shocked. However, both Rayner and Henry Bustle's first impression of the young man's character had to be delved into further, especially as there was a distinct possibility that their man might well have been involved in the kidnapping of Estelle Roland. He was therefore escorted back to Scotland Yard for further interrogation.

"I don't know anything about any missing girl," the man pleaded, when sitting opposite the Chief Inspector and Sergeant in a basement interview room.

"Surely, the lodger who shared the same room with you at The Horse and Jockey would have confided in you Benny, we are not complete fools," Rayner suggested, "And we believe you and McBride argued over something to do with the kidnapping of Miss Roland, that resulted in you slashing his throat, before fleeing down to the docks where you could hide out for a while." Rayner thought how convenient it would have been for the lodger to leave the public house with no one giving a second thought when seeing him.

The prisoner remained in denial and shook his head, showing signs of nervousness by fidgeting on his seat and continuing to insist he had no knowledge of the murder or kidnapping.

"It's very simple, my friend," the senior detective continued, "Either confess to all that you know and escape the noose, or we shall have no option but to charge you with the murder and may the Lord have mercy on your soul."

"I ain't going to admit to something I ain't done and that's the truth."

"How long have you known Jimmy McBride?"

"Just a few months, when he moved in."

"And how did you two get on with each other?"

"Okay, I never really saw a lot of him, when I was in, Jimmy was usually out, and it was the same t'other way round. The only real time we spent together was when we were training with Blackie and at the Sunday morning fights."

"Were you ever matched together in the ring?"

"No, but I've fought most of the others and suppose my turn with Jimmy would have come sooner or later."

"What about the others who lodge there, how well do you know each other?"

"We don't, everybody keeps to themselves. You see, it don't pay to get over friendly because we could be fighting each other if ever Blackie put us up, so we all go our different ways, except as I said, when we are training."

"What about McBride's friends, did he have any?"

Whistler shook his head and declared that, as far as he knew, his room-mate was a loner and didn't mix socially.

Richard Rayner then nodded for Bustle to take the lad to the cells. He wanted the prisoner to spend some time alone, considering his position.

"What do you think?" the Sergeant enquired, having secured Whistler, and made his way to his Chief Inspector's office.

"Actually Henry, I believe the lad. I just don't think he's the type to slit anybody's throat. He might well get up to some mischief if there were a few guineas to be earned, but murder goes against what I have seen of him."

"I agree, shall I get hold of the others that's lodging down at The Horse and Jockey?"

"No, I'll get Claude Davey and his lads to sort them out. I prefer you to get back on to finding out who has been committing those burglaries in Whitechapel."

It was with some dismay that Bustle left, being of the opinion that his time would have been better spent working on the Investigation Richard Rayner was conducting. But he also knew, the sooner he concluded the task given him, the sooner he could return to helping with the kidnapping and murder.

Not surprisingly, Frederick Morgan and his wife, Sally-Anne, had spent a sleepless night and sat in silence at the breakfast table, both looking like a couple of zombies. The Chief Superintendent was having some difficulty, having to remain at home without being involved in the search for his daughter and his patience by now was on the brink of snapping.

"If those bastards harm one hair of her head Sal, I swear..."

"So, you keep saying, Frederick, but all I want is for our girl to come home to us unharmed."

The doorbell rang and the butler, James, could be heard answering the door. It was Emily Pratchett, Sally-Anne's co-owner of the circus who had earlier visited the stricken couple on the previous night. Both women had agreed for Emily to perform a solo act, until her business partner had dealt with the ordeal she was going through at present.

When entering the dining room, she naturally asked if there had been any news and both husband and wife shook their heads.

"How did the show go last night, Em?" Sally-Anne quietly asked.

"A full house again, Sal, but don't you worry none about that. Everybody sends their hopes and prayers for you to get Estelle back quickly."

The lady of the house showed her appreciation by smiling, but her eyes confirmed her inner anxiety.

"If anybody can find her, it's Richard Rayner," Emily Pratchett suggested, having met the famous detective on several occasions and having seen him at first hand, recover her own niece when she was kidnapped up in Cumbria on a previous occasion.

"Not without me being there to direct him," an agitated Frederick Morgan spurted out, "I should be back at Scotland Yard, organising the searches for my little girl."

"Our little girl, Frederick," his wife corrected, "But you know what Richard told you makes sense, you need to be here in case that vermin deliver a ransom demand."

"So, he thinks Estelle is being held for a ransom," Emily asked.

Sally-Anne nodded, but then the front doorbell rang again and shortly afterwards, they heard the butler call out from the hallway in a voice filled with anguish.

All three left the room and hurried to where James the butler was standing, looking out through the open doorway.

"What is it, Jimmy?" Morgan asked.

His servant didn't answer and just stood there with his back to the others. And then they all saw the pitiful figure, pale faced and wearing dishevelled clothing. It was the ghostly looking person of an extremely tearful, Estelle.

Two other men had been seen with Jimmy McBride leaving Salisbury Court, after leaving the carriage in which they had supposedly abducted Estelle Roland, just prior to the young street fighter being murdered in his room at the public house. Rayner had little doubt that one or both of those men had been responsible for killing McBride, but for what reason. If the girl had been incarcerated inside the bundle the old gardener had seen being carried across one of the saddles of the horses they were riding, then they would surely have taken her directly to wherever it was they intended to keep her prisoner. He tried to imagine a sequence of events that might have taken place after they had left the carriage behind. Whatever the motive behind the murder of the young street fighter was, the killers could not have gone far, before securing the girl and then journeying to The Horse and Jockey and committing the heinous atrocity against their associate. That meant the victim of the kidnapping had to be kept prisoner somewhere close to both Salisbury Court and the public house.

He requested a street map of the Whitechapel district and noted the time Doctor Albert Critchley had decided when the murder had taken place – two hours before having been discovered by Henry Bustle and Blackie Jones, which was at one o'clock that lunchtime. The girl had been taken at nine o'clock that morning and Rayner estimated it would have taken about ten minutes to transport her to Salisbury Court, arriving at ten past nine. It was therefore apparent that during a period of just short of two hours, between 9.10 a.m. and 11.0 a.m. the kidnappers had left the carriage and taken the girl to a safe house. Allowing twenty minutes to transfer her from the carriage to the horses, after ensuring she wouldn't be seen and taking one horse out of its attachment to the vehicle, which would cut the time down to approximately one and a half hours. Richard Rayner estimated that the girl was being kept somewhere in which it would have taken forty-five minutes to have gone on to The Horse and Jockey, that was, if they had walked and less than that if they had journeyed on horseback, which was very likely.

Looking at the street map that contained both Salisbury Court and York Street where The Horse and Jockey was located, he then worked out the approximate distance a horse could canter in forty-five minutes. Rayner then drew a circle around the location of the public house and viewed the street information contained within that same circle. To the north was Whitechapel High Street and to the south, Cable Street. The furthest point to the west was Mansell Street and to the east, Turner Street. Somewhere within that circle, both Estelle Roland and the killers of Jimmy McBride, were located, but the same area resembled a spider's web containing a conglomerate of back alleys and streets. At least it was a starting point for searches to be made and Rayner was about to send for Sergeant Claude Davey, when the man himself appeared in the doorway of his office, looking a little flustered.

"We've just heard from Mr. Morgan sir, his daughter has returned home."

By the time the senior detective arrived at the Morgan's residence, Estelle was resting in bed with a doctor in attendance, having been sent for by Sally-Anne. The Chief Inspector was a little surprised by the look of vexation on the Chief Superintendent's face, having expected a joyous reception.

"This is excellent news sir," he said, "How is she?"

"The filthy bastard raped her," Morgan instantly snapped back, leading the way into the downstairs drawing room, with James the butler in close attendance.

Rayner was sympathetic but received the news without passion. After all, it wasn't his daughter who had been subjected to such an ordeal and his responsibility was to apprehend those responsible and to do that, he had to remain totally objective.

After a moment of silence, he asked where the girl was, and Morgan confirmed she was being medically examined upstairs in her room.

"Is she well enough for me to talk with her?" he then asked.

"I swear Rayner, I shan't rest until I've caught this bastard and chopped off his balls."

"I understand how you are feeling at this time, but we are..."

"Do you Rayner, do you really. I doubt that," the former Major in the Coldstream Guards, responded, "I mean every word I say."

"I'm sure you do sir, but we have to catch them first."

"According to Estelle, there was only one of them, a lone wolf who kept his face covered up throughout the whole frightening ordeal. She was kept in some kind of attic room and after he'd had his pleasure with her, blindfolded her and then dropped her off at the bottom of our drive."

Morgan then poured a couple of glasses of whiskey and handed one to the Chief Inspector, before finally sitting down.

Rayner had seen similar rage on Morgan's face before, but never so intense. There again, the Chief Superintendent had never experienced his daughter having been kidnapped and raped before.

"Why has he returned her home?" the Chief Inspector quietly asked.

"Because, after what the bastard did to her, he knows if he hadn't, he was already a dead man."

"No, what I mean is, by doing so, it flies in the face of the motive we were considering."

"You mean ransom money."

Rayner nodded.

"So, what's going on inside that devious thinking head of yours, Richard?"

"We know there was more than one who took Estelle from the front of the Ragged School, and I find it difficult to accept she was kidnapped just for the purpose of taking advantage of her."

"The filthy bastard took advantage of her when the opportunity was there."

"Maybe so, but what was the real reason for taking her in the first place?"

Morgan thought for a while and then suggested, "As you said, initially they took her with the intention of demanding a ransom, but then having defiled her in the way he did, his conscience pricked him, which is more than what's going to happen to him, once I get my hands around his scrawny neck."

Rayner stood and stepped across to the log fire burning in the large open fireplace, before making mention of the murder of Jimmy McBride at The Horse and Jockey public house.

"I believe that he was killed because he went against the intentions of the others involved, whatever those were."

"The defilement of my little girl."

"Not necessarily, I'm still not sure of what the actual motive was behind the kidnapping but I'm fairly confident now, it wasn't to extract money from you."

He then went on to explain how he had identified the possible areas in which Estelle might have been kept incarcerated, confirming that detectives were already searching for premises that might have been used.

"It's a bit late now my old mucker, the rats would have already flown," Morgan suggested.

"I have no doubt, but if we can locate where she was held prisoner, that might help us to identify those responsible."

"Whatever, but one thing is certain, there is no longer any requirement for me to stay here now, so I need to get back to work as soon as possible. I need to catch this bastard if it's the last thing I do."

Spotty Finkel was a small, fragile looking creature for which the years hadn't been kind. He walked with both shoulders slumped forward and his face was a similar colour to burnt ashes found in a fireplace hearth. Henry Bustle discovered his informant walking along a thoroughfare just off Commercial Road in Whitechapel and as soon as the elderly little vagrant caught sight of the detective, he tried to accelerate his pace to get away.

"What's your hurry, Spotty," Bustle called out.

The man stopped and turned to wait for the Sergeant to approach him.

"I'm late for work Mr. Bustle," he said, in a wavering sort of whisper.

"Work Spotty? You haven't got a bleedin' job mate."

The vagrant, who had spent most of his life surviving on the streets, straightened his back, allowing his pride to cover his facial features and insisting, "That's where you're wrong Mr. Bustle, I do some cleaning at the Pied Piper in Reynolds Street and get handsomely paid for it."

"You mean you clean out the spittoons there in return for a couple of jugs of ale."

The Sergeant's man just sniffed and returned his upper body to its previous posture, looking down at the pavement.

"Well, at least you are doing something useful, even if it isn't guarding the Queen at Buckingham Palace. What do you know of loads of copper being shifted my little rat-faced friend?"

Spotty just looked up at him and repeated, lowering his voice even more, "Copper you say?"

"That's what I said, you might have heard the rest of it, if you'd put a shovel to good use and cleaned out those allotments you call earholes."

"I'm a bit short at the moment, Mr. Bustle."

The Sergeant quickly handed over a florin, that rapidly disappeared somewhere on his man's person.

The inconspicuous individual then glanced around to ensure no one else was within hearing distance, as was his habit, before mentioning that he might be aware of a metal dealer that had recently been making a lot of money by moving on bales of copper wire.

"I don't know who Sammy Grealish's moneyman is Mr. Bustle, but he can't seem to get enough of the stuff."

"Who's this Grealish bloke, strange I've never heard of him."

"He's new at the game Mr. Bustle and when he first opened his yard, he got burgled twice in a week and has been struggling since, so I think that's why he's taking in the copper wire."

"Where's his yard, Spotty."

The informant looked sheepish at the detective, resulting in another two florins exchanging hands.

"Apart from getting pissed, you could afford to get a bath now, Spotty, before you're arrested for being a health hazard. The location of the yard, mister."

"Hord's Place, by the Sailors Church."

"And who's supplying the copper?"

"Come on Mr. Bustle, I'm taking all the risks 'ere."

"Two more bob you little runt and that's it. Now, the names."

"I've only got one name Mr. Bustle, Archie Green, but he and his mates hold out at the Horse and Jockey in York Street."

Chapter Six

Henry Bustle had been raised amongst the stench coming from the blocked drains and open cesspools that were common features in the backstreets of London, but Richard Rayner was still having some difficulty in becoming accustomed to such unsavoury presence. On occasions, the additional odours of animal excrement covering the muddy thoroughfares, and the waft of human urine raised the level of fumes to an unbearable challenge, attacking the nostrils like a swarm of invisible bees. And then of course, there was the unbreathable air itself. An atmosphere of soot and smoke was a constant aggravating feature that resulted in many of the population suffering from lung conditions. It was commonly known amongst the local inhabitants that you could tell how long sheep had been grazing in Regent's Park by the colour of their coats, changing over a period of days from white to black.

There were however, refuges and respite away from this unsavoury medley of consequential communal habitation, one being a myriad of public houses located on virtually every corner of every street, in which the local people could drink away their distress and impoverished style of life. Drunkenness and street brawling were a common feature in the backstreets, requiring police attention more than any other anti-social act.

The illegal sport of bare-knuckled fighting was another popular attraction that drew fans of the sport into its grip like a magnet, encouraged not only by the sight of bloodied bouts, but also the chance to wager what little coin they possessed on individual favoured pugilists. Such recreation was also favoured by the opportunity to drink cheap ale during the various entertainments on display, before returning home to their wives with flushed faces and for the many, more pleasant thoughts. The Law had required participants fists to be covered for the past thirty or forty years, but such a regulatory requirement was ignored by those who promoted such contests, and it was common knowledge that the police were reluctant to enforce such restrictions on a sport they themselves admired, some even participating in.

The backyard of Blackie Jones's public house was a hive of industry, with a group of half a dozen or so fit looking young men, some forming a circle and throwing a well-worn medicine ball at each other, attempting to strengthen biceps and stomach muscles. A few of the landlord's charges were engaged in hardening knuckles by punching buckets filled with gravel with clenched fists, and the landlord was presiding over his money-making youngsters, stood in the middle of the activities and vocally encouraging each to move the ball more quickly.

When the outside gates suddenly burst open and the two unwelcome visitors appeared for all to see, the training session stopped abruptly. Richard Rayner and Henry Bustle looked as though they meant business and as if fortuitously, a woman's voice could be heard at the same time, shouting out from the back door of the building.

"Ere' Blackie, there's two coppers just been sniffing around, asking about little Archie." It was the landlord's wife, a rounded woman with a flushed face.

Rayner just smiled, before asking, which of the young fighters was Master Green, but before the landlord could deny any knowledge of the name called out, a small but stocky built lad suddenly barged into the senior detective, pushing him to the ground before heading for the same open gates used by the Scotland Yard men. His attempt at escape though was cut short by Henry Bustle's clenched fist, that was dug deep into his solar plexus, resulting in the would-be fugitive collapsing to the cobbles, gasping for breath. The young man was strong, but not as experienced or physically capable as the Sergeant, who quickly pinioned both arms behind his back and secured his wrists with a pair of handcuffs, before lifting the helpless individual back on to his feet.

Richard Rayner turned to Blackie Jones and doffed his hat, suggesting the landlord continued with his training schedule, before both he and Bustle disappeared with the unfortunate young man who was still trying to force some breath into his lungs.

Archie Green would have been in his early twenties; a young man who from his gaunt facial features and vacant eyes, had experienced his fair share of poverty. He sat in the interview room at Scotland Yard, looking extremely forlorn, with his head bowed and constantly sniffing, the result of a cold he'd contracted. The prisoner looked far from being a future street fighting champion and there was an air of pauperism about the individual, the kind that both detectives had seen many times before and was a part of London's daily life.

"I take it you have already spent the money you received from your recent copper wire business," Richard Rayner remarked.

"I ain't done nothing," came the disenchanted reply.

"I am talking about the proceeds you and your mates have been taking from your escapade of burglaries recently and it seems from the rags on your back, you have spent your ill-gotten gains, unwisely." Rayner felt it unnecessary to waste time developing any rapport with the young street fighter, preferring to leave the prisoner in no doubt as to the reason for his arrest.

Archie Green just shrugged his shoulders but said nothing in response.

"We know all about the antics you and your mates have been getting up to Archie, but that's not the real reason you are in here. We want to know what part you played in kidnapping that young girl from outside the Ragged School the other morning. Tell the truth and it might reduce your sentence."

The prisoner looked up at Richard Rayner and shook his head, before pleading, "I don't know anything about any kidnapping and that's the Gospel, I thought you was coming at me over McBride's slit throat."

Rayner glanced up at Henry Bustle, who was standing directly behind Archie Green, with the intention of unnerving him. There was no need and the Sergeant quickly realised that.

"Well, I'm certain you will be telling us it was self-defence and that you had no other option but to use your knife, and we shall probably accept that, but you do know that kidnapping and rape could see you get the noose as well as murder."

"Rape? I don't know what you're talking about, I ain't raped or kidnapped anybody and that's the Gospel. Me and Jimmy had a barney, that's all and he came on to me with an iron bar, and that's the Gospel as well."

These verbal admissions had come to Rayner quite unexpected, but as the prisoner was talkative, the senior detective decided to go with the flow, the murder of Jimmy McBride now taking precedent over the other matters.

"So, what happened to the iron bar, Archie, we never found that in the room."

"I took it with me and slung it in the river, together with the blade."

"The blade you used to slit his throat."

"I've told you; he came on to me first. I had no choice."

"I think you had better start at the beginning, such as how many burglaries have you and your mates committed when you thieved that copper wire."

The prisoner shrugged his shoulders.

"Well, I shall tell you; nineteen in total. Does that equate with the number you have inside your head my friend?"

"About that, I suppose, I can't count past ten."

"Very well, so what was it you and McBride had a barney over?"

Green appeared to be keen on sharing the details of that incident and willingly explained that, after selling off the latest batch of stolen copper wire, the murder victim had divided the cash they had been given, unfairly in his favour.

"The cheating scoundrel handed a fiver to each of us and kept a tenner for himself. When we argued with him up in his room after returning to Blackie's place, he refused to put right what he'd done and threatened to split my head open with that iron bar. He reckoned he was worth more because he'd fingered the places for us to hit and when I told him I wasn't having it, he came at me, so I used the blade on him, that was all there was to it and me and the others divided the money he'd kept from us and scarpered. If I hadn't done him in, he'd have put me under the sod."

"You were seen that morning riding horses away from a carriage left in Salisbury Court and one of you was carrying a large package."

"We never had any carriage and that parcel you're on about was some of the wire our man couldn't take off us at the time. We stuck it up in the attic at the pub."

"What man? Who was fencing it for you, Archie?"

"I ain't no snitch, Mr. Rayner."

"You have no choice, Archie. The only way you are going to escape the hangman is by being fully co-operative with us, and to honestly tell us everything about everybody involved in those burglaries and that murder."

"It wasn't murder, it was self-defence, you said so yourself."

Without warning, Henry Bustle jerked the man from out of his seat by both shoulders and slammed him against the wall. With his nose almost touching the other's, he growled, "You've heard what the Chief Inspector has said, nothing short of telling all is going to save you from the drop, so let's have it. The name of your fence."

"The metal man, Sammy Grealish."

Bustle looked across at Rayner who nodded his acceptance of what Archie Green had just disclosed.

"And the names of your two mates."

"I've already told you, Jimmy McBride and a geezer calling himself, 'Brigand'."

"What kind of a name is that?" the Sergeant asked.

"That's all we knew him as, and that's the Gospel. He came into The Horse and Jockey one day and told us he was recruiting for a few jobs in Whitechapel and would we be interested. That's what my grouse with McBride was, because it was Brigand who set the jobs up for us, not him, so why should he get more of the share out. I'm telling you Mr. Rayner that's how it was, I know all about there's no honour amongst thieves, but that took the biscuit."

Richard Rayner asked where they could find this Brigand individual, and Master Green swore an oath that he had no idea and that they only used to see him at the public house.

After securing their prisoner in a cell, the two detectives made their way up to Rayner's office on the first floor and Henry Bustle suggested that if the man Green was to be believed, those burglars who had been creating bedlam across the Whitechapel district, had nothing to do with the kidnapping Investigation.

"So it seems, Henry, and we are right back at the beginning, but at least the Commissioner will have something positive to tell the media in the morning." They then both left to visit the yard belonging to the metal dealer, Sammy Grealish, who was apprehended and later dealt with. A large quantity of the stolen copper wire was recovered from the dealer's yard, and returned to the rightful owners, much to Rayner's delight, but the real reason for Archie Green's arrest remained a conundrum. Nothing had been forthcoming that would help identify the kidnapper of Estelle Roland.

All the loose ends as far as the murder of McBride and the copper wire burglaries were concerned, had been tied up nicely, except for the identification of the man referred to as 'Brigand'. However, that part of the Investigation would have to wait, knowing that his priority was now to concentrate on tracking down the man who had kidnapped and raped Frederick Morgan's daughter. There was also the Tower Bridge murder to be kept under consideration, but to focus his full attention on that atrocity would mean putting more distance between the detectives and the rapist of Estelle Roland.

Of course, Richard Rayner empathised with the anger his Chief Superintendent was feeling but did not need the man's obsession for revenge to interfere with the ongoing Inquiry. Having said that, it had not been Rayner's young son, Matthew, who had been subjected to such a traumatic ordeal and the detective wondered how he would feel, if the boot was on the other foot. He recalled the shock he felt when first discovering he had an orphaned son, following the brutal murder of the boy's mother and would always remain thankful for his wife, Clarice's understanding, by agreeing for Matthew to live with them and help raise him as though he was her own. It had also helped when the couple's domestic staff had also taken the lad to their hearts, having witnessed at first hand the pain and grief their master and mistress had suffered when losing their only daughter, Rose, to Cholera not long before Matthew came on the scene.

The youngster had quickly settled into his new life and attended a private school of teaching in Richmond, close to where the family residence was located. The usual practice was for either Richard or Clarice Rayner to take their son to school each morning and collect him at the end of the day. However, recently the fourteen-year-old had insisted he could make his own way home and his father had reluctantly agreed, appreciative as his work commitments had increased quite dramatically in recent weeks.

When it transpired on the same afternoon that Archie Green had been arrested, that young Matthew Rayner had failed to arrive home at the usual time, the butler, Albert Winkler, became concerned. After an hour went by without there being any sign of the youngster, it was Mrs. Uddlestone, the Rayners' cook, who advised the elderly servant to contact their mistress at the college where she worked. But before doing so, Albert directed the stable boy, Jonas, to take him in a carriage to the missing lad's seat of learning, only to confirm from the caretaker there, that Matthew had been seen leaving the premises at the usual time.

It was dark when the concerned butler reached Kings College in The Strand and found Clarice Rayner in her laboratory, putting the finishing touches to the model of a human face she intended using at a presentation to students the following day. When the butler related his anxieties to his mistress, she immediately grabbed her coat and suggested they should immediately report the missing boy to her husband at Scotland Yard.

Richard Rayner's life was about to change, quite dramatically.

Chapter Seven

As the late afternoon bowed its head towards the early evening, it became obvious the boy had been the subject of some misadventure and a concerned Richard and Clarice Rayner had to finally accept that something untoward, perhaps sinister, had happened to the light of their lives. The Chief Inspector prayed his son had not been snatched in the same way as Estelle Roland had been taken, or that any other ill will had befallen him, but as the darkness closed in, his fears were beginning to transform into reality.

Ironically, as news of the boy's disappearance began to spread, it was Richard Rayner who had to reluctantly remain at home and await the delivery of any anticipated correspondence from those who were responsible for taking his son.

Frederick Morgan naturally displayed immense sympathy for his Chief Inspector, having so recently experienced what Rayner was now having to confront. The Chief Superintendent made it quite clear that he would immediately take personal charge of the search for young Matthew and committed every available detective and patrolling constable to make enquiries across the whole of London. In addition, Henry Bustle was dispatched back to Whitechapel to seek what information he could from the Sergeant's many contacts.

Thankfully, the headmaster of King Alfred Collegiate School in Queens Gate Terrace, Richmond, a Mr. Bartholomew Parker, was still working late in his study when Morgan disturbed him. He was a small, rounded gentleman with a short moustache and smartly dressed in a winged collar and dark suit. After explaining the disappearance of Matthew Rayner, the senior detective suggested that perhaps the incident was the result of some kind of schoolboy prank but was quickly assured that would not have been the case. The headmaster confirmed that young Matthew had been seen stepping through the school gates at exactly 4.05 p.m. that afternoon.

"From what his form master tells me Chief Superintendent, young Rayner is an extremely mature and articulate boy, not the kind who would play silly pranks, especially one that would cause so much grief for his parents, sir."

That was all Frederick Morgan wished to know and after politely thanking the man, turned to leave.

"You must find the boy quickly Chief Inspector," Mr. Parker suggested, "For the sake of the school's name."

The Welshman glared at the headmaster and snapped back, like a terrier with its prey in sight, "It's Chief Superintendent sir, and yes, we shall find the boy, but for his sake and for no other reason."

After leaving, Morgan stood outside the front gates of the school with Jack Robinson at his side.

"Are you wondering sir, if the boy might have had some kind of accident on his way home," the young Sergeant suggested.

"No, I am not. I have no doubt that Master Rayner has been taken by some fiendish individual, Robbo and I am fearful for his safety."

"The most direct route he would have taken to reach home would have been across that parkland in front of us sir," the Sergeant suggested.

"I'm aware of that Robbo," his senior answered, "And there's every chance the kid might have been snatched when crossing over there."

Jack Robinson could see the vindictive determination in Morgan's eyes. The Welshman's facial features were a personification of an individual pursuing a quest for retribution.

"We have to catch this bastard," the Chief Superintendent quietly whispered, staring across at the open acreage.

"Would you like me to arrange for it to be searched, sir."

"No, we'll do it ourselves, now."

Both detectives followed a path that took them across the middle of the open land, until they reached a copse of trees at the far end. The path they were following led them straight through the centre of the woodland, where their Bullseye lanterns illuminated their way, and it was just as they were about to exit the trees at the far end, that Jack Robinson suddenly stopped. Turning to Morgan he confirmed there was what looked like, a schoolboy's satchel resting against the trunk of a tree just a few feet to their right.

When the senior detective opened the item, the name of Matthew Rayner could be seen neatly written on the inside of the flap. Amongst several exercise books there was surprisingly, a sealed envelope addressed to 'Detective Richard Rayner'.

"Do you think we should open it sir, or take it to the Chief Inspector, as it's addressed to him."

"Of course we bloody well should, Robbo, it might just contain a note from the kidnappers."

Inside the envelope was a folded letter that read:

'We ave your boy Rainer and lets see how much you value his life. You ave 'til three o'clock tomorrow afternoon, the 4th of the munth, to deliver ten tousand in cash to Waterlue Station. The muney is to be contained inside a leather case and left beneath the clock just inside the entry to the station. Any tricks and you wont see your kid agaen'.

Morgan read the demand twice, before placing the note and envelope inside his jacket pocket and deciding they should make Richard Rayner aware of what they had discovered.

There was no time to spare and both detectives ran back across the parkland, to where they had left their carriage and within a few minutes they were knocking on the front door of the Rayners' residence.

A distraught Chief Inspector read and scrutinised the written instructions, before making a surprising comment.

"Very clever," he remarked to no one in particular.

"What's clever about it, Richard?" Morgan enquired.

"They have chosen one of the busiest venues in London."

"What do you make of the writing?"

"It's disguised, notice the spelling errors that have been made quite deliberately, but the grammar depicts it was written by an educated person."

"That's not much help to us. I take it you are not prepared to part with such an amount."

"It matters not, we couldn't lay our hands on that amount of cash, even if we had it," Clarice Rayner explained, sitting next to her husband on a couch inside the downstairs drawing room.

"No, we could not," Rayner confirmed, "But the person making the demand would be aware of that, they have quite deliberately given us a task that is impossible to fulfil."

"What's puzzling me is how these jackals knew we would find that satchel as quickly as we did," Morgan confessed.

"They didn't, I suspect they expected it would be found in a day or two, just to add to our anguish and fear that by not being in a position to respond to the instructions, we would be subjected to more pain."

"But for what reason, Richard?" Clarice asked.

"I'm not sure dear, but it all seems to be very strange, and I suspect whoever is behind this is the same person responsible for abducting Estelle. At present, the only motive they seem to have, is to cause us the utmost grief."

"Well, they are succeeding," his wife remarked.

Turning to Frederick Morgan, she asked what steps he was taking to trace Matthew's whereabouts and find out who the kidnappers were.

The Chief Superintendent recognised that there would not have been many people about in the parkland when the youngster was taken but confessed his intention was to make a plea for any witnesses in the local newspapers.

"I don't suppose you have a tin plate of Matthew's face," he asked.

"Yes, we have several," Richard Rayner replied, "But I am not sure if that isn't exactly what the kidnappers are looking for."

"I don't understand."

"I do not believe this is about demanding money, but rather a ploy to cause distress to us, in the same manner as Estelle's disappearance did to yourself and Sally-Anne. That being the case, it might well be that the same people would be encouraged by any publicity they might receive for their evil atrocity."

Morgan thought about what his Chief Inspector was saying for a few moments and then suggested that Rayner return to work and join him in the hunt for those who were causing so much bedlam.

"What do you think we should do about the demand for the ransom?" he sympathetically asked.

"They will be expecting us to react in some way and I have to think of the safety of my son, dependent on what course of action we take."

"What if we cover the drop-off point tomorrow and you leave a suitcase containing blank pieces of paper."

"These vermin would expect us to do exactly that, knowing that I could never raise that kind of cash in such a short period of time. Having said that, I see no other option but to play their game, and in the meantime, I think we should make more enquiries at Matthew's school to see if anyone there noticed any strangers loitering near to the entrance prior to my son being taken."

"I'll go back there now and start with the caretaker," Jack Robinson suggested.

"And I will see you at Scotland Yard, Richard, first thing in the morning," Morgan added, before both detectives left, but not before the Chief Superintendent had tried to reassure Clarice that he would do all in his power to recover the boy and bring to justice those responsible.

There was little sleep that night for Richard or Clarice Rayner and their thoughts remained with the nightmare their son would have been going through, replicating the same dilemma the Morgans had experienced. And yet, in a strange way, Rayner was convinced the kidnappers' purpose was not to harm the boy and that they were targeting himself as well as Frederick Morgan. He gave a great deal of consideration to how they were going to respond to the demand made the following afternoon, and by the time he finally came to a decision, the dawn had arrived with low lying heavy clouds threatening the winter's first snow.

Denmark Street was a peaceful narrow side street in Whitechapel, resulting from the vast majority of terraced houses being void and awaiting demolition. The dwelling at number five however, was still occupied and owned by Maisy Winthrop, a Madam responsible for managing a brothel at that address. Naturally, and because of the nature of her business, it was Maisy's habit to constantly peer through her curtains, watching out for any undesirable individual who might be intent on visiting her premises. She was a confident and vigilant woman who kept her profit-making ventures behind closed doors, the majority of her customers being known to her and comprising of men working at the nearby docks.

On the afternoon following the disappearance of Matthew Rayner, Maisy Winthrop noticed an incident that uncharacteristically gave her grave cause for concern. Through the downstairs curtains, she watched a carriage stop in the street, just up from the lady's business premises and saw a man leap from the vehicle, looking a little agitated. He was joined by the driver before both men then struggled with a third person, forcing the individual out of the carriage on to the pavement. Much to Maisy's surprise, the one who appeared to be objecting to being manhandled was nothing more than a young boy, with a hessian sack placed over his head. Eventually, the men managed to force their prisoner down an alleyway that divided the brothel from the next-door dwelling that the Madam knew was empty.

Knowing the three girls that worked for Maisy were resting upstairs, she stepped out through her front door and cautiously made her way down the same alleyway until reaching the rear gardens. She then inquisitively leant over a broken wooden fence to try and view the inside of what used to be the kitchen through a grime covered window but couldn't see or hear anything. Although it was against her better nature, the woman decided it best to find a patrolling constable and report what she had seen. She then turned and began to retrace her steps back down the alleyway, when suddenly she was confronted by one of the men she had earlier seen molesting the boy.

He aggressively asked what she was doing there and without hesitation, Maisy answered, "Looking for my bleedin' cat, what do you think? The bleedin' thing has got out." She then hurried past the man and made the street. But instead of returning to her own house, the woman quickly made her way down Denmark Street, heading towards the docks.

It wasn't long before she came across a constable walking towards her and quickly told him about what she had seen.

Constable George Bullock was at first reluctant to believe the woman's story, but after seeing how genuinely concerned she appeared, sent her on her way, promising to look into the matter.

Five minutes before the designated hour of three o'clock, everyone was in position inside the entrance hall of Waterloo Railway Station. Detectives dressed as porters and other rail workers were poised in readiness, with Frederick Morgan and Henry Bustle seated on a bench close to the large clock beneath which the ransom money was to be left. The location was extremely busy, with travellers moving to and from the only two platforms facilitating incoming and departing trains, which benefitted the detectives' concealment.

As three o'clock struck, Richard Rayner could be seen stepping through the archway over the entrance and slowly walking towards the clock. He was carrying a brown leather suitcase and when arriving at the designated place, stopped and looked around, assuming that the kidnappers would be watching his every movement. The Chief Inspector was armed, just in case, and after carefully lowering the suitcase to the floor, stepped away and began to walk back towards the exit.

Rayner had only walked a short distance, when unexpectedly, he heard some commotion coming from beneath the clock. Turning his attention to the scene that was ongoing, he could see a young street ruffian being manhandled by Frederick Morgan. The lad was grasping the suitcase and detectives were appearing from everywhere.

"I ain't done nothing mister," the urchin was pleading, wincing at the tightness in which Morgan was grasping his arm.

"Who paid you to pick up that suitcase boy?" Rayner asked.

"A tall geezer gave me threepence to take it to him."

"Where?"

"On the bridge, Waterloo Bridge."

"What did he look like and be quick about it."

The lad was nervous and did his best to stutter out a vague description of a man wearing a green cape, but that was all the young ruffian could disclose.

Without speaking another word, both Rayner and Bustle raced outside towards the bridge, with half a dozen other detectives following. When they got there, because of the crowds of people present, it was nigh on impossible to identify any individual and Rayner's suspicions were quickly realised.

"It seems our man is still playing games," Bustle remarked.

"I agree Henry, but I did anticipate this was how it was going to play out in the end."

The problem Rayner now had, was that he genuinely feared for the life of his son.

When they got back to where Morgan and the others were still holding on to the boy who had given the name of Harold Smith, which was probably false, Rayner suggested he be released, satisfied he had told the truth. The street urchin left, having been given another threepence for his troubles.

Upon returning to Scotland Yard, they all regrouped in Frederick Morgan's office and the usual pipe filled with Atlantic Shag tobacco was lit up, causing most of them to begin coughing.

"So, what now, Rayner?" the Chief Superintendent enquired, "We're no closer to catching these vermin or getting your boy back."

Rayner repeated his earlier suggestion that he believed the motive behind both kidnappings wasn't for monetary gain, but rather connected with some bizarre intention of revenge.

"I think we should search through the records in the basement and see if we can find somebody who we have both dealt with in the past, and who is likely to commit these atrocities as a way of paying us back for having been incarcerated."

Morgan nodded, but then the short meeting was interrupted by a knock on the door and the Desk Sergeant from downstairs entered the office.

"Sorry to interrupt Mr. Rayner sir, but your butler is downstairs, asking to speak with you urgently."

"I'll come," the Chief Inspector confirmed, wondering what other disturbing incident had taken place, knowing that Albert would not have been sent to Scotland Yard by Clarice, unless it was of some urgency.

He found the elderly servant sitting on a bench in the main reception area and upon seeing his master approaching, the butler instantly got to his feet.

"I am sorry sir, but it's Master Matthew."

"What about him, Albert?" Rayner feared the worst.

"Well, he's come home sir."

"Elaborate more Albert, is he alright?"

"Oh yes, he says he was dropped off at the main gate and apart from being a little shook up, appears to be fine sir."

As the dusk was quickly approaching, Frederick Shoemaker, a lamplighter employed by the Holborn District Council, had started his round early and had just three more streetlights to illuminate. When walking close to the London Dock, between Wells and Fell Street, with his pole resting on his shoulder, the elderly worker suddenly noticed what looked like a bundle of rags lying on the Embankment, close to the river's edge. Not wanting to miss an opportunity to recover anything that might be of value, the old lamplighter cautiously made his way down towards the water's edge. When reaching the object he was intent on examining, he gasped and stepped back at the sight of a woman's face staring upwards and directly at him. She had a gaping wound across her throat and the old man almost dropped his pole, as he scampered back to the street, yelling for help.

When Henry Bustle and Jack Robinson arrived at the scene, they found two constables standing near to the body, talking to the old lamplighter who looked as though he had just seen a ghost.

Constable George Bullock told Bustle that he thought he knew the dead woman, explaining that she had approached him the day before and gave a brief account of what she had told him.

"She lives at 5, Denmark Street, which I suspect is a brothel, sarge."

"Did you get any description of those two men, or of the boy she spoke to you about?" Bustle asked.

"No, she couldn't give me any, but I went up to the house at number six, where she reckoned they'd taken the boy but found it empty. I put in a full report with all the details."

Henry Bustle then turned to Jack Robinson and suggested he went and fetched the pathologist, Doctor Critchley. He was already beginning to wonder if the incident was connected in any way with the Matthew Rayner kidnapping.

Chapter Eight

By the time Jack Robinson had returned with the pathologist, Henry Bustle had visited 5 Denmark Street, to see if he could get the dead woman identified but had got no response to his call. He was trying hard to replicate how he thought Richard Rayner would respond and act if he was present, and upon arriving back at the scene, stood back to allow Doctor Critchley to make his usual cursory examination of the body, in the same manner he had seen the Chief Inspector do, so many times previously.

It was quickly established that the woman had been dead for only a matter of a couple of hours, and Bustle continued to walk in the senior detective's shoes by noting every other feature visible at the scene. Finally, after arranging for the victim to be removed to the mortuary at St. Mary's Hospital, the Sergeant told the doctor he would inform Chief Inspector Rayner of the circumstances as soon as he could.

During the time that Bustle was taking charge of London's most recent murder, Richard Rayner was hastily making his way home, anxious to see his son, Matthew, and upon arrival found the lad being comforted in the drawing room by Clarice. She was obviously elated, and the fourteen-year-old boy appeared to be physically none the worse from his ordeal but had obviously been shaken by his experience. When his father asked a couple of questions regarding anything his son could tell him about the men who had taken him, the boy tried hard to relate everything he knew, but his obvious exhaustion made it difficult for the youngster to remain fully rationale, prompting Clarice to interrupt the conversation.

"Might I suggest Richard, that Matthew should be allowed to have his supper before taking a bath and going to bed.   You can continue your Inquisition in the morning, when I am sure Matthew will be far better equipped to help you, after a good night's rest."

"Of course, dear, we shall speak further in the morning Matthew, but thank God you are home safe." Rayner was feeling a mixture of relief that his son had been returned to them, and anger at the person responsible for taking him in the first instance. Whatever help Matthew could eventually provide, the senior detective was more determined than ever, to get his hands on the culprits who had brought about so much grief to his family. However, when divorcing himself from the emotional atmosphere that was now gripping his home, the renowned detective felt a great deal of confusion as to the true purpose behind both Matthew's kidnapping and that of Estelle Morgan. It was quite evident that the purpose behind the atrocities wasn't sourced by any of the usual motives and the person he would now be urgently attempting to track down had some hidden agenda that was foreign to his pursuer. At least his son was home safe and sound and the fact was, that by returning Matthew to them, the kidnapper had given them the best witness they would have in assisting with uncovering his identity.

"I can't say as I'm surprised my old mucker," Frederick Morgan remarked, when first being told of Matthew Rayner's safe return by his father the following morning, "It has to be the same bastard who took my Estelle, although he raped..." Morgan broke off and then looking directly at Richard Rayner enquired in a quiet voice, "They didn't do..."

"No, he wasn't touched," the Chief Inspector answered abruptly.

"Well, let's be thankful for small mercies."

"Matthew tells me there were two men, one who kept a sack over his head and the other who drove the carriage they used to abduct him. He recollects they took him to what he assumed was an empty building somewhere, but then overheard the pair discussing a woman who had seen them. It was then they returned him to the carriage and took him some distance to another room that he thought from what he could hear and smell, was over some kind of kitchen or cooking location. He thinks from the odours that reached him it could have been a tripe shop."

"At least that's something for us to go on."

"But there's more." Rayner then went on to describe how Jack Robinson had eventually confirmed the latest murder victim was a woman known as, Maisie Winthrop, who lived at number 5, Denmark Street, Whitechapel. He reiterated what Constable George Bullock had told Henry Bustle and was wondering if the incident was related to the information shared by Matthew, particularly when telling his father, he had overheard the two kidnappers suggesting they had been seen by a woman.

"And you think that those two miscreants could have done away with our lady in case she took what she knew to the police," Morgan enquired.

"Yes, I think there's every possibility, but strangely, one of the men who returned Matthew gave him a personal message for me. He told him to tell me that, Brigand predicts the storm will soon be a tempest."

Morgan sat back in his chair and reached for his pipe, giving notice that his office would soon be enveloped by the stench of his favoured smoke.

"Does the name, Brigand, mean anything to you?" he finally asked.

"No and I was going to ask the same question of yourself."

The Chief Superintendent considered the name thoughtfully, before conceding that it meant nothing to him either.

"I reckon we are dealing with some prat who is completely bonkers."

"On the contrary," Rayner responded, "I think he is a highly intelligent individual who plans every move he makes extremely carefully. What has become obvious to me, is that he is desperate not to be caught and if I am right about the murder of Maisie Winthrop, is prepared to kill to avoid detection."

"Don't you think that murder is a bit dramatic for a crackpot who is just playing games with us."

"I fear the reason he needs to remain free of capture, is because he is planning some finality to his activities by committing some heinous crime that is far more serious and perhaps devastating than he has done so far."

"Such as killing either or both of us."

"Perhaps, but I doubt that somehow, only because he could have already attempted that. No, it seems that he prefers at present to cause us as much pain and suffering as possible, which might very well be leading up to whatever his final atrocity is going to be. That's the only pattern I can think of that seems to be logical and makes sense."

"Nothing this prat has done so far, makes sense to me, my old mucker."

The large, magnificent crystal chandeliers added to the spectacular scene inside the Grand Ballroom at Claridge's in Brook Street, Mayfair. It was a formal affair with an array of ladies dazzling ankle length gowns on display, in contrast to the gentlemen's smart black tie evening attire, as the participants twirled around the spacious floor. The orchestra continued to play, and the atmosphere was of great joy and merriment as the majestic annual dinner for the surgeons working at the New Women's Hospital, continued into the night.

Sir Reginald Hammond was the Head of the Gynaecology Department at the hospital, a distinguished fifty-two-year-old gentleman with silver hair and a full beard to match. Being highly reputable and widely recognised for his research in his specialised subject, the eminent surgeon had gained greater respect from his colleagues since gaining the confidence of the Queen herself. The man's charismatic presence was usually admired by those whose company he chose, and yet, on this particular celebratory evening, Sir Reginald appeared to be uncharacteristically subdued, sitting to one side and sharing his wife's company.

"You seem to be miles away dear," Lady Barbara Hammond quietly whispered, sitting upright and looking adorably enchanting in her silver gown, "Is there something worrying you?"

"What? No, no, of course not my dear, I was just enjoying to the full this splendid cigar I purchased from Robert Lewis's Tobacconist earlier this afternoon, especially for this occasion, and of course, admiring some of our younger members enjoying the pleasant company of their ladies."

"Then might I persuade you to take this bemused lady of yours for the next Polka."

"Of course, dear, nothing would give me greater pleasure."

As the couple began to revolve around the room, the male half of the partnership suddenly saw his young assistant enter the ballroom and sit with a group of other junior doctors. But to leave the dance at that moment might have caused some embarrassment to his wife, so Sir Reginald continued to remain the dedicated gentleman.

"Oh, go on Reggie, go and speak with young Toby, I know you are absolutely bursting your buttons to speak with him," his understanding wife offered.

"Are you sure dear, it's just that..."

"I know dear, yet another experiment you cannot wait to hear the results of."

He smiled appreciatively and kissed her on the cheek, before leading her back to their table.

When Tobias Corncrake saw his senior approaching, he instantly leapt to his feet, knowing exactly what would be required of him.

Sir Reginald nodded, indicating for his assistant to follow him out into the hotel's foyer, where they could both enjoy some privacy and where the two men stood alone, facing each other. Trying to retain some control over his enthusiasm, the senior surgeon lit up a second cigar, one that he had failed to notify his wife he had also bought from the reputable tobacconist in Covent Garden. He could see from the smile on young Tobias's gleaming face, the tests had met with a positive result.

"It went well?" he enquired.

"Better than that, we achieved complete fertilisation that went beyond the time scale."

"How far beyond?"

"Exactly twenty-two minutes past the scheduled ten minutes."

Sir Reginald's eyes lit up, knowing they were on the brink of bringing to the world of medicine, the very first case of successful artificial insemination inside a female. The Knight of the Realm had spent the past two years working hard with his small team of scientists at The New Women's Hospital to achieve what had just taken place.

"What temperature did you maintain?" he then asked.

"The same as you suggested, sir."

"Excellent young man, you have done well, now we can move forward to the next stage with confidence."

"Introduction to the cervix."

"Or fallopian tubes or possibly the uterus, but that's for us to perfect. But first we shall require a real-life recipient." Sir Reginald slapped his assistant on the back and then demanded that the success achieved should not be shared with anyone at present, much to the younger man's gratification.

As each day passed by, Richard Rayner and Henry Bustle became more frustrated by their failure to identify any individual who might have been holding a grudge against the Chief Inspector in particular. After delving through numerous files in the basement at Scotland Yard, the result was always the same, the vast majority of those miscreants they had dealt with were dead, having been dispatched by the hangman. Even Frederick Morgan spent a great deal of time dwelling over his past, right back to his Army days, recalling one or two fellow officers he had been involved in personal skirmishes with, but no one as far as he was concerned, had any reason to have carried animosity towards him over such a lengthy period of time. Finally, all three detectives had to concede that nothing would be further gained by continuing with that part of the Investigation.

It was late, when Henry Bustle found himself sitting opposite Sidney Pike in an interview room inside Highgate Prison. In fact, the visit was the last scheduled for that day and the Sergeant's rank had been the only reason he had been authorised to attend so late in the day.

Prisoner Pike was a colossus of a man with a full black beard and hair that touched his shoulders. The man had been convicted of manslaughter some years before, having been arrcstcd by Richard Rayner, a fact he was reminded of by his official visitor.

"How long have you been inside here now, Sid?" Bustle enquired.

"Seven years and two months," the man replied, "And I'm not hopeful you've brought a free pardon with you. Why are you here, Mr. Bustle?"

"I'm here to represent Mr. Rayner, who as I'm sure you recollect, saved you from the noose."

The convict said nothing and just stared across the table at the Sergeant.

"You do recall Sid, that it was Richard Rayner who persuaded the judge to spare you from the hangman."

The convict nodded.

"Well, you might just be able to repay the favour."

"How's that when I'm stuck in here until they carry me out in a box."

"I want you to think carefully over the past seven years if any other prisoner passed through who held more than the usual amount of hatred towards the Chief Inspector. Somebody who perhaps might have made some threats towards Rayner. Does anybody come to mind?"

The prisoner sat for a while in silence, obviously trying to recall and then remarked, "There were a few who mentioned his name and you know how it is, swear they would get even once they got out, but it's usually all bullshit and nothing comes of it."

"What about an individual who you thought might not have been bullshitting and was capable of carrying out his threat."

"Nobody."

"Perhaps a quiet geezer who you might have thought would have the inclination to perhaps kill to get even with Rayner."

"Nobody."

By the time Bustle returned to Scotland Yard it was late and a light was still burning inside Richard Rayner's office on the first floor. He found the Chief Inspector at his desk, still pondering through a few files but without success. When told of his Sergeant's recent disappointing visit to see Sidney Pike, Rayner thanked him for trying and stepped across to his blackboard. Reading from the chalked notes he'd made, the senior detective reiterated that Estelle Morgan had been incarcerated for a matter of three days before being released, albeit she had been unmercifully raped during that time. His son had been kept from him for that same period, before being dropped off at the gates of his home and following the murder of Maisie Winthrop, a Madam from Denmark Street in Whitechapel.

"We are assuming Henry, that the woman was killed because she actually saw the kidnappers with Matthew and could have possibly identified them."

"What if that wasn't the case and Maisie Winthrop's death wasn't connected to the kidnappings?"

"There are too many coincidences for that to be the case, but the point I'm making is that to have committed such an evil act in the woman's case, must mean that her killer was desperate to avoid detection. Can you think of any other villain who would commit murder to avoid being caught for kidnappings where they returned the victims to their homes safely without having been paid any ransom money? It would be the same as a burglar stealing jewels and making good his escape, only to return the stolen goods the following day."

"I take your point, but where does it get us?"

Rayner returned to his desk and sat down, his mind obviously toying with several possibilities but recognising only one that appeared to be logical.

"There were two kidnappers, one who did the actual abductions and the other who drove the carriages, perhaps an assistant. Therefore, it is highly probable that only one of them is seeking his revenge, possibly paying the other to assist him, would you say?"

"That seems fair to assume."

"So, I believe we are looking for two different characters; the planner who has set up what has taken place, and his labourer who is being employed to do the donkey work."

"And you are going to ask me where I would go to employ such a person."

"Yes."

"Anywhere north of the river, with Smithfield and Whitechapel being the favoured districts."

"I think we should concentrate further on those two areas, asking the right questions of the right people, in an effort to identify any individual who has recently been kept busy by some other unknown character."

"You mean I should."

"Both you and Jack Robinson."

"And might I ask sir, what you will be doing in the meantime."

"Setting a trap for our man to fall into, Henry."

Richard Rayner had already decided that the man he sought was determined to cause him further distress, perhaps far more intense than ever before. An act of criminality that would, if successful, possibly leave the Chief Inspector deranged, such as an attempt on his wife's life, or even his own existence being the prize sought after by the culprit of one murder and two kidnappings. That being the case, he wasn't willing to wait like a sitting duck for anything to happen and preferred to take his chances by somehow setting the man up in a way that he, Rayner, had control of what would take place. The senior detective wasn't quite sure how he was to go about it but was convinced of what his next course of action should be.

When he arrived home that same night, he discussed his thoughts with his wife, Clarice, and suggested that it would be safer if she and Matthew were to visit her mother, Marjorie Peach, who lived in Brook Street, Mayfair. At first, Clarice was reluctant, but when her husband explained it would afford him a better state of mind knowing they were out of the firing line as it were, she agreed to write a note to Matthew's school, excusing him for a few days, and leave the following morning.

"It would also mean you staying away from the college, Clarice," he explained.

"Yes, I know dear, but your wish is my command and Mr. Detective, you had better catch this individual quickly," she said, raising a glass of wine.

After arranging for his wife and son to be transported to Mayfair the following morning, the senior detective arrived at Scotland Yard believing that an idea which had developed in his mind overnight, might just work, provided the powers that be, would agree to his suggestion. It took a good hour before Frederick Morgan finally declared his support for what was in his Chief Inspector's mind, and he wasted little time in arranging for Rayner to see the Commissioner.

"Don't be disappointed if the old man thinks your proposal outlandish," the Chief Superintendent advised, as both men climbed the stairs leading to the top floor, with Morgan still feeling dubious, although his Chief Inspector remained optimistic. Richard Rayner was hoping that the murder of Maisie Winthrop would add weight to what he was about to put to the Head of the Metropolitan Police.

Chapter Nine

After being summoned into the spacious office, both detectives stood before Sir Edward Bradford who was seated behind his large ornamental desk with his back to a window.

"I can allow you five minutes only I'm afraid gentlemen, as I have an important meeting with the Home Secretary at half past nine," the Commissioner instructed, glancing at his time piece grasped in one hand, "So please continue Mr. Rayner and be quick about it."

The Chief Inspector hastily gave an attenuated account of both kidnappings, before placing emphasis on his belief that the same perpetrators were responsible for the murder of the Madam from Denmark Street. He concluded by reiterating his belief that the motive behind the first two atrocities was one of revenge against himself and Frederick Morgan, or either one of them.

"But I favour that I am his principle target sir," he added.

"What makes you think that?"

The Chief Inspector repeated the message delivered by one of the kidnappers by his son, that 'Brigand predicts that the storm will soon become a tempest'.

"Also, according to one of the men we arrested for the copper wire burglaries and murder of James McBride in Whitehall, those were instigated by a man of that same name, Brigand."

Frederick Morgan glanced across at his Chief Inspector, unable to hide a look of surprise. He was hearing that snippet of information for the first time.

"I'm not sure I follow what you are inferring, Mr. Rayner," the Commissioner confessed.

"I suspect the burglaries were a ploy to distract us during the time this Brigand fellow was planning his escapade of kidnappings."

Sir Edward sat back in his chair and eyed both detectives a little dubiously. He then asked, "Pray tell me, Mr. Rayner, what evidence have you that the murder of this woman in Whitechapel is connected with the kidnapping of your son?"

"None sir, but there are too many coincidences to leave much doubt." Rayner then described how his son had overheard his captors mention that a woman had seen them and how Maisie Winthrop had reported the incident to a patrolling constable.

"Very well, so what are you proposing."

"I believe that the man we seek is planning another atrocity against myself sir," Rayner explained, "One that has far more serious repercussions than the atrocities he has committed so far, perhaps even my own murder." He then continued to explain that his intention was to use himself as bait and allow his stalker the opportunity to strike at a time when Rayner would be sufficiently protected. He continued to share his considered views that an element of jealousy was possibly a part of the killer's motivation, and therefore believed the greatest inducement to lure their man into a pre-arranged trap, would be if the publicly known detective was awarded some special honour to be presented at a ceremony that received wide newspaper coverage prior to it taking place.

"If I am correct in my assumptions sir, and if the man we seek is being driven by a degree of malicious resentment towards me, the temptation might be sufficient for him to swallow the bait and attempt to prevent any such presentation from taking place."

"And what kind of special honour are you thinking of Chief Inspector, a knighthood perhaps?" The Commissioner was being facetious, but Rayner remained persistent.

"I'm not sure, but I strongly suspect that the killer's actions are the result of some form of bitter resentment towards myself, and he would naturally want to spoil any attempt to glorify my name."

"And yet, he returned your son to you."

"Yes, and that is why I truly suspect I am his only target, sir."

"If what you say is true, what if this individual decides to attack your family again."

Rayner explained how he had moved his wife and son to a place of safety.

Sir Edward then turned to Morgan and asked for his thoughts, rising from his chair as if in a hurry to depart.

"I support Mr. Rayner's suspicions sir," the Chief Superintendent answered, "And his plan to catch this cretin, but we would have to be careful when choosing the venue for the presentation of this fictitious honour, whatever it might be."

The Commissioner called out for Miss Collins, his elderly secretary, before requesting the lady to bring him his hat and coat.

"Very well, I shall authorise whatever action you decide should be taken, but for now gentlemen I must really be on my way."

Both Rayner and Morgan turned to leave, but whilst Miss Collins was helping Sir Edward with his coat, the Head of the Metropolitan Police suddenly called them back.

"I have an idea that might assist in this lark you are suggesting. Come back at midday and by then I should have obtained the necessary approval required."

Both detectives nodded and made their exit.

Jack Robinson, who had been making enquiries into the Tower Bridge murder at the direction of Richard Rayner, was waiting in his office when the Chief Inspector returned. But first, the young Sergeant explained that he had experienced great difficulty in tracing the manufacturer of the carriage used in the kidnapping of Estelle Roland, without a maker's plate being available.

"Not to worry Jack but thank you for trying. What of our other victim, Raymond Carter."

"The gentleman lived at 225, St Paul's Road, Islington sir, with his wife, Alice, and their two young children, Esther and Elizabeth. I arranged with Inspector Downing for Mrs. Carter to identify her husband at the mortuary and naturally she was devastated."

Robinson then went on to explain that, although he felt it was more conducive to leave the lady to her privacy to grieve her husband's death, he did manage to confirm that the victim had no known enemies as far as she was aware.

"She described him as being an enthusiastic worker who was extremely ambitious and was actually disappointed when his contract ended upon completion of the bridge."

"What did she mean by ambitious, Jack?" Rayner asked.

"I'm not sure sir, I guess she was referring to the manner in which he approached his work."

"Very well, you were right to allow her some space for the time being, but we shall need to see her again, perhaps in a few days, once she has partially recovered from what must have been a shock to her."

"Yes sir."

"But we need to know more about Mr. Carter's background. Which individuals were closest to him during the time he was working on the bridge and who did he socialise with? Any snippet of information that would give us a better idea of the kind of character he was, Jack."

As much as Frederick Morgan detested being kept waiting unnecessarily, he could do nothing to avoid being kept sitting for two hours with Richard Rayner in the corridor outside the Commissioner's office. The Chief Superintendent was like a cat too close to the fire and constantly referred to his pocket watch, much to Rayner's irritation. He was about to stand and leave when Sir Edward finally appeared, having obviously been delayed by an extended lunch with the Home Secretary.

"I do apologise for keeping you waiting gentlemen," Sir Edward offered, as he stepped into his office, followed by his secretary grasping a folder of papers in her hands, and both Richard Rayner and a slightly flustered, Frederick Morgan.

"Considering what we discussed this morning, I do believe an opportunity to set a trap for your man has presented itself."

The Commissioner then went on to explain that in celebration of her Jubilee year that had taken place two years previously, the Queen had authorised the presentation of what was known as the 'Jubilee Medal' to members of the Metropolitan Police.

"Tomorrow evening, I am to attend at the Guildhall to make presentations of belated medals to a dozen or so officers who were absent from the initial ceremony."

"Forgive me, sir," Morgan interrupted, "But I wasn't made aware of such presentations." The Head of the Detective Branch was thinking of how much a medal such as that described by the Commissioner, would have impressed his wife, Sally-Anne.

"No, you would not have been Mr. Morgan, the medals were only distributed to uniform officers."

The Welshman was tempted to argue that point, but suddenly remembered he was in the presence of a man who could end his career with a snap of his fingers, so just nodded his understanding.

"Very well, now then what I have in mind, taking all aspects of Mr. Rayner's suggestion into consideration, is that I shall present one of the Jubilee Medals to yourself Chief Inspector, but it will be a special medal awarded for the excellent service you have provided in the past and for those outstanding achievements attributable to yourself."

"But it will be fictitious, as we suggested, sir," Morgan outlined, not feeling comfortable about Richard Rayner receiving such an honour without himself being recognised.

"No, it will be quite genuine, as I believe Mr. Rayner is well worthy of such an honour in any case."

The green-eyed monster appeared for a fleeting second and Morgan had some difficulty in disguising his obvious envy.

"Thank you sir," the Chief Inspector acknowledged, humbly.

"Don't thank me, Mr. Rayner, thank the Home Secretary, for it is he I have had to seek approval from." The Commissioner then continued by explaining that the presentation ceremony was scheduled to take place the following day in the evening, and it might be a good idea to publicise the event in the local newspapers, placing a great deal of emphasis on Rayner's participation and the true objective of the exercise being to apprehend a kidnapper and the killer of Maisie Winthrop.

"Of course, in normal circumstances I would not be happy about informing the newspapers of a ceremony such as this, unless it was for our benefit you understand, but obviously you require your man to be notified of the event I take it."

"Yes sir, that is an excellent idea," Rayner remarked.

"Then I shall call a press conference this afternoon here at Scotland Yard and try and persuade those in attendance to assure me, the story will find a place on tomorrow's front pages."

Rayner then asked how many people were anticipated to attend the event.

"The recipients', their families and friends, which I would guess would total about thirty or forty people, no more than that, unless your plans to set the trap require more, then we can provide a captive audience of our own people."

Rayner glanced across at Morgan, inviting his senior to make any comment, but the Chief Superintendent hadn't yet had time to digest all that the Commissioner was suggesting.

"I suspect that if our man turns up, he will come at me with some kind of weapon and there might well be two of them, so I suggest we must make it look easy for him to commit what atrocity he has in mind."

"He might just throw a bleedin' bomb at you, Rayner," Morgan quipped, resulting in a look of disdain from the Commissioner.

"Somehow, I don't think so. If my suspicions are correct, the individual will want to identify himself to me, before trying to cause me harm or end my life and that might be difficult for him with so many police officers present."

"Or should he attempt to kidnap you like my Estelle and your Matthew," Morgan suggested.

"You have a point, Frederick," Sir Edward remarked, "But now gentlemen, go and make whatever plans you need and let me know what requirements, if any, will be necessary to ensure the trap you set will be satisfactory."

Both detectives nodded and left, with Morgan leading the way.

"Why is it, you always get the accolades, Rayner," the senior man quietly said, as both men were returning to the first floor, "I mean, you'd have thought the old codger would have pinned some of those bleedin' medals on the chests of a few detectives, who work just as hard as the uniform lads."

"I agree sir, but it was probably down to a limited number of medals available."

"Or rather the bleedin' cost."

"I shall donate the medal I am presented with to the department as a whole," Rayner suggested, coyly.

"Don't talk like a prat, you will wallow in it, like you always do."

It was the following morning when the residents of London awoke to see the first snow of the year had fallen on the city, covering it with a white blanket, having made its presence known throughout the previous night. As was the case when such adverse weather came visiting, carriages and bicycles were hindered, struggling to manoeuvre about the streets and resulting in fewer people using transport to attend their workplaces. Nevertheless, that wasn't the case for one particular nursing sister who was employed on the wards at The New Women's Hospital in Marylebone Road.

Catherine Jacobs had been working at the hospital for the past four years and was in the habit of gaining access to the rear of the building by walking across the grounds at the back of the establishment. And that early morning excursion to work was no exception. The sister was about to begin the twelve-hour dayshift, having taken advantage of having a day's leave, following a two-week night duty commitment.

The snow was still falling, as she hurriedly made her way through the rear gates and glanced up through the mist at the vague outline of the building sitting on top of a slight incline. Following the narrow path that crossed the grounds to the rear double doors of the hospital was difficult to negotiate, as she marvelled at the surrounding wintry scene. But she persevered, passing a small copse of trees to her left, at first not noticing a man standing just on the edge of the small, wooded area. Then, as the path she was following took her closer to the individual, only then did he come within her vision.

He was tall and wearing a dark cloak with his back to her, but completely motionless. The hospital employee called out to him, asking what his business was, and prompting him to turn with a start, looking extremely fearful. Then she could see he was grasping a knife in one hand. Her first instinct was to run through the drifts for the safety of the hospital but decided that would be futile, as the man could easily have caught her, so courageously decided to approach him.

"According to the Desk Sergeant, he's one of the surgeons at the hospital," Henry Bustle was explaining, as he and Richard Rayner were making their way as best they could by carriage to Marylebone Road.

"And the culprit was caught red-handed, Henry."

"Yes sir, apparently he was discovered by one of the sisters at the hospital standing over the deceased with the murder weapon in his hand."

"Do we know who the culprit is?"

"Another surgeon, apparently. Again, according to the Desk Sergeant, the sister called for help and a couple of the other doctors took charge of the man. He's being taken into custody as we speak."

"What was the weapon?"

"A knife by all accounts and I understand that was recovered at the scene. Doctor Critchley has been informed and will meet us there."

By the time the detectives arrived in the grounds of The New Women's Hospital, the snow had stopped but Rayner's driver, Constable Studley, was compelled to stop the carriage at the back gates, leaving the Chief Inspector and his Sergeant with no other option but to walk across the snow-covered ground to the same copse of trees where Sister Jacobs had first sighted the killer, armed with the murder weapon.

There were two constables standing close to where the victim lay, and Rayner could see that the pathologist had already arrived and was crouching over the body making his initial examination.

"Good morning doctor," the Chief Inspector greeted, but received no response, the elderly physician completely immersed in carrying out his duties.

After a short while, Doctor Critchley got to his feet and finally acknowledged Rayner's presence with a nod of his head.

"It seems apparent that Sir Reginald died from two or more stab wounds to his chest, but I shall know more once I've conducted the post-mortem."

"Sir Reginald? You know the man?"

"Yes, this is Sir Reginald Hammond, Richard, an eminent Gynaecologist at the New Women's Hospital and a surgeon who is occasionally summoned by the Queen and other members of the Royal Family, or so I have been led to believe."

Rayner looked at Doctor Critchley and was about to ask, if he was absolutely sure, but then realised that of course he would be. The murder of a victim with such reputable credentials would undoubtedly become of interest to the Commissioner and other dignitaries, possibly even the Home Office, possibly even the Prime Minister. All Richard Rayner could think of was that interference from such sources would be a hindrance to the subsequent Investigation.

"Any time of death?"

"It's difficult in this freezing weather, but certainly not more than three or four hours ago, but again, I shall be able to be more accurate back at the mortuary."

Rayner turned to one of the constables and asked if they had spoken to anyone at the hospital and one of them confirmed, only the sister who had come across the murder and a couple of doctors who had detained the man responsible.

The senior detective then enquired with the same constable, if he was aware of the name of the man taken into custody.

The officer opened his notebook and read out the name of Tobias Corncrake.

"Apparently sir, he worked under Sir Reginald as his assistant at the hospital."

Rayner then asked Albert Critchley if he was aware of Mr. Corncrake, but the pathologist confirmed he wasn't.

"Sir Reginald is well known in medical circles, Richard, and I am aware he was very popular with the board of governors at The New Women's. From what I have read about him, he has been involved in a great deal of complex research into the female anatomy."

"A subject close to my own heart, if I might say sir," the Constable remarked, with a grin across his face and provoking Rayner into throwing a look of distaste in his direction.

"Sorry sir," he apologised, stepping back a yard or two.

"Keep your comments to yourself," Henry Bustle snapped, "And keep your mouth shut until spoken to."

"Sarge."

"One more thing, Richard," Doctor Critchley said, "From the blood splatter on his chest, I believe he was killed here."

"Yes, thank you doctor, the quicker we get the body back to your mortuary the better." The Chief Inspector then directed the constables to arrange for the departure of the deceased.

"Have you spoken with Sister Jacobs yet, Richard," the pathologist enquired.

"That's my next step doctor."

"Then allow me to introduce you to her, she worked at St. Mary's for a time, and I found her to be an excellent, hard-working nurse."

"With an unblemished character."

"Oh yes, of course."

Chapter Ten

The pathologist led the way towards the back entrance of the hospital building and as the three men trudged through the snow, Henry Bustle quietly asked Richard Rayner, if he intended spending a great deal of time investigating the surgeon's murder. They still had to make arrangements in connection with that evening's attempt to capture the killer of Maisie Winthrop at the Guildhall presentation ceremony.

"After all, this does appear to be cut and dried, sir," the Sergeant added.

"Maybe so, Henry, maybe so, but when a man is facing the noose I believe we should do all in our power to unravel every detail of what he is to be arraigned for."

Doctor Critchley found the lady they wished to interview drinking tea with the matron, who apologetically left after the pathologist had introduced their two visitors.

Richard Rayner began by congratulating the sister on the courage she had shown earlier when confronting the killer and allowed her to finish her tea, before suggesting she began to relate what had happened from the time she first entered the hospital grounds.

Whilst describing the course of events, Catherine Jacobs couldn't stop herself from trembling, obviously still in shock and the senior detective decided to spare the woman as little further anxiety as possible, by keeping the interview short.

"I intend asking only a few questions at this time, sister," He explained, "So, tell me, when Mr. Corncrake first saw you approaching him, how did he initially appear, what kind of expression was on his face, perhaps fright or relief or even confusion, or perhaps threatening towards you."

She looked up at the ceiling and then explained, "I recall at first, he looked strangely relieved and then fearful, before he dropped the knife on to the ground."

"Did you see anyone else nearby, or when you first entered the hospital grounds?"

She shook her head and answered, "No sir."

"Were you personally acquainted with either of the men, Mr. Corncrake or Sir Reginald?"

"Everyone knew about Sir Reginald sir, but I didn't know him personally, or the other man holding the knife."

"And just to clarify what you have told us, when you first laid eyes on Mr. Corncrake, he was standing upright with the knife in his hand."

"Yes sir, and with his back to me, as I have already said."

Rayner gave her a reassuring smile, recognising that the lady had been subjected to a distressing ordeal and must be wishing she had stayed at home that morning.

"Thank you, sister, one of my officers will call on you later to take your statement, but in the meantime I suggest you go home and rest until you have recovered from this dreadful experience."

After leaving the matron's office, the Chief Inspector and his Sergeant met up with Constable Studley who confirmed he had managed to bring the official carriage to the front of the building.

"We need to make plans for this evening, sir," Bustle once again reminded Rayner, sounding a little frustrated at spending so much time on what he obviously felt was unnecessary.

"Yes, you are right Henry. We shall return to Scotland Yard, and I would prefer if you then went to the Guildhall and see what you can come up with. I need to speak with our Mr. Tobias Corncrake as a matter of urgency."

"It seems to me to be cut and dried," the Sergeant remarked, once again expressing his opinion, but also knowing how fastidious Richard Rayner was.

Jack Robinson was given a brief account of what had taken place earlier that morning in the grounds of The New Women's Hospital in Marylebone Road, before being led by Chief Inspector Rayner down to the cell block in the basement of Scotland Yard. When entering the cell at the far end of the corridor, they found the prisoner, Tobias Corncrake, standing looking up towards the small barred window set high in the opposite wall, as if wishing he was a bird and could fly away.

After the introductions, they requested that the suspect went with them to a nearby interview room, but even before leaving to retrace their steps, Corncrake professed his innocence several times. The tall, thin young man, with a pale face and small mouth spoke articulately. He boasted a thin moustache, fair in colour that matched his bushy hair and whiskers covering his chin, confirming an attempt to grow a beard. The man's eyes were slightly sunken and watery, and he walked with a natural straight posture that indicated a previous life in the military, which was not the case. The man's open facial features certainly did not give the impression he had just murdered someone in cold blood with a knife.

Once all three were seated around a small table, Rayner asked his first question, remaining his usual cold and clinical self, when engaged in such an intense interview.

"Tell me, Mr. Corncrake, what exactly was your relationship with the deceased, Sir Reginald Hammond."

"We have been working for the past two years on a theory of what we called, 'Artificial Impregnation' and had made incredible advances..."

"In relation to women I take it."

"Yes, Sir Reginald believed that by taking the sperm from a male subject and maintaining it in a frozen state until a certain time when it could be impregnated into a woman's cervix you could induce the woman's eggs to be fertilised."

Rayner looked disbelievingly at the prisoner, before remarking, "Creating a pregnancy without there having been any sexual connection between the man and woman."

"My God, such an act would surely be against the teaching of God Himself," Jack Robinson claimed, in a voice filled with astonishment.

"It is a method we were trying to create that would be greatly beneficial to women who couldn't get pregnant by natural means," Corncrake offered.

"In other words, a form of Black Magic, or Witchcraft," a disturbed Sergeant Robinson commented.

The prisoner bowed his head, shaking it from side to side, before trying to explain that it was neither.

"A medical scientific exploration meant only to benefit humanity and for that reason, I believed in what Sir Reginald was trying to achieve. I admired the man greatly and was proud to work at his side. I certainly had no desire to kill him."

"Please explain what you were doing when you were found standing over the dead man with the murder weapon in your hand," Rayner demanded.

"Yesterday evening we all attended the Annual Surgeons Ball at Claridge's in Mayfair, and it gave me the greatest of pleasure to inform Sir Reginald that earlier that day we had succeeded in achieving test tube fertilisation of a woman's eggs by artificially impregnating with a man's sperm. It was the first time we had seen such success..."

"How was that possible, in layman's terms if you please, Mr. Corncrake."

"Temperature and timing; the temperature of both elements has to be exactly right when impregnation takes place, as is the time for when the eggs are right for fertilisation."

"I see, please continue."

"Well, we were both overjoyed and later that evening, Sir Reginald suggested we should meet in the laboratory early the following morning, so we arranged to be there at dawn. By the time I had prepared the necessary equipment for repeating the experiment, it was six thirty and still there was no sign of Sir Reginald. So, I made my way to the rear exit of the hospital, which overlooked the direction in which he always approached and saw a man I first thought was Sir Reginald walking away from the cluster of trees, towards the back gates."

"What made you think it was Sir Reginald?" Rayner asked.

"He was of the same build, but I couldn't see his face beneath a large hood he was wearing, but I was surprised he was making his way towards the exit. So, I stepped out into the snow with the intention of calling out to him and it was when I was passing the trees that I noticed a figure lying on the ground. When I approached, I saw it was, much to my horror, Sir Reginald, and there was a knife lying near to his side. I picked it up and was in shock I suppose and just stood there, trying to come to terms with what I was seeing. It was then that the nurse called out to me, and you know the rest."

"Why did you drop the knife, when you were disturbed by the woman?"

"I wasn't disturbed. As I said, I was in shock and realised how it must have looked, so from fear I suppose, I dropped the knife because of the way it looked."

"Where did this other man, you say you saw, go to?"

Tobias Corncrake shook his head and suggested, "He must have left through the back gates, I didn't see him again."

"Through the same gates as Sister Jacobs stepped through but has made no mention of seeing anyone other than yourself."

"Then he must have disappeared somewhere else, but I am not lying sir, he was there and I saw him walk away."

Jack Robinson looked sceptical at his Chief Inspector, who told the prisoner that unless they found the man he had referred to, it was looking extremely bad for him.

"All the evidence points towards you having been responsible for Sir Reginald's death Mr. Corncrake, but we shall persevere in trying to discover who this other man was, if indeed he ever existed," Rayner promised.

The prisoner slumped back in his chair, before repeating his innocence and asking what purpose would be served by him killing a man he admired and respected.

"That sir is for us to find out, but in the meantime, Sergeant Robinson will return you to your cell and we shall speak again later."

"How long do you intend keeping me here?"

"Oh, Doctor Corncrake, possibly until you depart from this world at the end of a rope."

Rayner then returned to his office and made a few notes about what Tobias Corncrake had said. He wasn't totally convinced that the man had been lying and from what the young surgeon had said himself, what possible motive would he have had for committing the murder. Rayner's initial impression had been that Sir Reginald's assistant had been telling the truth, but then a surprising incident cast a shadow over the Chief Inspector's reasoning.

During the time Jack Robinson was leading the prisoner back along the corridor towards his cell, suddenly and without warning, he was violently pushed to the floor and Corncrake turned and ran towards where the Detention Sergeant was standing, near to the door that gave access to the backyard.

Robinson cried out, but by the time his colleague had turned to see what was happening, he was also struck a physical blow, sending him reeling backwards and the escaping prisoner flew through the door, disappearing from view.

The detective managed to retrieve his feet and immediately chased after the fugitive but by the time he reached the backyard, there was no sign of the man. He promptly made enquiries with the constable on duty at the back gate but was told no one had been seen going in or out of the yard and Robinson's first thought was that losing a prisoner in custody, was a sackable offence.

When Richard Rayner was first told of the unfortunate incident in the cell block, the forlorn look on Jack Robinson's face was quite clearly visible. Remaining calm and level-headed, he ordered the young Sergeant to organise a search across the immediate area surrounding Scotland Yard and within a few minutes, detectives and constables were back on the streets, hastily attempting to retrieve the escaped prisoner. Officers were also dispatched to The New Women's Hospital in Marylebone Road, to make enquiries there. When Henry Bustle finally appeared, having organised matters at the Guildhall, he also joined in the search.

"It's a sacking offence, Rayner," Morgan shouted at the Chief Inspector, "And young Robinson deserves no less, my old mucker. Of all the stupid…"

"Perhaps, but I think he's already paid the penalty for his negligence, and surely we are all allowed one mistake."

"That's not a mistake man, it's bleedin' sacrilege, losing a prisoner is bad enough, but from our own cell block, come on now, the old man is going to go through the roof when he gets to hear about it, never mind the amount of embarrassment we shall all be subjected to, once the newspapers get hold of it."

Richard Rayner had no answer to that last remark, knowing that Jack Robinson's future would be in the hands of the Commissioner. They needed to get Corncrake back into custody as soon as possible, otherwise he was fearful that his young Sergeant would have undoubtedly worked his last shift.

Eventually, the searches were called off, without there having been any sign of the fugitive and if there had been any doubt as to Tobias Corncrake's guilt, that no longer existed, especially as far as Frederick Morgan was concerned.

"That young man's shenanigans will guarantee he gets the noose," the Chief Superintendent told Richard Rayner, but the senior detective still wasn't so convinced.

Evening was upon them, and by the time the doors to the Guildhall were opened for the recipients and their families to enter the vast room, more than twenty armed plain clothes officers were already in position, some concealed on surrounding balconies and others disguised as attendants. A small stage had been erected at one end of the room with a row of chairs for various dignitaries and a lectern had been placed just in front of them, put there for the use of the Commissioner who was to make the presentations.

When putting his idea forward, Richard Rayner had genuinely believed that the honour being awarded to him would be fictitious and had felt humbled by the Commissioner's stated intentions. For obvious reasons, he was the only individual taking part in the ceremony who was attending alone, and without his family being present. Now the scene had been set and his trap was ready to be sprung. The newspapers had carried a picture of the celebrated detective on their front pages earlier that morning, explaining how Scotland Yard's finest was to receive a special honour for his outstanding past achievements. All that could have been done to lure the kidnapper to the event that was about to take place, had been. They could only hope now that the man they sought would have received the news and was tempted to use the occasion to further his own ends.

The principle and only detective in the audience, sat on the front row, having chosen to be the last to be awarded and surrounded by the other officers who were to receive the accolades. He was also armed with a loaded pistol in a shoulder holster concealed beneath his suit jacket and arrangements had been made for the star of the show to give interviews to the press following the presentations. And that meant it was to be a long night, during which he had to remain aware and fully on his metal. If he was wrong about his assumed profile of the killer, then so be it. But Rayner felt confident the man he sought would make an appearance, either during the ceremony or towards the end.

The Commissioner opened the proceedings by welcoming everyone and making a short speech recognising the gallant duty those officers present had performed, as he had done so two years earlier when making similar presentations. Then each officer was called up onto the stage and awarded with the Queen's Jubilee Medal, before being congratulated and shaking hands with Sir Edward. There were thirteen recipients in total, and Richard Rayner was the last. But then an incident occurred as the seventh in line was called to receive his medal.

A man unexpectedly appeared from nowhere and leapt up on to the stage, to stand next to the Commissioner. To everyone's disbelief, it was the escaped prisoner, Tobias Corncrake, who screamed at the audience that he was completely innocent of the murder of, Sir Reginald Hammond, and begged for the Commissioner and his officers to listen to his pleas of innocence.

As officers quickly moved in towards the fugitive, Rayner was taken aback by this surprising interruption, thinking firstly of how it would affect the intentions of the killer of Maisy Winthrop, and whether, if he was close by, might be frightened off by such a turn of events. By the time the senior detective reached the stage, Corncrake had been arrested by four or five officers and most of the participants were out of their seats, causing a general kerfuffle, resulting in some chaos amongst the audience.

The Commissioner just stood there, speechless and in obvious shock, and it was Rayner who ordered his men to shackle the young surgeon and take him to Scotland Yard. But then, just as efforts were being made to remove the former escapee from the stage, what looked like a wine waiter with a full black beard and wearing formal clothing, walked across the front of the first row of people and quite deliberately stared across and up at Rayner who had remained on the stage. The man shaped his hand as if it was a gun with the forefinger representing the barrel and his thumb, the hammer and manoeuvred it, as if firing a bullet directly at the Chief Inspector.

Rayner was again, for the second time that evening, taken by complete surprise and once the action of the waiter had dawned on him, could see the same man disappearing through a side door.

"Stop that man with the beard," he yelled at a small group of officers who were acting as attendants, but it was too late. His tormentor had brazenly delivered his bizarre message and had escaped the attention of those who were looking to arrest him.

The door the man had last been seen stepping through, led onto the street outside and Rayner was quickly joined by Henry Bustle and half a dozen other armed detectives.

"He's dressed formally as a waiter and is sporting a full black beard," he yelled out, before dispatching men in all different directions, but he knew it would be hopeless. Any individual who had the audacity to do what this man had just done, would have planned his escape route with great attention to detail. However, both he and Bustle quickly made a search of some of the adjacent streets, knowing it was a futile exercise.

"Did you recognise him," the Sergeant enquired.

"No Henry, the lower half of his face was covered by that monstrosity of a beard, but he had dark eyes and dark brown hair swept back with side whiskers I think, and he was of average height and build. He was obviously well disguised, but I must confess, his ballsiness caught me completely off my guard."

"He was undoubtedly telling you that if that had been a real gun in his hand, he could quite easily have bumped you off."

"Yes, Henry, I do believe he was. One thing is for certain though, he doesn't want me dead, just yet."

Chapter Eleven

"The question is simple enough to understand, Mr. Corncrake, if you are innocent and have nothing to hide, then why did you hit Sergeant Robinson here and run?" Richard Rayner was asking the question with a great deal of incredulity in his voice. At least, the quick return of the escapee to the cells would mean that Rayner's younger detective who was sitting next to him, would be keeping his job and position, or that was the most probable outcome.

"I was frightened and panicked because no one believed what I was saying." Looking directly at Jack Robinson, the prisoner then apologised for his misguided course of action.

Rayner's man just looked at him, a little ruefully, not being in the mood to accept any apology. In fact, the way young Robinson was feeling at that moment, he would have preferred to have been left alone with the hospital physician in a cell for ten minutes.

The fact that Tobias Corncrake had been instrumental in creating the diversion that allowed the killer of Maisy Windthrop to physically behave in the manner he had performed at the Guild Hall, had not gone unnoticed by the Chief Inspector.

"Very well, then pray tell us where you spent yesterday, after you took flight."

"I visited a friend and stayed at his house, and it was he who suggested I should prove my innocence by giving myself up."

Rayner smirked at the prisoner, before enquiring, "Would this friend of yours favour kidnapping a young lady and boy by any chance?"

Corncrake looked genuinely puzzled and confessed he had no idea what Richard Rayner was insinuating.

Jack Robinson was also a little surprised at what the senior detective was suggesting.

"I believe there is more to you sir, than the individual you are trying to portray yourself as being," Rayner then suggested, "Therefore, tell me more about your involvement with Sir Reginald Hammond in this research project you were conducting at The New Women's Hospital."

"I had the privilege of working with the man for the past two years. He was a genius in his field and…"

"Were there others involved in the work?"

"Yes, Simon Cartwright, a junior doctor and a nurse, Phylis Cameron, but the direction of the experiments came from either myself or Sir Reginald."

"I see and are you aware of anyone who might have held a grudge against Sir Reginald, or perhaps envied in some bizarre way, the success of the project you were engaged with."

"None, nobody outside our team was aware of the results of our work. That was a condition Sir Reginald always imposed on us, not wanting to disclose anything until our research had been completed one way or another."

Jack Robinson shifted in his seat and enquired as to where the money came from to finance such a project, one that he still believed represented some kind of heathen practice.

The young surgeon sat back and quietly explained that financial backing had been approved by the Board of Governors who were responsible for running the hospital and that every year, bids for further support were made and either rejected or authorised.

"The latest success you previously mentioned, concerning the fertilisation of the female eggs, who else was aware of that achievement?" Rayner asked.

Corncrake shook his head. "No one, I only told Sir Reginald on the evening before, at the Annual Ball."

"I take it, Cartwright and Cameron were aware."

"Yes, of course, they both helped me with the experiment, but I'm fairly confident they would never have shared what we had achieved with anyone else outside the laboratory."

"Is it possible, either or both of those could have done away with your boss?"

Corncrake shook his head and claimed that he very much doubted that would have been the case.

"Both Simon and Phylis regarded Sir Reginald in the same way as I did."

Richard Rayner then stood and explained they would need to speak again with the prisoner, but at a later time. He then indicated for Jack Robinson to return Tobias Corncrake to his cell and smiled when his young Sergeant replaced the pair of handcuffs on his man's wrists and secured shackles to his legs, ensuring the previous incident would not be repeated. But before Rayner left the interview room, the young surgeon pleadingly asked if he believed in his innocence.

Rayner looked at him indifferently and then said in a quiet voice, "As a matter of fact, Mr. Corncrake, yes, I do."

After returning to the first floor, the Chief Inspector went to update Frederick Morgan on what had taken place and found his Chief Superintendent sitting at his desk, wincing in obvious discomfort. The smokescreen in Morgan's office had reappeared and the senior man was contently adding to the obnoxious smell, justifying his nickname of 'Puffing Billy'.

"I take it your condition has returned, sir," the Chief Inspector remarked, sensitively.

"With a vengeance Rayner and I feel as though I'm paying the price for a previous life of debauchery."

Morgan had been a long sufferer of haemorrhoids, an ailment he preferred to put up with, rather than seek the services of a surgeon. It was also a condition he preferred not to discuss, frequently maintaining that what was his private business had nothing to do with anyone else, even Richard Rayner.

"Why don't you..."

"Enough Rayner, my piles are mine alone and I shall deal with them as I please."

"Of course, only I was about to suggest..."

"What about that bastard downstairs, has he been given his just dessert, a bleedin' good hiding? He should have both his legs broken to stop him from running again."

Rayner sat down and quietly explained the reasons why he wasn't convinced that Tobias Corncrake had murdered Sir Reginald Hammond.

"He might well be a highly intelligent individual, but he is also extremely fragile in disposition, and I just cannot envisage him having the nerve to stab a man twice in the chest. I truly believe that he is also incapable of lying and if anything, is vulnerable to any kind of pressure we put on him."

"So is my Aunt Fanny, Rayner, but she managed to drown half a dozen kittens in a canal once."

The Chief Inspector had no response to that informative remark, so continued to share his views relevant to the Investigation.

"I believe we need to delve more into the background of the victim and perhaps some of the hospital staff, before jumping to anymore conclusions."

Morgan stood from his chair and immediately his face became contorted by the pain from which he was suffering, having momentarily forgotten about his medical condition.

"I knew it, I bleedin' well knew it. There was me thinking with the man caught standing over the body with the murder weapon in his hand and covered in blood, there was every chance he was the killer, but of course, anything so simple as that goes against the grain with you Rayner, doesn't it."

"Corncrake didn't have any reason to murder the man he highly respected and had worked with for the past two years."

"So he says."

"We need to find what the motive was behind the murder, and I understand that the deceased had a wife who I would like to talk to next, before deciding on Mr. Corncrake's guilt or otherwise."

"You do know, the jasper killed was privy to the Queen herself, and the Commissioner is being pressurised to get a result from them that govern our lives."

"In that case, we best charge the man downstairs and allow the real killer to go free then. Is that your interpretation of where we are at present?"

"Don't be impertinent man, that bone picker downstairs isn't going anywhere except to the hangman, unless you come up with a better suspect."

Rayner smiled, before leaving, thankful to breathe some clean air in the outside corridor. It wasn't unusual for the former Major in the Coldstream Guards to get through a tin of Atlantic Shag tobacco in a day, whenever he was in discomfort and the disgusting stink that came from his habit, certainly kept people away from his door. However, he knew Frederick Morgan well enough to know that he wouldn't claim to have found the killer, unless Rayner was convinced they had the right man.

The residence of the late Sir Reginald Hammond was located in Elm Tree Road, St John's Wood; a large three-tiered building shaped like a parallelogram that stood before a spacious triangular forecourt. A stone wall enclosed the cultivated gardens, and two large wrought iron gates gave access to a short driveway that led to the front of the house.

"How the other half live, sir," Jack Robinson remarked, as their carriage approached the house.

A young maid, dressed in black with a white frilly apron opened the door and following the usual introductions made by Richard Rayner, stepped back for the two unannounced visitors to enter a large square shaped hall with a black and white tiled floor and an interior balcony encircling it.

"I will see if madam is available sir," the girl confirmed, before disappearing through a ground floor door on their left. When she returned, she offered to show the two detectives into the drawing room.

Lady Barbara Hammond was sitting in a large soft armchair at the side of a blazing log fire, dressed in all black and obviously in mourning. She was grasping a lace handkerchief and holding it to her face. The room was the largest Rayner had seen inside a private house, with its walls decorated by various sized gold framed scenic oil paintings, most of which depicted hunting scenes. There were the usual soft chairs and sofas and small tables supporting expensive ornamental clocks, porcelain figurines and cut-glass objects of rare beauty. There was a large Aspidistra plant in one corner that appeared to dwarf the small table upon which it was resting, and a smell of lavender seemed to permeate throughout the room.

"Forgive me gentlemen if I do not stand to greet you, but I am sure you will understand I am not at my best at present," the lady of the house explained, in an articulate voice.

Rayner immediately apologised for disturbing the widow at such an inconvenient time and quietly explained that he was making enquiries into her husband's untimely death.

Lady Barbara referred to her maid by the name of Lillian and requested she arranged for the butler to bring her visitors some refreshments. Turning to the men from Scotland Yard, she then offered, "Tea gentlemen, or perhaps something a little stronger. At this time of the day, it is my habit to take a sweet sherry and you are quite welcome to join me."

"We are obliged My Lady," the senior detective answered, "Sherry would be just fine."

Lady Barbara waited for the maid to disappear and then requested the Chief Inspector to ask his questions. She was a tall, slim, elegant looking woman with a pale face that reminded her visitors of fine porcelain with high cheek bones and shiny fair hair that was secured on top of her head. Richard Rayner could not help but be impressed by the lady's demeanour and posture, noticing how straight backed she sat on the edge of her chair with both hands clasped together on her lap. He thought it strange how people blessed with extreme wealth and aristocratic upbringing, always seemed to behave in such a manner.

"Forgive me My Lady but did Sir Reginald ever discuss his research work at the hospital with you."

"Yes, quite often, we shared many common interests and Reggie would often refer to the many charities I am involved in. In return, he often sought my counsel relative to the work he was undertaking."

"So, you were aware of the intricacies of the project he was currently undertaking at The New Women's Hospital."

"Not in so many words Mr. Rayner, but he would often share some of the details with me. It was his ambition to help those poor wretched women who wanted children but failed to succeed."

Robinson was about to remark that there were literally hundreds of women living in the impoverished backstreets of London who wished they couldn't have any more children, but bit his tongue.

"Did you know Mr. Tobias Corncrake, who I believe was his closest assistant."

"Of course, Toby is an enthusiastic gentleman who would do anything to help my husband's cause."

"Forgive me yet again, if you find my questions disturbing but were you aware that Mr. Corncrake has been arrested for your husband's murder."

"Yes, so I was informed by the constable who brought me the dreadful news, but I find it difficult to believe that he would have done such an horrific thing, sir."

There was a knock on the door at that precise moment, and the butler entered the room, carrying a small silver tray with three glasses of sherry, before handing one to each of the room's occupants.

"Thank you, Charles," Her Ladyship spoke in a quiet voice.

"Is there anything else, madam."

"Not at present."

After the butler had left, Rayner continued with his next question, asking if Lady Barbara knew of anyone who might have held a grudge against the late Sir Reginald.

She answered quite decisively.

"No, no one, Mr. Rayner, Reggie was a popular and learned man who was well respected in the highest circles."

"What of his fellow surgeons and doctors who worked at the hospital, perhaps someone who might have been jealous of your husband's success."

"No one to my knowledge, sir."

Rayner could see that the lady's eyes were beginning to well up and sat back to sip his sherry, allowing the woman some respite and the opportunity to also address her own glass. Having seen that Jack Robinson had quickly consumed his beverage, he thanked Lady Barbara for her patience and co-operation, before standing to leave, signalling his Sergeant to do the same.

"I might well need to speak with you again My Lady but do not wish to intrude any further on your grief at this particular moment in time."

"That is very kind Mr. Rayner, but please do and please, I beg of you, catch the monster who has done this to us."

"You have my word My Lady, I shall bring the fiend to justice."

"So, you have doubts about young Toby being your man."

"We are at an early stage of the Investigation, and I have to keep an open mind, madam but at present, like yourself, I have my doubts, yes."

She smiled somewhat nervously, before ringing a small bell, summoning the return of the butler who escorted the two detectives from the room.

"Why is it, that such a graceful and charming lady such as that is subjected to the torment of losing her husband in such an horrific way," Jack Robinson asked, as they travelled back to Scotland Yard, "I truly admired the courageous way in which she behaved, at a time when she must have been suffering from the greatest of traumas, sir."

"Isn't it always the case though Jack, when murder most foul is committed the real victims of such atrocities are those who are left behind."

"Yes, but it seems to be so unfair."

"The killing of a human being by another human being is never fair, Jack."

"Except when lawfully executed, sir."

"Of course, but I fear that Lady Barbara cannot be of much help to our cause because she is not aware of any individual who would have reason to murder her husband, but like you, I did appreciate her fortitude in seeing us. She obviously wants the culprit caught as much as we do, but I suspect she knows a little more about her husband's background than she is prepared to confide in us."

"Then you are not convinced that Tobias Corncrake was responsible."

"No, my initial thoughts are that this murder was pre-planned by a person or possibly a group of people who had a strong motive to bump off Sir Reginald."

"Do you think that motive is connected with the work he was doing sir."

"Yes, I believe so, but as I told Lady Hammond, it's too early to draw any conclusions and we must keep an open mind."

When they arrived at the headquarters building, they found both Frederick Morgan and Henry Bustle stepping into a carriage in the backyard. As soon as Morgan saw Rayner, he leapt back out of the vehicle and hastily approached his Chief Inspector, looking extremely anxious.

"We've only just heard Richard, there's been a fire at your place and the brigade are there. We were just on our way to find you."

"Has anyone been hurt do we know?"

"According to the first reports, there are casualties apparently."

Chapter Twelve

At Richard Rayner's direction, Constable Studley didn't spare the horses and within a few minutes, all four detectives had arrived at the Chief Inspector's residence. They were met by an apprehensive Albert the butler, after coming to a jolted halt at the foot of the steps leading to the front door. The air was filled with the smell of acrid smoke and the elderly servant directed his master to where the stables were at the back of the house, confirming that was where the fire had taken hold.

"I fear all is lost sir," the elderly butler confessed, sounding extremely pitiful. But Rayner's first concern was regarding those who had been injured, and when enquiring found his head servant too agitated to sound coherent.

As the butler led the way, Rayner suddenly stopped, causing Frederick Morgan and Henry Bustle to almost collide into his back. Seemingly, as an afterthought the master of the house turned to face his head servant. Looking calm and reassuring he directed Albert to calm down and take a deep breath.

"Yes, get a grip man," Morgan advised.

The old man did so and immediately apologised.

"It's young Jonas sir, he's been hit over the head something bad." The butler was referring to Rayner's stable boy.

"Where is he now, Albert?"

"We carried him into the house sir, and... and before the brigade came, and... and I sent for Doctor Collins, same time as I sent the boy to tell you sir, and..."

"Where is Jonas now, Albert?"

Doctor Collins has taken him to the hospital sir, he looked awfully bad, sir." The doctor being referred to was Herbert Collins, the family physician.

Richard Rayner then scurried off towards the stables area, followed by the others and where he was greeted by the sickening sight of smouldering wood and the charred remains of what had once been a well-cared for structure. There were members of the local fire brigade still in attendance with hoses and buckets and one of them, who introduced himself as being Gabriel Chance, approached the head of the household and explained that Rayner's coachman, Nicholas Withers, had managed to get the horses extracted from the stables before it turned into an inferno, with some help from Tillie the maid.

"Any idea Mr. Chance, what started this?" the Chief Inspector enquired, looking forlornly across at the incinerated ruins.

"It was quite deliberate Mr. Rayner and from the speed in which the flames took hold, I suspect some kind of accelerant has been used. That young stable boy of yours and the livestock were lucky to come out of this alive."

"When did it start?"

"We were first told a couple of hours ago and by the time we got here, the fire was well established. Mind you, if we'd have been earlier sir, I doubt we could have done much more by the speed in which the fire spread."

Rayner thanked him and then noticed Tillie the maid and Gabriel Chance standing close by, both servants with their blackened faces showing the effects of being traumatised.

"I understand you did a fine job," the master remarked to both servants.

"Aye sir, we managed to get all of them out, thanks to this little girl here," the coachman quietly confirmed, nodding towards Tillie, "That was all except one sir, the mistress's pony, Patch, she seems to have gone missing."

"I don't quite follow," Rayner said, looking a little bemused.

"Well, we haven't had time to look for her as yet, but she was missing from her stall when we went in to lead the rest of them out."

The Chief Inspector glanced across at Morgan, both men having the same thoughts. So was Henry Bustle and immediately walked away to search for the missing pony. Patch was a Christmas gift Richard Rayner had bought for Clarice a couple of years beforehand and the black and white trusted horse was doted on by his wife. Rarely a weekend passed by without the lady of the house taking the pony out for a run across the surrounding open fields.

"Where are the rest of the horses, Gabriel?" Rayner then asked.

"They're safe enough sir, we've put them on the far side of the house and John is looking after them," John being the assistant stable boy.

Morgan then asked his senior detective for a quick word in private, and both men stepped away from the others.

"You do know who is responsible for this, Richard," the Chief Superintendent whispered.

"Of course, it has to be our friends again, the kidnappers, but we need to speak with young Jonas and find out exactly what happened to him, as soon as possible."

"You also need to hire some security around your home. I fear these delinquents might well return."

Rayner nodded but was having some difficulty in thinking clearly. His mind was filled with anger and a lust for revenge against the people who had brought such distress into his home. He recalled the individual who had pointed a finger at him during the kerfuffle at the medals ceremony and regretted not having acted more quickly at the time. At least those he sought had proven how vulnerable he was, having entered the grounds of his private residence and committed so much damage, let alone the atrocity they might have inflicted upon his stable boy.

His thoughts were interrupted by Henry Bustle calling to him from a short distance away. Rayner looked up and could see his friend standing on the other side of a hedge separating the cultivated area of the gardens with an open field. The Sergeant was also waving his arm, beckoning the group to join him, which they did.

"I think I've found her," the Sergeant claimed.

There lying on its side, was Patch, sadly not moving and certainly not breathing.

Both Gabriel and Bustle turned her over, only to find a spike had been driven into the pony's head causing instant death.

For a moment, it was as if time itself had stopped and the group just stood there in disbelieving silence, looking down at a scene that was so woeful, so agonising, it was beyond belief. Then their rejection of reality was abruptly interrupted by Morgan hissing in anger and placing a hand on Richard Rayner's shoulder.

Gabriel swore out loud and Tillie the maid openly wept.

"I shall not rest until I have got these evil bastards under lock and key," Rayner vowed, glaring into Frederick Morgan's eyes.

"You and me both, my old mucker."

But the most arduous task was having to inform his wife of what had happened to the pony she had loved and adored, a commitment that Clarice's husband wasn't relishing having to undertake.

It was Doctor Herbert Collins, who Rayner spoke to first after arriving at St. Thomas's Hospital with Frederick Morgan, just as the family physician was about to leave. The elderly medical man, who had originated from Edinburgh, had not lost his natural accent and had known the detective since he was a young boy, having attended to his parents when they were alive.

"He has concussion and a nasty wound to the back of his head, Richard" he explained, "I have recommended he remains calm and sedated and stays with us for a minimum of three days at least."

"Can I speak with him, Herbert?"

"Of course, he's in that ward across the corridor, but refrain from over taxing him, apart from his injury the lad has suffered quite a shock to his system."

Rayner nodded, and both detectives made their way into where young Jonas Tomkins was resting in one of a line of beds, most of which were occupied. A nurse was attending to the patient and the young stable boy resembled an Egyptian mummy, covered in bandages concealing his head and most of his face. At least he recognised his master as soon as Richard Rayner appeared and tried to raise himself off the bed.

"You must lie still and rest young man," the elderly nurse ordered.

"Yes, do as nurse tells you Jonas and remain where you are for as long as it takes for you to recover," the detective advised.

Rayner then turned to the attending nurse and confirmed he had been given permission by Doctor Collins to speak with the patient for a short time, upon which she smiled and left.

Both detectives moved to either side of the bed and Morgan was the first to question the injured lad, asking if he knew who had attacked him in such a manner.

The youngster spoke quietly but coherently and confessed, "I didn't see anybody sir, all I remember is walking across the yard intending to check the mangers in the stalls and that was it. The next thing I knew, I was in here."

"Think carefully Jonas, just before you were struck on the head, did you see or hear, or even smell anything unusual?" Rayner asked.

The lad stared up at the high ceiling, before answering in the negative.

"Can you cast your mind back over the past few days for me and try and remember if you came across any strangers lurking about, or anything that appeared to be odd to you."

Again, he gave the enquiry some consideration, but to no avail. Jonas was regretful he couldn't help further but wasn't in any fit state to remember anything with clarity.

"He must have hit me over the head with a shovel sir, or an anvil, it certainly feels that way."

"One last question son, when was the last time you saw Patch?"

"Earlier in the arternoon sir, when I took him for his walk around the yard, like I do with the others. Why, has he gone missing or something."

Rayner described what had happened to the pony and the location where he had been found by Henry Bustle.

The young lad closed his eyes and sighed. His master knew just how fond he was of Clarice's mount and could see how the news distressed him.

"Why in Gawd's name would anybody want to do that to such a lovely hoss," he remarked.

"There's no sense or reasoning about what's in the mind of such an evil individual, Jonas."

"When you finds them sir, I beg of you, slit their throats for me."

Rayner smiled down at the patient and suggested he continued to rest, reiterating what the doctor had told him and insisting that he stayed where he was until he was well enough to return to Richmond.

"And don't worry none, son, I promise..."

"Does the mistress know sir - I mean about Patch."

"No, not yet, but I shall tell her at the first opportunity, now rest and if there's anything you need just send a message to Albert. I'm sure the rest of the staff will be coming to visit you shortly."

At the same time as Morgan and Rayner were visiting the stable boy, Henry Bustle, at the direction of his Chief Inspector, had accompanied Jack Robinson to The New Women's Hospital, where they first spoke with Simon Cartwright, the junior doctor who had been a member of Sir Reginald Hammond's team of researchers. Although the young man wasn't in a position to cast any further light on the death of their former leader, he did confirm that most of the instructions given to him and Nurse Phyllis Cameron, came directly from Tobias Corncrake. Doctor Cartwright's information was verified by the female member of the team who was a quietly spoken lady who gave the impression she was highly efficient in her work.

Before leaving, Bustle asked the nurse, who the most important physician at the hospital was, in Sir Reginald's absence.

"That will be Sir Giles, Sergeant," she answered, without hesitation, "Sir Giles Lamfrey, he is responsible for the general running of the hospital."

"So, he would be the individual responsible for approving the research being undertaken by Sir Reginald."

"I'm not sure, but he is the man who hires and fires staff members, including us if we should ever upset him, God forbid."

"Where can we find this Sir Giles Lamfrey, nurse?"

"In his office on the first floor."

Bustle thanked both Phyllis Cameron and Simon Cartwright and left to go in search of the gentleman whose name had been given to them.

When making their way up a set of stairs with iron railings, leading to the first floor, Jack Robinson mentioned how quiet it seemed, every hospital he had visited previously always seeming to be busy with porters and other members of staff, usually industriously running about like headless chickens.

"It's a women's hospital remember Jack," Bustle explained, "And I suppose only the most serious cases are admitted here."

"That's more reason why I would have thought it would have been noisier, you know how they like to cackle on." As soon as Robinson had jocularly made that inference, he realised it had been the wrong thing to say to Henry Bustle, remembering his colleague had recently lost his own wife who he had loved dearly. But the more experienced detective chose not to respond, and the younger man immediately apologised for having spoken so thoughtlessly.

They found Sir Giles office easily enough and knocked on the door bearing a plaque with the senior physician's name on it. After receiving approval to enter, they found the man they wished to speak with, sitting in a soft chair in front of a gas fire, reading a medical journal spread across his lap.

Henry Bustle did the introductions and both detectives were offered chairs.

The man who, according to Nurse Cameron, oversaw hospital affairs was physically small in stature with a bald head, except for a strip of dark brown hair around its circumference. He spoke lucidly and reminded his visitors of Frederick Morgan, being Welsh and speaking in a similar dialect, although not as loud or as brash as their Chief Superintendent. He also had a defined moustache, trimmed and was wearing a white ankle length coat over a suit, winged collar, and tie.

"I take it gentlemen, this is about the dreadful demise of my friend and colleague, Reggie Hammond. An appalling atrocity that has absolutely stunned everyone working here at The Women's."

Bustle allowed Jack Robinson to take the initiative when questioning the Knight of the Realm, and the younger Sergeant explained that they were investigating the murder and was Sir Giles aware of anyone who might have held a grudge for whatever reason, against the victim.

"No, I do not, Sergeant. Reggie was a most popular member of the staff and was enjoying phenomenal success in his latest research project. He is going to be greatly missed I can assure you."

Although Jack Robinson was much younger than Henry Bustle and certainly not acquainted with Richard Rayner for as long as the older detective, he was closer to their Chief Inspector's methods of working and on occasions was known to mimic the senior detective. He had learned from the famous detective that in the majority of cases, it was far better to adopt a subtle approach to an inquiry than just diving in feet first and doing his best to put the fear of Christ up any witness or suspect, as was the case with Frederick Morgan.

"Forgive me, sir, but we are trying to come to terms with how the administrative requirements of the hospital actually work, particularly with regard to the distribution and allocation of funding various projects, and I was wondering if you could assist us."

"Of course, Sergeant. It's quite simple, the hospital is divided into two main categories, patient care for which I am responsible, and research for which Sir Reginald was in charge. We are all accountable to the board of governors who decide how the annual budget is to be divided. We place our bids as it were, and according to what the board feel is in the best interests of the hospital, funds are allocated accordingly."

"So, you yourself have no say in how much expenditure is authorised for a research project, the likes of which Sir Reginald was undertaking."

"That is perfectly correct."

Bustle had a question and enquired as to what would happen to the exploration of artificial insemination now that the leading figure into that research was no longer with them.

Sir Giles shrugged his shoulders and confessed, "I hadn't given that much thought, I suppose it will be disbanded until some appropriate leading physician decides to continue where Reggie left off."

"And would you be willing to continue with that particular research yourself, sir?"

"Heavens no, I'm afraid I have neither the knowledge or inkling to undertake such a demanding proposition and apart from that, I am kept extremely busy in directing the day-to-day commitments of the hospital, Sergeant."

Henry Bustle then nodded at his colleague, who thanked the physician for his time, before turning to leave.

"I take it you have no idea who committed this dreadful act," the man in charge enquired.

"No sir, but we shall eventually," Jack Robinson confidently declared.

"I truly wish you well gentlemen, and if I or any other member of my staff can be of further assistance, please feel free to return."

"Thank you sir, you have been most gracious."

Both visitors then left, intending to return to Scotland Yard in the hope of meeting up with Richard Rayner to see if he had got any further in identifying the individual who was causing him so much grief and distress. Their Chief Inspector had a problem, of that there was no doubt, and Robinson and Bustle wondered how long it would take for the most successful detective in the force to track down the culprits.

Chapter Thirteen

"There's nobody with any apparent motive working at the hospital that wanted Sir Reginald dead sir," Jack Robinson explained to Richard Rayner, "It does seem that what Tobias Corncrake has told us is true, his senior was a very popular gentleman."

"What about this fellow, Sir Giles Lamfrey, what exactly was his relationship with the victim?"

Robinson reiterated what the hospital's most senior physician had told them during the earlier interview, adding that he believed the man was genuinely upset by the incident.

Henry Bustle was more concerned at that time about the arson at Rayner's stables and enquired as to how the Chief Inspector's wife had taken the news.

"I take it she knows about the pony."

"As you would expect, Henry, I'm afraid she is devastated. We need to find this blighter as quickly as possible but it's going to be difficult. The man works in the shadows and strikes when and where you least expect. By the way, have you any ideas where I might find half a dozen good men who would be willing to patrol my property around the clock."

"That could easily be arranged sir, according to how much you are willing to pay them."

"I would make it well worth their while."

"For how long were you thinking of employing them?"

"For as long as it takes to put these people behind bars."

"Then leave it with me and I shall have men in position before tonight," Bustle promised, before leaving the office to make the necessary arrangements.

Rayner then stepped across to his blackboard and stood staring at snippets of information recorded.

"The name Brigand refers to one of a group who commit heinous felonies such as robbery and larceny," Jack Robinson explained.

"Yes, I know what it means, Jack," Rayner said, writing the word across the top of the board, "But I wonder if our man has just selected that name randomly, which I suspect is more likely."

"I have been trying to remember if anyone we have dealt with in the past used the same word, but for the life of me, cannot recall such a person."

Rayner suggested the young Sergeant shouldn't tax himself further, as he was now convinced the man they sought had not had any previous dealings with them, in any official capacity. He explained further that he suspected the man was possibly an associate from his own past, who would not have been known by that name at that time, although the senior detective was speaking from assumption and not actual known facts.

"It could be anybody Jack and the purpose behind his attacks on myself could be anyone's guess."

"I have a strong suspicion you have a plan on how we are going to catch this creature."

Rayner turned away from the blackboard to face his young Sergeant and confirmed, "What I have in mind is to investigate individuals I was acquainted with prior to joining the police, but offhand I cannot recollect any individual who would wish to carry such a torch of hatred and bile as this chap.

Robinson nodded in agreement, wondering what he could possibly do to assist.

As if recognising his colleague's frustration, Rayner suggested he could only progress those enquiries alone and that the Sergeant would be better employed continuing to assist Henry Bustle in delving into the murder of Sir Reginald Hammond.

It was the senior man's intention to begin his new initiative as far back as his days spent at the Royal Grammar School in Guildford, close to where he lived with his parents. If that proved to be fruitless, then he would focus his attention on his university life at Oxford, as both student and lecturer, convinced that whatever information he was seeking lay somewhere within those two phases of his personal history. His initial aim was to visit his old school and check the name of Brigand against school registers appertaining to the time he was there, but then he recalled reading somewhere of an old pupil who attended the Royal Grammar at the same time as he did, a former pupil by the name of Jonathan Mytton. He tried hard to think back to where he had seen the name published and had wondered at the time if it could have been the same individual who he had known at the school. No matter how much energy he spent in attempting to recall where he had seen the name, all that Rayner could recollect was that it had been contained in a newspaper article, celebrating some success achieved by his old school associate, if of course it was the same man.

"You need to get your nose on the ground to catch this bastard, Rayner," Morgan bawled out from the open doorway, interrupting the Chief Inspector's train of thought, "And I don't think you'll catch the vermin sitting here in the warmth."

From Morgan's caustic manner, it was obvious the man was still suffering from his haemorrhoids, and Rayner gave the usual response when subjected to sarcastic bites from Morgan.

"Then I bow to your suggestions, sir."

"Get Bustle to rattle a few more cages up at the prison and go with him to shake up a few memories."

"Somehow, I don't think the answer lies there."

"So, where do you think it lies, it certainly isn't at that blackboard you are constantly nursing."

Richard Rayner knew only too well, this was Morgan's way of trying to motivate his Chief Inspector in upping his game, in an effort to catch the man who had just burned down his stables, violently struck his stable boy over the head and unmercifully slain his wife's favourite pony. But then, it suddenly struck him like a bolt from out of the sky. The miscreant he sought could never have personally visited his home or known about the favoured pony or the lay out of his stable block, and yet such information would have been necessary to have committed such atrocities.

He stepped across to the blackboard and picked up a piece of chalk. 'Analytical Thinker', 'Ability to Research', 'Amenable Character' and 'Well Educated', were the words he scrawled across the slate.

Morgan watched and once Rayner had discarded the chalk, commented, "That's your description of him, is it. Not much to go on, might I suggest."

"No, you're missing the point. Our man has an uncanny ability to research and plan his next move, as he has shown with the kidnappings and arson attack at my home. He also has the kind of character that can extract necessary information from people, perhaps without them even knowing the importance of what they were disclosing."

"Similar to the way we interview people."

"In a way yes, but what all of these characteristic traits point to, is a man who has received a high education and has previous experience in putting those assets to best use."

"I'm still at the starting gate, Rayner," Morgan confessed, looking a little perplexed.

"In what walk of life would such a person develop such talents?"

"Commercial business, if he was successful."

"Or the Diplomatic Service."

"Or in politics," Morgan suggested.

"No, I doubt that because of another aspect concerning this individual. As an elected politician, I suggest it would be unlikely he would have the time to engineer and commit such atrocities, even as a successful businessman he would be limited. But in the Diplomatic Service, he would have the freedom and privilege of working whenever he chose."

"That's one hell of a long shot, Rayner."

"Yes, I know, but it seems to make sense to me."

"And only you."

Rayner focused back on the name of Jonathan Mytton and asked both Frederick Morgan and Jack Robinson, if the name meant anything to either of them, but both men shook their heads. If only he could remember where he had read it.

When returning home later that same evening, Richard Rayner found his wife Clarice awaiting his arrival in the drawing room. The butler Albert explained that his mistress had returned with their son, Matthew, and the boy had retired for the night in his room. He also mentioned that Henry Bustle had called with four heavily built gentlemen who were now patrolling around the outside of the property and seemed surprised when the master of the house confirmed that the men were there in a professional capacity.

"Forgive me sir, but are they armed?" the butler asked, looking somewhat nervously at his master.

Rayner chuckled and told the old servant that he had no idea.

"Only if they are sir, I hope they will avoid any accidents."

"Now don't worry Albert, I'm sure Sergeant Bustle knows what he's doing and if his men are carrying weapons they will be well acquainted as to their use."

"Of course, sir, shall I tell cook to serve dinner?"

"If you please."

Clarice quickly explained, in between taking sips of sherry, that she decided her place was at her husband's side, no matter what dangers were present, and she would prefer to be at home than be safely tucked away elsewhere.

"I mean Richard, why should these vermin force us to change the way we run our lives..."

"I hear what you say, Clarice, and love you all the more for it."

It was following dinner, that the Chief Inspector summoned his butler again, and asked if he could recall ever seeing the name of Mr. Jonathan Mytton in a newspaper article in recent weeks.

Albert answered without hesitation.

"Yes sir, I remember distinctly the name having been ringed by yourself in a copy of the Chronicle and placed the edition in a drawer in the library in case you found it to be important. I recall the gentleman had been awarded the Queen's Medal for Bravery. Shall I fetch it?"

"If you would Albert," a relieved Richard Rayner said, instantly remembering now what the article was about. Jonathan Mytton had pulled a drowning boy from out of a canal and as a result had been hailed as a hero.

When the butler placed the article in front of his master, Rayner remembered what had initially attracted his attention to it, according to the author of the report, the gentleman receiving the accolades had attended The Royal Grammar School, Guildford, prior to going to Cambridge where he studied Military History. It was undoubtedly the same Jonathan Mytton he recalled at the same school. In addition, the article contained one other snippet of interesting text, confirming that Captain Mytton of the Household Cavalry was the officer in charge of the security of the Royal Mews at Buckingham Palace.

"Well blow me down," Rayner gasped.

"What is it dear," his wife asked.

"I might not be required to return to Guildford after all, dear."

Early the following morning saw the senior detective standing at the main gates of the Royal Mews asking to see Captain Mytton, after showing the guard on duty his identification card. Following a short wait, Richard Rayner was allowed access into the Royal establishment. He had visited the premises on one previous occasion, when it was thought the life of a member of the Royal family might have been in danger from Irish dissidents, and soon observed that nothing much had changed. Everywhere was immaculately clean, with rows of stalls and soldiers busy with their daily duties, including the constant maintenance of the official carriages. He was even led into the Administration block and taken to the same office, where on his previous visit he had spoken with the then young officer in charge.

Captain Mytton was obviously a lot taller than when Rayner remembered him as being a young pupil at school, but his facial features were immediately recognisable and both men shook hands in greeting.

"I have read many excellent reports about your amazing work at Scotland Yard, Richard," the officer remarked, "You have most certainly had an illustrious career."

"And it appears you have also, Jonathan. The reason for..."

"Come and let me show you what we are about here at the Mews." The captain then stood and led the way out of his office, down the stairs and into the open yard, before introducing his visitor to several of the resident horses and staff members responsible for caring and grooming them. It was noticeable how the troopers displayed the utmost respect towards their senior officer and another surprise came Richard Rayner's way, when Jonathan Mytton spoke to a middle-aged cavalry man with three stripes on his arm.

"We shall take the open Landau, Ernest, if you please," the captain directed.

Within a few minutes, both the man in charge of the Royal Mews and the senior detective from Scotland Yard were sitting in an immaculately kept carriage being pulled by two impressive white stallions with a cavalry officer in full uniform, mounted and following behind. The small procession travelled through the streets of London, attracting looks from the populace and of course, Richard Rayner was aware the charade was a way in which his old schoolfriend could impress and he appreciated the gesture. But this was the last thing he required, being anxious to find out whether Mytton had any knowledge of a man known as Brigand.

Few words were spoken during the short tour, any conversation being drowned out by the noise coming from the carriage wheels, except when the captain explained they were sitting in a carriage frequently used by King George IV at the time he was seeking a divorce from Caroline of Brunswick. It was all so interesting but the Chief Inspector's patience was being tested and he needed to discuss the subject of his visit urgently.

After returning to the mews, his old schoolfriend was the perfect host and ordered tumblers of malt whiskey to be supplied forthwith, before finally apologising for not having enquired earlier as to the reason for Richard Rayner's visit.

"I'm not sure if you can be of help to me. Jonathan," the Chief Inspector confessed, "But I am trying to trace an individual who might well have attended at The Royal, at the same time as we were there. I know very little about him, except he might have been known by the name of Brigand."

The captain looked directly at his visitor and surprised Rayner by naming one former pupil by the name of, Herbert Winkler.

"He was known as Brigand and still is, that's what the others call him when he attends the reunions. Wasn't he with you when you were embarrassingly lost on some mountain up in Cumbria I seem to recall?"

Of course, the incident Jonathan Mytton was referring to was immediately called to mind and Richard Rayner remembered instantly the youngster, Herbert Winkler, a name he had forgotten about many years previously…

…How strange it is when an ordeal brings fear to an individual, everything appears exaggerated. For instance, when the temperature drops, the cold air suddenly feels colder than it actually is, as was the case for the two boys lost on the fourth highest mountain in Britain, Scafell, on that mid-week afternoon. The lateness of the hour could be measured by the darkening sky and the mist covering Scafell Pike. It was only natural that the fourteen-year-old, Richard Rayner, felt some trepidation, but was doing his best to hide his true feelings from his younger friend, Herbert Winkler. He had to play the leading role in attempting to get off the mountain before the darkness of night was upon the two boys, especially as he was a school prefect and would be expected to take charge in any such crisis.

The older boy stood and looked around him, wondering what the best path to tread would be. The last they had seen of the others had been from a fair distance away, when the group unexpectedly disappeared down a small ravine. But when Rayner and Winkler reached that same point, there was no sign of the teachers' or other pupils. Trying to perform responsibly, he assured his young friend that all would be well, provided they continued following a downwards slope, but the encumbrance that had been the reason he had lagged behind the main party of young climbers, was still present. He was wearing a pair of borrowed boots that were a size too small, and by now his impaled crippled feet were similar to a couple of hot furnaces. The young Rayner's only respite had come when the two boys had stopped for a brief moment to examine an ancient stone with hieroglyphics that neither understood. As for young Herbert Winkler, well, he had dawdled only because he was idle, but none of that mattered now, they were lost and the dusk was approaching rapidly.

Before following the same narrow, rocky gulley containing pieces of jagged slate of all sizes, Rayner took one last look at the mist covered pike crowning Scafell; a ghostly apparition that appeared sinister and unwelcoming. He still wondered why this specific mountain had been chosen as a final objective for that year's school outing, having been told the excursion was intended as a character-building exercise. Well, the long laborious climb up to the summit had certainly been sufficient for that but now, things hadn't gone as planned and two of the party would soon be reported as missing, presenting yet another challenging situation, if only to survive.

Both youngsters were aware they were many miles from any civilisation and Master Winkler's constant weeping and nervous disposition wasn't helping the older boy to concentrate, resulting in Rayner continuing to offer reassurance, but to no real effect. He remained confident though, if they continued to descend they would eventually get off the mountain, needing to achieve that before the arrival of the advancing darkness.

Both boys' persevered, following the small, narrow ravine downwards and moving as quickly as they physically could, with Richard Rayner leading the way in a great deal of pain. However, those whose company they sought weren't to be seen again and by the time the rocky gulley they were following came to an end, the darkness of night was upon them, and they could just about make out they were now standing in a sloping field. The taller of the two, continued to suggest they carried on, in their effort to lose height. Alas, by the time they reached a man-made stonewall it was late and the moon had made an appearance, casting some subdued light that was to benefit the lost boys.

At least the wind had dropped, which was a good indication they had progressed further down from the apex of the mountain, but the temperature had fallen and the two lost souls were beginning to feel the effects of the Cumbrian Autumnal night air.

Young Winkler wanted to spend the remainder of the night where they stood, but Rayner insisted they should continue with their descent.

"I'm sure we will soon come across a farmhouse or other dwelling where we can seek help," he suggested.

So, they continued, following the decline feeling cold, hungry and exhausted, until the smaller of the boys suddenly tripped over some unseen object and went sprawling down the hillside, disappearing into the darkness.

Rayner quickly followed his friend's cries for help and found the lad propped up against yet another stonewall, crying in pain and grasping a booted ankle. Their involuntary escapade was now turning into a nightmare.

Carefully, he helped the injured boy to his feet, but the victim of the mishap had difficulty in putting any weight on his one foot, suggesting he'd sprained an ankle. Neither was there anything close by that would have supported Master Winkler, so they continued their flight towards safety as best they could.

After another mile or so the descent began to flatten out and they reached a narrow lane with tall hedgerows that could be vaguely seen on either side. Both youngsters' spirits were raised, realising that finally they had managed to escape the clutches of Scafell.

Suddenly a flare lit up the night sky, some distance away.

"Look Winkler, I think that's meant for us," Rayner said, excitedly, "I wager it's the mountain rescue looking for us."

Both boys continued to gingerly hobble along towards where the flare had been seen, their optimism increasing with every step, until finally, they could hear voices not far from where they had reached.

Figures appeared in front of them, and they immediately stopped walking, their legs unable to move another step and giving Richard Rayner little respite from the agonising torture his feet were being subjected to. Soon afterwards they were confronted by members of their own young party of climbers who had been frantically searching for their two lost friends. But there was no welcoming party, only succour and the release of great frustration from the two teachers who had led the school outing.

When the young Richard Rayner finally returned home, the one aspect of his trip to Scafell that made an impression was a trip to the local doctor who diagnosed septic nerves in both his feet, resulting in them being treated with Salva and having to wear slippers for the next three weeks...

The school trip to Scafell Pike had been nothing short of the most undesirable in Rayner's childhood.

Chapter Fourteen

When Richard Rayner finally returned to the present, having recalled the memory of that dreadful and frightening night during a school trip to the Cumbrian Mountains, he found Jonathan Mytton staring across his desk directly at him, looking rather inquisitive.

"Forgive me, Jonathan," he quickly apologised, "I was remembering that ordeal you mentioned but please tell me, what reunions are you referring to?"

"Why, the school annual reunions of course, I never miss them, unless I have engagements abroad, but young Winkler is always there, repeating his story how you and him narrowly escaped death by spending the night on the highest mountain in England. I do believe we have a different version of that story each time Brigand tells it and I suspect the chap has a tendency towards exaggeration." The captain chuckled, a little sarcastically.

"After coming off Scafell, we were quickly rescued by the teachers and other youngsters in the party."

"Ah, I thought so, but on the last occasion I heard the description shared by our mutual friend, you both apparently almost froze to death, having spent the whole of the night exposed to nature's elements. I suspected the miscreant was pulling the wool somewhat, but he is the only individual I know who is referred to by that nickname."

"Have you any idea where Master Winkler can be located now?"

"Sorry old chum, I only ever come across him at the reunions, but I suppose I could ask around, although I presume you are best suited for that purpose with your reputation and all." Mytton laughed, causing Rayner to smile, but the senior detective's mind was now working rapidly, trying to recall when he had last cast his eyes on Herbert Winkler and trying to fathom out why he should hold any grudge against him, but failing to identify any reason. His initial belief was that their old school associate could not possibly be the same man he was so urgently seeking to find.

After thanking his friend for his hospitality, Rayner left the Royal Mews feeling somewhat disappointed and yet bewildered. His latest discovery contained a great deal of doubt and cynicism in his way of thinking, although the rare use of the name, Brigand, continued to tease his faculties. But for what earthly possible reason would young Herbert Winkler kidnap Frederick Morgan's daughter and his own son, murder an innocent woman in Whitechapel and set fire to Rayner's stables. It made no logical sense and was a dilemma that continued to needle him throughout the return journey to Scotland Yard. The renowned detective continued to think back to that disturbing time spent with the innocuous schoolboy, when in his early teens, and by the time he had reached the back yard of the police headquarters, was convinced that the individual mentioned by Captain Mytton, was an innocent party.

After entering the building from the backyard, instead of making his way up to his office, Richard Rayner decided to collect his post from the front Desk Sergeant, a habit he undertook on a daily basis.

"Ah, Mr. Rayner sir," the officer behind the desk in the public reception called out, when first seeing the Chief Inspector approaching, "There's a young lady wishing to see you by the name of Miss Clarissa Farthing, and I've taken the trouble to put her in your office. Henry Bustle is in attendance."

"Did she say what she wanted to see me about, Thomas?" the detective enquired.

"No sir, I did ask but she wouldn't say, except that it was important and she would only speak with yourself," the Sergeant explained, lowering his voice, "She's wearing a nurse's uniform and wasn't left standing at the gate when they gave out the good looks, if you take my meaning sir."

Rayner nodded and took his small parcel of correspondence from the officer, before climbing the stairs. When he reached his office, he found Henry Bustle in conversation with a young dark-haired lady who was undoubtedly pleasant on the eye.

After introducing himself, the senior detective asked how he could help his unexpected visitor and she looked coyly towards his Sergeant.

"Have no fear, madam," Rayner said, reassuringly, "Anything you wish to tell me is safe in the presence of Sergeant Bustle and won't go beyond these four walls."

Miss Farthing looked sheepishly down at the floor, as if reluctant to speak and the Chief Inspector assumed that she was there to divulge an extremely sensitive matter. He asked if she would like some refreshment, offering the woman tea or some other beverage, but she politely declined. He then sat in a soft chair opposite the lady and waited patiently for her to tell him the reason for her unexpected visit.

Henry Bustle, also felt a little self-conscious and having received a nod from Rayner, stepped across to the senior detective's desk and sat down behind it, leaving the Richard Rayner and his young visitor sitting in front of the log fire.

"I take it from your attire, you are a nurse by profession," the Chief Inspector remarked, stating the obvious.

She nodded and looked up, before confirming that she worked at The New Women's Hospital in Marylebone Road.

"I work on the surgical ward sir," she said, quietly, "And shouldn't be here by rights, but thought it was important to let you know, something that Sir Reginald told me a few weeks ago."

"Please, go on."

"I do not wish to place any aspersions on anyone sir and fear I might get into trouble by speaking with you."

"Fear not, Miss Farthing, as I have already made clear, our conversation is in the strictest confidence."

She smiled and thanked him, seemingly encouraged by Rayner's assurance.

"I was in love with Sir Reginald sir, and still am, and I suppose you could say, proud to have been his mistress."

Strangely enough, Richard Rayner wasn't surprised by that confession and remained looking indifferent, preferring to refrain from making any comment, to encourage his visitor to elaborate further.

"Well, it's like this sir, he confided in me about a number of matters connected with his work at the hospital and frequently took me out for lunch whenever our individual commitments allowed, of course."

"And I take it, his wife was not aware of your association with her husband." It was an insensitive remark, but one that Rayner felt was necessary to make in the early stages of the interview.

"Glory be sir, no, there was a time when I would have welcomed that, but now, I would rather die than have Lady Barbara discover the truth. I have never met the woman and have no intentions of doing so. We were always very discreet when spending time together. I would surreptitiously make my way down to the Jolly Teapot in Marylebone Road and Sir Reginald would meet me there. He was such a kind man who treated me with the utmost respect and even now, I find it difficult to believe he is no longer with us."

Rayner nodded and smiled supportively.

"Please go on, Miss Farthing," he prompted.

"Well, it's like this sir, about four or five weeks ago, we were both enjoying each other's company in the Jolly Teapot, when Reggie, I mean Sir Reginald, told me he was having some difficulty with a former friend of his. A lady friend, sir."

Again, the senior detective just nodded, but was beginning to feel intrigued by what he was anticipating was about to unfold.

"Reggie confessed that a long time ago, he had an affair with this lady and that now she had suddenly decided to blackmail him, threatening to tell his wife if he didn't pay her two hundred pounds for her silence."

Rayner glanced across at Henry Bustle, who remained stone-faced, although the Sergeant was obviously interested as was the senior detective. A failure to blackmail someone could very well be recognised as a motive for murder.

"And who was this lady, did he say?"

"Oh yes sir, it was Lady Margaret Plumb, the wife of Sir Oswald Plumb, the chairman of the Board of Governors at the hospital."

"Do you know if Sir Reginald paid the money being demanded by Lady Margaret?"

"No sir, he hadn't paid her a penny at the time he shared the secret with me and was in fact, extremely annoyed at the situation the lady was putting him in, calling her a vixen who was determined to ruin his life."

"Perhaps she felt justified in seeking recompense," Henry Bustle callously remarked, from where he was sitting behind Rayner's desk. Having recently lost his beloved wife, and having been a devoted husband and father, he found any mention of extra-marital affairs deplorable, but on this occasion was ignored by both Rayner and their visitor.

"Forgive me, Clarissa, if I might call you that, but why are you telling us this?" the Chief Inspector enquired, watching closely for the lady's reaction.

The nurse appeared to be taken aback by the question and she looked more concerning at the senior detective, before explaining that she thought it was possible that the former lover of Sir Reginald Hammond, might well have been responsible for killing him, after he had refused to pay her demand.

"I see, and did he mention the lady to you again, after that first occasion."

"He did sir, only last week when we were alone at my home in Smithfield. I asked him directly if she had furthered her demand for money, and he told me that she was still threatening to tell his wife and her own husband of their affair and that he was adamant he would not pay her a single penny. When I brought up the subject, he appeared very distraught, and I had never seen him like that before. In fact, sir, he offered violence towards the lady."

"In what way, exactly?"

She lowered her voice and continued to explain that her former lover threatened he would strangle the woman, if she continued to harass him.

"Do you believe he was capable of doing that, Clarissa?"

"I'm not sure sir, he was very upset at the time."

Rayner sat back in silence for a few moments, considering the information shared with him. The circumstances would most certainly have given credence to Sir Reginald attempting to end Lady Margaret Plumb's life prematurely, of that he had no doubt, but was dubious that a female blackmailer would succeed in stabbing him twice in the chest, in retaliation. However, it did stand to reason that, should the besieged gentleman be pushed too far, he could have arranged for some other villain to have done his dirty work for him and the attempt to silence Lady Margaret had failed, hence the motive for the fatalistic act of revenge. But Rayner was unconvinced.

He thanked Nurse Farthing for sharing what she knew with him and again, assured her of its confidentiality, before requesting that Henry Bustle escorted her back downstairs to the exit door.

"Was I right in coming to you, Mr. Rayner?" she asked, after standing from her chair.

"Yes, you have done the right thing, Clarissa, and I am extremely grateful, but just one more thing. I have referred to you as Miss, assuming that you are not married yourself."

"You assume correctly, sir."

"Then tell me, is it at all possible that someone close to you might have discovered about your own affair with Sir Reginald?"

"No, that could never have been. No one knew of our...arrangement."

"Are you absolutely certain?"

"As certain as I can be, as I said, we were very careful."

"Thank you."

When Henry Bustle returned to Rayner's office, the Chief Inspector asked his Sergeant what his thoughts were concerning the news they had just received.

"Revenge could be a possible motive sir, yes."

Rayner was sitting at his desk, trying hard to visualise the kind of woman who would risk her own social position in return for the payment of two hundred pounds. Blackmail was a dirty business, as far as the Chief Inspector was concerned and he accepted that the woman, Lady Margaret Plumb, could only be an individual without scruples, although that didn't mean she was a cold-blooded killer.

"Do you want me to find out where they live and bring her in?" Bustle asked.

"No, not yet, Henry, when dealing with the aristocracy we must be certain of our facts and not go flying in, unless we are absolutely certain of what we are about. I do believe though, we should meet with her husband to try and find out what his relationship was with Sir Reginald, in his capacity as chairman of the board."

"You suspect he could have found out about his wife's illicit affair and taken his own revengeful act."

"Possibly but ask Jack Robinson to find out more about the background of both of them before we go blundering in."

Reminding Richard Rayner of Eres, the Greek Goddess of Chaos, Frederick Morgan then appeared in the open doorway and enquired as to the purpose of the visit from the lady who had just left the building.

The Chief Inspector briefly told him of what Clarissa Farthing had shared with them, to which Morgan instantly suggested that in all probability, either Lady Margaret or Sir Oswald Plumb, or both of them, had been the perpetrators of the murder. However, Rayner had his own thoughts on the subject, and it showed by the look of indifference in his facial features.

The senior officer then asked if any progress had been made to identify the kidnappers and Richard Rayner explained about his visit to see Captain Jonathan Mytton and the fact that an old school associate, Herbert Winkler, was popularly known as, 'Brigand'.

"But as far as Winkler is concerned, it doesn't make sense. I recall the lad wouldn't say boo to a goose and if our Brigand is the same individual involved in the copper wire burglaries, I cannot see little Herbert having either the inclination or capability of being involved in such crimes."

"But a number of years have passed by since you last saw him, Rayner, or so I am assuming."

"Yes, but also, he would have no reason for wanting to harm myself or my family."

"Perhaps a third party is involved, one who you have dealt with in the past and is close to this old school mate of yours."

"Perhaps."

"In any case, you need to find him and decide one way or another."

Up to that point, Rayner had been prepared not to waste time searching for an individual who he was convinced could not possibly have been involved in the kidnappings and the murder of Maisy Winthrop. However, Morgan did have a point and if only to satisfy his own curiosity, decided to track down Herbert Winkler and find out more about his recent past.

Morgan then enquired how the enquiries were progressing into the Tower Bridge debacle and was told by Rayner that so far, Jack Robinson had met with little success, that particular Investigation having been shelved until they had brought the murder and kidnappings Inquiry to a successful conclusion. And then of course, there was the slaying of the hospital surgeon.

"At present, I am prioritising what we need to be looking at," Rayner added, "And I believe this Brigand individual needs to be identified above all else before he commits a further atrocity."

Morgan nodded his understanding and then suddenly remembered, "Isn't the name Winkler, the same as your old butler, Rayner?"

Of course it was and such a fact had escaped the renowned detective's attention. How he had failed to recognise that fact was beyond him. As far as he was aware, Albert Winkler had never been married, having worked for Richard Rayner's father before agreeing to serve his present master, following Rayner's marriage to Clarice. It was an uncommon name and there was every possibility that the two men were related in some way. That was a strong possibility he would have to address.

"Yes, it is, and I shall need to question Albert, as soon as I get home later this evening."

"Don't take this the wrong way, but you said yourself that the vermin who set fire to your stable must have had some form of inside knowledge about the layout. Could it be…"

"I will know soon enough, sir."

Number 45 Cavendish Square was just off Oxford Street and contained a small number of houses, all set in their own gardens and obviously owned by people who were fairly well off. Where the Plumb family resided was facing a central area of green open spaces, a two-tiered building with balconies and a short gravel driveway leading to the front door.

A smartly dressed maid with red hair tied in a bun, answered Richard Rayner's call and when the senior detective requested to see Sir Oswald Plumb, they were invited into the hall, while the young lady went to see if the master of the house was available. But as the maid turned to leave, a woman's voice rang out, asking who the visitors were.

"Two detective gentlemen from Scotland Yard, madam," the maid answered, directing her voice at an open door, that obviously led to the downstairs drawing room.

A lady appeared, tall with dark hair platted across the top of her head. She was slim in build and wearing a black ankle-length dress.

"I am Lady Margaret Plumb, gentlemen, can I be of assistance only Sir Oswald is busy at the moment entertaining some people from his horticultural club."

Rayner was tempted to conduct an in-depth interview with the lady of the house there and then but thought it better if for now, his business with her husband remained discreet. He apologised for calling unannounced at such an inconvenient time and suggested he would call again at a later date, when the lady's husband was available.

"Can I ask you Chief Inspector, what you wish to see my husband about." Concern was written all over her face and Rayner decided to take advantage, briefly explaining that his business was for Sir Oswald's ears only.

Lady Margaret appeared to be a little abashed by her visitor's manner, and then unexpectedly turned to the maid and asked her to bring her husband to the drawing room.

"I am sure that my husband would prefer to know the nature of your visit now, rather than be kept wondering. I do hope he has done nothing wrong."

"No milady, not your husband," the senior detective said, teasingly.

Chapter Fifteen

The chairman of the hospital's board of directors was a lot older than his unexpected visitors had envisaged and Richard Rayner, having estimated the lady of the house to be in her mid-thirties, recognised that Sir Oswald Plum was twice her age. The distinguished gentleman greeted the detectives warmly and inquisitively, before inviting them to take a chair each in the drawing room.

Once all three were seated comfortably in front of a roaring fire, Lady Margaret discreetly left, although the Chief Inspector had no doubt she would be listening to the conversation from the other side of the closed door.

The feeble looking Sir Oswald spoke quietly but in a high-pitched voice, enquiring how he could be of help to Scotland Yard.

"Forgive us for this intrusion sir, but we are investigating the unpleasant murder of Sir Reginald Hammond," Rayner explained, "And we have recently become acquainted with some information that we think you might be able to help us clarify."

Henry Bustle instantly glanced across at his Chief Inspector with some concern, wondering if the story related by the nurse, Clarissa Farthing, was about to be disclosed to the husband of the victim's former lover. Such an indiscreet course of action would have been so unlike Richard Rayner, considering his solemn promise of confidentiality made to the informant.

"Ah, a dreadful incident Mr. Rayner," the elderly man with thinning white hair and a slightly darker full beard answered, "Sir Reginald did some outstanding work for the hospital and will be greatly missed."

"Yes, I understand he was a popular individual whose research was of the utmost value in the field of Gynaecology."

"Yes, indeed."

The Chief Inspector was expecting an offer of refreshments to be made, but none was forthcoming.

"So, I take it you have a suspect in mind," Sir Oswald continued, with genuine interest.

"There are several at present, but might I ask what your relationship was with Sir Reginald, friendly or perhaps antagonistic."

"Ah, I see, might I assume I am a suspect then?"

"Not necessarily sir."

"There was certainly no animosity between us, I always found the fellow to be amicable and quite sincere in his intentions to progress in his selected field. In fact, I always supported his applications for further funding when required."

Rayner sat forward on the edge of his chair with both hands clasped together and enquired, "Am I not correct then in assuming there was some friction between Sir Reginald, and some other member of the board."

"I have just made my position clear, most certainly not sir, we all admired the man for his achievements and I regarded him as a friend. Both he and his wife often called upon us, and on several occasions dined with myself and Lady Margaret. We often returned their social niceties by calling at their residence."

"And your wife sir, what was her opinion of Sir Reginald and Lady Barbara?"

"That's a question you should put to my wife sir, but I believe you will find her assessment of the couple was quite favourable."

"Thank you and I am most grateful for your time, Sir Oswald. I shall not intrude any further." Rayner stood to leave, followed by Henry Bustle, but then asked the Knight of the Realm, one more question.

"Now that it appears Sir Reginald's research is doomed to be discontinued, what exactly will happen to the funding already provided?"

Sir Oswald had no hesitation in explaining that the money would undoubtedly be transferred to the work being conducted by the Director of the hospital wards and maintenance, Sir Giles Lamfrey.

Again, Rayner thanked the man and left, with his Sergeant at his side. His intention had been to plant a few seeds of anxiety and discomfort in the mind of Lady Margaret, and he was quite satisfied that had been achieved. The senior detective intended leaving the lady to dwell somewhat on the short conversation with her husband for a couple of days and then interview her at Scotland Yard, and certainly not within the comfort of her home.

"So, Henry, what is your first impression of the Chairman of the Board and his enigmatic wife?" the Chief Inspector asked, as they were transported back through the streets of London.

"I cannot see him being our killer sir, that's for sure. I don't think he has enough breath to close a door."

"And what of his much younger wife."

"Let's say, from what I have seen, I wouldn't like to cross her path when her bloods up. She certainly rules the roost as it were."

Rayner smiled. "I fully concur Sergeant."

Following dinner that same evening, Clarice Rayner joined her husband in the library, where she found him scrutinising pages in a reference book recording the antecedents and positions of a number of well-known surgeons practicing in the

London area. He was particularly interested in those employed at the New Women's Hospital but was surprised to find no mention of any individual, except the main administrator, Sir Giles Lamfrey.

"I'm surprised Sir Giles is the only one on record," Clarice commented.

"The hospital is fairly new dear, and it could be this ledger I have is somewhat out of date, but nonetheless, it wasn't really important and I do need to have a talk with Albert."

After being summoned, the butler appeared carrying his master and mistress's usual glasses of after-dinner brandy on a silver tray, which he placed on a small table at the side of Richard Rayner.

"You wanted to see me sir," the elderly servant enquired.

"Yes, Albert, it was just that I was wondering if you had a relative by the name of Herbert Winkler, your namesake. I am trying to trace a young man of that name who attended the same school as I did, and I am sure you would agree that Winkler is not exactly a common surname."

"I have a nephew by that name, sir."

"And would you know if your nephew attended the Royal Grammar School in Guildford?"

"To my knowledge, I believe he did, yes sir."

"Ah now, it might well be myself and your nephew are old acquaintances from the school. In fact, we both shared quite a traumatic experience when on a school trip one particular year."

"Yes, he has told me, when you were lost on a mountain up in Cumbria, sir."

Rayner nodded, a little bemused by the fact, after all the years the old man had worked for him, he had never had any idea that his butler's nephew was indeed the same young whipper snapper he had led off Scafell, on that fearful night so long ago.

"Do you ever see your nephew, Albert?"

"Aye sir, I hadn't seen him for a long time but just recently he has visited me on a couple of occasions, if that's alright by you, sir."

Rayner noticed how solemn looking his butler had become and knew it had nothing to do with fear of having not first sought approval before seeing his nephew at the house. The old man had been in the Chief Inspector's employ since he had first moved into the dwelling following his marriage to Clarice, and before that, had worked for his parents together with Mrs. Uddlestone. the cook. In addition to that, his aged butler would have known that neither Rayner or the lady of the house would have had any objection to having his relative visit, or anyone else if it came to that. No, something else was bothering the man and the detective could sense it.

As if reading her husband's mind, Clarice asked Albert, whether Herbert Winkler was in good health.

"Oh yes, perfectly good health, Madam, thank you," came the quiet reply.

"Then why is it Albert, you look so forlorn?" she asked.

"We have known you for many years, and you must be aware of how your loyalty and friendship has led us to regard you as a highly respected member of our family," Rayner added, "Whatever is disturbing you, we wish to help if we can."

The butler remained standing there, looking down at the carpeted floor, like a small child having just been scolded.

"Do sit with us, Albert, for a short time and tell us what it is that's causing you grief," his master offered, placing the glass of brandy into the old man's hands, which was greatly appreciated.

Both Rayner and his wife then sat for a few moments in silence, waiting for their head servant to disclose all.

He began to nervously tremble, before subduedly confessing, "I do believe sir, madam, I have made the gravest of errors."

Both smiled back at him, encouragingly and in an effort to solicit more from their butler and friend.

The old man's watery eyes looked at them, before continuing, "It's like this sir, young Herbert called here about two weeks ago and I sat him downstairs in the kitchen. He told me that he was having a run of bad luck when visiting the turf, having lost the inheritance left him by my brother, Granville. He told me that he was no longer addicted to that soul destroying habit, Heaven forbid, and was trying to start his life over by finding a more reliable and conducive occupation."

"Did he say exactly what his intentions were?" Rayner asked.

Albert nodded and answered, "Yes, he told me he was looking for a position in banking and had been offered a post by a Mercantile bank in Norwich and had accepted. He also said that he would soon be taking that up."

"So, what is it that is disturbing you now?"

The butler sighed before explaining, "Herbert called again last week on the day before we had the fire at the stables and asked if he could see the horses we maintained, so, thinking it was harmless enough, I took him round back to meet the stable boy, only Jonas wasn't there. So, I took him inside to see the stalls and allowed him to meet each of the horses, including Patch, madam's pony."

"And, then what happened?"

"Nothing sir, but strangely enough, once Herbert had seen the horses, he left saying he had just remembered he had arranged to meet a friend in Piccadilly."

"Did he call again after that?"

"No sir, I haven't seen him since that day," the butler admitted, still looking anxious and concerned.

"Then what is it that's troubling you, my old friend?"

"I truly believe, and may God be my judge that for whatever reason, it was Herbert who set fire to the stables. I cannot tell you why I think that sir, him being my own flesh and blood and that, but just know it was him."

Both the master and the lady of the house sat in silence for a little while, trying to come to terms with what they had been told. The same old question came to Rayner's mind, why would Herbert Winkler want to cause so much grief to his old school associate.

He then asked his butler if he was aware of his nephew's nickname from school, but without actually mentioning the name of Brigand.

The old man shook his head, remaining daunted by his feelings of self-incrimination.

"Do you know Albert, where Herbert can be found now?"

"No sir, he never said, but I assumed he was living somewhere in London."

"Did he mention the name of the Mercantile Bank in Norwich?"

"No sir."

"Then might I suggest we forget all about the matter and I strongly advise you to stop blaming yourself for something that might not have taken place." In trying to reassure his butler, Rayner added, "Personally, I find it difficult to believe that your nephew would commit such an atrocity. He most certainly has no justifiable cause to have created so much grief for us."

"Do you wish for me to work my notice sir," the old man sorrowfully offered.

"Heavens no, we are your family Albert, and you can rest assured we are here to support you through thick and thin. Now take that empty glass back to the drawing room and replenish it with some of that excellent brandy so I might join Mrs. Rayner in our usual nightcap. Would you like another, dear?" he asked of Clarice, who smilingly declined the offer.

Albert stood and thanked both of his employers for their understanding, before bowing and quietly leaving the room.

Clarice then turned to her husband and enquired as to what course of action he now intended to take, believing that their butler's suspicions were justified.

"I do believe I need to track down Albert's nephew dear as quickly as possible, if only to reminisce about old times."

It was Richard Rayner's driver, Constable Jacob Studley, who first noticed some disturbance taking place at the front of Scotland Yard, just before he was about to turn the carriage down the side street leading to the backyard. There were two fire pumps positioned at the entrance gates and uniformed police officers making their presence known by hurrying in and out of the headquarters building. The Chief Inspector also noticed the ongoing activities through the carriage window and called to his driver to continue, after he had left the vehicle.

The first senior officer Rayner met was Inspector Partridge, who was standing on the front steps demonstrating with a fireman controlling one of the pumps.

"All you are attempting to accomplish now sir, is to flood the bleedin' place," he overheard the officer say, "The fire is out, and the only damage being caused is by you and your men."

When the Inspector saw the senior detective approaching, he instantaneously shook his head.

"What's happened, Percy?" Rayner enquired.

"A bomb went off in the front reception sir, but from what we can see there's not much damage been caused, except what these blokes are now doing."

Although surprised by what had taken place and immediately thinking that in all probability, the culprits were most likely to have been Irish dissenters, Rayner asked if Chief Superintendent Morgan had been informed.

"He was down here not so long back sir but appears to have disappeared. He might have gone back upstairs to his office, or to see the Commissioner who also made a brief appearance earlier."

"Was anyone injured?"

"No sir, according to Sergeant Butler behind the desk, no one was near the thing when it went off."

Rayner nodded and continued to enter the front reception area. There was still a lot of smoke lingering, and the sickly smell of cordite was prominent in the air. Various constables were busily engaged in completing several tasks under the direction of the Desk Sergeant, and apart from some noticeable signs of scorching around the desk area, it seemed to the senior detective that no other real damage had been caused, except for the floor that was flooded resulting from the use of the water pumps.

When he reached the first floor, Rayner found Frederick Morgan standing in his office, together with Henry Bustle and Claude Davey. All three were studiously gazing down at the desktop, closely examining some remnants of what the Chief Inspector assumed were brown paper remains of what the bomb had been secured inside.

"Well then, for once we can't blame the Paddies for this one, Rayner," the Chief Superintendent declared, "From what we have here, it seems that the explosive device was meant for you, my old mucker."

Morgan showed him a particular segment of paper showing the parcel had been addressed to, Detective Richard Rayner, at Scotland Yard. The details were handwritten and the Chief Inspector immediately recognised the script was similar in appearance to that found in the note discovered close to Matthew's school, following his son's kidnapping.

"I reckon this thing was meant to go off when you were opening the parcel, and for some reason, detonated prematurely."

"Have we recovered anything else from downstairs?" Rayner asked.

"A few bits and pieces that I've put on my desk next door. I'll show you."

There was an array of metal objects covering Morgan's desk and the Chief Inspector warily examined each of them, noting the presence of burnt-out pieces of wire and what he identified as being small percussion caps. He then asked the senior officer who had recovered the display before him.

"Bustle and Davey mostly, why do you ask?"

"They did an excellent job, because what we have here is the leftovers of a home-made bomb, which I suspect from the percussion caps, contained a couple of sticks of dynamite. I am amazed that no one was seriously injured by the explosion."

"Then might I add, from my military experience those sticks of dynamite might well have been old stock, losing their impact when detonated."

Rayner noticed the part of a clock face, badly burned but not sufficiently defaced to prevent the time the device was supposed to have detonated, from being visible.

"It appears the bomb was supposed to have gone off at nine o'clock."

"It was more like eight o'clock when the bloody thing exploded."

"Then for some reason, it must have shorted but it does appear that the manufacturer intended causing me some harm. How was it delivered?"

"By the first post this morning. This cretin is beginning to test us to the limit Rayner, and it's about time we got his lily-white arse in our cells, my old mucker."

"Yes, I couldn't agree more sir, and I suspect we are closer to doing just that, than you might think," the intended victim replied, with a look of earnest determination in his eyes.

Chapter Sixteen

Richard Rayner didn't need anyone to remind him of how fortunate he had been to have escaped serious injury or worse on that particular morning, but the one major lesson he had learned from the experience was that his enemy had displayed a determined intention to kill him. The device that had exploded prematurely had been addressed personally to him, and that in itself unnerved the senior detective. But why, was still the question haunting him. The fact that it was highly likely his stalker was an old school associate, Henry Winkler, disturbed him even more so and he was finding it difficult to come to terms with such an alarming situation.

One other certainty that had resulted from his enquiries over recent days, was that any doubt he might have held regarding his butler's nephew having been responsible, had now disappeared. The reason for Winkler's vengeful acts were no longer important to Richard Rayner, it was now imperative that he tracked the man down before he'd had the opportunity to commit another attempt on the detective's life. The story given by the man to his uncle, alleging he had obtained employment with a bank in Norwich, was dismissed by the Chief Inspector as probable fiction, with the suspect knowing that his intended victim would in all probability extract that bead of information from the butler, and would therefore be nothing more than a red herring. The individual who had been performing as if he was some inexperienced hunter who kept missing his target had now, in Rayner's mind, become the hunted. Albeit the senior detective suspected the man had been playing a bizarre game with him, he needed to authenticate the ruse that Winkler had given his Uncle Albert. Jack Robinson, who had been making little headway in the Tower Bridge murder, was dispatched to Norwich to conduct whatever enquiries were necessary to confirm his butler's nephew's statement of employment, one way or another.

"I also want you to check with our records, Jack, to see if Herbert Winkler has come to our notice at all in the past," he added.

The Sergeant nodded and suggested he would complete that task, prior to leaving for East Anglia.

After the younger Sergeant had left, Rayner then studied his own notes made earlier on his blackboard, focusing his mind on his previous pattern of thinking that had led him to conclude that his man might well have held a position in the diplomatic service. He had no factual evidence to support that belief, only that it appeared to be rational and logical when considering all the circumstances surrounding the time Winkler had been active, and the amount spent on his planning and guardianship of the kidnapped victims, including his own son. It was time to go down that route and he explained his line of reasoning to Henry Bustle.

Repeating what Frederick Morgan had also said earlier, Bustle suggested that such an idea was only a remote possibility, but his Chief Inspector was not to be deflected from having his suspicions confirmed or otherwise and told his Sergeant to grab his hat and coat.

The interior of the Foreign Office in Downing Street was no stranger to Richard Rayner, having visited the Head of the Secret Service, Sir Nigel Ponsonby, on many previous occasions. The tall, slim former Major in the British Army had grown a beard since the senior detective's last meeting with him and signs of insufficient sleep were prominent from the dark rings around his eyes. Ponsonby's usual boyish features were also absent and it appeared the country's top spy had aged at least ten years since their last meeting. Richard Rayner could only assume that the gentleman, whose father happened to be the Private Secretary to Queen Victoria, had recently been involved in some highly stressful operation. But it was not the Scotland Yard man's place to probe as to the reason for his friend's physical deterioration.

Smartly dressed and articulately spoken, Sir Nigel welcomed his two visitors and immediately poured measures of Scotch malt whiskey into three tumblers, before handing one to each of them.

"Although it's always good to see you Richard, and you, Sergeant Bustle," the man whose office they were in, complimented, "I do suspect that Scotland Yard has unravelled some major issue that is a threat to the country's security."

Rayner noticed how Sir Nigel's hand was shaking when he handed the glass tumblers to his visitors, and the Head of the Secret Service saw the concern on Rayner's face.

He returned to his seat behind his desk and sat back, before loudly exhaling.

"Forgive me gentlemen," he softly said, "But I am only just recovering from a bout of Jaundice that has unfortunately kept me bed ridden for the past damnable month or so. In fact, I fear I am still suffering from the effects of an illness I would never wish on anyone else."

"I'm sorry to hear that Nigel and wish you a speedy full recovery."

"Thank you Richard, and fear not, that will be achieved, I am only back at my desk because every ship needs its captain, as they say. So, what treasonous episode of conspiracy against the Empire has brought you here today my old friend."

All three took sips of their whiskey, before Rayner continued.

"Nothing as serious as that, Nigel, I assure you."

"Then I am disappointed my friend. How can I be of help this time?"

"We are trying to trace a gentleman by the name of Mr. Herbert Winkler who I suspect might just hold a position in the diplomatic service."

The department's top agent slowly manoeuvred across his office and sat on a soft chair in front of a blazing fire, inviting his guests to do the same.

"I confess the name means nothing to me, have you any idea of what exactly your subject is responsible for in the Foreign Office. As I am sure you are aware the diplomatic service covers a vast area of important fields of responsibility."

Rayner nodded, before suggesting that, if his assumption was correct, in all probability, Herbert Winkler, could very well be engaged on the home front. He based that premise on the man's activities having been confined to the London area.

"Ah, that makes it a little easier." Sir Nigel returned to his desk and picked up his telephone, asking the person on the other end to summon Giles Catchum, to speak with him.

The Deputy Head of the Diplomatic Service was a short, rounded gentleman, with fairly lengthy wavy grey hair and, unlike his senior, was clean shaven. After being introduced to the detectives, it was Sir Nigel who put to Mr. Catchum, the name Richard Rayner was enquiring about.

"Yes of course, Master Winkler is employed downstairs in the Foreign Visitors' Department and to my recollection, has been with us for at least the past five years or so."

"Could you divulge what his responsibilities are sir?" Rayner asked.

"Yes, he holds a junior position and is responsible for assisting more senior personnel with accompanying Foreign dignitaries when visiting Britain in an official capacity, arranging accommodation, personal security and that sort of thing."

"And are you aware of his current commitments, sir?"

"I am afraid I am not, Chief Inspector, but if you give me a moment I shall endeavour to find out, if you think it is important."

"I do sir, and I am extremely appreciative."

After Giles Catchum had disappeared, Sir Nigel enquired as to the nature of his friend's interest in Herbert Winkler.

I'm not sure yet, Nigel, but if the man is the same individual we are trying to trace, then quite simply I believe he is trying to kill me."

Ponsonby just sat there, staring across at the Chief Inspector in utter disbelief. The Head of the Secret Service was well aware that Rayner was not the kind of man to exaggerate or over-react and was immediately taken aback by the response to his enquiry.

It transpired that, surprisingly to everyone except Richard Rayner and according to Giles Catchum, Winkler has been on sick leave for the past two months and no date was yet available to confirm his return to work. Having been told of the suspect's current circumstances, the Chief Inspector became more convinced that the man who had spent the best part of a night lost on Britain's third highest mountain, all those years before, was the same man they were seeking. Alas, the only problem remaining was the absence of any noticeable motive for any of the atrocities he had committed, except of course, for the murder of Maisy Winthrop, who Rayner had also been persuaded, had been slain from fear of the lady possibly identifying the kidnappers.

Having enquired as to Herbert Winkler's recorded home address, he was told that the Foreign Office employee lived in lodgings at 105 Manning Street, Bermondsey and that his vetted landlady was known as Mrs. Betty Kilgallon.

At the senior detective's request, both Sir Nigel Ponsonby and Giles Catchum, agreed not to disclose any details of the detectives' visit, until Rayner had been given the opportunity to take his man into custody and the Chief Inspector thanked them before leaving, knowing precisely where his next call would be made, and once again wishing his old friend a speedy recovery.

Having passed over Southwark Bridge, they could see the Pratchett and Longfellow Circus in the distance and Richard Rayner was reminded of just how fortunate Frederick Morgan had been in marrying the lady, who at that time was Sally-Anne Longfellow, now one of the richest women in London, together with her business partner, Emily Pratchett.

Henry Bustle must have been thinking the same because he made mention of it and his Chief Inspector remarked on what a shrewd lady, Mrs. Morgan was, in addition to being extremely likeable.

"But Henry, when we stop in Manning Street, I want you to approach the front door alone, just to confirm that our man is there."

Bustle nodded, understanding that Rayner was concerned that if Herbert Winkler caught sight of him, it might encourage the man to run.

"Where will you be sir?"

"Not far behind you, but hopefully concealed."

At the senior detective's instructions, the driver stopped the carriage a hundred yards or so from the terraced house they were intending to visit. Most of the fronts of the residences had hedges, offering Rayner the opportunity of some temporary concealment, at the same time as his Sergeant approached the front door of number 105.

A middle-aged lady answered the door, wearing a pinafore and grasping a broom.

"Mrs. Kilgallon?" Bustle enquired.

"Yes, and who might you be."

The detective introduced himself and enquired if Herbert Winkler was at home.

"I understand he hasn't been well for some time, missus and I'm an old friend of his."

"In God's name Sergeant, whoever has told you that is still in the Middle Ages. Master Winkler hasn't lived here for nigh on a year now."

A disappointed Henry Bustle asked if she had any idea where the lady's former lodger had moved to.

"No idea, he left here owing me a week's lodgings, so if you find him, tell him I'm not best pleased."

"Have you seen him at all, since he left?"

"Naw, if I had, I'd have put this broom across his head."

"What kind of a lodger was he, Mrs. Kilgallon, when he stayed here, I mean did he keep regular hours or was he more like a fly by night type."

"I never had any trouble with him, but he was rarely here. He had some secretive job working for the nobs in the Foreign Office and he always told me that his work was demanding."

Bustle tipped his hat and thanked the lady for her help, before walking away.

"Don't forget, if you see him, tell him..." she called after him.

"I shall missus, have no fear."

On their way back to Scotland Yard, Rayner confessed to having not been surprised that their man had moved on.

"It certainly adds more credence to our suspicions about him, Henry."

"I'm beginning to dislike this bloke already, and I haven't met him yet."

Jack Robinson was waiting for them in Rayner's office when they returned and confirmed that there was no official record of the man they were seeking.

"It would appear Herbert Winkler has never come to the notice of Scotland Yard sir."

"Very well Jack, thank you, and forget about travelling to Norwich, we have just confirmed that he has been working for the Foreign Office for the past five years."

Robinson was relieved, not looking forward to having to spend a few days away from his wife and child.

"We seem to be back at the starting gate," Bustle remarked.

"Not quite Henry, at least now we have a strong suspect, but I fear we shall have some difficulty in tracking our man down."

"Well, your guess about him working as a diplomat was spot on."

"Yes, but I suspect he won't be returning to work until he has accomplished whatever it is, he is trying to achieve."

Jack Robinson asked if the other two had learned how Winkler had been paid during his employment at the Foreign Office.

"Obviously by cash in hand," Bustle rightly suggested.

"Yes, but how. What I mean is, did he call at a wages office to collect his pay, or was it delivered to wherever his domicile was."

Rayner expressed his understanding of what his junior Sergeant was implying and immediately directed Henry Bustle to return to Downing Street and find out the information Robinson required from Giles Catchum.

"Although, I should imagine Jack, he wouldn't be paid during his absence from work, but it's worth delving into."

"There's no chance of him drawing a penny when he's not there," a pessimistic Bustle remarked, before leaving to carry out Rayner's instruction.

Although the senior detective was aware that the men would still be patrolling the outside of his property, he still felt uneasy not being personally present at

Clarice and Matthew's side, so left his work early to remedy that situation, taking a loaded firearm with him. And yet, when he reached his home, yet another unexpected surprise was awaiting him.

Clarice handed a sealed envelope addressed to 'Detective Rayner' that she explained had been found on the front doorstep by Albert the butler, earlier that day. The writing on the envelope was similar to that contained on both the package containing the bomb left at Scotland Yard and the note relevant to his son's kidnapping. Suspecting that the item could well be another booby trap intended for the addressee, Rayner quickly placed the envelope into a bucket and carried it out into the gardens. He also took a paper knife with him and was watched closely by Clarice, well distanced from the house.

"Now dear, I would be grateful if you would please stand back while I examine this little gem."

"Be careful, Richard."

Crouching over the bucket, he cautiously lifted the envelope off the bottom and with both hands began to feel around the edges but found nothing suspicious. He then carefully moved his hands over the outside to feel what was contained inside and could only detect the shape of what appeared to be a folded piece of paper. Finally, he slid the paperknife inside the item and began to slowly slit open the top, relieved when he'd finished without his suspicions having been realised.

Having cautiously taken the note from its enclosure, he opened it, only to be surprised by the nature of the wording written inside.

Chapter Seventeen

"To all intents and purposes, my old mucker, this Devil's disciple is intent on taking your life," Morgan declared in a loud boisterous voice, that penetrated from behind the usual smokescreen occupying his office, "Therefore, I agree with Bustle for once, it would be complete madness to meet him unarmed and on your own." The Chief Superintendent continued to stare down at the handwritten missive delivered to the Rayner residence the day before, and both the Chief Inspector and his Sergeant were wondering how the hell he could read it, through all the heavy smog being generated by the Welshman's pipe.

"Might I suggest, I remain close by sir, armed and in disguise," Rayner's right-hand man put forward, a suggestion that his senior found difficult to reject.

"Very well, Henry, I truly appreciate all the concern but as long as you ensure you remain invisible."

Rayner then took the same note from the top of Morgan's desk and after coughing read the contents aloud.

"You now know what I am capable of doing," he reiterated, "And the time has come for us to discuss my requirements. Meet me on Waterloo Bridge at ten o'clock tomorrow evening alone, and all will be revealed. I have placed a bomb in a chosen place that is densely populated and any tricks, or your failure to comply will result in many deaths for which you will be responsible." Rayner paused before referring to the fact it was signed, 'Brigand'.

"That signature tells us that Herbert Winkler is still unaware that we know his identity."

"So what?" Morgan asked.

"I suppose it's of little importance but might be useful in some way, should matters go wrong this evening."

"And what about this bomb the reprobate mentions. Is there any way in which we can discover its location?"

"I suspect that is a ruse to encourage me to comply and attend the meeting alone," Rayner suggested.

"And what if it isn't?"

"Then we are facing an impossible task to find its location in such a short space of time." Again, the Chief Inspector paused before suggesting that it was his belief that their man would turn up in some form of transport and would wish for Rayner to accompany him elsewhere, more private and where they could talk without fear of being apprehended.

"Which means he'll be armed, Richard," Morgan remarked, "It's much too risky, my old mucker." It was most unusual for Frederick Morgan to look so concerned and Richard Rayner appreciated the sincerity behind his Chief Superintendent's anxiety.

"Probably, but I do not believe we have any choice, that's if we wish to get our hands on him."

"At least agree to putting some other supporting officers surreptitiously close to Waterloo Bridge, so we have all the escape routes covered."

Rayner shook his head and reiterated his belief that their man was a careful and meticulous planner and would be extremely observant before showing himself.

"The slightest indication that we have officers in the vicinity of the meeting will undoubtedly scare him away, and as you have suggested yourself, his threat of having planted another bomb might not be a ruse. I don't think we can take that risk."

"Then I suggest you go armed yourself."

"For what purpose? I doubt I would ever be given the chance to use a firearm and if he was intending to kill me, surely he would have attempted that before now. In his missive he states that all will be revealed, which to my way of thinking can only mean he wants to talk and nothing else."

"But talk about what, for Christ's sake?"

Rayner shrugged his shoulders and then, turning to Henry Bustle, he re-emphasised his request that no rash action should be taken once Winkler had shown himself, but if the man did require Rayner to go elsewhere, then it would be wise to have a carriage nearby and cautiously follow.

"The man we are hoping to capture is very cunning," he continued, "Even with his selection of timing, knowing that at ten o'clock in the evening there will be very little traffic on the streets, which would make it more difficult to be followed unseen. You will have to be extremely careful Henry."

Morgan then stood from his seat and stated that he needed to run all of this past the Commissioner.

"He needs to know what we are about, and we shall need the old man's blessing to go ahead with it."

"Did anyone see the person who delivered the letter, sir?" Henry Bustle asked.

"No, it was found on the front doorstep by Albert."

Morgan then asked if the Chief Inspector was absolutely certain of his butler's loyalty and was told in no uncertain terms that there was no doubt or misgiving concerning the elderly servant's honourable intentions.

Henry Bustle then produced the stiletto type knife he always kept strapped to one leg and offered it to Richard Rayner.

The senior of the two smiled back at him and shook his head.

"I would be more likely to stab myself with that Henry, but thank you for the thought."

"I have never been able to fathom out how any reasonable and sane thinking human being, could even consider carrying such a gruesome instrument of death as that on his person, Bustle," Morgan declared, bringing a wry smile to Richard Rayner's face.

It was then that Jack Robinson joined the others and told Rayner that he had been back to the scene of Sir Reginald Hammond's murder. The young Sergeant was convinced that the killer had been lying in wait for the specialist gynaecologist, prior to stabbing him to death.

"I've searched every part of the ground and undergrowth inside that copse of trees and could find nothing, sir. I'm convinced the assailant didn't come from the hospital, otherwise I have no doubt he would have been seen."

"Pure assumption Robbo," Morgan snapped, "And we don't pay you to assume, matey."

"Or she, Jack," Rayner remarked, "It appears that the eminent surgeon was not void of female admirers."

"A philanderer," Henry Bustle added.

The Chief Inspector told the younger Sergeant to concentrate on the backgrounds of both Sir Oswald and Lady Margaret Plumb.

"Try and find out all you can about them, Jack. I suggest that at the moment they are our strongest suspects but make your enquiries surreptitiously. What of the Tower Bridge murder, have we made any progress yet?"

"No sir, that one is a complete mystery at the moment."

Rayner nodded, knowing that he urgently needed to address that incident as soon as they had resolved the current ongoing Investigation.

The City of London was glistening beneath a recent fall of snow and there was an eerie silence about the way in which, what few local people were about, walked the pavements. A few carriages could be seen crossing Waterloo Bridge, mostly hackneys transporting client's home after an evening's entertainment, but the adverse weather had undoubtedly persuaded the vast majority to stay at home. Richard Rayner had been absolutely correct in his assessment that the streets would be quiet at that time of night.

Henry Bustle was in position early, crouched over a metal brazier full of red-hot coals on the corner of Wellington Street, from where he had an unobstructed view of the bridge. Big Ben had already chimed the third quarter of the hour and the disguised Sergeant, dressed in woollen rags, muffler and a soft working man's cap, glanced down at his time piece confirming it was five minutes to ten o'clock.

On the opposite side of the thoroughfare, he watched covertly as Richard Rayner walked slowly on to the bridge, dressed in a heavy frock coat and top hat. He noticed the Chief Inspector was carrying a cane, which was unusual and assumed it was the only weapon Rayner had thought of taking with him. Bustle was hoping that what was about to take place would be quickly over, standing in the shadows and continuing to rub his gloved hands over the top of the blaze, trying to keep as warm as possible in the freezing conditions and keeping an eye on his senior detective's movements from beneath the peak of his cap. He was rightfully ignored by the senior detective who nonchalantly strolled past him, but undoubtedly aware of all that was going on around him.

When Rayner had reached the halfway stage across Waterloo Bridge, he stopped to look across at the black icy water of the River Thames below, stamping his feet and still grasping his cane in a leather gloved hand. A pitiful looking lamp lighter walked past the Chief Inspector, followed by a man and woman, but there was no sign of anyone intent on approaching him.

Big Ben finally struck out ten o'clock and at that precise moment only Richard Rayner remained on the bridge, alone where he stood. Five more minutes went by and still there was no sign, until Henry Bustle's attention was drawn towards an enclosed carriage with curtained windows, moving slowly towards his position. The one-horse transport past where he was standing, and the Sergeant cautiously noticed the driver on top was concealed beneath a heavy hooded garment. Bustle continued to watch as the vehicle continued on to the bridge, until stopping close to where the senior detective was still gazing out across the river.

Rayner was ready for whatever would take place next and turned to face the carriage, watching with interest and alertness as the door swung open. A man's voice could be heard coming from inside the darkness of the interior.

"Step inside and join me, Mr. Rayner."

The detective remained where he stood and enquired, "And who might you be, sir?"

Suddenly, a face appeared, the face of Herbert Winkler, hatless but looking through protruding eyes.

"You know very well, who I am, Rayner, now come inside man." The barrel of a pistol was pointing directly at the Chief Inspector, leaving him with little choice.

Winkler backed off, as Rayner stepped up into the carriage.

"Close the door," was the next directive and the Scotland Yard man obeyed.

The carriage then took off under the whip and rocked from side to side as it approached the far end of the bridge, the horse struggling to retain its grip on the snow-covered cobbles.

As soon as Henry Bustle saw his Chief Inspector enter the carriage, he waved to Rayner's driver, Jacob Studley, who was waiting nearby and quickly brought the official carriage up to where the Sergeant was waiting.

"They've crossed the bridge Jake," was all that Bustle had to say for the constable to follow in haste. Unfortunately, by the time they reached Belvedore Road at the far end, the vehicle carrying their Chief Inspector had disappeared from sight.

The look of anguish and concern on Bustle's face was obvious and he directed 'Jake' to drive around in the hope that their quarry might have stopped somewhere close by, but still there was no sign. That initial part of the operation had failed miserably and the senior detective was alone, to deal with his own situation without there being any intended help to support him.

"It's been a long time, Rayner," Winkler pointed out, "Since those heady days at the Royal," referring to the school they had both attended.

Rayner just stared at the man, confidently, as if they were on their way to attend a banquet given by London's Mayor.

"Pray tell me, Winkler, what game are you playing?" the detective asked, not taking his eyes away from the barrel of the pistol still pointing at him and not knowing whether Henry Bustle had managed to keep them in sight or not, "I must confess I am surprised you have been responsible for this charade of yours."

"Oh, it's not a charade my old friend, in fact, it's quite serious."

"Yes, I can see why your pitiful little brain would think that, having kidnapped Estelle Morgan and my son, Matthew, and of course murdering in cold blood that poor wretched woman from Denmark Street. You do realise that every police officer in London is now looking for you, so why add to your growing list of criminal atrocities."

"The brothel keeper was unfortunate, leaving us with no other option, but the kidnappings and that small blaze we created at your home, were only gestures to show you exactly what we were capable of doing, should you wish to reject our offer."

"Our offer?"

"Alright, my offer."

"And was that also the case, when you cruelly killed my wife's pony, you black hearted heathen."

"Enough, are you not interested in hearing my proposition, Rayner?"

"Of course, but I very much doubt I shall be interested in becoming your accomplice in whatever mad scheme you have been busy nurturing. Tell me, Herbert, whatever happened to that innocent young boy I once saved the life of on Scafell." Rayner was trying hard to deflect Winkler's attention from his present position of strength and to cause him to drop his guard, if only for a second.

"He grew up Rayner and you and I both know, you didn't save my life, I could have got off that mountain on my own; you just happened to be there in the same predicament."

"Something very drastic must have happened to you, to turn you into the monster you have become."

"Don't push it Rayner, I would not hesitate to send you on your way without any conscience."

"Yes, I believe that of you but why so much hatred towards myself and my family?"

The other man sat back relaxing more and then insisted, "I do not hate you or anyone else if it comes to that my old friend, far from it, you have something I require and that I believe could make us very rich, if you were willing to participate in what I have in mind, but you must hear me out first."

The detective suddenly felt a sensation of loathing towards this individual who had caused him so much grief in recent days, but needed to retain a look of indifference towards him.

"Really, so what is it that has driven you to commit kidnapping and murder?" Rayner could sense the carriage was slowing down and noticed that Winkler's finger was now resting on the trigger guard of the pistol he was holding.

Without warning, he grabbed the barrel and quickly managed to wrench the weapon in an upwards arch with one hand, at the same time striking the man across the face with his walking cane. But Rayner's timing was not quite right, and instead of knocking his man senseless, only managed to graze the side of his head.

Herbert Winkler fought back, screaming as he tried to maintain his grasp on the pistol butt, but failed and the weapon went flying out of the open window.

Both men then grappled with each other, with Rayner's hat following the pistol and his cane dropping to the floor of the carriage, until the detective managed to sit astride his opponent and began to pummel his face, not noticing that the carriage had stopped.

The door flew open and the next thing that Richard Rayner experienced was pain, as his head exploded and he fell into a deep pit of darkness, having been struck by a heavy cosh. His attempt to escape had been far too slow and now he was about to pay the price for that grave misjudgement.

Chapter Eighteen

Consciousness welcomed Richard Rayner with a violently throbbing head and a wave of nausea that restricted his thinking abilities. He was in complete darkness and his body was lying prone with both arms stretched around some kind of pillar. Only when he tried to move his limbs did he realise that both wrists were tightly secured together and he remained in that position, waiting for the insufferable pain in his head to ease, but it continued in similar fashion to an anvil being constantly struck. At first, he thought he was in the middle of a nightmare, but then his brutal discomfort told him otherwise and slowly his recollections began to surface until finally, he was overcome by sickness.

As the mists began to clear, the detective became capable of processing his thoughts, although the violent headache refused to subside. His old schoolboy associate, the insignificant Herbert Winkler, had suddenly become an extremely dangerous man and the first realisation felt by the Scotland Yard man was that he had made a grave error in not taking greater precautions prior to meeting the deviant on Waterloo Bridge, as had been suggested by Frederick Morgan. Things had not gone according to plan and he could only hope now that Henry Bustle, and the rest of the detective branch would have the ability to find him. They certainly wouldn't be lacking motivation, but what was certain in Richard Rayner's mind was that he had underestimated this individual from his past and was now extremely vulnerable, a feeling that was foreign to him and not at all welcome. He had to remain calm and clear headed, which he was finding difficult in the circumstances, resulting from the constant pounding in his head.

As the dawn approached, every detective in Frederick Morgan's department was out on the streets, searching throughfares and buildings close to Waterloo Bridge for the missing Chief Inspector. Richard Rayner's top hat was found lying in the snow and close to a loaded pistol, which it was assumed had been used to enforce the kidnapper's requirements and confirmed the senior detective had resisted his captors. Unfortunately, neither item gave any indication of where the missing man had been taken and the search continued in vain.

Morgan, who was leading the pursuit, had attempted to send Henry Bustle home to get some rest but such a directive was always likely to be disobeyed and the closest friend to Rayner remained with the others, looking, seeking and trying hard to fathom out the direction in which the carriage he had failed miserably to follow, would have gone after leaving the bridge.

When Clarice Rayner was told of the incident involving her husband, she also insisted in joining the search and Morgan was helpless in trying to stop her.

Eventually, as the first signs of daylight began to sweep across the London sky, uniformed officers were dispatched to assist, until virtually the whole of Scotland Yard was deployed in, what many were feeling, was an effort to save Richard Rayner's life.

"My God, Clarice, I shall never forgive myself if anything happens to him," an exhausted Henry Bustle declared, as his reddened eyes peered into his friend's wife's eyes, "I should have acted more quickly."

She was gracious when accepting that it had not been the Sergeant's fault.

"Richard knew what he was doing, Henry, and I know my husband would have left us some kind of sign to show where he has been taken. We just have to find it somehow."

That didn't help the guilt riddled man much and he was desperate to make amends, imagining every other officer pointing a finger of blame at him.

By midday, every square foot surrounding Waterloo Bridge had been searched without success; residents had been disturbed and questioned and both pedestrians and coach drivers had been stopped and interrogated, but there had been no sightings of the missing detective.

When the surrounding darkness began to lighten with the coming of the dawn, Rayner could see that he was being kept prisoner in what looked like a large and spacious disused warehouse of some kind. He could hear the movement of people in the far distance and suspected he was confined somewhere in one of the docks, either the London Dock or St. Katherine's Dock, it mattered not. The excruciating pain inside his head had subsided and twice he had vomited on the ground that was partially covered with strands of straw. Apart from a few packing crates sparsely littering the floor, nothing else of significance could be seen and it was with some relief he heard the two wooden doors being opened at the far end.

Herbert Winkler and another resembling a dock worker came within his vision, after closing both doors behind them. Rayner watched the leading protagonist approach with a wide grin across his face, still having problems in accepting that this individual was indeed the nephew of his butler, Albert.

"How are we feeling this morning, Rayner," his tormentor enquired, insincerely, "I take it you are far more susceptible now to listen to my proposition."

Richard Rayner remained silent, but made a point of staring the man down, as he drew closer.

"You should have been prepared to listen to me in the carriage last night and that would have saved you all this pain and suffering my old friend." Winkler was now standing just a few feet away, his companion standing back further and grasping an iron bar in one shovel-like hand.

"What do you want from me, Winkler?" the detective asked, knowing that any attempt to escape would be futile. Even if such an opportunity came his way, Rayner doubted he was fit enough to go far. He had already decided to try and buy some time by attempting to appease his captor, until his whereabouts became known to his colleagues, if that was at all possible.

"Your time, Rayner, that's all we are asking for."

"Then you obviously have it."

"I want you to recall what you have already mentioned, when we lost the others on that mountain during that awful school trip."

"Do we have to continue conversing with both my arms wrapped around this post, Winkler," Rayner pleaded.

"For now, yes. Think back to just after we lost sight of the rest of the group, it was still light at the time."

The detective winced, as the ropes binding his wrists continued to dig into his flesh.

"I remember," he confirmed.

"And we inadvertently came across a large rock with an inscription carved in the stone."

Rayner vaguely remembered the incident and recalled seeing, what he thought at the time were ancient hieroglyphics carved into the rock that Winkler was referring to. He also recollected they had stopped to copy what they saw on a piece of paper. There were about five or six different features and at the time, being a young schoolboy interested in the subject of Ancient History, he suspected they were of Saxon origin.

"What of it, Winkler?"

"Where is the sketch you made of that rock now, Rayner?"

"I have no idea, if you remember we were both severely admonished by the teachers when returning to safety and I never gave that paper another thought. I have no doubt it has been lost in time. Why would you be interested in that, all these years after."

"Well, my friend, I never forgot it and I later recalled the nature of those hieroglyphics and in fact, was able to sketch them down myself. I later managed to translate them, with some help from the British Library here in London and discovered that you were correct in your assumption that they were Saxon."

"Good for you."

"They indicated that there existed what they referred to as a 'treasure pit'."

Rayner shook his head, confused and not really understanding the purpose of what Winkler was attempting to explain.

"An Anglo-Saxon treasure pit man, that would undoubtedly be worth thousands, if not millions to the person who discovered its concealment."

Now the detective was beginning to understand what this crusade of violence had been about.

"I have returned to Scafell on a number of occasions and tried to retrace our steps but as yet, have failed to find that same rock."

"I'm not surprised, considering that neither of us had any idea of where we were at the time."

"Well, you know what they say, two heads are better than one and I want you to come back there with me and try and find that same rock. I've read all about your achievements as a detective and if anyone can find it, you can. In return, I am willing to share half of what we manage to dig up."

So, that was what all of this had been about, the fantasy of a mad man. Richard Rayner loudly exhaled, before remarking, "All of this for a fool's errand to become rich."

"It's not a fool's errand my friend, it is a conquest I have been committed to ever since that unfortunate incident."

"Of course it is a fool's errand, utter madness to think that treasure is buried on Scafell Mountain. You Winkler, have been blinded by your own greed and you honestly believe I would be prepared to help you with this fallacy, after kidnapping my son and setting fire to my home."

"Regretfully, that was the only way I knew how to attract your attention."

"Then why kidnap Chief Superintendent Morgan's daughter as well?"

"Ah, that was a mistake, I confess I made it based on the false assumption that the girl was somehow related to you. You see, I have watched you for some time now, noting every move you made, and you know something Rayner, you are very much a creature of habit. The girl was my first choice of victim after I had seen you take her to and from the school where she worked, but alas, as I have said, I misjudged her relationship with both you and your wife. In any case, I released her, as I did your son. It was only to make a point."

"After you callously raped the girl."

"We must all take our little pleasures, Rayner, when they are presented to us on a plate. She was begging for it."

"You are a liar Winkler, and her father would disagree with you. Frederick Morgan is a determined gentleman who won't rest until he has hunted you down and inflicted on you the same pain and suffering you caused to his daughter."

"Well, Mr. Morgan hasn't been very successful so far, now has he?"

Rayner then suggested that if he gave his word as a gentleman, that he would not try to escape, Winkler could cut his bonds that were beginning to become excruciatingly unbearable.

"Sorry my old friend, I cannot do that."

"Then do you think I could have a drink of water."

"Yes, but later. Firstly, I want you to think about my offer."

Rayner paused, knowing if he agreed immediately to this hair-brained idea that had been obviously tormenting his man for some time, his insincerity would become apparent. So, he just agreed to think about it and nothing more.

Herbert Winkler then made a surprising announcement. He unexpectedly crouched down on the floor just a few feet from where Rayner was standing, tied to the pillar. He looked up at his prisoner with a sad facial expression and explained how his mother had died when he was an infant, and how he had been raised by his father, a man who had worked hard throughout his life to pay for his son's education.

"Even after he died from the Consumption, my papa left me fairly well off and I had every intention of making him proud by investing his money wisely."

"So, what happened, Herbert?" Rayner gasped, his throat parched and his tongue beginning to swell through the lack of water.

"I became addicted to the turf, Rayner, that's what happened. Initially, I won on my selections but then began to lose heavily."

Winkler's eyes dropped to the floor and he lowered his voice as he continued, "I tried to walk away, believe me I tried with all my heart, but couldn't and continued betting until every penny I had was in the bookmakers' coffers."

"And now you think you can retrieve your position in society by grabbing a load of treasure that might not exist."

"Oh, it exists alright, Rayner, I have done my research and let me tell you, Scafell was known to have been a burial site for the tribal leaders in that part of the country, those who retained all the riches discovered during that period, and it's common knowledge that when one of them was buried, all of their wealth and riches went with them."

This was sheer lunacy, as far as the detective was concerned and the man crouching down before him had undoubtedly become mentally unbalanced. But there again, no normal sane individual would have become so obsessed by what could only be regarded as a myth.

"I need some water," Rayner croaked, now having difficulty in speaking.

His captor looked up at him without speaking for a few seconds, and then turned to his associate and nodded for him to see to his prisoner's requirements.

The man was only gone for a few seconds and returned carrying an old bucket but filled with fresh water that was a life-safer for the detective.

After drinking his fill, Rayner thanked both men and then asked Herbert Winkler, how he could be so sure that he would succeed in finding that same piece of rock that his captor had failed to trace.

"Because of whom and what you are, Rayner. You have a gift for uncovering things and I do confess to having been jealous of your success, but know that you are far more capable of finding that location than I could ever be," he admitted, standing upright from the floor.

"As I said, I need to think about it."

Having successfully obtained one small concession, the Scotland Yard man attempted to gain yet another.

"I beg of you Herbert, loosen these bonds, I cannot feel my fingers or concentrate properly, and the pain around my wrists is excruciating."

"Then you will just have to bear it for a little longer, until you give me your answer."

Both captors then turned and left Richard Rayner to his own counsel and helpless position.

Henry Bustle was sitting in Richard Rayner's office with Jack Robinson. Both detectives were looking extremely frustrated and despondent. The older of the two Sergeants was attempting to think in the same way as he thought their Chief Inspector would, asking himself how Rayner would react in similar circumstances.

"They would have taken him to some isolated place where there was no danger of anybody seeing them," Robinson suggested.

"They might have done," Bustle answered, staring across the room at Rayner's blackboard. He then stepped across to it and rubbed it clean of his senior detective's notes, before putting a piece of chalk to good use by mimicking what he thought, Richard Rayner would have done, but recording in his own hand details of the two kidnappings, the murder of Maisy Winthrop, and the burning down of the stable block in Richmond.

"That doesn't tell us anything we don't already know, Henry," Robinson indicated.

Bustle stood staring at what he had just written down on the slate and then turned to face his colleague, before confirming, "Yes it does Jack. Tell me, where did Maisie Winthrop live?"

"In Denmark Street, you have just written that down, Henry."

"And where was her body found?"

"On the Embankment, close to Norfolk Street."

"Exactly Jack, we need to speak to the pathologist."

Robinson was naturally confused but followed his colleague out of the building, intrigued by what possible pattern of thought was now formulating in the more experienced man's mindset.

After arriving at St Mary's Hospital, both detectives made their way down some steps leading off the central Quadrangle, where the mortuary was situated. They found Doctor Albert Critchley tidying up, having just completed a post-mortem and Henry Bustle asked if he had completed his examination of Maisie Winthrop's body yet.

"Of course, days ago Sergeant, I understood that Mr. Rayner was coming to discuss it with me."

"I'm afraid he's otherwise engaged at the moment doctor but is it possible you could confirm if the woman was killed where she was found, on the Embankment."

"That is what I included in my report to Richard Rayner, the answer is no, and due to the lack of blood at the scene I believe she was killed elsewhere and then transported to the Embankment."

"How long had she been dead before you examined her?"

"As I told you before, no longer than a couple of hours, perhaps less but no sooner than an hour and a half would be my calculation."

Bustle then turned to Jack Robinson and enquired how long he thought it would take a horse and carriage to reasonably travel from Denmark Street to Norfolk Street, close to where the murdered victim was found.

"About half an hour, Henry, why?"

"Let's just say, she had been lying on that Embankment for about an hour before she was found, that would mean her death would have occurred about half an hour away from the scene."

"If what you say is correct, yes, but I don't follow."

"She wouldn't have been killed in Denmark Street because there would have been too many people about, which means she was killed elsewhere between that location and where her body was found."

"That's highly probable, Sergeant," the pathologist remarked.

Still speaking to Jack Robinson, Bustle asked, "What is the remotest area in between those two locations?"

Robinson shrugged his shoulders, and then, as if suddenly coming to life, cried out, "Good God, Henry, I believe I know what you are getting at."

Both detectives then hurriedly left the mortuary, leaving Albert Critchley a little bemused and wondering what on earth had happened to Richard Rayner.

Chapter Nineteen

It was Henry Bustle who insisted they called at Scotland Yard to arm themselves just in case his suspicion that Richard Rayner might be held captive somewhere in the docks area, had credibility.

"It might be wise to notify Mr. Morgan, Henry, and get some help before we go down there," the younger Sergeant suggested.

"No Jack, if we were to do that you know what Frederick Morgan is like, he would go charging in with a hundred or more constables and that might possibly start a riot amongst the dockers, or put the Chief Inspector's life in danger, or even result in the kidnappers leaving and taking Richard with them."

"But we don't even know if he's being kept there, and the docks is one hell of a place to search."

"Not really Jack, remember we will be looking for a structure that's not being used, and there can't be many of them standing void in the London Dock or St. Katharine's."

Bustle had a point and Robinson agreed, accepting that it would be far more professional if just the two of them made a surreptitious search around each of the two docks, the two oldest of London's gateways to the commercial outside world. There were of course other docks, but they were too far down river to be a part of Henry Bustle's speculation.

It was early afternoon when the two detectives finally arrived at the main London Dock and stood for a while, observing the activities from nearby Pennington Street. They continued to watch as various transports entered and left a row of warehouses opposite where they were standing, until Bustle suggested they made their way into the dock itself.

The usual flotilla of various sized vessels was moored at or close to the quayside, being loaded or unloaded, or waiting to be attended to. But they weren't of interest to the two Scotland Yard men, and they walked through the many groups of stevedores, porters and other workers pushing and pulling crates of produce, scrutinising the large open storage buildings on their left. Then they came across one structure where the large wooden doors on the front were closed and secured by a padlock.

Bustle was followed by Robinson down the side of the building, looking for an open window or other means of entry, but what they required to do wasn't going to be easy, as everywhere was battened down. So, their only option was to obtain some assistance and the older Sergeant left Jack Robinson, while going in search of a crowbar. Seemingly ignored by the labourers busy at their work, he quickly returned having found what they required and wasted little time in prising open the lock on the front doors. Within seconds, both detectives found themselves inside the building, which they found to be empty, apart from a few wooden crates scattered around the dirt covered floor.

"This is the only place here, that would have suited the kidnappers' purpose, Jack," a disappointed Bustle confessed.

"I know, but let's take a look next door at St. Katherine's."

Still surprised that they hadn't yet been confronted by one of the dock supervisors, they walked back along the quayside to Nightingale Lane that separated the London Dock from their next intended location. St Katherine's Dock comprised of two separate loading areas, the East and West Docks that were both adjacent to a basin used for holding vessels back, prior to being allocated moorings at either location.

Having entered the East Dock, the scene was similar to what had confronted them at their last search area, only every warehouse they passed by was in use and there appeared to be more men busily working there. At Bustle's suggestion, they made their way behind the quaysides into Upper East Smithfield, a cobbled thoroughfare where more warehouses came into view. They followed the building line until reaching a break where the two docks were divided and continued towards the far end of the West Dock, where Upper East Smithfield joined Little Tower Hill. There was less bustle and noise at this point, the buildings being situated at the furthest point away from the quaysides and moorings, and yet again, the very last building on their left and on the same corner, appeared to be void.

An extremely tired but determined Henry Bustle, was reluctant to forcibly enter yet another building, sensing that they were about to meet with more failure. He casually walked down the side, where he noticed a row of small windows set high, just below the roof line and suggested that Jack Robinson, being the younger of the two, should leap up the side of the brickwork and try and see inside, with a little help from the older Sergeant.

Albeit his colleague tried, when standing on Bustle's shoulders, he just couldn't get enough purchase to reach the line of windows, so rather than just accept defeat, the older Sergeant grabbed a couple of wooden crates from nearby and placed them one on top of the other. Having scaled those, Bustle then helped the younger man back up onto his shoulders and that resulted in Robinson successfully reaching the grime covered glass panes. At first, he couldn't see a thing and told Henry Bustle it was hopeless, not relishing the thought of trying to climb through one of the small enclosures.

"Here, use this," his colleague suggested, waving the crowbar up for Robinson to grasp, which he did.

The sound of breaking glass seemed to reverberate around the district, but at least the observer could see most of what was inside, another apparent empty skeleton of a warehouse. But then, just as he was about to climb down, Robinson noticed some movement on his left inside the building, close to one of several pillars that were supporting the roof. It was Richard Rayner, looking extremely incapacitated with his head bowed down and both arms wrapped around the same pillar.

Upon seeing his Chief Inspector, Jack Robinson almost collapsed off Henry Bustle's shoulders in his effort to return to the ground.

"He's inside there, tied to a pillar," the young man gasped.

Bustle instantly ran to the front of the building with the crowbar and within a jiff, had prised the lock open, but before stepping inside the older Sergeant paused to look around the immediate vicinity to make sure they were not being watched by any undesirable. Both detectives then grasped their guns and entered, closing the wooden door behind them. They found Rayner standing alone and totally immobile, close to the entrance and Bustle quickly instructed Robinson to keep watch in case the kidnappers returned.

Richard Rayner looked pale and tired but found enough strength to welcome his friend with a wry smile, who produced his stiletto blade and cut through the rope securing his Chief Inspector's wrists.

"Thank the Lord, we've found you," Bustle remarked, "I take it, it's Herbert Winkler who is responsible for this."

Rayner nodded and immediately reached down and took a drink from the bucket left earlier by his tormentors. He had little strength and what skin was left on his wrists had been badly chaffed, but the senior detective knew they had to move quickly and tried to walk only to stumble to the floor. Propped up by Bustle, both men joined Robinson at the doors, when Rayner stopped to stamp his feet, trying to quickly get some feeling back into them. There was nothing he could do about his aching back and burning wrists at that time and when his friend suggested they should get him to hospital, he instantly rejected the idea.

"We cannot leave here without those two jackals who we have spent so much time trying to hunt down, not now that we have them in our grasp." Having seen that his two men were both armed with firearms, he explained that he had been taken at gunpoint, "And I will explain everything later, but for now we have to wait for them to return, Henry, which they surely will."

"They'll smell a rat as soon as they see the locks bust at the front," Bustle suggested.

"Then we shall just have to take them outside."

"You are in no fit state to take anybody, Richard."

"Don't be impertinent, I can easily..."

"Grab his other arm Jack and let's get him away from here," Bustle directed.

Once outside, Rayner was hit full in the face by an icy wind that was blowing down Upper East Smithfield, and was quickly propelled across the thoroughfare to the opposite side where they found a hedgerow that divided the street from the perimeter of the Royal Mint.

After helping Richard Rayner to rest against the base of a tree and out of sight from the front of the disused warehouse, both Sergeants remained concealed behind the hedge in readiness for what was to become a lengthy vigil. To make matters worse, and as the dusk approached, the temperature dropped dramatically, prior to another fall of snow and Henry Bustle, in addition to watching the street, kept an eye on his Chief Inspector, for whom he was concerned might not last very long in the freezing conditions. But knowing how obstinate Richard Rayner was, had no other option but to leave him resting in the open.

Eventually, as the weather deteriorated, Bustle became more concerned and suggested to Rayner, they needed to get him under cover and in the warmth.

"I think it best Richard, if Jack helps to walk you over to the Mint, where at least you can get some shelter."

"Leaving you to deal with these reprobates on your own, is that it, Henry."

"They won't be expecting me."

"Stop fussing Sergeant, I shall be alright, but it's going to take the both of you to deal with these two."

As he was quietly speaking, the sound of turning wheels attracted their attention and glancing over the hedgerow, Jack Robinson could see a horse and carriage heading down Upper East Smithfield, towards their position.

"This might be them," he quickly announced, optimistically.

"Black painted carriage with curtained windows," Rayner enquired.

"Yes, it has to be them."

"Take no chances gents, if they produce firearms, don't hesitate to respond accordingly," was Richard Rayner's final directive, before both Sergeants checked the loads in their guns and watched as the carriage drew nearer.

The vehicle stopped right outside the front of the disused warehouse and the driver climbed down from his perch, to be joined by another man who leapt out from inside the carriage. Both men were about to walk around the transport to enter the building when both Bustle and Robinson broke cover.

"Stay exactly where you are," Bustle shouted out, pointing his pistol at the men, "We are from Scotland Yard and you are both under arrest."

Herbert Winkler froze and suddenly looked like a man having an apoplectic fit. His associate began to raise his hands in the air.

"Cuff them both Jack, while I cover them."

As Jack Robinson moved towards the pair they had apprehended, Winkler suddenly produced a pistol from his overcoat pocket, but before he could level the barrel at the younger of the two Sergeants, Henry Bustle fired and shot him twice in the chest. The man dropped his weapon and collapsed to the ground.

At the same time, his associate dropped his arms and produced a meat cleaver from inside his overcoat and ran at Robinson, screaming like some wild animal, but was stopped in his tracks by another two bullets that struck home, one entering the front of his head and the other penetrating his chest.

It was over, and not in a manner Richard Rayner had been hoping for. He managed to find his feet and joined his two Sergeants in the street, who were both standing over the men they had just inadvertently killed. Strangely enough, the senior detective felt some bizarre sympathy for both men and with a little difficulty, managed to crouch down over the prostrate figure of his old school associate. The man was still alive, but from the blood that was oozing from his gaping mouth, Rayner knew Henry Winkler was soon to meet his Maker.

"I never thanked you Rayner, for helping me get off that mountain you know," the injured man gasped.

"No, I don't think you did, Herbert."

"Tell me truthfully, did my idea appeal to you?"

"Truthfully, it would have done, if I had believed it to be true," Rayner answered.

Winkler smiled and then his eyes rolled before departing from this world, having failed to complete his desperate ambition to become a rich man once again.

"What was all that about, sir, if you don't mind me asking," Henry Bustle enquired.

"It's a long story Henry, but at the end of the day, quite a sordid tale of one individual's despair and misery."

It was with some relief that Albert Critchley went out of his way to attend to the senior detective, after being admitted into St Mary's Hospital and being allocated a private room with the blessing of Rayner's elderly friend and physician. And the senior detective was delighted when being told he need only be detained for rest and recovery for a couple of days, to allow himself to be rehydrated and for the wounds he had suffered to both wrists to begin to heal. In a way, the Chief Inspector felt like some charlatan, lying in his sick bed and feeling quite well, except for the soreness coming from his injuries, and although he appreciated the doctor's advice, he was quickly becoming restless and impatient to return to work.

Within minutes of being transported to the hospital by Henry Bustle, both Clarice and his son, Matthew, had been in attendance with an extremely thankful wife fussing over her husband as though he'd been absent for years rather than a couple of days. But the man of the moment fully understood his wife's concerns and in return left nothing out when sharing the circumstances of his most recent ordeal.

When the small family reunion was joined by Frederick Morgan and his wife, Sally-Anne, the quiet atmosphere inside the small private room quickly changed to one of laughter and uplifting mirth, as the Chief Superintendent endeavoured to make light of what had taken place.

"I knew all along you would finally track that bleedin' psychopath down," Morgan quipped, instantly feeling his wife's elbow in his ribs and having to apologise for his slip of the tongue.

"It was Henry and Jack who were the real heroes in all of this," Rayner humbly pointed out.

"Richard, if we are over taxing you, you must say and we shall leave you to rest," Sally-Anne offered, anxious that the patient's health should come before anything to do with his and her husband's work.

"I can assure you Sal, having you here is the best thing for my recuperation," Rayner nobly confessed, "Yourself and my dearest wife here, who I regret deeply for the trauma she has had to endure during all of this."

It was all very amicable and enjoyable, until Doctor Critchley made yet another appearance, just to check on his patient's condition. After taking the detective's temperature and checking on the heavy bandaging around his wrists, the doctor remained with the others, listening to the crude jokes and quips made by Frederick Morgan, much to the distaste of Sally-Anne.

Rayner asked Clarice how their butler, Albert, had taken the news of the untimely death of his nephew and she assured him that, although saddened by the outcome, their elderly servant seemed to have taken it in his stride.

"But dear, there was one small incident I forgot to mention earlier. We had a lady call at the house yesterday morning asking to see you and I told her that you were engaged away from home at that time," Clarice explained, "When I asked if I could be of assistance, she told me that her business could only be conducted with yourself and left, saying she would call back in a few days' time or try and contact you at Scotland Yard."

"Did she leave a name?"

"No dear."

"What did this woman look like, Clarice?"

"She was tall with dark hair and a pale face, and her hair was plaited on top of her head, quite heavily pinned down. She was articulately spoken and quite attractive, Richard, and smartly dressed. I suspect she was a member of the aristocracy."

It was the mention of the visitor's hair being plaited and worn on top of her head that attracted Rayner's attention and he immediately looked across at Frederick Morgan.

"What is it my old mucker?"

"It seems that everyone just recently seems to know where we live, and Clarice's description fits that of Lady Margaret Plumb."

"The wife of the Chairman at the Women's Hospital?"

"Yes."

Turning to Albert Critchley, Rayner asked how well he knew Sir Oswald and Lady Margaret Plumb.

"I'm afraid we have never met," the physician replied, "Now I must get on and advise you to rest as much as possible and while you have the opportunity." The doctor then made his exit, leaving his patient looking a little concerned about the news of Lady Margaret's visit to his home.

"Why do you think she wishes to speak with you, dear?" Clarice enquired.

"I've no idea, but I am more concerned by the fact she knows where we live and that I am not at home with you and Matthew. Have the men outside left, Clarice?"

"Yes, Henry Bustle called late last night and told them their services were no longer required. I paid them off on your behalf dear and they were quite satisfied, asking if we should ever require their services again to get hold of them through Henry."

Rayner could sense red lights flashing through his mind. Something wasn't right and he found the visit to his home by Lady Margaret Plumb, extremely disturbing. This was a woman who he was convinced knew more about the murder of Sir Reginald Hammond than she would probably be willing to disclose. Without having any logical reason for doing so and completely against the doctor's advice, he made his decision and leapt out of bed, much to the surprise of everyone else.

Chapter Twenty

Richard Rayner appeared to be oblivious to his wife's pleas, as they accompanied young Matthew in their private carriage towards home. Clarice was begging her husband to go back to the hospital forthwith and follow the advice of Doctor Albert Critchley, but surprisingly and so out of character, Rayner was adamant he could not rest until he had discovered the reason behind Lady Margaret Plumb's earlier visit.

"But what harm could the woman do to us, Richard?" his wife asked.

The Chief Inspector looked drawn and although the short walk to his carriage had left him breathless, his priorities had changed in the last few minutes.

"It's not so much the threat she might have towards us dear, but rather what she knows about the murder of Sir Reginald Hammond. That woman is a principle suspect and I need to know the reason why she called at our home, when she could quite easily have contacted me at Scotland Yard."

"I think you are being rather silly, Richard, and selfish. You heard what Doctor Critchley said, you need to rest as a matter of priority."

"And I will do that I promise Clarice, after I have spoken with this woman."

After leaving his wife and son at their home, Rayner then directed his coachman, Nicholas Withers, to take him directly to Scotland Yard, where he knew that Henry Bustle would be waiting for him, having asked Morgan to ensure his Sergeant was given the instruction.

The Chief Superintendent was also there, together with Rayner's man, and demanded to know the reason for his Chief Inspector's odd behaviour, as soon as he walked through the door.

Rayner could offer no logical explanation, except he suspected there was something sinister behind the woman's earlier visit to his home, and Morgan suggested that in that case, he and Bustle could speak with Lady Margaret, after his senior detective had returned to the hospital to continue with his recovery.

"I can assure you I am feeling absolutely fine, sir," Rayner explained, "But I need to put a few urgent questions to the lady in connection with Sir Reginald's death."

Morgan was in no mood to argue further, his mind having to concentrate on his own medical condition and the recent flare up of his haemorrhoids, from which he was still suffering unmercifully. He quickly succumbed to the Chief Inspector's reasoning, advising him to return to the care of Doctor Critchley as soon as he had spoken to Lady Plumb. The Head of the Detective Branch also needed no reminding of Richard Rayner's handicap from the bandaging on his wrists, partially concealed by his shirt sleeves.

Having sent his coachman home, the Chief Inspector instructed his official driver, Jacob Studley, to take himself and Henry Bustle to the home of Sir Oswald and Lady Plumb in Cavendish Square. He was like a runaway horse with the bit between its teeth, and once having made a decision he considered fundamental to his own way of thinking, was not for turning.

On the journey, his Sergeant pointedly asked what it was that was causing his Chief Inspector so much anxiety concerning this enigmatic female member of the aristocracy.

Rayner looked at Bustle with a forlorn expression on his face and declared with the utmost candidness, "Henry, I strongly believe that woman might well have murdered Sir Reginald in cold blood and is now planning some devious way of avoiding arrest. Even now, we might be too late."

Such a short statement took Bustle by surprise but knowing the way in which Richard Rayner worked and the methods he used when analysing certain situations, had every confidence that he was correct in his suspicions. It was rare indeed, when he had known the senior detective to be wrong and from the sound of Rayner's voice, his Sergeant was left in no doubt they were about to apprehend a female killer.

When they arrived at their destination, the door was opened on this occasion by a young butler who could not have been older than thirty, with a pale face and red hair, the same colour as Frederick Morgan's.

Rayner immediately asked to see Lady Margaret Plumb, but was quickly and politely told that the mistress was not at home.

"Then I need to speak with Sir Oswald."

"I'm sorry sir, but neither Sir Oswald or his wife are at home at present, and I can only advise you to call back at a later time."

"When are they due to return?" Rayner asked, becoming impatient. Nothing irritated him more than an obstructive servant, whether from loyalty or for any other reason.

"I'm afraid I have no idea sir, they left for the continent earlier this morning."

That surprised both Rayner and Bustle and it showed on their faces.

"Whereabouts on the continent are they visiting, can you tell us that much," Rayner enquired.

"I'm sorry I cannot sir, as I have said, I suggest you call back on another day."

"Then pray tell me, for how long does Sir Oswald and his wife usually stay away when they travel to the continent?"

"Usually about three to four weeks, sir."

Rayner then glanced at Henry Bustle, before stepping closer to the young butler and quietly asking for his name.

"Charles Rickinshaw, sir," the man volunteered without hesitation.

"Then Charles Rickinshaw, I want you to listen very carefully to what I am about to say. I have told you who we are and rest assured, unless you disclose to us the exact location of where Sir Oswald and his wife have gone, your immediate future will be spent in the most uncomfortable and traumatic conditions you can imagine, in a place where there are bars at the windows and wooden planks to sleep on. Do I make myself clear?"

"They have a villa in a small village called Celerina, outside St. Moritz in Switzerland, sir, and that is all I know."

"And how were they travelling?"

"In a carriage to Folkestone, where they were due to catch the ferry across to France. They would then journey across land into Switzerland, sir."

"Thank you, now that wasn't so bad, was it."

Richard Rayner left to return to his carriage, followed by Henry Bustle.

"It looks like you were right sir," the Sergeant remarked, "And the birds have flown. Does this mean a trip to Switzerland?"

"No Henry, we have no idea where exactly their villa is, apart from being somewhere in wherever Celerina is situated. However, if in three weeks' time they have not yet returned, then perhaps such a journey will become necessary."

"If I was a betting man, my money would be on that pair having disappeared for good."

"We shall see."

When the two detectives arrived back at Scotland Yard, they unexpectedly came across Jack Robinson just leaving Frederick Morgan's office, next to Rayner's. The young Sergeant was looking extremely abashed, as if having just been admonished for some misdemeanour and when Richard Rayner asked what had taken place, the troubled man whispered that it was nothing to be concerned about.

"Then come with me, Jack," his Chief Inspector said, before leading the way into his own office, followed by both Robinson and Bustle.

"Close the door," he directed Henry Bustle, before turning to Robinson and once again asking, "Now Jack, explain to me why you look as though a horse has just trodden on your foot."

The Sergeant's facial features resembled a child who had just been caught out opening its presents before Christmas morning, and in response whispered, "I've been sworn to secrecy sir."

"Jack?"

"He's threatened to hang me by my private parts sir, from the roof of the building if I ever made any mention downstairs about his piles."

For an instant, Rayner looked confused and then had some difficulty in stopping himself from laughing out aloud.

"I do believe Jack, that everybody working at Scotland Yard is already aware of the Chief Superintendent's affliction. Now then, to work gentlemen."

The Chief Inspector stepped across to his blackboard and noticed for the first time the details earlier written in chalk by Henry Bustle.

"I forgot to ask you before Henry, how did you manage to discover where I was being kept imprisoned down at the docks?"

"By applying your own methods of deduction, we eventually worked out that dockland was the most favoured location." Bustle then went on to describe how he and Jack Robinson had come to that conclusion, albeit the work had been successfully undertaken by the older Sergeant and Jack had been a virtual observer.

"Well, my thanks goes to the both of you, and I am in your debt for what you did."

The younger Sergeant was about to put the record straight but was quickly prevented by a defiant glance from Henry Bustle.

Turning to Jack Robinson, Rayner then requested him to check with the Ferry Ports at Folkestone to confirm that the Plumbs had left the country earlier that morning and the young man immediately left to fulfil that task, remembering not to make any mention to his colleagues about Chief Superintendent Morgan's embarrassing condition.

Richard Rayner then wiped his blackboard clean, in readiness to begin making more notes of what they had learned so far, in particular, facts relating to Sir Oswald and Lady Margaret Plumb. But before he could start, the office door opened and Frederick Morgan appeared, standing in the doorway as if he had a broomstick stuck down his breeches.

"There's been an incident at The New Women's Hospital," he loudly voiced, "That young man, Corncrake, has been found hanged in the room he rents there."

It was a pitiful sight that greeted Rayner and Bustle, inside the small room located on the top floor of the hospital building. Tobias Corncrake had been left in the same position as when he was discovered, and a janitor was in attendance with a constable. The wretched man was hanging from a hook driven into the ceiling and a rope attached and wrapped around his neck. Initially it appeared that he had jumped off a single bed resting up against one wall and Rayner had no hesitation in cutting him down with Henry Bustle's knife.

On a small table in one corner of the room there was a handwritten note, explaining that the young surgeon was sorry for his decision to take his own life and including several personal remarks made for the attention of family members. But there was one sentence contained in the suicide note that attracted Richard Rayner's attention, that read:

'I can no longer bear up to the demands of others and go to my Maker looking for peace and tranquillity of mind'.

"An unusual statement to make in the circumstances, don't you think, Henry?"

"The man's mind must have been under severe pressure and in all probability sir, he didn't know what he was saying at the time."

"I'm not convinced, Mr, Corncrake did not appear to me to be other than an individual who was clear minded and fully aware of his faculties. Something has happened that has driven him to taking this tragic course of action Henry and whatever that was, it took place following his departure from Scotland Yard."

He then turned to the janitor who was standing just outside in the corridor gossiping with the constable and asked who it was that had found Tobias Corncrake.

"It was a couple of hours ago now sir, when Bridget the cleaner couldn't get any answer from the room, cos she wanted to clean it and she knew that Mr. Corncrake was inside there, cos she'd seen him go in earlier."

"How did Bridget gain access to the room eventually?" Rayner asked, pointedly.

"She never sir, she sent for me, and I sent for Sir Giles and it was him who opened the door and that's when we found him. Horrible it was sir, I don't mind telling you."

"Sir Giles Lamfrey?"

"That's the man sir, he's our boss."

"And where is Sir Giles now?"

"He went back to his office to wait for the police sir and hasn't come back up yet."

They found Giles Lamfrey sitting in his office, naturally looking a little shaken but managing to smile when Richard Rayner did the introductions. The man who oversaw the running of the hospital repeated virtually what the janitor had already told them, before the senior detective asked if he was aware of anything that might have been troubling Tobias Corncrake recently.

"Nothing that would cause him to commit suicide, Chief Inspector," the man answered, "But I did notice how young Corncrake appeared to be...confused, for want of a better description."

"In what way, sir?"

"I spoke to him shortly after he had been released by your people and he seemed to be somewhat distant, it's difficult to say, but I thought in all probability he was recovering from having spent so much time with the police, and of course the tragic death of Sir Reginald must have been playing on his mind, or so I imagine."

Rayner then enquired as to what the future had held for Tobias Corncrake, after the obvious closure of the research project he had been conducting with Sir Reginald and the others, and Sir Giles shrugged his shoulders, before explaining, "Of course, he would have been disappointed, as we all were, but his immediate future as a surgeon at this hospital was secure enough, but the subject never came up in our brief conversation."

At that moment, the janitor appeared once again and informed Rayner that a pathologist from St Mary's had just arrived and was asking to see him.

"That will be Doctor Critchley." He thanked Sir Giles for his time and left.

"You do believe this was a suicide sir?" Henry Bustle asked, as the couple made their way back to the top floor, after sensing that Rayner appeared to be showing more commitment to this obvious event than he would have done in normal circumstances.

"It appears to be the case, Henry, but let's wait to see what Albert Critchley has to tell us."

When they re-entered the dead man's room, they found the pathologist making his initial examination of the body that was now lying prostrate on the bed. They waited until the physician had finished and Rayner asked what his first thoughts were.

"That you should be in hospital, Richard, resting. My God man, what on earth possessed you to leave your sick bed."

"Other matters of far more importance, doctor," Rayner answered, "Now, what have you to tell me, if you please." The Chief Inspector sounded agitated and regretted his manner as soon as he had spoken.

"It appears that strangulation is the obvious cause, and it seems that the victim has been dead for somewhere in the region of three hours."

"Suicide then?"

"I could only confirm that after a post-mortem."

"You have found no other injuries on him?"

"No, not as yet."

Rayner then noticed two empty glasses resting on a small bedside table, items he hadn't noticed previously and picked one up to sniff the inside.

Prompted by an inquisitive look from Henry Bustle, he confirmed that they had both contained wine, or so he believed.

"But wrap them up Henry, and I think we shall take them with us back to Scotland Yard."

Still, the Sergeant thought that Rayner was over-reacting to an incident, the cause of which appeared to be quite obvious. But, of course, the way in which the senior detective's mind worked would have been a complete mystery to many of those who didn't work closely with him.

Chapter Twenty One

"According to the customs officers at Folkestone sir, both Sir Oswald and Lady Margaret Plumb left the country on the eight o'clock morning ferry destined for Calais."

Rayner thanked Jack Robinson, and recorded those details on his blackboard, before leaving his own office to update Frederick Morgan on the events at The New Women's Hospital.

It was obvious from the way in which the Chief Superintendent shuffled about in his chair and from his distorted features that he was still suffering greatly from his most recent attack of inflamed haemorrhoids.

"Isn't it time now that you had something done finally about your problem, Frederick," Rayner suggested, with all good intentions and feeling a great deal of sympathy towards the other man.

"Mind you own bleedin' business Rayner and concentrate on what you are about to tell me."

The Chief Inspector then gave a brief account of what he had observed at the scene of Tobias Corncrake's alleged suicide, before mentioning the contents of the handwritten note left by the young surgeon, in particular, the sentence that referred to his inability to bear up to the demands of others.

"An unbalanced mind Rayner, nothing more than that," Morgan suggested, continuing to shuffle uncomfortably in his chair.

"That may have been the case sir, but there was also the presence of two empty glasses that had contained wine in the same room in which Master Corncrake was found."

"So, what is so remarkable about that?"

"It indicates that our man had a visitor to his room, just prior to taking his own life, which seems strange in the circumstances."

"Perhaps he wanted to get pissed before doing the dastardly act and one glass wasn't enough."

"But there was no bottle present, which tells us that whoever shared that drink with young Corncrake, left and took the remainder of the wine with him, or with her." Rayner paused, before continuing, "It just adds some uncertainty to what I believe we are supposed to accept was the course of events."

"And pray tell me, what are you insinuating by that exactly."

"I'm not sure."

"You don't believe that this young man took his own life."

"I have no doubt he was responsible, but why when he had no real reason to do so. Let's just say I am not totally convinced that his death was as straightforward as we are being led to believe."

"Perhaps that particular assignation had taken place sometime before he lost his mind and decided to top himself."

"Perhaps, but I have checked with the Detention Sergeant downstairs and he was only released from here just four hours before he was found strung up."

"So, you think he was murdered. For Christ's sake Rayner, this is like pulling teeth."

"Or having haemorrhoids removed sir," the Chief Inspector impudently offered, soliciting a look of wrath from the suffering man, "It could very well be that Doctor Corncrake was coerced into taking his own life and if that was true, then we have to address the question as to why that should have happened."

"Rayner, you are making a mountain out of a mole hill, my old mucker, and I would thank you for not referring to my own personal situation."

"I apologise sincerely sir; I shouldn't have said that."

Morgan nodded his acceptance and then asked what his Chief Inspector intended doing next.

"I do believe a visit to the mortuary might be beneficial."

The recent physical commitments were beginning to tell on Richard Rayner and by the time he reached St. Mary's Hospital, his legs felt leaden and he was finding it difficult to think clearly. Every ounce of his self-motivation was being challenged and the senior detective was constantly convincing himself that he had to push on, if they were going to get to the bottom of those events that had taken place. The death of Tobias Corncrake possibly being connected in some way to that of Sir Reginald Hammond, was the principle question he was now faced with. Of course, if indeed that was the case then again, why and how? Had the young surgeon genuinely fallen into such a quagmire of deep depression in such a short space of time, his mind had become unbalanced as Frederick Morgan had suggested, or had he been coerced into believing such a drastic course of action was necessary. Had there existed an outside influence that had propelled him beyond his possible fear of losing his job at The New Women's Hospital. If the latter was the case, then Rayner believed whatever had been shared with the young man just prior to his suicide, it had to have been of devastating effect.

"Ah, Richard, I was hoping you would visit eventually." Albert Critchley was standing in the centre of his examination room, wearing an ankle length brown leather apron and his words of welcome were sincere.

"You have something for me, I assume doctor."

"Yes, I do believe I have, let me show you." The doctor then led the way into his office that was adjacent to the examination room, where Rayner could see that the pathologist had been busy with several test tubes and Bunsen burners littering his desk.

After inviting the Chief Inspector to take a seat, Albert Critchley explained, "It was the 18th century philosopher, Edmund Burke, who once said, 'Under the pressure of the cares and sorrows of our mortal condition, men have at all times called in some physical aid to their moral consolations'."

Rayner smiled, recollecting the quote from his university days and remarked, "Corncrake was a drug addict then."

"That I cannot answer, but he certainly had sufficient mescaline in his system to subject him to hallucinations and possible psychosis."

"So, the man was after all, out of his mind but perhaps involuntary?"

"Involuntary, I cannot be definite, but most certainly he would have become unbalanced temporarily. You may already know that mescaline is found in seeds grown on the outside of the cactus plant, which when dried out are eaten or boiled and consumed as tea. They can also be ground down and administered in capsule form as a white powder, but it matters not, it always has the same effect."

"And I take it, these are blood samples taken from Tobias Corncrake."

"Yes, the colour of the litmus papers I have been using have confirmed the presence of the drug in his system."

"Apart from hallucinations doctor, what other side effects can be produced from taking mescaline?"

The doctor shrugged his shoulders and continued, "Psychosis, as I have already mentioned, possibly anxiety, a rapid heartbeat and physical muscular spasms."

"I was thinking more of psychological side effects, apart from hallucinations."

"I'm afraid my knowledge does not go beyond the immediate effects of the drug when taken."

Rayner stood and stepped across to the door, looking out into the examination room where Corncrake's body lay beneath a white linen cover. Then turning to face the doctor again, he enquired, "Could the resulting hallucinations be responsible for an individual to contemplate or commit suicide?"

"That would depend on the strength and quantity of the drug being taken, but if sufficient, I believe it could. As with most drugs, including those used in medicine, they tend to seek out the weaknesses in a person's character. If for example, the recipient has a tendency to be depressed then that condition could be exacerbated after being administered, or if the tendency is towards being positive then the same might apply."

"You mentioned the drug could be administered as a tea, what if it was disguised in a glass of wine?"

"Most certainly yes, I believe that would be possible, I take it you are referring to the glasses found in his room."

"Yes, is it possible to test those for traces of mescaline?"

"Of course."

"Then I shall arrange for them to be transported across to you."

It seemed to be a pointless exercise meant only to challenge Jack Robinson's reasoning and rationale when he entered the premises of Baggott and Ridgeley Hospital Supplies that was situated on the Strand. In normal circumstances the Sergeant accepted whatever task he was given without question, but on this occasion he failed to see the purpose or logic behind Frederick Morgan's most recent instruction. It was customary in circumstances where an individual had died in the workplace or other location other than their home, for the police to be notified and usually a constable would attend and make what necessary enquiries were required for the coroner. However, on this occasion no uniformed officer was available and the Chief Superintendent had been asked to provide one of his officers to assist. Hence a reluctant Jack Robinson had been dispatched, believing that such a use of a detective's time was wasteful. But there again, who was he to argue with the powers that be.

When the young Sergeant arrived he was met by a Mr. Nicholas Baggott, who introduced himself as being a partner in the company, the other being Mr. Clayton Ridgeley who had suffered a heart attack and had died when sitting at his desk in his office on the upper floor. As far as the detective was concerned, there were no apparent suspicious circumstances and his visit was just routine, as he explained to the now, sole owner of the supplies company.

After making a note of what details Robinson would need when compiling his report to the coroner, he asked Mr. Baggott what exactly his business involved, and was told they supplied ancillaries, such as bandages, medical instruments, and other requirements to The New Women's Hospital in Marylebone Road. Naturally, that attracted the detective's interest and he enquired as to the individual the company dealt with at the hospital.

"That would be Sir Giles Lamfrey Sergeant, a most amicable gentleman who I have had the pleasure of meeting on a number of occasions, although dear Clayton was responsible for that side of the business," Baggott explained, referring to his recently departed partner.

"And is The Women's the only hospital you supply, sir?"

"Yes, and I believe we are their only suppliers of ancillaries."

"Might I see your most recent inventories recording the supplies you have provided."

"Of course."

When Richard Rayner returned to Scotland Yard, following his intriguing conversation with Doctor Critchley, he immediately made his way to the general office on the ground floor and instructed Henry Bustle to take the two wine glasses across to the pathologist for examination.

"Jack is waiting to see you in your office," the Sergeant remarked, "And I've no idea what he's discovered, but he looks like the cat that's got the cream."

When Rayner finally entered his office, he found his younger Sergeant pacing the floor.

"So Jack, you look as though you have something of interest that requires my urgent attention," the Chief Inspector said, when hanging up his coat and top hat on a peg near to his office door.

"I'm not sure sir," the Sergeant answered, "It's just an idea I have regarding the financial dealings involving the business conducted at The Women's Hospital." Robinson then produced a sheaf of papers and spread them on top of Rayner's desk, describing how he had visited the supply company on the Strand and gave a detailed account of his conversation with Nicholas Baggott.

"These are handwritten copies of materials purchased by Sir Giles Lamfrey on behalf of the hospital," he continued.

Rayner sat at his desk and studied them, before remarking, "Lists of items supplied by Baggott and Ridgeley showing the cost of each item charged."

"Yes sir, and I was wondering if those same prices were the same as those actually paid from the hospital's funds by Sir Giles."

The Chief Inspector glanced up and declared, "I hear what you are implying Jack, but that is a serious accusation."

Robinson nodded his acquiescence and tried to explain the reasons for his suspicions but could only confirm that he had a gut feeling and nothing else.

"What exactly are your concerns regarding this innuendo, Jack?"

"Well sir, I was thinking that if for instance, there had been some fiddling going on between Sir Giles and the deceased man, Clayton Ridgeley, and if Sir Reginald Hammond was a part of such a conspiracy, then there might be a motive for murder if our victim threatened somehow to reveal what was taking place to the board of governors at the hospital, or perhaps even the police." The young detective was speaking in haste, as if he needed to get his hypothesis off his chest before running out of time.

"That's a lot of if's young man," Rayner remarked, and sat back in his chair, remembering the contents of the suicide note left by Tobias Corncrake, particularly the words confessing that the young surgeon could no longer bear up to the demands of others. Should Jack Robinson's wild guess be proven to be accurate in reality, then it was more likely that Corncrake could have been involved in such criminal activity and was being blackmailed by the likes of Sir Giles Lamfrey. But there was only one way to find out whether his Sergeant was on the right track and Rayner told his protégé to grab his hat and coat.

When they arrived at The New Women's Hospital in Marylebone Road, the detectives found the man in charge of the institution's daily routine, sitting behind his desk in his office. When Rayner and Robinson entered, they were warmly welcomed initially by Sir Giles.

"I presume gentlemen, your unsolicited visit can only mean that I can be of further assistance to you, so pray tell me, how can I help you further," the Knight of the Realm offered.

"Please allow me to thank you Sir Giles for the valuable help you and your staff have given us so far in trying to identify the killer of Sir Reginald," Richard Rayner humbly put forward, not wanting to disclose the real reason for their visit just at that very moment. In fact, the Chief Inspector thought he noticed a look of disguised relief in the other man's eyes, just for a fleeting second, which was followed by a courteous smile.

"We all want the same thing Mr. Rayner," Lamfrey expressed, articulating with both hands to emphasise his point, "And naturally, we will assist in whatever way we can." He then offered the detectives a seat, but the senior man from Scotland Yard politely declined, explaining that their visit was to be of a short duration.

"Our enquiries are progressing satisfactorily," Rayner lied, yet again, "But as a matter of routine, we need to view the last audit of the hospital's financial records, which I believe you have in your possession, is that not correct sir?"

Sir Giles nodded but looked inquisitively back at the senior detective.

"You suspect those could have something to do with Reggie's murder then?"

"Not necessarily, but I'm sure you understand that we have to cover all angles, as I said, it's a matter of routine. Tell me, was Sir Reginald ever involved in any of the financial business conducted by the hospital?"

"No, that would have gone far beyond his remit."

"I see, well in that case I am sure our examination of the books will only be cursory if only to please the Commissioner. If you would be so kind sir."

"Of course." Sir Giles then stepped across his office and took a large ledger from one of the shelves inside a cabinet at the side of where the detectives were standing and handed it to Richard Rayner.

"You will see that the last audit was conducted by Prigg and Sanderson, the hospital's accountants, last August I believe but might I suggest you complete your examination here and now Mr. Rayner, as these records are not supposed to leave the building."

Rayner had taken possession of what the purpose of his visit was truly about and had every intention of scrutinising the records back at Scotland Yard. He therefore rejected the suggestion put forward and confidently confirmed that he would give Sir Giles a receipt for the item, promising to return the records the following morning.

"I must confess, this is highly irregular sir," the man in charge of the hospital declared, looking just a little anxious.

Again, the Chief Inspector smiled and pointed out, "Most things are when we find ourselves investigating a murder Sir Giles. I can assure you this will not leave my possession until I return it to you tomorrow and once again, I fully appreciate the co-operation you have shown us throughout this difficult Inquiry." At that he turned and left, followed closely by Jack Robinson and before the man whose office they were in, could make any further comment.

Chapter Twenty Two

It was late that same evening when both Richard Rayner and Jack Robinson finally completed their examination of the entries contained in the ledger handed to them by Sir Giles Lamfrey. Each individual handwritten record consisted of the date of supply, the products delivered, and the cost of each order procured. There were several different suppliers named, but the Scotland Yard men were interested only in those connected with the company of Ridgeley and Baggott.

When compared with the list of supplied items given to Jack Robinson by Nicholas Baggott, they identified discrepancies on each of the supplies, showing inflated charges made in the hospital records. In fact, when totalling the exaggerated amounts taken from the hospital funds, the unexplained difference came to no less than just over six thousand pounds over a five-year period.

"A King's ransom, Jack," Rayner remarked, when placing the ledger into his own office safe, "Well done, it appears that enthusiastic nose of yours has not only unravelled a magnanimous deception and monetary fraud, but has also provided us with a possible motive for the murder of Sir Reginald Hammond."

"Thank you sir, I'm just relieved that I haven't been wasting your time. Shall I arrange for Sir Giles to be arrested now?"

"No, it's far too late and I see no reason for a gentleman of his stature to disappear in the meantime. I don't think he suspected we were on to his little profitable game, but I would like to know if our Tobias Corncrake was involved in this scheme and if so, in what way."

Robinson suggested that he should further interrogate the surviving partner in the supplier's business, Nicholas Baggott, to ascertain whether he was aware of what had been going on, but Rayner was reluctant to take that course of action at present.

"From what you have told me earlier, you were fairly happy that this was an arrangement between Lamfrey and Ridgeley."

"Yes sir."

"Then let's not risk putting the cat amongst the pigeons, prior to speaking with Sir Giles in our official capacities." Rayner then suggested they should go and get a good night's rest, intending to arrest the man in charge of the Women's Hospital first thing the following morning. What remained a mystery to the senior detective was the purpose behind the hasty departure from the country of Sir Oswald, the chairman of the board of governors at the Women's Hospital, and his wife Lady Margaret. Unless of course, Sir Oswald had also participated in Lamfrey's scheme and was in fear of being put in the dock. Perhaps the reason for his wife's efforts to speak with Richard Rayner, at the time he was confined to a hospital bed, were somehow connected with that affair and had nothing to do with the murder of Sir Reginald Hammond. However, the behaviour of the couple was the most frustrating problem Rayner was now facing, unless of course, their race to the continent had been a genuine attempt to take a leisurely break, although he very much doubted that had been the case. How was any of this connected with the principle atrocity they were investigating. Apart from the obvious fraud, all they had at that time consisted of assumption and no actual evidence that pointed towards any individual having had cause to commit the murder of the gynaecologist or the procurement of Tobias Corncrake's suicide.

When Richard Rayner and Jack Robinson arrived the following morning at The New Women's Hospital, they were informed by the matron that Sir Giles Lamfrey was engaged with his daily rounds of the wards and were asked to wait in an outside corridor. However, the Chief Inspector took the opportunity to seek out the man they had come to apprehend and surreptitiously watched the principle member of the staff visit various patients' beds, accompanied by a small group of junior doctors. From his distant observations, he could see that the man he wanted to take back to Scotland Yard, went about his professional work with an air of confidence and efficiency, and when he finally stepped through the exit doors only to find himself confronting the detectives, Rayner suggested they should go to the privacy of the surgeon's office to continue with their conversation.

"Can this not wait, Mr. Rayner, until I have finished my rounds."

"I am afraid not sir," the senior detective insisted, "I do believe it would be beneficial for you to speak with us in private."

Sir Giles looked a little affronted and after hesitating, instructed one of his staff to continue with his round in his absence. But they never reached the man's office and as soon as they were out of sight of the junior doctors, Rayner explained that he was being arrested for a number of fraudulent claims made against the hospital.

"This is preposterous," Sir Giles Lamfrey claimed, but to underline his authority and make it quite clear as to what was taking place, the Chief Inspector instructed Jack Robinson to handcuff the surgeon.

"Please, I beg of you gentlemen to allow me some dignity if I have no other choice but to go with you," the prisoner pleaded.

Rayner felt that Lamfrey was not the kind to resist arrest and agreed to allow Sir Giles to leave with them without there being any physical indication of his apprehension.

Strangely, no words were exchanged on the journey back to Scotland Yard and the senior detective noticed how quiet the man who was now in his custody, appeared. All Sir Giles did during the trip was to stare out of the frost covered windows of the carriage, failing to enquire further as to the reason for his demise.

After entering through the back door of the police headquarters building, the prisoner was taken immediately to a basement interview room, where he was seated behind a small table, with Sergeant Robinson facing him, whilst Richard Rayner disappeared back to his first-floor office. When he returned just a few minutes afterwards, he was holding the ledger previously given him by the man in charge of the hospital, together with the sheets of recorded transactions obtained from the company of Ridgeley and Baggott.

He began by asking the hospital's representative, how often he dealt with the supply company.

"We frequently order quantities of various ancillaries from them, or so I believe," the man answered, "Bandages, pins and small items such as that."

"Apart from yourself, does any other member of the hospital staff have dealings with the same company of Ridgeley and Baggott?"

Sir Giles looked away and stared for a moment at the wall, showing signs of feeling utterly deflated and before quietly answering, "No, only myself."

Rayner then opened the ledger and placed the sheets of paper at the side of the book, before referring to an entry made five years previously. But then, and quite unexpectedly, was interrupted by a surprising declaration made by Sir Giles.

"There's no need, Mr. Rayner, I am fully aware of what you are about to tell me sir. You have found discrepancies in the invoices going back over a number of years."

Rayner nodded. "You do not deny that you have been fraudulently over charging the hospital for goods ordered on their behalf."

Sir Giles looked pitifully at the Chief Inspector and sighed, "I deny nothing Mr. Rayner." He then paused before continuing in almost a whisper, "I am a ruined man sir, and see no reason now why I should lie to you."

"Would you agree that the total sum of monies obtained from this scheme of yours, amounts to about six thousand pounds over a five-year period."

"I have no idea, but if you say so, yes."

Richard Rayner sat back in his seat, before quietly enquiring if Tobias Corncrake had been involved in any way with the unlawful practice.

At first, it appeared that Sir Giles was about to deny the allegation, but then nodded and explained, "Before Toby was seconded to Reggie's research team, he worked under me as a junior and it was during that time that he participated in entering a number of records in that ledger, in return for a small renumeration. You will find several entries in his handwriting."

"And Sir Reginald Hammond, was he involved in any way?"

"Heaven forbid, no, Reggie was far too scrupulous, his only vice was women."

"So, you had no reason to kill him," Rayner suggested, pointedly.

Sir Giles looked astounded at the suggestion and quickly responded by claiming, "No, of course not. I had nothing to do with Sir Reginald's murder and that is the truth. I am being completely honest with you Mr. Rayner about a slight diversion away from honest practices, and as a result I am fully aware that my professional life is now at an end, so why should I deny anything that I was responsible for."

"Then, returning to Tobias Corncrake, I suspect you had a conversation with him in his room at the hospital and just before he committed suicide, am I correct."

Again, Sir Giles turned away to stare at the wall, obviously recollecting his thoughts and Rayner waited patiently for his response.

"Yes, after his experience with yourselves and having been arrested as a suspect for Reggie's murder, the lad was extremely disturbed and told me that he was intending to tell the police everything he knew about our previous little scam."

"And what did you say to him, in reply."

"Nothing, what could I say. The man was determined and it appeared there was nothing I could do or say to dissuade him. I begged him to rethink but he was quite adamant that he needed to clear his conscience, so I left and you know the rest."

"Not quite, Sir Giles, I believe there was something more that took place during that short meeting." Rayner then stood and much to Jack Robinson's surprise, left the room.

Henry Bustle was waiting in the Chief Inspector's office, looking his usual indifferent self and when Richard Rayner enquired if he was aware of the result of Doctor Albert Critchley's examination of the two wine glasses, the Sergeant reported that the pathologist had found traces of the drug, mescaline.

"Thank you, Henry," the Chief Inspector said, before turning to leave.

"Have we our killer, sir?" Bustle asked.

"I'm not sure Henry, I need to put more pressure on our good doctor downstairs."

When Rayner returned to the interview room, Sir Giles Lamfrey was sitting looking down at the floor, dejected and obviously wondering what his future now held for him. He resembled a man with the shadow of the noose hanging over him.

"Tell me sir, what was the purpose in drugging Tobias Corncrake, when you were having that conversation with him, before he so surprisingly took his own life."

"I know nothing about that," the man replied.

"Please, Sir Giles, do not insult my intelligence. Doctor Corncrake took his own life just three hours after being released from here. During that time, a hallucinatory drug was administered to him, and you were the only individual that met him just prior to his death."

The now disgraced Knight of the Realm stared back at his inquisitor and remained silent.

"We have evidence that shows the drug, mescaline, was concealed in a glass of wine and given to the junior doctor without his knowledge, do I really need to continue?"

Sir Giles shook his head and realising that Richard Rayner had cornered him like a fox in a trap with nowhere to escape, made his confession.

"As I have already told you, he was quite determined to ruin me and for a moment, I didn't know what to do to prevent him from doing what would have been a disastrous outcome.

"For you, you mean."

"Of course, but you must believe me, my only intention was to temporarily incapacitate him until I had been given some time to think about what I could do to dissuade him from taking such a course of action. I most certainly had no idea that he would contemplate suicide when being under the influence of the drug."

Richard Rayner stood from his seat and leant across the table, glaring down at the prisoner, before making his feelings known.

"Doctor, I do not believe you. You knew exactly what the effects of mescaline would be, the fact that such a drug could induce hallucinations on your victim..."

"A victim, he wasn't a..."

Rayner slammed the top of the table with an open palm and raised his voice.

"Yes, Tobias Corncrake was a victim of complicity to control his mind in such a way, he would take his own life and you were fully aware that such a mental condition could have that result...weren't you."

Sir Giles could not verbally respond to Rayner's insinuation and once again turned away, unable to look him in the face.

"To be capable of orchestrating such an act of cruelty, places you into a category of evilness that would never fall short of committing murder."

"But I never murdered him, I wasn't even present when he took his own life."

"I believe that much, but you procured his suicide and I believe callously stabbed to death your competitor, Sir Reginald Hammond, for reasons I have yet to establish, but strongly suspect it was something to do with the monies he was receiving for continuing his research project."

"You have no evidence of that, Mr. Rayner."

"No, but if there is evidence to be found, I can assure you I will find it and see you pay for your dastardly crime by visiting the hangman, sir."

Rayner then turned to Jack Robinson and instructed him to take Sir Giles Lamfrey to the cells. But before the Sergeant could do so, the eminent surgeon once again denied any participation in the killing of Sir Reginald Hammond.

"I swear to you Rayner on everything I hold dear, I did not murder Hammond and am completely innocent of that debauchery."

"That sir, is an unusual word to use by a man who has just openly confessed to having been complicit in the suicide of an innocent young man."

At the same time as Richard Rayner was climbing the stairs with the intention of returning to his office, he met Henry Bustle heading towards the ground floor general office.

"Go and get your hat and coat Henry, the time has come for us to take off the kit gloves my friend."

"Where are we going sir?"

"Back to that damned hospital to seek out the real killer of Sir Reginald Hammond."

Chapter Twenty Three

The snow was falling once again, making the thoroughfares more hazardous than before, as the dusk added to an atmosphere of wintry hostility. Richard Rayner's official carriage stopped outside the front doors of the hospital and both he and Henry Bustle alighted, before stepping into the dark reception area. The interior was quiet, but they found a solitary porter manning the front desk and requested to see the matron.

"I'm afraid matron has gone home for the day sir, as is the case with the majority of staff," the elderly janitor confirmed.

Rayner then asked to speak with Doctor Simon Cartwright but was told that the junior physician had been absent from the hospital for a number of days, although the porter confessed to not knowing the reason.

As the detectives were speaking with the employee, Nurse Phylis Cameron suddenly appeared, her shoulders covered in a woollen cloak and hurriedly making her way across the reception area towards the exit doors. She looked a little flummoxed when the senior Scotland Yard man addressed her, asking if she could spare him the time to answer a few further questions. She agreed, seemingly reluctantly and sat on one of the rows of wooden chairs intended for patients' visitors. With Rayner and Bustle either side of the young lady, the Chief Inspector immediately asked if she knew the reason why Doctor Cartwright was not in attendance at the hospital.

Nurse Cameron shook her head and quietly admitted that she had no idea but had not seen Simon Cartwright since the demise of Sir Reginald Hammond.

"Very well miss, so please tell me what exactly your relationship was with the deceased man?"

"I don't understand what you mean sir," she answered.

"Was it purely professional, or, and forgive me for being personal, but it is necessary to ask these questions I can assure you. Did you have, or have you ever had an intimate liaison with Sir Reginald?"

Phylis Cameron sat bolt upright, clasping both hands on her lap and abruptly answered, "Our relationship was solely professional, I can assure you, Chief Inspector." It was obvious the suggestion had made the lady feel uncomfortable, but from Rayner's instinctive impression, he did not believe her.

Lowering his voice, so the porter who had remained behind the front desk was unable to overhear the ongoing conversation, the senior detective persisted in explaining that it was of the utmost importance the nurse was telling the truth.

"We are dealing with a murder, Miss Cameron, and I have to inform you that any misguiding declarations made to us could result in a serious view being taken, so much so, any such obstruction could be penalised with a term of imprisonment."

The young lady looked down and began to shake her head.

"Was your association with Sir Reginald ongoing at the time of his death, or perhaps a thing of the past?"

"It was nothing more than a flirtation that ended months ago sir, and that is the absolute truth. I am now engaged to be married to someone else and am fearful should he find out."

"Then that someone else is a lucky man, if I might say so, but forgive me, was anyone else aware of this assignation. I take it from what you have just said, your fiancé was not aware. As I have explained, it is most important that you tell us the truth."

"No sir, no one. It was nothing more than a young girl being carried away by a passing phase with her employer and when I told Reggie I no longer wished to continue, he was very understanding."

"Yes, I bet he was," Henry Bustle quipped.

"Very well, I can assure you that what you have told us will remain completely confidential."

"Thank you, I appreciate that sir."

Both Rayner and Bustle stood, to allow the nurse to continue on her way and watched as Phylis Cameron approached the exit doors, but then she suddenly stopped and retraced her footsteps.

"There is one thing though that might be of some significance, Chief Inspector," she whispered to the senior detective, "I believe that Reggie was an extremely jealous man."

"In what way miss?"

She looked towards where the porter was still leaning across the desk and then at their immediate surroundings before continuing, "Well, please do not think I am being conceited, but in recent weeks I have been pestered a little by Simon Cartwright, during the time we have spent working in the laboratory."

"Please elaborate further."

"Simon is what you might regard as being an immature and unstable individual and at first it was just small innuendos he made, little suggestive remarks that were nothing more than what I regarded as being a schoolboy's fantasy."

"He approached you to be his lover."

"Not so direct as that, but he asked me out for dinner on several occasions, although I am sure his intentions were honourable, but after a short while he became irritating and eventually I had cause to complain to Sir Reginald."

"And what was his response."

"I was embarrassed when he confronted Simon and told him to leave the team and he would obtain a replacement."

Rayner threw a glance towards Henry Bustle and then enquired, "When did this take place, in relation to the murder being committed."

Without hesitation, the nurse answered that it had been on the day before the eminent surgeon's body had been found in the hospital grounds.

"And do you think, such a drastic course of action is the reason why it appears that Doctor Cartwright has been missing from his work."

"Simon remained working with us for some days after that dreadful incident and has only been absent for the past couple of days sir, as far as I am aware."

"Thank you, Miss Cameron, have you an address for Doctor Cartwright?"

"No, but if you give me a moment, I can find it for you."

Adam Street, where the junior doctor was in lodgings, was situated in Wapping and to get there the detectives had to cross over the River Thames via the London Tunnel. When they arrived, they found it to be a fairly respectable residential location and number 106 was one of a row of terraced houses with an iron railing separating a small, well-cared for garden, from the street itself.

A short, plump, middle-aged woman with greying auburn hair tied in a bun answered the door and after the usual introductions, Richard Rayner confirmed that she was in fact the landlady. After enquiring, he was told that Doctor Cartwright had two rooms situated on the top floor, before the Scotland Yard men were led up flights of stairs on to the top landing.

Mrs. Hutchings indicated the door giving access to both rooms occupied by the man they wished to speak with, before nervously disappearing back downstairs.

It was Bustle who loudly knocked and a voice from inside the room asked who it was calling.

"Chief Inspector Rayner from Scotland Yard, Doctor Cartwright, a word if you please."

"I have already spoken to your people Chief Inspector, so can it not wait until I am fit enough to return to work," the same voice pleaded. The physician sounded a little agitated, which didn't go unnoticed by the detectives.

"I am afraid not sir, and I would be obliged if you would open the door."

Whilst speaking, Rayner stepped back to allow Henry Bustle to silently try the door handle, but the obstruction was locked.

"I am very ill at the moment Mr. Rayner and would appreciate seeing you when I am feeling more accommodating."

At that, the Sergeant kicked the door wide open and both detectives entered the room, to find the junior doctor sitting on the edge of a bed pressed up against a wall. He was dressed only in singlet and trousers and naturally was taken by surprise by the unwanted visitors' method of entry.

Before any words were spoken, Bustle lifted the man from the bed and slammed him against a wall, before pinioning both arms around his back and securing his wrists with a pair of shackles.

"You know why we are here," Rayner suggested, at the same time nodding for his Sergeant to make a cursory search of the room.

"I have a bloody good idea, it has to do with that slime ball's just desserts," Cartwright answered, taking the Chief Inspector by surprise, mostly from the vitriolic sound of his voice.

"I do believe the time has come for you to give us your side of the story, Doctor Cartwright, or do we have to go through the tedious process of producing the evidence we have that proves you are the killer of Sir Reginald Hammond."

The room's occupant shook his head, and then quite unexpectedly began to weep.

Henry Bustle produced a handwritten receipt from inside the drawer of a bedside table, which was for the purchase of a long-bladed knife and was dated on the day prior to Sir Reginald Hammond's murder. The same day as, according to Nurse Cameron, Cartwright had been dismissed by the eminent surgeon.

Rayner showed the same item to the prisoner, suggesting the knife referred to was the same one recovered by the body of the victim by Tobias Corncrake.

The doctor said nothing in response.

"And you were prepared to see your younger colleague take the blame for your atrocity and be hanged for a crime you committed."

Again, Cartwright didn't speak but looked defiant at Richard Rayner, or at least tried to, but the Chief Inspector was confident they had finally captured their man.

It was a despondent young gentleman who sat in the interview room at Scotland Yard, being quizzed by both Rayner and Bustle. After having accepted his fate, Simon Cartwright explained that, following Sir Reginald Hammond's insistence that his services were no longer required and knowing the reason was only because of the man's jealousy towards himself and Phylis Cameron, he had decided to succumb to his own bitter hatred and dispatch the senior surgeon on that cold and wintry morning.

"At first, I just wanted to give the scoundrel a good kicking," he continued, "And waited for him to come to work. I told him what I thought of his disgraceful behaviour towards women, and he just smirked and told me to grow up and find a position cleaning the sewers."

"But you purchased the knife the day before, which to my thinking, shows that you were planning on using it on Sir Reginald."

"I admit I was planning to accost the man the following morning, but initially it wasn't my intention to end his life. I took the knife for self-protection."

Rayner knew that a judge and jury would have difficulty in believing such a statement of mitigation, but made no further comment, continuing with the interview.

"And it was then you lashed out with that knife."

"The arrogant bastard turned his back on me and started to walk away, still cursing me as though I was some kind of vermin standing in his way. I just lost my temper and called him back. When he turned to face me again, it was then I stabbed him in the chest, which was only what he deserved." Simon Cartwright paused, before continuing.

"You must understand, Mr. Rayner, we all worked extremely hard to achieve that scoundrel's objective, one that only he would get the acclaim for if successful. But that didn't bother us, Toby Corncrake was in awe of him and if we succeeded, I knew it would not do my own career any harm. So, we worked day and night in that laboratory, sometimes taking a twenty-minute break in a twenty-four-hour period."

"This sounds very admirable doctor, but at the end of the day you took another man's life unlawfully and that my friend amounts to murder in accordance with the law."

The prisoner looked down at the floor and then quietly asked, "Will I hang for this, Mr. Rayner?"

"That sir, will be a matter for a judge and jury, but I shall not lie, I believe your situation looks extremely dire and the fact you remained silent throughout the time an innocent man was put in peril of being blamed for your crime, will not I fear, help your cause."

Following the interview with the self-confessed killer, Rayner and Bustle updated Frederick Morgan on the course of events, bringing a look of relief to the Chief Superintendent's face for the first time since the slaying of the kidnapper of his daughter, Herbert Winkler.

"At the rate you're going Rayner, there won't be any bleedin' doctors left at the Women's my old mucker. Now, what about the other problem, have we got any further in resolving the dangling man off Tower Bridge."

The last thing Richard Rayner felt like undertaking at that very moment, was yet another complex Inquiry, still feeling the effects of his incarceration at the hands of his old school associate and his bandaged wrists were still painful to manoeuvre.

"One mystery still remains I believe," he quietly remarked, "The roles that Sir Oswald and Lady Plumb played in all of this."

"I doubt there's much of a mystery there, Rayner," Morgan suggested, "It seems obvious to me that the woman was worried that you might inadvertently disclose her relationship with that fornicator, Sir Reginald Hammond, and the safest thing she could have done was to hide her husband away for a bit, hence the trip to wherever it is they've skipped off to."

Rayner agreed that did seem logical in the circumstances and indicated that the Tower Bridge murder would now get his full attention.

"But not until you have undergone a few days' rest, Richard," Morgan suggested.

It was then that the Detention Sergeant appeared in Morgan's office doorway and informed the Chief Inspector that Sir Giles Lamfrey wished to speak with him.

"Do we know what about, Cyril?" Morgan asked.

"No sir, the gentleman has made it quite clear he wishes to speak with Mr. Rayner alone."

"He can speak to me instead," the Chief Superintendent instructed, before turning to Richard Rayner and suggesting he went home and remained there for a few days, until fully recovered.

"A few words with the man won't make much difference sir," Rayner responded, "If only to find out what exactly he wishes to tell me."

Morgan nodded and then flippantly suggested that the man in the cells downstairs probably wanted to confess to the Tower Bridge murder.

"If only," Rayner answered, before leaving with Henry Bustle at his side.

Chapter Twenty Four

When Henry Bustle escorted the disgraced senior surgeon to the interview room in the basement cell block, Richard Rayner was already sitting there and finding it difficult to stay awake. He had been tempted to step into the back yard and take some evening air to refresh himself, but his impatience to learn what the eminent and disgraced surgeon had to tell him prevented him from taking that course of action. As Sir Giles Lamfrey settled into a chair with the Sergeant standing behind him, the Chief Inspector noticed he had a twinkle in his eye and was naturally curious about what kind of plea for mercy the prisoner was about to make.

"I know my position now is a helpless one, Mr. Rayner," Lamfrey began, "And I am aware sir that I must take whatever punishment is bestowed upon me."

Rayner nodded and sat back, waiting patiently with both arms folded across his chest and forcing himself to remain focused.

"But I am in possession of certain facts that I believe would be of interest to you."

"And pray, what facts would those be sir."

The prisoner held up a palm and continued, "All in good time, I beg of you to indulge me for a little while to explain a set of circumstances, which I am asking you to help me with."

"I am listening, Sir Giles, but finding it quite onerous."

The man then went on to describe that, although he had remained a bachelor throughout his life, many years previously he had been involved with a woman who, at the time, had been working as his secretary.

"Miss Marcia Graham was the most beautiful lady I had ever clapped eyes on and we quickly fell in love. Although we co-habited for a couple of years, we had to keep our relationship secret owing to my position at Guys Hospital where I had a position at the time, and we managed to do that, until things between us began to go wrong. Marcia became pregnant."

"So, you did the honourable thing and married the lady," Henry Bustle suggested, already knowing the answer.

Sir Giles then went on to explain that, knowing that would have been the right thing to do, his career had to come first and being married with a child would have in all probability, been detrimental to the professional advancement he was looking for at that time in his career.

Bustle could not help but throw a look of disgust, Richard Rayner's way.

"Go on, Sir Giles," the senior detective prompted, but having to force himself not to yawn.

The doctor then explained that he came to an agreement with Miss Graham and she agreed they should separate, leaving their cohabitation to live in a bedsit in Islington, paid for by her former lover and where she eventually had the child, a son she named Egbert.

"She gave the boy her own name of Graham with my blessing and allowed me to visit them both whenever I had the opportunity over the following twenty years or so. In addition to keeping the lady comfortable, I also paid for the education of my son and that was the principle reason I appropriated those funds from the hospital. Eventually, they both moved into a house in Mayfair, for which I continued paying the cost and inevitably, I became confronted by financial difficulties. But let me be clear sir, I am not offering those circumstances as an excuse for what I have done, I can assure you."

"Please continue Sir Giles."

"Well, after completing his primary education, I was hoping that Egbert would go to university. I suppose a part of me was hoping he would follow in my footsteps, but the boy had no inclination towards obtaining a career in medicine or any other calling if it came to that."

The prisoner then paused, before asking Richard Rayner for a glass of water, which Henry Bustle left to fetch for him.

He then continued to explain that his son then found employment at a high-class restaurant in St. John's Wood, serving tables as a waiter. The establishment was known as the 'Nourriture exquise', a French restaurant owned by a Parisienne gentleman by the name of, Jacques Duboir.

"At first, Egbert appeared happy at his work, until a day came when his mother told me that he was becoming involved in, what I can only describe as being an unusual and improper engagement."

"By that you mean criminal activity."

The prisoner's eyes looked down at the tabletop and the Chief Inspector again prompted him to continue with his story, by asking the nature of the improprieties being committed.

Lamfrey explained that, from what the boy's mother told him, the owner of the restaurant, Monsieur Duboir, was involved in forcibly bringing young girls from France to London and employing them in various brothels and other eating establishments as prostitutes and waitresses in return for a commission demanded as payment for their protection. Marcia Graham was aware that their son had become involved in some way, helping to orchestrate the ongoing practice of slave labour in return for generous amounts of reimbursement.

"How did his mother become aware of that, Sir Giles?" Rayner asked, "Did the boy tell her?"

"No, his pay was a mere thirty pounds a year and suddenly he was buying fancy clothes and other expensive items that were way beyond his financial capability. What Marcia wanted me to do was to speak with Egbert and try and find out the truth and attempt to dissuade him from continuing with whatever notoriety he was becoming involved in."

"And did you?"

"Yes, we spoke at length and that was how the details of his involvement became known to me. But although he never admitted such to me, I was left in no doubt that this Duboir fellow had some kind of hold over him, or the attraction of greater wealth was too tempting for him to stop. However, it was Egbert who eventually came to me at the hospital and told me that his conscience was preventing him from continuing with his escapade, and that he intended going to the police and telling all that he knew. He asked if I could possibly find him a small position where I was employed, and I said I would try."

"And did that happen?"

"Oh yes, I was quite willing to employ him as a junior porter to begin with, but on the day following his visit to speak with me, tragically his young life ended." Sir Giles paused to take a deep intake of breath, and Rayner noticed the man's eyes beginning to well up.

"Regretfully, Mr. Rayner, my son was found dead in an empty building in Newgate Street, Smithfield, near to the Christ's Hospital."

Sir Giles paused yet again, and the senior detective could see the memory of what he had just described was having an emotional effect on the man, so sat back and waited for him to recompose himself.

"I apologise sir, for there is much more to disclose that has been tormenting me since I lost Egbert."

"Take your time," Rayner suggested, "And take a few more sips of water."

After a short delay, the prisoner continued to describe more of the circumstances in which his son had been found, explaining that his body was found hanging from a beam in the upstairs room of a void house that was due for demolition in Newgate Street.

"There was a note found in the same room allegedly written by Egbert, confessing his desire to end his own life, but when I was shown that same missive it wasn't my son's handwriting and his mother agreed with me."

"When did this happen?"

"Last year, the second of March. I am convinced Mr. Rayner that my son was murdered and went to speak with Jacques Duboir on several occasions but was prevented from doing so by some of his henchmen."

"Tell me sir, who found the body?"

"A patrolling policeman, in the middle of the night but I'm afraid I never got to know his name, Marcia was informed by an Inspector from Cannon Street police station."

"And I take it, the police accepted that the boy had committed suicide."

Sir Giles nodded, "Yes, but he was murdered, of that I have no doubt. Of course, I made a number of representations, telling people of my concerns but no one was prepared to listen."

"And you now wish for me to investigate the matter."

"I am begging you sir. I do know from personal experience how committed you are towards your profession, obviously that is the very reason I am in here, and I know that if anyone can shed some light on my son's death, you can."

Rayner stood and stepped across to the far wall, turning and leaning back with both hands in his trouser pockets, the exhaustion he had earlier been feeling now having disappeared. Silence prevailed for a short period of time and the senior detective observed how distraught Sir Giles Lamfrey had become. The man was highly intelligent and certainly not the kind of person to have misgivings about any kind of situation, especially regarding the death of his own son, or so Rayner believed. He was also aware that, because of the accepted circumstances of the incident, there would undoubtedly have been a post-mortem and that would have been performed by Albert Critchley at St. Mary's. Finally, he returned to his seat and looked apathetically into Lamfrey's eyes, stating that he would look into the matter, but could not promise anything at that stage.

"That's all I can ask of you, Mr. Rayner and believe me, I will make it worthwhile, no matter what the outcome. I swear I will share with you details of another criminal enterprise that has resulted in yet another murder of a young man."

"I only deal in facts, Sir Giles and do not appreciate being teased by empty promises. I have already told you I shall look into your son's demise, so in return tell me what exactly you mean by another criminal enterprise."

Lamfrey looked reluctant at first to disclose anything further but convinced himself that he had to trust Rayner, and that it was necessary to expand on what he had already told the Chief Inspector.

"There was a construction engineer by the name of Raymond Carter, recently found hanging from Tower Bridge Mr. Rayner, and who lived in Islington, close to Marcia and Egbert, before they moved to Mayfair. I know the names of the people responsible for that."

The senior detective looked inquisitively at the man who had suddenly sprung quite a surprise on him and was tempted to ask a whole string of questions but was reluctant to do so. If Lamfrey was playing some kind of game, which Rayner doubted that he was, then to show more than a little interest might just be playing into his hands. But there again, it mattered not whether the Knight of the Realm was being sincere or otherwise, there could be no doubting his story concerning his son's death and there was an obvious need to investigate the circumstances of that further. Therefore, if Sir Giles was falsely making out that he knew more about the Tower Bridge murder, just to obtain Rayner's help in uncovering the truth about Egbert Graham's untimely death, then it was not relevant because the senior detective would never turn his back on such allegations made. However, if the same man was being genuine then his knowledge concerning the murder of Raymond Carter would be an invaluable bonus.

On their way to see Doctor Critchley at St. Mary's Hospital, Henry Bustle asked his Chief Inspector if he believed what Sir Giles Lamfrey had told them back in the interview room.

"Only a thorough investigation into Egbert Graham's death will reveal that, Henry," the senior detective expressed.

"And what about his claim to know who topped the man on Tower Bridge?"

Rayner looked across at Bustle and suggested that they would soon find out.

The detectives had to wait patiently for some time, while the elderly pathologist searched his records to find the post-mortem details of Egbert Graham.

"I vaguely remember the incident, Richard, but for the life of me cannot recall the details. Ah, here it is, a gentleman whose name was recorded as being Egbert Giles Graham." The doctor then read out the personal details of the deceased, before handing a copy of the police report to the Chief Inspector.

"As you can see, the coroner recorded the cause of death as being one of suicide," he continued to confirm.

"Yes, but what were your findings doctor," Rayner enquired.

"According to my own report, he died of asphyxiation and there were rope marks around the neck. The spinal cord had been clearly broken but mention was made of uncertain and vague impressions around the pharynx; the throat."

"Can you recall more about those particular impressions?"

"Yes, I can now. I believe there were two or three vague bruises either side of the pharynx, but unfortunately they were unidentifiable."

"Perhaps the size of thumbs being pressed against the throat."

"I remember they were too vague to determine whether that was the case and from what I remember, the marks had been partially corrupted by the burns made by the rope."

"Which means they could have been caused prior to the rope being placed around the neck."

"Yes, and that was exactly the problem. You see, it was possible that the imprecise nature of the impressions meant that they could have been placed there as a result of several causes, by accident or otherwise, so I was not in a position to confirm one way or another that the deceased had been unlawfully strangled or that his death was self-inflicted."

"But you could not rule out the possibility of him having been murdered?"

"No, Richard, you are quite correct. It is all in my report submitted at the time."

"Yet another verdict of convenience by the coroner," Henry Bustle remarked.

"That might be so, Henry."

Rayner thanked the pathologist before leaving, disappointed that even the slightest suggestion of foul play had not been investigated thoroughly by the police, to ascertain the truth behind Master Graham's death.

By the time they got back to Scotland Yard, it was getting late, and after wiping his blackboard clean and making a few notes in chalk concerning the life of young Egbert Graham, Rayner sent Bustle home before making his own way back to Richmond.

It was a very tired looking Clarice who welcomed her husband home, smiling in her usual warm way, but also confessing to having delivered two sequential lectures that afternoon to a hall filled to capacity with students.

"In fact, Richard, I have only been home for a few minutes before you arrived dear."

Rayner grasped his wife's hand and after instructing Albert the butler to inform cook downstairs that they preferred to dine after resting a short time over sherry, he led Clarice into the drawing room to recover before a blazing log fire.

"The problem you have my dear, is that you are obviously extremely popular with your students," the detective remarked.

"Hush Richard, it had nothing to do with my magnetic charm or the enticement of my lectures. One of the other members of staff had fallen sick and I was asked to fill in for him and that's all there was to it."

"Then I do believe this gives me the opportunity to invite my wonderful wife out to lunch tomorrow, shall we say midday. I could collect you from college if that is convenient and was thinking about trying out a French Restaurant I have been hearing so much about, over in St. John's Wood."

Clarice sat upright in her chair and smiled appreciatively.

"In that case, Mr. Rayner, I shall ensure it is convenient, thank you."

Chapter Twenty Five

The location of the 'Nourriture Exquise' restaurant in Portland Terrace, had been well selected, favouring the centre of residences belonging to some of the wealthiest people in London. Its frontage was fairly impressive with bunches of colourful artificial grapes hanging in the window with draped velvet curtains on either side. A brightly coloured canopy was positioned over the front entrance, giving the establishment a continental appearance and Richard Rayner assumed that tables and chairs would be placed on the pavement when the weather was more appropriate.

"It looks exquisite dear," Clarice whispered, as the couple were ushered to a table in one corner of the dining room by a smartly dressed waiter, carrying a white towel over one arm.

"Yes dear, I confess it does, let's just hope the food is as good as the decor."

The detective sat with his back to the wall from where he could observe everything going on and at the same time was facing his wife, who really didn't care where she sat. It was such a refreshing change for Clarice to accompany her husband out for lunch and she had been looking forward to the occasion since Rayner had first made the suggestion. He had also been reluctant to disclose the real purpose of the visit, knowing that once his wife became aware she would begin to act like a detective, whereby he preferred her to be natural, which was excited, joyous and only there to enjoy the cuisine.

It was early for lunchtime diners and apart from Richard and Clarice Rayner, there were only two other couples occupying well-spaced-out tables and within seconds of being seated, a filled water jug and glasses were placed before them. When asked if they wished to see the wine list Clarice shook her head, not wanting her mental faculties to be diminished in any way for the afternoon's work that was waiting for her back at the college.

They both ordered mixed salads for their starter, followed by a Boeuf Bourguignon for Rayner and a Cassoulet for Clarice, which was a meat dish with white beans. The food proved to be what the lady had been hoping for and she suggested that the establishment could become one of their regular visits. Still, her husband failed to disclose the real reason why they were there and continued with small conversations throughout the meal, dividing his attention between his wife and his surroundings, but Clarice was no fool and quickly suggested in a whisper that Rayner had some hidden agenda connected with their lunchtime visit.

"I will explain later dear, but I am enjoying our little excursion away from work." Up until then, the only thing he had noticed that appeared out of the ordinary was a very young female dressed in a waitress's costume, who appeared a couple of times from the kitchen, looking extremely downcast and emaciated, unusual for an individual working in an eating place, or so he thought.

During their main meal a gentleman in a white suit approached their table and enquired if everything was to their satisfaction. Monsieur Jacques Duboir was a slim individual, small in height but broad shouldered. The restaurant owner had black hair plastered down with a thin moustache that twitched as he spoke. Rayner noticed a red carnation pinned to the lapel of the man's suit jacket and nodded appreciably, making special mention of his Boeuf Bourguignon.

"I do believe this is the finest Bourguignon I have ever tasted, Mr....?"

"Duboir at your service monsieur, I am the owner of this establishment and we are here only to please our clientele. The steak is braised slowly in red wine with the bacon and onions, and we add the tomatoes at the very end of the cooking process."

"Then my congratulations to the chef," Rayner said, before taking another mouthful.

Jacques Duboir then turned to Clarice and with a charming smile, enquired if she was enjoying her Cassoulet.

"It is delicious, monsieur, thank you."

He bowed and turned to leave, after remarking that he would leave them to enjoy their meals in peace, but Rayner hadn't yet finished talking to him.

"Forgive me, Monsieur Duboir, but your English is very good, whereabouts in Francais do you originate from?"

"Paris, I studied culinary delights at the Sorbonne, before coming to London to open this restaurant."

"How wonderful," Clarice remarked.

"Have you other restaurants in England, other than this one?" Rayner enquired, being careful not to sound over enthusiastic.

"No monsieur, but I intend to expand once this business has been established and enables me to do so."

"Then I wish you well sir."

After the restaurant owner had disappeared into the back somewhere, Clarice leant across the table and whispered, "He does appear to be an amicable gentleman, Richard, surely you are not..."

Rayner shook his head and whispered back, "All will be revealed after we have left dear but do continue to enjoy your meal."

When transporting Clarice back to Kings College on the Strand, Rayner apologetically disclosed all to his wife, who was surprised that the man who had conversed with them in broken English could possibly have been a brutal killer, as her husband was suggesting.

"It takes all sorts dear," he suggested.

"And did you learn much Richard, from your short conversation with Mr. Duboir."

"His character does appear to fit in with what Giles Lamfrey told us dear. I believe that beneath the charm on display, Monsieur Duboir is an ambitious man who might well be capable of murder, if it meant expanding his coffers."

"I find that hard to believe, although I appreciate we have only crossed his path for a brief few seconds."

"Yes, but you are not a detective, Clarice."

"And you are not a scientist, Richard," his wife bit back.

"Forgive me dear, I did not intend any insult or disrespect."

"And that is the answer to all insults and innuendos."

They both laughed and Rayner stretched across the carriage to kiss his wife on the cheek.

After dropping a very pleased Clarice off at the front gates of the college, the Chief Inspector directed his driver to take him to Cannon Street police station, where he intended speaking with the Duty Inspector there.

Gilbert Forsythe was a larger-than-life man, robust in build with bushy side whiskers that met across the top of his mouth. He spoke loudly in a Gloucestershire accent and displayed all the signs of a former military man. The Inspector in charge of the police station welcomed his visitor from Scotland Yard warmly and immediately offered Richard Rayner a tumbler filled with dark rum, which the Chief Inspector politely refused, not having ever drank the navy's favourite tipple at any time during his previous life.

"Then how can I help Scotland Yard sir?" the likeable officer enquired.

Rayner gave an attenuated account of the circumstances surrounding the death of Egbert Graham, mentioning in particular the purported suicide note left at the scene of the incident.

"Well now, you are in luck Mr. Rayner, sir," the Inspector suggested, "I recall that incident very well. The victim seemed to be far too young to have committed suicide and I told the coroner so, but who are we to challenge the decision of one of the most powerful men in London."

"So, there was some doubt as far as the verdict went?"

"I suppose you could call it doubt, but it was only my own personal view that it was unlikely the lad had topped himself if only because of his age, but there was no evidence to show any foul play had taken place. Give me a moment and I'll bring out the file, it should still be with us."

At that Inspector Forsythe stood and left the room during which time his visitor studied several framed photo prints of various individuals on his desk, people who Rayner assumed were members of the Inspector's family.

When he finally returned with a folder the man in charge of the police station began to peruse through the contents until coming across a crumpled suicide note, allegedly written by the hand of Egbert Graham. He handed it to Richard Rayner, commenting that it appeared the deceased had written it and there had been nothing to suggest otherwise. But Rayner thought differently.

After scrutinising the contents, the Chief Inspector asked if he could keep the note together with the rest of the documentation and take it back to Scotland Yard with him.

"You suspect he was murdered then," Gilbert Forsythe remarked, still a little bewildered as to why a senior detective from Scotland Yard would be interested in what had been recorded as an obvious suicide, especially that officer being Richard Rayner.

"It's early days Inspector but have no fear, from the circumstances presented at the time no blame will be apportioned to the original Inquiry."

"Well, I'm relieved to hear that sir," the officer bawled out, standing once again from his seat and offering his hand to his visitor, who shook it.

"If there is anything else I can do to assist, you know where I am sir."

Richard Rayner thanked him and left to return to the police headquarters.

Surprisingly, when the senior detective entered the front reception to gain access to the stairs leading up to his office, the Desk Sergeant called him over.

"You have a visitor sir," he whispered in a manner that appeared as though he was about to disclose a secret of the utmost importance.

"What visitor Sidney?" Rayner asked.

"It's Mrs. Morgan sir, I've put her in the interview room across the way there, at her request." The Desk Sergeant winked, which the Chief Inspector found to be mystifying.

Sally-Anne Morgan was standing facing the far wall when Richard Rayner entered the room, completely perplexed by the fact the woman was there to see him and not her husband who was domiciled on the next floor up from them.

"Sal, has something happened to Frederick?" he immediately asked.

"No, not as far as I know, Richard," she answered, "I wanted to speak to you in the strictest confidence."

"Then you shall, so how can I help," he asked, inviting her to take a chair but she preferred to stand, explaining that she wouldn't be staying long.

Speaking in a lowered voice she explained, "It's his piles Richard, you must know the agony he has been going through lately."

Rayner nodded, still wondering what his Chief Superintendent's medical condition was to do with him.

"He desperately needs to have surgery and believe me I have tried everything to convince him to go to the hospital and have them removed once and for all, but you know how stubborn he is."

Again, Rayner nodded, in anticipation of whatever was coming next.

"Now, Richard, you are the only person he will listen to and I am begging you to persuade him to take the right course of action."

"I've already tried Sal, but he won't listen to me."

"Then promise me you will try harder. He's becoming a real pain in the arse now Richard, and when he comes to the circus to pick me up, even some of the others have noticed how his demeanour has changed. I mean, he walks about with a gait that's straighter than my stilt man."

The Chief Inspector was finding it difficult not to laugh at the manner in which Sally-Anne described her husband's circumstances but could see just how serious she was. There was little doubt that Mrs. Morgan was at her wits end as far as the man she was married to was concerned.

"I will try and have a word with him again, Sal," he promised, "But I cannot guarantee anything because of what you have said yourself, he is extremely stubborn."

"Well, if this fails Richard, I will personally be firing a bullet up his arse and that should do the trick," she offered, smiling, "You are my last hope and his, and for God's sake don't let him know I have instigated this."

"You can be sure of that, Sal."

After she had left, Rayner finally made his way up to his office where low and behold he found Frederick Morgan waiting for him. The Chief Superintendent had a flushed face and a glint of irony in his eyes.

"Well Rayner, what did that scheming woman want," he bawled out, taking the senior detective by complete surprise.

"Who are you referring to sir, might I ask," he answered, placing his top hat and coat on to the usual peg stand near to the closed door.

Morgan leapt to within a few inches of Richard Rayner and screamed out, "My wife sir, as you bleedin' well know. What collusion is ongoing between the pair of you, and the truth mind you or so help me..."

Rayner had to break the promise made to Sally-Anne Morgan and quickly. He realised to remain loyal to the Head of the Department's wife would only be detrimental to his own physical being, and hastily advised Morgan to calm down.

"Trust me sir, your wife only has your best interests at heart," he just managed to splutter out, before a fist would certainly come flying in his direction.

Morgan lowered his voice but remained in his threatening position.

"She's been on about my piles again, is that it mister?"

The Chief Inspector side stepped around the inflamed Welshman and retrieved his seat behind the protection of his desk, before explaining as sensitively as he could, "She worries about you and is concerned that if you continue to refuse to get something done to remedy your ailment, you will only suffer more greatly in the future."

"So why has the vixen come to you to discuss my personal affliction, what in God's name is going on, Rayner?"

"Because she is desperate to help you and thinks I am the only person you will listen to. Obviously, she is misguided on that score and I told her so."

Morgan instantly resembled a balloon that became deflated and stepped back across the room to lean with both hands on top of Rayner's desk.

"I told Sally-Anne that I had already tried to convince you of what the right course of action was, but that your stubbornness prevented that from happening. But, in order to appease the concerned lady I promised to have another word with you, and that's all there was to our conversation...sir."

The Chief Superintendent winced again, as he straightened from the desk and sighed loudly. He stood there for a few moments, as if frightened to move and provoke further discomfort, looking away from his best detective and shaking his head. Finally, he succumbed to common sense.

"I apologise Richard," he quietly offered, "I know you both have my best interests at heart, but damn it man and between you and I, the bloody thing frightens me to death."

"The thought of the surgeon's knife, or the realisation that your ailment is not going away?"

"The thought of everybody knowing the reason why I would have to stay off work for a few months, mister."

Rayner then reminded his senior man of the time when Morgan had become addicted to morphine and on that occasion had been forced to put his trust into others. The result was lots of care and support until he had finally overcome his addiction without the world knowing about it.

"Frederick, I can fully understand your concerns, but there are times when we all have to ignore what others might think and do the right thing for our own and the sake of others. You have everything you could possibly wish for with Sally-Anne, and surely it can only be right that you show your support for her feelings by ridding yourself of that which is obviously making your relationship so stressful." Rayner felt like some kind of Father Confessor, a role that was foreign to him, except when interviewing a prisoner downstairs in the cell block.

"I know you are right, Richard, but it's hard you know..."

"Then take comfort from the thought of future years being pain free from that dreadful condition from which you frequently suffer."

Morgan nodded and turned to leave but was stopped by Rayner, who then briefly updated him on the recent course of events regarding Giles Lamfrey and the death of his son, Egbert Graham. At least that helped to take the afflicted man's mind away from his medical condition, if only for a short spell.

Chapter Twenty Six

Having made those few early enquiries into the premature death of Egbert Graham, Richard Rayner found himself being sympathetic towards Sir Giles Lamfrey's dilemma and could understand the surgeon's concerns regarding the loss of his son. There were a number of questions left unanswered, including the note left by the deceased purporting to have been written by Master Graham, a forgery if his father was to be believed, and Rayner had no reason to doubt the man's assessment. There was little doubt in the senior detective's mind that a fresh Inquiry should be conducted, if only to confirm Lamfrey's allegation that his son had been murdered as the result of his participation in some sordid business dealings conducted by the restaurant owner, Jacques Duboir.

Another important issue to be considered was the presence of indistinguishable marks referred to by Doctor Critchley around the victim's throat region and the fact they had been placed there prior to the hanging. Also, the question of whether or not Duboir was the kind of individual to orchestrate the abduction of young females from the continent, to be deployed as waitresses and prostitutes in London, or perhaps further afield. His own opinion, having only briefly spoken with the restaurant owner, was that he most probably was that type of underhanded person. Was Duboir capable of committing murder? That was a question that could only be answered by instigating further investigation. There was little doubt that individually, each of the factors now being considered by the senior detective, might have been regarded as having been insignificant in isolation, but with them all being connected to each other, together they strongly supported what Lamfrey was alleging.

The Chief Inspector spent some time alone in his office, analysing the complexity of the circumstances he had been presented with. It was fairly obvious that if the Investigation was to progress in a search for the truth behind the now doubtful suicide of Master Graham, the focal point had to be the man, Duboir, and the centre of his existence, the Nourriture Exquise restaurant. But any enquiry made there would be difficult without having the services of an insider or employee working for the Frenchman. Having decided upon what Rayner believed was the only course of action open to him, he sent for Henry Bustle and Jack Robinson.

When the two Sergeants arrived, their Chief Inspector updated them on every aspect learned so far, before outlining his future intentions.

"How well do you think you could play the role of a silver service waiter, Jack?" he asked the younger of the two.

Robinson hesitated, before confessing that he had no idea what would be required of him.

"Then we shall teach you, or rather, I shall arrange for a trusted friend to instruct you in the art of that occupation."

"I take it sir, you wish for me to apply for a position at the restaurant in Portland Terrace."

"You assume correctly, Jack. If what Sir Giles has told us is correct then Egbert Graham was employed by Monsieur Duboir, before becoming involved in the darker side of the Frenchman's business and we need someone to walk in the victim's footsteps and try to obtain as much information as possible regarding what exactly is going on there."

"You are quite satisfied now that the young man was murdered?" Henry Bustle asked.

"Knowing what we have now been made aware of Henry, I believe we would be irresponsible not to treat the man's death as anything other than murder most foul."

Rayner then went on to explain to Jack Robinson that he knew of a reliable Italian friend, Alberto Greco, who owned 'The Seven Hills of Rome' restaurant in the Strand, where he and Clarice often dined and that he would make arrangements for the young Sergeant to receive some instruction in silver service waiting at tables. He was quite confident that Alberto would assist and the sooner he introduced Robinson to his friend, the better.

Later that same evening, all three detectives were enjoying dishes of pasta after Senor Greco had agreed to undertake the assistance requested by the Chief Inspector. In fact, Jack Robinson was quite enthusiastic, looking forward to quickly learning a trade that had never been within his personal compass previously. By the end of the following day, the Italian restaurant owner reported to Richard Rayner that his pupil was sufficiently skilled in becoming an adequate waiter.

By the time the undercover detective was ready to apply for a position at the Nourriture Exquise in St. John's Wood, he had already been briefed by Rayner on what story he was to share in his effort to be successfully recruited. Even Jack Robinson's attire had been carefully selected for the occasion, comprising of a casual jacket and trousers with a loose-fitting tie and large cloth cap. He was also made to wear deliberately scuffed shoes to add to his appearance of an out of work waiter and was naturally apprehensive when stepping inside the restaurant for the first time. In addition, and in further preparation for the operation that was to take place, Henry Bustle arranged for temporary lodgings, in the form of a one room bedsit in Commercial Road, Whitechapel, with a female acquaintance he had known for a good many years, and after his colleague had actually moved into his new address under the name of Ronald Polo, the stage was set for the young man to fulfil his task with as much professionalism as was possible.

Having asked one of the waiters to see the owner, Jack was eventually led into a back room where he was surprisingly confronted by an Englishman who spoke with a local London accent. The man was seated at a small desk and resembled a well-built ruffian with a bushy beard that covered most of his chest. His eyes matched the colour of his dark hair and heavy eyebrows and Robinson knew immediately from the description that this wasn't Monsieur Duboir.

"What do you want with Mr. Duboir?" the man asked, in a gruff voice.

"A job," the detective answered, trying to look desperate and speaking quietly, "I was hoping he might be in need of extra staff and although I am a waiter by trade, am willing to do anything for a few coppers, sir." That opening explanation gave him confidence and he was happy the man with the beard genuinely believed him. But then his optimism was wrecked when the man replied, "We ain't taking on at the moment, you'll have to look elsewhere."

Robinson was tempted to persist with his application but realised that to do so would not be in keeping with the character he was portraying, so thanked the man for his time and turned to leave.

"Wait," was the next directive.

The detective turned to face the man again.

"What's your game, matey?" It was a challenging question, obviously to see how the applicant would respond, and Robinson was aware of that.

"I don't follow," he calmly replied.

"What name do you go by?"

"Polo, Ronnie Polo and that's my real name."

"And where and when did you last work?"

"At the Seven Hills of Rome Italian restaurant in the Strand, four months back." Again, Robinson spoke with confidence, knowing that any enquiry made with Alberto Greco would be positively met. But he also knew his biggest test was yet to come.

"Why did you leave there?" The bearded man was staring directly into the applicant's eyes.

The detective from Scotland Yard had to follow the advice given by Richard Rayner and this was the crossroads that the Chief Inspector had suggested would eventually either achieve success or total failure. He deliberately hesitated, before quietly answering, "The Italian didn't pay me what he had promised so I took a subsidy from the till."

"You were fired then for thieving."

"Yes, but I only took what I thought was owed to me."

Suddenly and without warning, the bearded inquisitor burst out into raucous booming laughter and Robinson had to wait until normality was restored. Then a cluster of questions was shot at him, including where he was living and the reason why he was applying for work at the French restaurant, which the detective answered assuredly and with conviction, knowing that if he was to be rejected it would have been when confessing falsely to having stolen from his last employer.

Finally, he was told to wait, before the bearded man stood and left the room, exiting through a door that obviously led to the kitchen at the very back of the building. He remained in the company of the waiter he had initially approached and who had stayed in the same room as a silent observer throughout the interview.

When the bearded man returned, he had with him a smaller and older gentleman, who was introduced as being Jacques Duboir, the proprietor.

The owner of the restaurant eyed Jack Robinson with a keen interest, before asking him whether he had been in trouble with the police before, to which the detective told him that he hadn't, except for an offence of begging when he was a mere knee-high street urchin.

The man in charge appeared to be more affable than his employee who had been asking all the previous questions and smiled, before asking if Ronnie Polo was married.

"No sir," he lied, abruptly and convincingly.

And then, the proprietor threatened Jack that if he was ever caught stealing from his business he wouldn't just be sacked but would suffer far greater physical retribution than he could ever imagine.

"You can rely on me sir, I swear." Richard Rayner's man had carried the day and was told that he would be hired for a three-week period only. If he was found to do his job as a waiter to Monsieur Duboir's satisfaction, then perhaps his employment would become more prolonged.

Jack Robinson nodded and thanked the Frenchman, before asking when he could start.

"As soon as we have arranged for you to have a uniform that will fit you. Be here tomorrow morning before midday and you can start then."

It was imperative the young Sergeant didn't go anywhere near Scotland Yard after leaving the restaurant and in accordance with Richard Rayner's instructions, was to remain at his lodgings until Henry Bustle contacted him, which took place later that afternoon, when his fellow Sergeant appeared dressed as an old tramp, which wasn't difficult for the Chief Inspector's right-hand man.

When calling on Richard Roberts, the Assistant Bridge Master, Richard Rayner found the gentleman seated in his office drinking tea with another smartly dressed individual whose appearance Richard Rayner could see was that of a member of the Aristocracy. The stranger was introduced by the likeable Welshman as being, Arnold Greensnap, his senior and the Bridge Master, the individual currently responsible for the structure. On this occasion, the senior detective found Mr. Roberts attitude to be a little more condescending than previously, which he thought was natural, being in the company of his boss and yet, Mr. Greensnap, who was in his mid-fifties, tall, slim with greying dark hair and side whiskers, stood to shake hands with their unexpected visitor.

"Forgive me for intruding unannounced," the Chief Inspector apologised to both men, but looking directly at Mr. Greensnap's assistant, "I was wondering if you might have remembered any untoward incident involving the deceased, Raymond Carter, since we last spoke."

"I would have let you know sir, if that had been the case," Richard Roberts quickly answered.

Arnold Greensnap looked interested in what Rayner was requesting and enquired as to the kind of untoward incident the detective was referring to.

Rayner accepted a mug of tea offered by Roberts and sat down to face the two engineers.

"Anything that might have seemed unusual at the time, no matter how trivial," he explained.

"I take it you have not yet made any progress then Mr. Rayner," the Welshman remarked, at the same time as Greensnap shook his head in response to the Scotland Yard man's suggestion.

"The difficulty we are experiencing at present is the lack of any motive for the murder. We are aware that Mr. Carter was deceased prior to being thrown off the bridge at the end of a rope, but the reason that happened still eludes us and I was hoping that something..."

"There was one very strange incident Mr. Rayner," Greensnap recalled. Turning to his assistant, he remarked, "You must remember Dick, that time we discovered a number of unskilled individuals claiming to be qualified construction workers."

It was obvious from Richard Roberts reaction that his memory was refreshed about something he had forgotten all about and he admitted to such.

"Yes, but wasn't there some kind of bizarre way in which those men were placed on the payroll. I seem to remember that Ray Carter was accused of being responsible for bringing in unskilled labour to do specialised work, but he denied being involved."

Rayner listened intently and with interest, before asking, "And what was the conclusion of that episode."

Roberts shrugged his shoulders and explained that nothing came of it.

"They were never paid and sent packing and that was the end of it."

"Can you recall how many men were involved."

"I would say about as many as twenty or so."

The senior detective stepped across to the open doorway and enquired if it was possible that other such individuals could have been introduced to the workforce during the construction of Tower Bridge, without actually being identified.

"It's possible," Richard Roberts confessed, "With a project as involved as this it was difficult to keep tabs on every person on the payroll."

"Just how big was the labour force during the construction."

Roberts glanced across at Arnold Greensnap and confirmed, "Around four or five hundred a day for the time it took to complete the work."

"Would that be for the complete duration of eight years?"

"Yes."

"I see, then twenty additional workers would have been a drop in the ocean, as it were. Thank you gentlemen, that has been most helpful."

Chapter Twenty Seven

Considering that winter was at an early stage, the night was extremely cold with the ground covered in snow, icicles hanging from lamp posts and a freezing fog coming off the River Thames, covering the whole of Southwark Bridge. The early evening revellers and pedestrians had long gone and the whole wintry scene languished in silence as the two dark figures slowly made their way towards the centre of the overpass, where they stopped and began to stamp their feet, prompted by the conditions.

Henry Bustle looked at his time piece and declared, "He's late sir."

"I rather think he is being cautious Henry," Rayner quietly answered, unperturbed.

It was then that Jack Robinson appeared from out of the mist, cloaked in a heavy overcoat beneath which he was still wearing his waiter's uniform and before confirming that the weather conditions were perfect for the clandestine meeting.

"What have we Jack?" the Chief Inspector enquired, a little impatiently.

"Well sir, apart from losing weight and working my fingers to the bone, not much has happened, until this evening when finally Monsieur Duboir asked me if I wanted to earn some extra money."

"That's interesting and only after a week of working for him," Bustle remarked.

"Yes, but it's helped by getting along with the other employees and Syd Froggatt, that's the man who interviewed me for the job sir, thankfully he seems to have taken to me."

"What more has been said, Jack?"

"Nothing sir, I just told him that of course I was interested but he didn't elaborate, except to say that I might be required to do some overtime away from the restaurant tomorrow night."

Rayner glanced at Henry Bustle who was trying to blow some warm air into his clasped hands and nodded.

"It sounds as though you have earned their trust," Rayner told the younger Sergeant, "But I prefer that we allow whatever they have in mind to take place without interference."

"Do you think that's wise sir," Bustle asked.

"I'm sure no harm will come to our young colleague here Henry, but we need to know Jack, exactly what they are up to and once we have that information then we can be ready to strike on the next excursion."

Robinson nodded his understanding of what was required, before asking how his family were.

"I went to see Lizzie and the bairn this afternoon and they send their love, Jack. I reassured her that it wouldn't be too long now before you're back at home with them."

"Thanks Henry, I best be getting back to the digs in Commercial Road, just to be on the safe side."

"Well done, Jack," Rayner said, "Let's meet again here at the same time, two nights from now and hopefully we should know by then what kind of people we are dealing with."

After Robinson had disappeared back into the fog, his two colleagues slowly made their way back towards where Rayner's driver was waiting with the official carriage.

"He seems to be doing okay sir," Bustle remarked.

"Yes, he does Henry, but we haven't really started yet. Let's just hope that tomorrow night will open a few more doors for Jack and he is able to pick a few golden olives off the tree."

The undercover detective was only halfway through his shift the following day and although dusk was approaching rather rapidly outside, it was still early. The restaurant was busy and Jack Robinson had just finished serving a young couple who had taken a window table, when he was approached by Sidney Froggatt who told him to make his way into the back room where Monsieur Duboir wanted to speak with him.

The business owner was sitting at the same desk used by Froggatt when initially interviewing the Scotland Yard man, and quickly gave Robinson his attention, asking if he was still interested in working some overtime later that same evening.

"Of course," Robinson answered, looking enthusiastic.

"Trust and loyalty are the two major aspects of the work we carry out here," the Frenchman commented, "And if you do well my friend and prove to us that you are capable of seeing and hearing nothing, then you will be well rewarded, financially that is."

"Are you expecting a big party of clientele after closing then monsieur?" the detective asked, trying to sound naïve.

Duboir smiled in response and explained that the work he expected Robinson to do had nothing to do with waiting on tables, but he would get to know more later.

"For tonight, I want you to stay with Syd Froggatt and do exactly as he tells you and provided there are no problems, you will be paid handsomely for about two hours work. Does that sound sufficiently attractive young man."

Robinson nodded and replied, "I am looking forward to it, monsieur."

The Scotland Yard man couldn't wait for the restaurant to close and the last of the customers to disperse and it was only natural that the remainder of that evening appeared to go by slowly. When finally the doors were closed and bolted, and the oil lamps doused, the man with the beard, Sidney Froggatt, told the newcomer to follow him.

Both men slipped out through the back door of the building where a carriage was awaiting them in an alleyway that ran along the backs of the shops and business premises. A man, unknown to Jack Robinson, was sitting on top grasping the reins and inside, one of the other waiters, another Frenchman by the name of Louis, who the detective had worked with during his week at the restaurant, was sitting inside. No words were spoken and as soon as the carriage door was closed they began to move until reaching Portland Terrace and before making their way across London towards the docks, not far from where the undercover detective was temporarily residing in Whitechapel. But they avoided that district and continued down towards St. Katherine Dock, where the carriage came to a halt and all three men sat in silence.

The newcomer to whatever scheme was planned, thought it would only be natural to begin a conversation with Froggatt and Louis, so decided to ask how long they expected to stay in that location.

"Be patient," the bearded man snapped back, "It won't be long now."

Robinson sat back, trying to take his mind away from the cold air inside the vehicle but watching as best he could, out of one of the frosted windows. At least the fog had lifted and visibility was a lot clearer than the night before, when he had met up with Rayner and Bustle on Southwark Bridge.

After about three quarters of an hour, the Scotland Yard man began to feel as though both his feet had been chopped off and began to stamp them on the carriage floor, trying to get some warm circulation back.

"Sit still," Froggatt hissed, "No noise, you'll get paid enough."

"How much longer Syd, it's getting more like an icehouse in here," Robinson remarked.

"Just keep your arse still," the man ordered, threateningly.

The detective looked across at the other waiter, Louis, who was smiling and shook his head as if to warn the complaining Robinson that he needed to do what he was told.

Another ten minutes or so passed by and the sound of Big Ben echoed around the city, indicating the midnight hour. Then finally, there was some movement outside. The carriage door opened and a dark featured man dressed in heavy clothing and wearing what looked like a skipper's cap on his head appeared. He spoke in French and was quickly chastised by Syd Froggatt, compelling the man to speak in English.

"They are ready and the transport is down on the quayside," the man resembling a mariner confirmed.

"Okay, get in," Froggatt ordered, before quietly telling the driver to carry on.

The carriage slowly moved down an incline before reaching the dock, which was shrouded in darkness. There was no moon that would have offered some respite from the night's intensity. Then they made their way past the line of closed warehouses until reaching the end of the quay where they stopped, and all of them left the protection of the vehicle to stand for a while looking across at the dark outline of a large vessel, moored close by.

Robinson could see another larger carriage parked just a few yards away with another man up top with his back to them.

"With me," Froggatt ordered, and immediately walked towards the vessel with Robinson and Louis following behind. The detective noticed how the Frenchman wearing the sailors cap, kept looking around as if expecting to see trouble suddenly appear from out of the shadows, and when they reached the side of the barge, it was he who spoke in his native tongue to a small group of men on board. They answered in the same language and then unexpectedly a line of human figures appeared and were forcibly pushed down a small gang plank on to the quayside. From what Robinson could see, they were all women and each looked petrified, although obviously compliant with the demands being made upon them.

Each of the restricted women had shackles around their bare ankles and were all wearing rags that were totally inadequate for the weather conditions, but shuffled along the quayside without complaint, until reaching the larger carriage. Robinson counted five of them in total and had no idea from where they had come, or the location it was intended taking them to.

Then one of the 'drovers' struck one woman who was lagging behind the others, across her back with a wooden stick, causing the poor wretch to cry out, before being kicked in a persuasive effort to quicken her pace.

Jack Robinson was tempted to take the weapon off the lout and give him some of his own medicine but had to restrain himself. This was just the beginning of his intelligence gathering operation and he had no doubt, his opportunity to avenge the victim of the beating would come soon enough. He also noticed the man Froggatt hand over a small package to the Frenchman with the mariner's cap, which he assumed was a cash payment for his services.

The five women were piled into the second carriage, together with one of the men off the barge and as soon as the doors were closed, Sidney Froggatt directed the driver on top to get moving. The same bearded man then quickly turned and made his way back to the other vehicle with both Robinson and Louis following closely behind. As they paced away from the moving carriage, the detective noticed the name of the vessel on its bow; 'La Angeline'.

"What do you want us to do now, Syd?" he asked, once all three were back in their own transport, the Frenchman having remained with the barge.

"You'll see soon enough, but for now keep it shut."

They soon caught up with the second carriage containing the women and Jack Robinson remained alert throughout the subsequent journey, making a mental note of every location they passed after leaving St. Katharine's Dock. Both transports moved down river, before crossing over New Blackfriars Bridge and continuing through the backstreets of Newington, until finally stopping in Ewer Street, a dark, quiet and narrow thoroughfare, typical of many built-up areas within the city centre.

Sidney Froggatt was the first man to leave their vehicle and quickly walked towards the other carriage, surprisingly joined by two other men who appeared to have come from a nearby enclosed alleyway.

Jack Robinson watched with interest as the women were led away, shepherded by the men down the same alleyway and supervised by Froggatt. When the man in charge returned to the carriage, he instructed both the detective and Louis to remain on the pavement and keep watch.

"Any sign of a copper, just yell out before scarpering, got it?"

Both men nodded and watched as he disappeared after the group that had gone before him.

Rayner's man was quick to make the entrance of the alleyway and in time to see the women be led across an open yard into a terraced house on the left, the only dwelling showing any lights. The door was closed after they had entered, and Robinson then turned to his fellow waiter and asked if he knew what it was all about, having mentally noted the number of the house fronting the street.

The man just shrugged his shoulders without making any comment.

"Who do you think those girls were?" the detective asked.

"Who knows, none of our business as long as we get paid," Louis answered him in broken English, constantly looking up and down the street.

"It might be if they're going to kill them."

The other man chuckled and then suggested, "Why should they bring them all the way from Holland to just kill them my friend."

The detective looked at him and smiled back.

"In that case, you are right. Can't see much harm coming to them if that's the case. They have probably been smuggled in to be used for prostitution." He was still probing to find out exactly how much the other knew about what was going on, but was told not to ask so many questions.

By the time Sidney Froggatt returned, an hour had passed by and both lookouts were standing and remaining observant, feeling the bitter cold of the night. When they returned to the restaurant, they were both paid three whole pounds for their assistance by the bearded man and told not to be late for work the following day.

Robinson was pleased with the way in which the operation had gone and had a lot to share with Richard Rayner the following night. But what he wouldn't have given for a hot drink by the time he reached his digs in Commercial Road, Whitechapel, but not having access to the kitchen he wrapped a blanket around his shoulders before making notes of everything that had happened and of what he had learned and observed. He was more than appreciative when the landlady unexpectedly appeared with a sealed crock pot filled with hot water for his bed and a bowl of piping hot soup.

Chapter Twenty Eight

On the same night that Jack Robinson had been keeping watch in Ewer Street with the French waiter, Louis, Richard Rayner had been suffering from a bout of insomnia, which was unusual for the senior detective who usually had the ability to sleep through until the morning arrived. The information he had been given at Tower Bridge concerning the victim, Raymond Carter, had been tantalising his thoughts and the more he attempted to analyse what Greensnap and Roberts had told him, the more he found it bizarre that a construction engineer would put his own job at risk by introducing unskilled labour. Although, according to the Bridge Master and his assistant, Carter had denied the allegation, it still rankled with the Chief Inspector, believing that if the man had been involved in such a caper, it could very well have been connected to the man's murder.

Finally, Rayner succumbed to the need for him to revisit London's most recent impressive structure and trying hard not to disturb Clarice, got dressed before apologetically awakening his stable boy Jonas, who had recently been discharged from hospital and who slept in his own private accommodation above the newly built stables. After hitching up a horse and carriage, the youngster drove his master to Tower Bridge, where he was told to wait for Rayner's return. By now, the senior detective knew the engineering marvel fairly well and made his way to the engine room, which was thankfully situated on the lower level. It was a few hours before sunrise, but there was sufficient illumination coming from various oil lamps to light his way.

When he arrived in the impressive wheelhouse, in which the movement of the bridge was enabled and monitored, he came across a middle-aged employee responsible for the night-time working of Tower Bridge. After introducing himself and assuring the gentleman of his true identity, the night-time worker disclosed his name was, George Peppercorn, and indicated a much younger individual he referred to as his assistant, 'Nobby'.

Whilst Rayner talked, the younger man never left a viewing window overlooking the river below them and Rayner asked of the man in charge, if he had personally known, Raymond Carter.

"Aye, I knew him, in fact, I knew most of the engineers and used to make the tea for them," the middle-aged man replied.

"Do you recall an occasion when it was alleged that Mr. Carter arranged for a number of unskilled workers to go on the payroll?"

"Aye and I wouldn't put anything past that shyster. If any of us had been caught at it, we'd have been sacked on the spot but that Ray Carter, well he had the luck of the Devil riding on his shoulder."

"You mean he was a villain then, in your opinion."

George Peppercorn scratched his head and then explained, "I wouldn't go as far as to say that, but he was what you would call a 'fly by night', the kind of geezer that was constantly looking for an easy buck or two."

"So, you yourself believe that he did bring in unauthorised labour."

"More than that, I bleedin' well know he did. Just before it all went up in the air, I came across him in the Duck's Bill, talking to a group of them and there was money changed hands, if you know what I mean like."

"The Duck's Bill?"

"A pub down in Lower Thames Street, just down the way there. One night it was, after work."

Rayner was fascinated by what he was being told and then pressed the night worker if he was aware of any other employee that was close to Raymond Carter, or who might have also been involved in the scheme that the dead man had been involved in.

"Nay, can't say as I can." Suddenly Peppercorn stopped talking and called out to his assistant in a loud voice, "Nobby, ten more minutes, any sign as yet?"

The younger man turned and called back, "Coming down from Southwark."

The man in charge then returned his attention to the detective and explained that a Spanish cargo ship was due to go under the bridge in ten minutes and it was time to raise the suspension part of the structure.

"Might I stop and watch how this machinery works?" the Chief Inspector asked.

"Aye but keep well clear, and don't touch anything."

At that, George Peppercorn began to pull on a number of levers and the huge cogs that were protruding through the wooden slatted floor began to turn. It seemed as though the whole room began to tremble as a multitude of ropes and pulleys burst into life.

"There was one geezer," the middle-aged man bawled out above the din, as he continued operating the levers, "One of the supervisors, Harold Browning, he seemed to be close to Carter, if anybody was."

"Any idea where I might find him?"

"Nay, but if you calls back, some of the boss men might know where he's living."

Richard Rayner felt that he needed to bottom out this line of enquiry and was appreciative of Peppercorn's candidness and honesty. He still remained where he stood though, interested to see just how this fine example of modern engineering worked in practice. In fact, the senior detective stayed and drank tea with Mr. Peppercorn and his younger assistant, until the sun began to rise and spread its yellow fluorescence across the surface of the river below them.

When the nightshift reliefs arrived, Rayner left after thanking Peppercorn for his assistance and hospitality and was fortunate to find Richard Roberts, the Assistant Bridge Master had arrived early in his office. Within a few minutes, the detective was supplied with the home address of the man he now wished to speak with, Harold Browning, and left, only to find a very tired stable boy asleep when perched on top of his private carriage.

"Scotland Yard if you please, Jonas, and when you return home, please inform Constable Brown when he arrives to pick me up that you have saved him the trouble and to meet me back at work."

Old Fish Street in Southwark contained a cluster of dilapidated terraced houses encompassing a yard with an open sewer running through the middle and a separate brick-built building containing toilets, each allocated to five families. Number 3/47 was a typical dwelling in need of repair and attention and certainly not the kind of house either Richard Rayner or Henry Bustle expected to see a former construction engineering supervisor residing in.

Although, as was usually the case, the Sergeant's appearance blended in well with the surroundings, Rayner's immaculate and pristine attire attracted glances from the local inhabitants and the Chief Inspector noticed an upstairs curtain move when Bustle knocked hard on the door.

An emaciated, thinly built woman with a pale face showing all the signs of having experienced a life of toil and hard labour, answered the call. She was wearing a well-worn grey grubby dress with a piece of hessian cloth tied around her waist and when asking what her visitors wanted, displayed a number of black teeth.

"We are sorry to disturb you madam," the senior detective said, sounding genuinely apologetic, "I am Chief Inspector Rayner, and this is Sergeant Bustle, from Scotland Yard. Am I addressing Mrs. Browning?"

"What do you want?" she asked, repeating herself in a quiet but slightly aggressive voice.

"We would like a word with your husband if we may."

"'E's not 'ere."

"Then be so kind as to ask him if he could come down from the front upstairs bedroom and speak with us and assure him he is not in any trouble, we only wish to talk."

She looked taken aback by Rayner's audacity and closed the door.

Turning to Henry Bustle, his Chief Inspector remarked, "It would appear we have to wait for a moment or two, Henry."

Bustle smiled, admiring the patience being displayed by his senior and knowing that when Richard Rayner was determined to converse with someone, they had little chance of avoiding him, unless they were deceased.

When the door opened again, a large, thick-set man appeared, wearing a collarless shirt and black leather vest. His trousers were secured by a piece of hemp tied around his waist, and he didn't look too pleased at receiving visitors that time of the day.

"What will you be wanting with me?" he asked, in a gruff voice.

His unkempt dark hair appeared ruffled, and the detectives noticed a piece of sticking plaster across his receding forehead and a formidable bruise beneath one eye, next to a bulbous nose that had been broken several times.

Henry Bustle recognised all the signs and indications of a back street bare-knuckled fighter

"Might we come in," Rayner suggested, "You might want to hear what we have to say beyond the hearing of your neighbours, sir."

Harold Browning stepped back to allow his visitors entry and both Scotland Yard men were taken aback by the stench of poverty and decay coming from within, as they found themselves in a cold dark room, with patches of linoleum covering the floor and a table in the middle supporting old newspapers, a substitution for tablecloths. There was an unlit lantern hanging from the ceiling and large patches of damp on the walls, next to sections where the plaster had fallen away. Naturally, the fireplace was filled with cold ashes, giving the appearance of not having had a fire lit for quite some time.

Browning offered them a seat on an old sofa set beneath the window with springs protruding through the covers, but Rayner politely declined, stating that they had no intention of disturbing the house occupier for long. If ever there was a bottom rung to the ladder of poverty, this was it and although Henry Bustle remained unphased, Rayner never ceased to feel sympathy towards people having to tolerate life in such inhumane conditions. At least, it appeared the interior was kept clean by the lady wearing sacking around her waist.

"I understand Mr. Browning that you were employed as an engineering supervisor during the construction of Tower Bridge."

The man just nodded, looking unmoved by the mention of his recent history.

"We are making enquiries into the brutal murder of Raymond Carter, one of the workers who I understand you knew quite well."

Browning shook his head and made no comment, but Richard Rayner could see from the look in his eyes, the name meant something to him.

"Does that mean you didn't know him, or don't believe he's been murdered," Henry Bustle enquired, impatiently.

"I had nothing to do with him," the man answered.

"But you did know him?" Rayner asked.

"Yeah, I knew him, he worked for me."

"Were you aware at the time when Mr. Carter introduced unskilled labour on to the site and arranged for them to go on the payroll?"

"No."

"I find that very strange, Mr. Browning, being as you were his supervisor."

"I said no, I knew nothing about that mister."

Richard Rayner then asked a question that he already knew what the reply would be.

"Have you any idea who would wish Raymond Carter dead?"

"No."

"Very well, thank you for your time."

Before the detectives turned to leave, Henry Bustle enquired as to how Harold Browning has come across his facial injuries.

"Fell over in the street," was the only answer provided, causing the Sergeant to smile.

And then Rayner stepped forward and surprisingly placed two one-pound notes into the pocket of the man's vest.

Browning stepped back and asked, "What's that for, I don't accept charity and I ain't no snitch."

"It's not for you, Mr. Browning, it's meant to buy a decent meal for your wife and some timber to light that fire with."

At that, the detectives quickly disappeared through the door.

"What in God's name did you give him that money for?" Henry Bustle asked.

"To soften him up a bit, Henry. His attitude is understandable considering the circumstances in which he now finds himself."

"Or because he was involved in killing Raymond Carter."

"You might be correct, but a little charity didn't hurt anyone, and in any case I was serious about helping that over worked woman of his."

"If you want my opinion, since being laid off when that bridge was completed, he's fallen on hard times that's for sure, but I reckon he earns a coin or two street fighting, from the marks he's boasting on his face and most probably spends it all on beer."

"Yes, thank you, Henry."

By the time the two detectives reached Southwark Bridge that following evening, the freezing temperatures were still keeping most people indoors and they found Jack Robinson had already arrived at the rendezvous. The young Sergeant was stamping his feet on the snow-covered ground and his breath could be seen spiralling upwards into the night air. His whole demeanour was one of enthusiasm and Richard Rayner guessed there had been some progress.

The undercover man gave a detailed account of everything that had taken place on the evening before, including the name of the barge, 'La Angeline' from which the five women had been taken, and the address in Ewer Street, Newington, where they were being held captive.

"Those poor souls were being forced to obey the scoundrels that were in charge of them," Robinson went on to explain, "And I would give my hind teeth to lay an iron bar across the backs of those louts, sir."

"You might get that opportunity yet, Jack" Rayner suggested. Turning to Henry Bustle, he continued, "We need to act with some urgency now Henry, just in case they intend moving those women on to another address."

"It sounds as though they've been kidnapped from France and brought across the channel."

"No," Jack quickly corrected his colleague, "The other waiter who was with me, said they had come from Holland and from his attitude, I suspect that Duboir intends to use them for the purposes of prostitution."

"These other men," Bustle made mention of, "Were any of them armed, Jack?"

"I didn't see any guns present, only wooden staffs, but with this lot, you never know. The main man, as I have mentioned before is, Sidney Froggatt, and when the time comes, he's going to be the difficult one to handle."

"Well done Jack, but I think it would be wise for you to continue in your role at the restaurant, until we have at least recovered those women you have mentioned."

"Very well, sir. Will you be raiding that house in Ewer Street tonight, only it might be they put two and two together and finger me as the informant."

"Don't worry, I intend grabbing hold of both Duboir and his henchman at the same time as we hit that house, but I think it would be beneficial if myself and Henry just took a look at the Ewer Street address. You say the house was up the alleyway on the left at the back of number twenty-three."

"Yes sir, next to an extended alleyway."

"Very well Jack, get yourself to bed and unless you hear from us beforehand, we shall meet here again at the same time tomorrow night."

After leaving Robinson, his two colleagues made their way back to Scotland Yard, welcoming the warmth of Rayner's office. There was a lot to discuss and plan and by that time the Chief Inspector had the bit well and truly in his mouth.

Chapter Twenty Nine

By the time Richard Rayner had reached Scotland Yard, he was having second thoughts about surreptitiously surveying the house in Ewer Street, knowing there might be a risk of alerting those responsible for keeping the five women in captivity. Part of him wanted to discuss further what they had been told by Jack Robinson, but exhaustion was beginning to dampen his enthusiasm. Once he and Henry Bustle had thawed out in front of the Chief Inspector's blazing log fire, it was late and although both detectives were tired, the senior detective told his Sergeant to make arrangements for a dawn raid the following morning.

After Bustle had disappeared from the office, Rayner once again addressed his blackboard, feeling a need to put everything they had learned into some kind of perspective. After recording virtually everything he knew in chalk, he stood back and began to put into perspective the whole intensity of the Investigation into the suggested murder of Egbert Graham, Sir Giles Lamfrey's illegitimate son.

Thanks to the alertness and courage of young Jack Robinson, Rayner now had a good idea of the criminal activities of the French restaurant owner Jacques Duboir and had little doubt that Graham's death was connected in some way with that particular enterprise. But the reason behind the murder remained elusive. He was confident that would become clear, once they had recovered the five kidnapped women and arrested the main man and his associates. It would be difficult to prove that the young man had in fact, been murdered and he would have to rely on pressure being applied to the miscreants, once they were in custody, but his first priority was to set those women free, once he had taken advantage of some well needed sleep.

However, turning his mind to the murder of Raymond Carter, there were many innuendos and suppositions present in Rayner's fatigued thought process, mostly connected with the victim having been involved in an activity that consisted of unskilled labour being introduced into the workforce during the construction of the bridge. The Chief Inspector strongly suspected that it was an unlawful project from which the man Carter would have taken commissions from individuals he found work for. And then there was the supervisor, Harold Browning, a most reticent gentleman who was obviously holding back on whatever he knew about what went on during the bridge construction. Having said that, it didn't appear from Browning's domestic circumstances, that if he had been involved in the same scheme as Jackson, he certainly wasn't paid a great deal of money for his efforts.

One question that the senior detective should have asked when talking with George Peppercorn at Tower Bridge, was whether those it was alleged had been introduced into the workforce by Carter, were British or foreign individuals. It was possible that they could have been forcibly brought from another country to work at the whim of those responsible for their employment. If that was to be the case, then could there be a link between Duboir's activities, the murder of Egbert Graham and that of Raymond Carter. It was all very complex and contained many possibilities without any clear evidence that the two atrocities were in fact linked. Rayner decided to continue treating both Inquiries as separate entities, until there was evidence to prove otherwise.

Finally, after everything had been arranged for the following morning's operation, both Rayner and Bustle left Scotland Yard to try and get some respite, if only for a few hours. The following day would soon be upon them and there was little doubt, they would facing more arduous tasks.

As even more snow began to fall and there were signs of the dawn arriving imminently, two carriages of constables left Scotland Yard led by Richard Rayner and Henry Bustle. The man in charge of the early morning raid had already decided to initially apply a cautious approach when arriving in Ewer Street, having surprised everyone by turning up, dressed as a rat catcher from the sewers.

The driver of the leading carriage was told to stop just a hundred yards from the enclosed entry at the side of number twenty-three, and everyone was instructed to remain inside the vehicles and that Rayner would blow a whistle if they were required. Upon hearing that signal, they were then to make the house in some haste, the one situated on the left on the other side of the alleyway but not until that moment. Having briefed his men, the Chief Inspector left with Henry Bustle walking at his side. Neither detective was armed, having been told by Jack Robinson that the men they were about to confront, were seen to carry only wooden staves, but naturally, Bustle had his stiletto knife strapped to his leg, just in case.

"That's the first time I've ever seen you unshaven and dressed like a garbage bin," Bustle whispered, as they stepped down the enclosed entry.

"There's a first time for everything Henry," Rayner quietly answered back, "Now remember to follow my lead."

By the time they reached the door indicated by Jack Robinson, the dawn was upon them and the snow had eased, changing the appearance of their immediate surroundings. The small back-to-back terraced house was in total darkness with all the curtains drawn closed.

Rayner nodded at Bustle, who then banged hard and loud on the front door. After a few seconds, he banged again, and again after that, until a woman's head suddenly popped out from a window on the upper level.

"What the bleedin' hell is going on down there," she screamed out. The woman was wearing a night cap and from what Rayner could see was in her mid-forties.

He waved a piece of paper at her, and shouted back, "From the district council missus, we need to access your house now. It's an emergency."

"Piss off and come back next week," she bawled out and disappeared, closing the window with a loud bang.

Again, Rayner nodded at Bustle, who then stepped back before kicking the front door off its hinges.

They found themselves in a dark front room and immediately heard noises coming from upstairs. A woman was screaming, probably the same one who had been yelling at them from the upstairs window, and a man could be heard grumbling.

Bustle had a truncheon grasped in one hand and Rayner kept his whistle concealed. Now wasn't the time to summon the cavalry, they needed to confirm that the five kidnapped women were still there. Then the front room was filled with a torrent of loud and abusive screams, as the detectives were confronted by the woman and a robustly built younger male, dressed only in his vest and trousers.

"Calm down missus," Rayner demanded, still holding the piece of paper in one hand for all to see, "We are only doing our job. This is a writ authorising us to enter these premises and exterminate the nest of rats that's been plaguing the neighbourhood."

"What rats, you cheeky bastards," the woman shouted back at him.

"Newington District Council has received a number of complaints from anonymous people claiming that the yard outside is rat infested and that they are coming from here. Now, what we..."

"What slimy bastards being spreading that shit about us."

"I've told you madam, they were anonymous, now what we need to do is to seek out where the nest is and once we have it, we can come back with the necessary poison to exterminate them. It's for everybody's benefit, including yours."

Henry Bustle could see that his Chief Inspector was actually enjoying the role he was playing and had some difficulty in keeping a straight face.

"You just get your arses out of my house now and take that scumbag paper you're going on about with you." She then turned to the man and demanded, "Arthur, see them out and I'll soon find out who's been using the spy against us."

"But ma, it looks official to me," the man remarked.

"Arthur, do as you're bleedin' well told and get these bastards out of my whack."

"Arthur, I suggest you stay exactly where you are," Rayner instructed, before turning again to the woman and explaining, "Listen lady, all we need to do is to look around and confirm whether or not you have a nest of rats living here. I'm sure you wouldn't know if they were, but we have to find out one way or another. It's the law and we ain't got no choice."

"Arthur, are you just going to stand there like a blob of jelly or move their arses out of here."

"Missus," Bustle interjected, "If you obstruct us in our work, you and any other person can go to prison, so don't be silly, it will take only a few minutes."

The Sergeant's threat appeared to subdue the woman and her son suggested that they should allow the council workers to do their job unhindered.

"Just you tell me what lying bastards have been spreading all this muck around about us then."

"We can't do that, because we have no idea madam," Rayner confessed.

Folding her arms across her chest, with her nightcap having slipped slightly to one side of her head, the lady of the house stood sideways on and then instructed Arthur to go with them.

"Thank you," Rayner said, tipping his workman's cap, "Let us start our search upstairs." Even then, he doubted the five women they were looking for were still present in the house.

Arthur led the way and as Rayner had surmised, after searching every bedroom, including the attic, there was no sign of what they were seeking, although he had taken notice of some indications that were visible. Before leaving, the Chief Inspector required the names of the man and woman, and was willingly told they were, Abraham and Violet Justin.

"It's only for the records you understand," he told them, before leaving, looking slightly embarrassed but thankful he had decided to keep the constables out of sight, and after assuring the woman and her son that they did not have a rat infestation problem.

The others were dispatched back to Scotland Yard and after disappearing from Ewer Street themselves, Henry Bustle suggested that Jack Robinson must have got the wrong house where the woman had been taken to.

"No Henry, that was the right house without doubt," Rayner answered, taking his Sergeant by surprise.

"But there was no sign, that house was completely empty, except for those two, who I shan't lose any sleep over if our paths never cross again."

"When we stepped into the back bedroom, what did you find?"

"Bare floorboards and a single mattress, that was all."

"Did you not detect the slight stink of human urine."

Bustle shook his head.

"And did you not see, scratched in small letters in the plaster at the side of the bed, the word, 'Helpen', which is Dutch for help. In addition to that I found this." The Chief Inspector then produced from his pocket a chocolate wrapper with the words, 'Willie's Cacoa' printed thereon.

"This is a popular chocolate bar manufactured in Holland, so what does that tell you my old friend?"

"Where did you find that?"

"Hidden beneath the mattress in that back room."

"So, they have been there."

"Undoubtedly, but there was no point in arresting that couple and warning those behind the enterprise that we are on to them, apart from putting Jack Robinson's life in danger. We need to find where these women have been taken and the only person in a position to do that, is our colleague."

Rayner then glanced out of the window and declared, "We have come far enough." He then called to their carriage driver to turn the carriage around and return to Ewer Street and to stop at exactly the same location as previously.

"I need you to watch that house, Henry, and to follow either of those two, should they leave. Hopefully, they might take us to where the women are being kept."

Bustle nodded and asked what the Chief Inspector was going to do.

"Arrange for Claud Davey to join you and then I have to make some enquiries on my own."

Having seen his Sergeant secrete himself in a shop doorway, near to the enclosed alleyway in Ewer Street, Richard Rayner hastily returned to Scotland Yard. There the senior detective found Claud Davey in the general office and dispatched him to meet up with Henry Bustle. Everything was happening at a fast pace and the Chief Inspector was soon being taken to his next location, which was Denmark Street, in Whitechapel.

After knocking on the door where the unfortunate Maisy Winthrop had once conducted her business, it was opened and Rayner was confronted by a middle-aged woman with red hair, tied up on top of her head. She was wearing heavy make-up and was wearing a flimsy ankle length coat over a dress.

The Chief Inspector immediately introduced himself and the woman answered, "You don't look like a plod to me, ducky."

The detective had forgotten about his appearance and quickly showed the lady his identity card, encouraging a look of suspicion from the woman.

"I assure you miss, I am not here to make any enquiries about the kind of business conducted from these premises," he earnestly explained.

"I don't give a hoot; we've closed down since poor old Maisie's passing."

"Yes, and I am the officer who caught the man who was responsible for that atrocity, and in return all I require is some help from you."

"Then you had better come in, ducky."

The red headed woman quickly explained that the girls who used to work for Maisy Winthrop had disappeared, following the Madam's untimely death and that she was living alone at the house.

Without mentioning any names, Richard Rayner described the fate of a small group of women kidnapped and forcibly brought to London for what he suspected was prostitution.

"I thought that perhaps you might have some idea where young ladies in that position would be concealed, before being required to work the streets."

"Well Mister Plod, believe me I detest scum that do that to innocent girls and would help you in any way I could, but I'm afraid I have no idea about what you are asking."

"Then thank you for your time, it was a long shot, and I shall just have to pursue other lines of enquiry."

Rayner turned to leave, but the woman told him to wait. She then produced a small piece of notepaper and wrote something on it, before handing it to the detective.

"I can't promise anything, but this lady might be in a better position to help you than I am. Only don't tell her that I sent you."

Rayner nodded and thanked the woman again before leaving.

Chapter Thirty

Richard Rayner wasted little time in visiting the Madam whose name had been disclosed to him by the woman living in Denmark Street, but unfortunately his pleas for assistance were firmly rejected. In fact, he spent a great deal of time calling at a number of known brothels in the district, particularly those in close proximity of the docks and by the time the late afternoon was fading towards night, his small crusade had been fruitless and he returned to Scotland Yard extremely frustrated and exhausted. What effort he had made to identify a possible location for the five missing women had met with complete failure as a result of prostitutes unwilling to speak with him. Perhaps Henry Bustle would have more joy, or so he hoped.

Frederick Morgan was far more amicable than he had been for the past few days, but was concerned about the man being held in the cell's downstairs.

"We have to charge him, Rayner, don't forget, Sir Giles is a Knight of the Realm and he's been banged up down there for over a week now. I'm expecting a writ of Habeas Corpus to be served on us at any moment my old mucker."

"I appreciate that sir, but once we charge him, he's off to Newgate and I would prefer he stayed with us, if only for another day or so."

"Will it be to our benefit, that's the question, Rayner."

"Yes, without doubt, I believe we are very close now towards solving the murder at Tower Bridge and a number of other atrocities we weren't aware of until recently."

"Okay my old mucker, two more days, but if we haven't charged the blighter by then, we shall have to kick him out, and that's the last thing I want to do. At the moment the old man hasn't said a word," Morgan continued, referring to the Commissioner, "But I'm expecting him through that door any minute."

Whereby, Richard Rayner had failed in his enquiries with the local brothels and street walkers, after being relieved by Claude Davey in Ewer Street, Henry Bustle felt a need to act unilaterally, believing it would be beneficial to converse further with Harold Browning but without being restricted by his Chief Inspector. The

Sergeant had his own way of working that often conflicted with Rayner's principles, although often obtaining the same results, and was convinced that the man who had been so unco-operative could be persuaded to tell all he knew by using a different tactic to that of the Chief Inspector. Strangely enough, as he was approaching the dwelling in Old Fish Street, he caught sight of the man he intended to confront, stepping out of his front door to walk ahead of him.

Bustle followed at a short distance, until seeing Browning was about to enter a corner public house, so called out to him.

Browning stopped and waited for Bustle to approach him.

"What do you want?" he asked aggressively, a response anticipated by the detective.

"Why, Harold, you don't seem too pleased to see me," Bustle taunted.

"I ain't, I've already told you and that other copper, I don't know nothing."

"And if you did you wouldn't tell me anyway would you Harold, because you are a yellow backed creature of habit that spends his days lurking in the shadows."

The unco-operative individual just looked at him, before spitting on the cobbles, but Bustle knew what he was doing and continued to lash the man with his tongue, accusing him of being spineless and unprincipled.

"Well, at least Harold old son, we've come to an understanding, which is something mate."

"And what might that be," Browning quietly said, stepping backwards a pace.

"That the only way you are going to tell me what I know is if I add a few more bruises to that ugly face of yours."

The man's eyes flared up and he clenched both fists.

"You can give me your best shot, scar face."

"Oh, it wouldn't take much to put you on the floor, before kicking your head in. I've always found sneaky bastards like you have always had a tendency to cry like an immature whelp when they cop one on the nose. All mouth and piss is what my old man used to say, and I reckon that describes you perfectly mate."

At that, Browning's right fist flew through the air, aimed at Henry Bustle's already disfigured face, the result of years of street fighting, but the intended blow missed the target, giving the Sergeant the opportunity to plant his punch squarely into the other man's stomach, causing his knees to bend and a desperate attempt to breathe.

Bustle then produced his truncheon and struck his opponent hard across the back of his neck, causing him to collapse to the pavement. He then struck him on the back of the head and stepped back to watch the blood flow from the wound, staining Mr. Browning's open-neck grey flannel shirt and his woollen jacket that had seen better days.

The injured man grasped the back of his head with both hands but was levered upwards to his feet by the strength of the Sergeant, who then slammed him up against a wall.

"Had enough friend?" Bustle whispered in the man's ear, but the injured man hadn't and brought up a knee, connecting with the detective's groin, resulting in

Rayner's man loosening his grip and stepping backwards, showing the pain he was feeling in his grisly face. That was one manoeuvre he hadn't been expecting.

One thing the Sergeant had learned throughout his days of fighting for survival in some of the worst slums in London, was that, once your opponent gains an advantage, that's the time to unleash all you have, and he did so. Both fists were like pistons, pummelling each side of Browning's face, Bustle's truncheon having fallen to the floor but no longer required. The man groaned, as the blows rained in one after another, each delivering more excruciating and stinging pain.

Harold Browning had met his match and slowly began to crumble to his knees unable to defend himself, when once again Bustle hoisted him up against the wall and asked if he had had enough.

The injured man's eyes were puffing up and his eyes were like two slits gazing back at his aggressor. He nodded and although he was a big man, Bustle managed to lift him over his shoulder and carry him into the public house, where he unceremoniously dumped him on to a bench in a corner of the bar room. He then called to the landlord to bring over two glasses of black ale, before sitting down next to his victim.

"God Almighty, who did that to you Harry?" the man with the drinks asked, in utter astonishment at the grotesque appearance of his regular customer's facial features.

"A ruffian just did that to him," Bustle answered on Browning's behalf.

"What ruffian was that Harry?" the bar tender asked.

Browning pointed a thumb at Henry Bustle and spoke through broken lips, "Him."

The inquisitor looked shocked and immediately offered to shake Bustle's hand.

"You must know how to handle yourself mister," he said, "Harry here is the hardest man in the district, and I would have bet this pub on no one being capable of doing that to him."

"Beginner's luck," Bustle remarked, looking unscathed and not even out of breath.

After the landlord had returned to his daily chores, the Sergeant turned to the injured man, who was trying hard to drink from his glass, and said, "Well then, Harry, now we've got to know each other a little better, how about telling me what you know about that caper Ray Carter was involved in."

Browning winced, and before speaking, pulled a loose tooth from out of his mouth, causing a small trickle of blood to run down his chin.

"Take your time and have another drink," Bustle suggested, which the other man did.

"You're a pugilist," Browning then suggested, hinting that the detective was a paid street fighter, similar to himself.

"No mate, just a kid who was brought up hard and rough, now what about Carter."

"He brought in a few idlers on occasions and used to get me to put their names on the payroll in return for a couple of back handers, that was all. I didn't kill him and that's the Gospel."

"I believe you, but who was he working for Harry, any idea mate?"

"No, but whoever it was, I know this much, Ray Carter was petrified of him."

"Did he ever mention him to you?"

Browning nodded and winced again, trying to make himself more comfortable by shuffling about on his seat and taking a long gulp of his ale, leaving blood on the outside of his glass and before confessing with some difficulty, "All he said to me was that the geezer was well to do and paid him top bat, but that he wasn't the kind of bloke you would want to cross."

"Did he ever give you a name?"

"No, he had no need to, and I didn't want to know anyway. When that little scheme was discovered by the boss men, that put an end to it and it was over, more's the pity."

"Our friend was garrotted before being strung up and thrown off that bridge. Any idea who would have done that?"

"Only the geezer Carter had been working for by bringing those foreigners into work."

"Were they all foreigners, Harry?"

The man nodded again and admitted, "A few Poles, Italians and some other foreigners, I only found that out by the list of names Carter gave me to copy on to the payroll."

"How come you never dropped in the shit when the boss men found out about what had been going on."

"I just told them I thought they were genuine skilled workers. We were getting close to finishing the construction in any case."

Bustle sat back and drank some of his own ale, satisfied that his man had been telling the truth and couldn't help him any further.

"Am I going to get locked up for this," Browning then asked.

Bustle smiled and in answering, pushed a rolled up one pound note into the other man's top pocket.

"No Harry, I think you served enough penal servitude already, but don't spend all that money we have given you on piss and think a bit more about the missus. Take your time and have another on me."

At that, Bustle stood and left.

Although Richard Rayner condemned Henry Bustle's methods of extracting information out of Harold Browning, he was pleased with what his Sergeant had to tell him.

"We need to know who this man is he reckoned Raymond Carter was working for, and by describing him as having been well to do might just put him closer to the social circle that Sir Giles Lamfrey mixed in."

"In fact, it might be Lamfrey himself who Carter was referring to," Bustle suggested.

"I don't think so, Henry. Why should an eminent and well-paid surgeon bother becoming involved in falsely supplying unskilled labour. That would be ridiculous. No, I truly believe that Sir Giles's involvement is merely information he has come across and his only personal concern is the circumstances surrounding the death of his son."

Having noticed the rawness of the flesh covering both of Bustle's knuckles, Rayner suggested he went home and had them attended to. He would meet with Jack Robinson on Southwark Bridge alone and meet up with the older Sergeant in the morning.

"I'll come with you, Rayner," Frederick Morgan suggested, having been stood in the open doorway of the Chief Inspector's office, unnoticed.

It seemed that the temperature was dropping more each night and there was a biting wind that numbed the faces of the two senior detectives as they made their way towards the usual meeting place, with Rayner hoping that Sergeant Robinson would not be late. He wasn't, and in fact, was standing in the usual place when the couple arrived.

According to the undercover detective, nothing of interest had taken place since that one excursion involving the abducted women, and work at the restaurant had continued as normal throughout the last couple of days with Jack Robinson waiting on the tables.

Although frustrated, Rayner suggested they had to remain patient and allow things to happen naturally. As long as Duboir and his henchman, Sidney Froggatt, were unaware of the Sergeant's true identity, there was every chance his services would be called upon again in the near future.

"But that doesn't help us to discover where these women are being kept," Morgan remarked, stating the obvious.

Rayner didn't answer him and was thinking of another avenue of inquiry. He suggested they should direct their attention towards learning more about, La Angelina, the barge used to bring them to London.

"There's every possibility the vessel is registered in Calais and if we can find out the names of the owners and captain responsible for sailing her, that might provide us with more valuable information to work on."

"I'm not optimistic that will be the case," Morgan admitted, "All you will get is a couple of frogs names, which won't tell us anything about the London end of the operation."

Of course, Morgan was right but Rayner felt so helpless. It appeared now that all avenues of the Investigation had been exhausted and that all they could do was wait until hopefully, Jack Robinson would be approached to go on another excursion. The problem with that was that the Sergeant might only be required to keep lookout again and no further progress would be forthcoming. The Chief Inspector made his feelings known to the other two.

Then Robinson suggested another idea.

"I'm convinced that the other waiter, Louis, knows more about what has been going on and is obviously trusted by Duboir. He might also know about the circumstances of Egbert Graham's death, as well as the location those women are being kept."

"Tell us more Jack, what's on your mind," Rayner asked, looking more optimistic.

"I know it's risky, but what if we somehow managed to get Louis into custody without him knowing the real reason for his captivity and then tried to open him up about Duboir's affairs."

"You're right Robbo," Morgan said, "But it's too bleedin' risky, for you I mean."

"I know he frequently visits an Opium den in Smithfield. Perhaps that could give us the reason we would need to get him in."

The Chief Superintendent turned to Rayner and asked what he thought about the idea.

"We would need to put to him, something that he feared more than what Duboir would do to him, should he open up to us."

"The noose," Morgan quipped, resulting in Rayner nodding, and the more the Chief Inspector considered the suggestion, the more he began to see some potential in what could be achieved.

"We might need to tell a few white lies to convince him," he then suggested.

"So, what's new, my old mucker."

Chapter Thirty One

Louis Bastien was a trusted servant of Jacques Dubois, having worked for the restaurant owner since the Frenchman had first come to London to open his business. In fact, Dubois regarded his fragile looking countryman in the same way as he would a brother, more so than Sidney Froggatt, who he employed more for protection than for any other reason. The unmarried waiter with the Mediterranean features only had two vices, he enjoyed smoking opium and frequently visited the same premises to fulfil his habit, and he enjoyed the company of homosexuals more than he did women.

As was his usual habit, when given a night off by Monsieur Dubois, Bastien made his way to his favourite haunt in Paternoster Row, Cheapside, a narrow-cobbled lane with red lights displayed outside the majority of dwellings there. The stench of humanity and decay would deter any stranger to the area from visiting unless their personal desires could only be satisfied at that location. And so it was, Louis Bastien stepped inside the one terraced house with a Chinese lantern on display over the front door. He intended smoking just one bowl of the drug before leaving and visiting a nearby secretive establishment frequented by a number of his homosexual friends.

The next hour or so, saw all anxiety and concerns leave the Frenchman's thoughts, to be replaced only by total relaxation and much happier and pleasant sentiments. Having smoked the bowl he'd paid homage to, a complacent and untroubled gentleman left the premises and began to walk along Paternoster Row, feeling light-headed and at absolute peace with the world. That was until, suddenly and without warning, someone grabbed him from behind and placed a piece of rag over his nose and mouth. Within a few seconds, Monsieur Bastien had collapsed to the cobbles, unconscious and never to learn who his assailant had been.

When the French waiter finally regained consciousness, he initially re-entered a world of confusion and bewilderment. It took some time for the discombobulated opium addict to return to full consciousness and when he looked up at a ceiling made of wooden planking, only then did he remember having visited his favourite place of leisure the evening before. He was lying prone on what appeared to be a pile of hessian sacks and the first noticeable sensations he felt through a thick fog enveloping his mind, was the unpleasant reek of dampness and decay. A grey light was infiltrating through a small window, confirming the night had passed, a period of time that was absent from the waiter's memory. As a result of the opium mixed with the drug used to render him senseless, he had spent the remainder of the previous night, comatose and in suspended animation.

He lay there, trying hard to recollect what had taken place during those missing few hours. After satisfying his habit he had stepped out into the cold air. Yes, then he had walked a few steps but after that; nothing. My God, he had been kidnapped but why and by whom. Quickly he felt for his roll of bank notes in his trouser pocket. It was still there, much to his surprise. And then he suddenly felt something touch his thigh. He turned and gasped at the sight of another individual lying next to him. It was a red headed woman, with a face as white as the snow outside. Her throat had been slit and she was dead.

Panicking, Bastien regained his feet and for a moment, stared down at the corpse, trying hard to focus his clouded eyesight. What in God's name had taken place in this gloomy confinement. He had to get away and desperately searched for an exit. He found it, a wooden door contained within wooden walls and lifted the latch. Thank the Lord it wasn't bolted and the terrified man flung the obstacle open, not looking back and stepping out into the early morning greyness, only to find himself on a canal towpath. Was this nightmare really happening to him. Quickly he hurried for a few steps, before stopping and looking back, disbelieving the sight that had greeted him back there, and could see his place of confinement had been a dilapidated wooden shack at the side of the towpath, but where was he. At that very moment he didn't care. He had to put some distance between himself and that place of horror, the structure in which the dead body of a murdered woman was lying, having appeared to have spent the night with him.

Beads of sweat were covering his forehead and as he turned to sprint away, Bastien was suddenly confronted by two men who appeared to have come from nowhere. One was smartly dressed, wearing a top hat and tailored frock coat and the other, less salubrious, resembling a common docker.

"Good morning sir, and where might you be going at such an early hour in the morning," the smartly dressed gentleman enquired, speaking fluently and with a hint of authority in his voice.

"Where am I?" the Frenchman asked in reply.

Richard Rayner nodded for Henry Bustle to look into the shack.

"We are detectives from Scotland Yard, and you appear to be lost. I take it you are on your way home sir," the senior man suggested.

"Yes, I have been out and I am on my way home, yes, thank you."

"Might I ask what you were doing inside that shed, sir."

"What?"

At that, Henry Bustle called back to the Chief Inspector and suggested he took a hold of the man they had just seen leaving the structure, to which Rayner grasped Louis Bastien's arm.

"My word, whatever have you been up to?" he enquired, looking towards Bustle who was standing in the open doorway of the shed.

"Search him, sir," the Sergeant requested, "There's a dead woman here who's had her throat cut open."

Bastien began to tremble, as Rayner removed a bloodstained stiletto type knife from his jacket pocket.

"What, I don't know how…"

"I think you had better come with us sir, it appears you have a lot to answer for."

While Richard Rayner was taking a terrified and confused French waiter back to his carriage, Henry Bustle helped Phebe Cunningham, the prostitute from Denmark Street, back to her feet and gave her a kerchief to wipe away the make-up on her face, in particular the artificially created bloody line across her throat. He reimbursed her with a couple of pound notes and thanked the woman for her invaluable help.

"Any time Sergeant, if it means catching the scum that did that to those poor girls," Phebe said, before Bustle directed her to another carriage that was waiting to return her home.

After disclosing his name and personal details, Louis Bastien was still quivering like a jelly in a gale force wind when he entered the basement interview room at Scotland Yard. The unsuspecting man's senses were still numbed by an overwhelming revulsion at what had taken place. The dead woman's face peering up at him from that pile of hessian sacks was a constant in his thoughts and he found it difficult to mentally circumvent such an horrific sight.

"I didn't kill that lady," he swore to Richard Rayner.

"Let us start at the beginning, Louis, when you say you lost consciousness last night when walking in Cheapside."

"I was attacked from behind and I remember a piece of cloth being pressed against my face. I must have been drugged."

"And where had you been before that incident?"

Bastien hesitated, but realising that his life was in mortal danger decided to co-operate as best he could.

"There's a small opium den in Paternoster Row where I called in for a smoke but I didn't kill that woman, you can ask anybody who was in there. I couldn't."

"So, when you were allegedly attacked, your senses must have been affected by the drug you had previously smoked, am I right in saying that?"

The Frenchman nodded, before repeating his denial concerning the woman he thought was dead, again adding that he had also been drugged by those who abducted him off the street.

"Then how can you be so certain that you did not commit foul murder, when you say you cannot remember anything my friend."

"I know who I am sir, and I am telling you I am not capable of doing such a thing."

Rayner smirked and glanced across at Henry Bustle, who was seated next to him.

"We saw you mate, leaving that shed at the side of the canal and found the murder weapon concealed in your coat pocket," the Sergeant confirmed.

Bastien became more excitable, denying having any knowledge of the weapon.

"I have never seen that knife before, you must believe me."

"I am afraid I am finding it difficult to believe a word you have said so far, Mr. Bastien," Rayner said, "But let us delve further into the circumstances of your current employment. You have told us you work as a waiter at the Nourriture Exquise in Portland Terrace, pray tell us who is likely to want you dead." It was a pointed question that caused the Frenchman to quickly become subdued.

"Nobody, I have no enemies," he quietly answered.

"As far as you are aware that is, but if what you say is true, which appears extremely doubtful, then someone has set you up to carry the can for the murder of that woman, surely."

The Frenchman appeared to go inside himself, offering no further comment and staring down at the tabletop, obviously in deep thought.

Richard Rayner then turned to Henry Bustle and suggested there was nothing more they could do, apart from charging the prisoner with murder most foul.

"And may God have mercy on your soul, sir," he added.

Such a remark seemed to shake Louis Bastien from his brief reverie, and he snapped back at the Chief Inspector, "I am going to hang for something I have not done."

"It would appear that way, unless you tell us the truth about what happened between yourself and that unfortunate lady, or of course, assist the police in another way, but I doubt that you are in a position to do that."

"In what way sir, how can I avoid the gallows. I have been telling you the truth."

Rayner sat back and signalled to Henry Bustle to sit back down, the Sergeant having stood to escort Bastien to a cell.

"It is a common practice in this country for a person to be allowed some leniency in return for having shown some remorse and having made some effort to become a good citizen, shall we say. If we could show the trial judge that you have helped us to solve another heinous crime then, I cannot guarantee it, but in most cases the court shows some sympathy towards the accused. It doesn't have to be a murder but would need to relate to some serious criminal activity, which I am confident you have no knowledge of. Therefore, I see no other future for you but to be sentenced to hang, the evidence is inexplicably overwhelmingly against you sir."

The prisoner sat in silence for a few moments and Rayner said no more, allowing the man to consider what he had just been told.

Bastien then enquired what guarantee he might have that, if he was to assist Scotland Yard, he would escape the gallows.

"I could not possibly give you any guarantee, except to say that precedent dictates that an individual who has shown remorse and has helped the police in the way I have described, is usually dealt with more leniently by the judge. But you are a waiter sir, how on earth could you possibly have any knowledge of the kind of criminal activity that would attract our interest."

Again, the man sat in silence, trying to come to terms with his conscience. He had always been loyal to his employer at the restaurant and would never have breached that trust in normal circumstances. But here he was, facing death himself by legal execution. In his mind, he was already standing on the gallows awaiting the inevitable, so all loyalty must be sacrificed for his own well-being and survival.

Rayner disturbed the Frenchman's thoughts by standing to leave but was prevented by Louis Bastien who whispered in a nervous voice, "There might be something that you would be interested in, provided you swear an oath to tell the judge what I am about to do and Heaven forbid, plead on my behalf that I be spared the noose."

The Chief Inspector deliberately yawned, playing out his role of indifference to the full.

"I am in a position to do that for you, but please Louis, continue."

The waiter then began to describe the activities of his employer, Jacques Duboir, describing how his fellow Frenchman had an arrangement for young girls to be brought to London, where he and his associates would keep them imprisoned in the most distressing circumstances, until they were completely void of resistance and left with no other choice but to do as requested in order to continue breathing.

"If this is true, for what purpose does this man, Duboir, inflict such trauma on these girls?"

"He uses them for various profitable callings including prostitution in London and other parts of the country, but I am also aware of a far more serious crime committed on the instructions of Monsieur Duboir."

"Do go on sir," Rayner invited, maintaining that look of indifference.

"There was a young man who we only knew as, Bert, I do not know his second name, but he came to work at the restaurant as a waiter last year and was soon recruited by Duboir to assist the others in bringing girls into the country. Although we were always paid well for what assistance we gave, this newcomer got greedy and wanted more than he was being paid. At first, Duboir instructed one of his men to beat up on the youngster, but when Bert threatened to go to the police and tell them about what was going on, he ordered his death. Would that suffice Inspector?"

"And you are telling us that this young man, Bert, was murdered at Duboir's instigation?"

Bastien nodded.

"Could his name have been Egbert?"

"I don't know, maybe."

"Very well, how and where was he killed?"

"I'm not sure but Duboir has a man working for him by the name of Sidney Froggatt and I was there when he was told to do away with Bert and make it look like a suicide."

Richard Rayner was pleased with how their ruse had gone so far, but still needed to urgently find out where the kidnapped girls were being kept. He didn't want to sound over enthusiastic when responding to Louis Bastien and quietly asked the man, "How do we know all of this actually happened and isn't a figment of your imagination, just to escape the noose."

"Go to Caroline Street off the Old Kent Road and you will see a field at the back of some houses. There's a house that stands alone in the field and that's where you will find five young girls who were forcibly brought by boat to London from Amsterdam the other night."

Henry Bustle asked how well they are guarded and was told by the Frenchman that he wasn't sure, only having been there on a couple of occasions, but there was an elderly woman and her son who live there and do Jacques Duboir's bidding for him.

"They have a dwelling in Ewer Street, Newington, but spend most of their time at the Caroline Street address when there are girls to watch over. I think some of his men visit now and again just to beat up on the girls and ensure they remain compliant."

"And terrified, I have no doubt," Bustle remarked.

"And when this Duboir fellow feels the time is right to put his merchandise to work, where does he take them," Rayner asked.

"I do not know sir; I've told you all I know."

"Just one more question Louis, how was this fellow Bert, murdered?"

Bastien shook his head, but confirmed he knew the young man had been killed because he read about him having committed suicide in the newspapers.

Again, Rayner indicated to Bustle to take the man to the cells and as the waiter was lifted from his chair, he turned to the Chief Inspector and asked if he had done enough to avoid being hanged.

Rayner looked at him unmoving and quietly declared, "If what you have told us is true young man, then I have every reason to believe you might regain your freedom very quickly, but first we shall need your written statement."

Chapter Thirty Two

"Well, did it work or not," Morgan demanded to know from behind his desk and staring across at Richard Rayner through two bloodshot eyes.

"Did what work, sir?" the detective asked, teasing his senior officer.

"The bloody pantomime we spent half of last night planning, what do you bleedin' well think I mean."

The Chief Inspector chuckled and gave Morgan a detailed account of what they had been told by Louis Bastien, including the house at which he'd suggested the girls were being kept.

"Then there's no time to waste, I take it we're going there now," the Chief Superintendent suggested.

"Yes, Henry is making the arrangements as we speak, but according to Bastien, the house is isolated in the middle of a field, so we shall have to approach it with some caution."

"More bloody shenanigans, what about firearms?"

"In the circumstances, I think we should all be armed."

"When do you intend taking out those creatures at that French restaurant?"

"As soon as we have secured the release of the women."

"Right then," Morgan said, grabbing for his coat and hat, "I'll get the armoury opened."

Jack Robinson continued with his role as a waiter at the Nourriture Exquise restaurant in Portland Terrace, St. John's Wood, serving what few customers were there for the lunch time servings. He noticed that the other waiter, Louis Bastien was missing and was wondering whether Richard Rayner's ploy had worked, but he wasn't the only individual who was missing the presence of the Frenchman.

Jacques Duboir approached him in the kitchen and asked if he had seen or heard from Bastien since the day before yesterday.

Robinson responded by telling the restaurant owner that he had no knowledge of where the French waiter was, except he did mention visiting some smoking establishment when it was his night off.

Duboir looked concerned and called on Sidney Froggatt to call at Bastien's lodgings to see if he was there.

"I suspect the fool had more opium than he could manage and is still sleeping it off," he added.

"How am I going to manage on my own," the detective enquired, looking genuinely put out by the other waiter's absence.

Strangely, Duboir looked hard at the undercover man, but then instantly relaxed and told him that he would assist until Bastien turned up.

When the roughneck, Froggatt, later returned and reported the missing man hadn't been seen at his lodgings since the previous early evening, Jacques Duboir became seriously worried and it showed by the manner in which he hurriedly served customers, in contrast to his usual gentile and smiling nature when working at the tables.

The building they were intending to visit could be seen from the Old Kent Road and Louis Bastien had been absolutely right in his description of its location. It was an isolated old red-brick farmhouse surrounded by open land. There was a narrow lane leading to the front door, but any individual or vehicle approaching the house could be seen as soon as they entered the thoroughfare.

Four carriages filled with detectives and uniformed officers stood stationery, overlooking the location and secreted from view, when both Morgan and Rayner discussed the most effective way in which they could gain access, using surprise as their best ally. A copse of trees could be seen at the back of the house, situated about a hundred yards or so from the building and it was decided to have half a dozen armed men covertly make their way around the perimeter of the field and take up positions inside the copse, using hedge rows and trees for cover. Henry Bustle was given the responsibility of leading that part of the operation and once they were in position, they were to quickly break cover as soon as the main party entered through the front door. It was of the utmost importance that the remainder, led by Rayner and Morgan, made the front door as quickly as possible. One noticeable and favourable feature was that there did not appear to be any guards outside, there to prevent anyone from approaching the building.

Following one final briefing given to Henry Bustle and his small contingency of armed men, Rayner made a note of the time on his pocket watch, allowing fifteen minutes for them to get into position.

"And remember to remain well out of sight of the house at any cost," he added, knowing that enthusiasm could sometimes make men careless.

As the minutes ticked away, Frederick Morgan began to become impatient, constantly asking the Chief Inspector how much longer they had to wait. Then, when Richard Rayner had decided that Bustle and the others should now be in position he climbed back into the carriage, followed by Morgan and an Inspector in uniform.

"Don't spare the horses Jacob," he called out to his driver, who responded by using the whip and leaving Caroline Street, turning into the narrow lane at the gallop, with the three other official carriages following closely behind. Within seconds Rayner and Morgan were at the front door that was swiftly kicked open, before they found themselves inside a narrow hallway with stairs leading off to their left and a number of rooms on their right.

Morgan was directing his officers to begin searching both downstairs and upstairs, when a woman appeared at the far end of the hall, coming from what appeared to be a kitchen. It was Violet Justin, who Rayner had last seen at the address in Ewer Street, when dressed as a council rat catcher.

"Well now, Mrs. Justin, you seem to be a woman who most certainly spreads her wings," the Chief Inspector remarked.

Initially, the woman failed to recognise him, screaming at Frederick Morgan and demanding the intruders left her home instantly. It was a replay of her behaviour when Rayner and Bustle had earlier visited the address in Ewer Street.

"Where are they, missus?" Morgan demanded to know, in his loud intimidating Welsh accent.

"Where's who?" she asked, with great disdain.

The sound of a door being forcibly crashed open from somewhere at the back of the building, confirmed that Henry Bustle and his team were about to join the party.

"Handcuff her," Richard Rayner instructed one of the other officers, just as the sound of a kerfuffle coming from the upper tier reached his ears.

Violet Justin's son, Arthur, then appeared, being forcibly dragged down the stairs by three police officers, one of whom suggested that the two senior officers needed to visit the bedroom at the back of the house.

When both detectives arrived, they saw five young women sitting on the bare floorboards near to a curtained window, looking in total shock. Each of them was in need of a bath and the stench that hit Morgan and Rayner was unbearable. There were several buckets on the floor, one filled with water and others with human excrement. The faces of all five women were pale and drawn, but more noticeably, their eyes were filled with terror in similar fashion to wild animals having just been caged. Three of the captives had both wrists tied together and it was obvious that all of them had been unmercifully physically abused and were in dire need of medical attention. They reminded the Chief Inspector of petrified rabbits in a warren, and he was struck by a wave of sympathy towards them.

Richard Rayner spoke in a quiet voice, trying to reassure the women by telling them that he and Morgan were police officers from Scotland Yard and that they were now safe. He continued to explain that arrangements would be made for them to attend at a local hospital where they would receive any medical treatment they required, before being transported back to their homes. He wasn't sure if any of them understood what he was saying, so repeated his message in French, hoping that perhaps one or two might speak that language. From the look on a couple of faces, he detected some relief and called for a couple of constables to escort the women to St. Mary's Hospital and place them into the care of Doctor Critchley.

"God Almighty, Rayner, who could do this to human beings," Morgan remarked, holding a handkerchief to his nose.

"A man who is about to reside in the cell block at Scotland Yard, before meeting the hangman," the senior detective replied.

It was Jack Robinson who first saw the official police carriage pull up outside the front of the French restaurant, whilst serving meals to customers seated close to the front window. When the two senior officers from Scotland Yard entered the eating house, he whispered, "In the back, but watch out for Froggatt."

Jacques Duboir had a plate of food in each hand and was just leaving the kitchen area when confronted by the detectives.

"You won't need those my old mucker, not where you are going," Morgan said, taking the plates from him and placing them on a nearby table.

"What is the meaning of this?" the restaurant owner enquired, portraying an innocent and confused look on his face.

"Jacques Duboir, we are detectives from Scotland Yard, and you are being arrested for the murder of Egbert Graham and for the kidnapping and unlawful detention of young women."

At the time that Richard Rayner was making his arrest, Sidney Froggatt, had stepped into the restaurant through the front door and was immediately confronted by Claude Davey and another detective who had been instructed to remain just inside the dining area. Without hesitation, the ruffian struck the Sergeant in the face, causing him to fall back and collide with his colleague. Froggatt then disappeared through a door leading to a staircase, chased by Jack Robinson.

Henry Bustle wasted little time in hastily following in Robinson's footsteps and leapt up the stairs, until reaching a dark landing. Voices could be heard coming from a room with the door open, situated on the left in a narrow corridor. And then the sound of a gunshot reverberated around the building, and the most experienced of the two Sergeants feared the worst.

Grasping his own pistol, he cautiously moved forward, crouching slightly and when nearing the open door, saw a figure appear, that of Sidney Froggatt. The man was looking back into the room he had just exited and was holding a gun in one hand.

"Drop it," Bustle loudly ordered, not hearing the screams of women coming from downstairs in the restaurant.

Froggatt looked like a desperate man, revolving around and glaring at Bustle with fiery eyes. He raised his gun and the Sergeant opened fire, placing two bullets into the man's chest.

Duboir's right-hand man was flung backwards on to the floorboards, his gun leaving his hand and spinning across towards where Bustle was still crouching. Picking Froggatt's firearm up off the floor, the Sergeant stepped over the fallen man and ran into the room, where he found Jack Robinson sitting on a bed, nursing a wound to his upper arm.

Bustle quickly snatched his colleague's tie from his neck and tied it tightly around his injured arm to stem the flow of blood.

"I see you haven't used your necktie, Henry," the younger man joked.

Bustle grinned, as he tied the knot around the injured arm.

"I'm okay, Henry, watch that scoundrel outside," Robinson suggested, but when Bustle returned to the fallen Froggatt, he found him still lying on his back in the outside corridor. Sidney Froggatt had drawn his last breath.

Arrangements were made for Jack Robinson to be taken to hospital and for Jacques Duboir to be escorted, shackled to a detective, to Scotland Yard. Apart from the injury sustained by the young undercover Sergeant, everything had gone according to plan and although there were still a few individuals still at large, Richard Rayner was satisfied they had captured the main perpetrators of what could only be described as a vile and horrific enterprise. He was also convinced that he had in his clutches, the man who had been responsible for murdering Egbert Graham, the son of Sir Giles Lamfrey.

"Mr. Rayner sir," it was the Detention Sergeant calling from the far end of the cell passage, "I've got an Arthur Justin banged up in here who wants to speak to the officer in charge of his case."

The senior detective turned to Henry Bustle and suggested it might be prudent to find out what Violet Justin's son wanted to say, before conversing with Jacques Duboir.

"Bring him to the interview room Henry and let's see what it is he wishes to discuss."

By the time the robust man entered the room with the Sergeant, Rayner was already there waiting and sitting at the usual table.

"I understand you wish to speak to me, Arthur."

The man nodded and quickly explained that, although his mother hadn't recognised Richard Rayner, he knew he was the same man who had previously called at the house in Ewer Street, dressed as a rat catcher. He had also recognised Henry Bustle who at that time, had no need to be disguised, his daily attire being similar to a person employed in the sewers of London.

"I'm listening, Arthur."

"Well, some people think I'm a little dim-witted Mr. Rayner, but you might be surprised to know I ain't and I want to tell you about something horrible that happened in Ewer Street."

Rayner raised his eyebrows and again, invited Arthur Justin to continue talking.

"I was doing the washing up when they came, and that man was with them."

"You mean Egbert Graham."

"I don't know his name, but I could hear them arguing about something in the front room and my mother was yelling at them to quieten down. Anyways, I went in to make sure she was alright and saw Syd Froggatt with his hands around the man's throat."

"What else did you see, Arthur?"

"The man couldn't breathe … and Syd kept choking him, until he passed out and fell in a heap on the floor."

"And then what happened."

"My mother asked if he was dead and Syd told her he was, God forgive, and that he'd been ordered by Duboir to do him in. He then asked my mother if she had any rope as he needed to take him away to make it look as though he'd done it to himself."

"And did your mother hand Froggatt a piece of rope."

"Yes, she got it from the shed out back and helped Syd carry the man in a blanket out to the carriage at the front of the house. When I told my mother that what I'd seen had frightened me, she just told me to forget all about it and keep my mouth shut, but it's been giving me nightmares ever since."

Richard Rayner leant forward and quietly commented, "You are certainly not dim-witted Arthur and in fact, I think you are a very brave man for coming forward and telling us about this. You have done the right thing my friend."

Justin sat back with a wide grin on his face and responded to the compliment by admitting that no one had ever called him their friend before.

"Are you willing for Sergeant Bustle to write down what you have told us and sign it for us," he quietly asked.

The man nodded and confirmed that he would have to make his mark, as he couldn't read or write.

"Well done Arthur, if there were more like you in the world today, it would be a far better place."

Rayner left his Sergeant to take the statement and went to see Frederick Morgan in the Chief Superintendent's office upstairs.

Morgan was enjoying his pipe, with a gleaming face and obviously delighted the way things had turned out.

"I need to update the old man, Rayner, but I don't think it would be wise to share with him the method we used to get Louis Bastien to talk." He was referring to the Commissioner.

"No sir, but I still need to talk with Duboir." Rayner then disclosed what Arthur Justin had shared with him and concluded by confirming they now had enough evidence to send the French restaurant owner to the gallows for the murder of Egbert Graham.

"Do you think this Justin fellow will give evidence in court?"

"Oh yes, he's a simple soul, but an honest one and of course, there is still the matter of the hanging man on Tower Bridge."

Chapter Thirty Three

Jacques Duboir sat in the interview room looking extremely smug, but all that was about to change when Richard Rayner joined Henry Bustle, carrying a folder of documents, which he placed on the table, looking stern and purposeful.

The Chief Inspector formally introduced himself and his Sergeant, before speaking about the kidnapping of five young women from Holland and being unlawfully imprisoned in the care of Violet and Arthur Justin, for the purposes of prostitution.

Duboir spoke for the first time by denying any knowledge of what Rayner was saying, speaking in his native tongue.

"La Angelina is the name of the vessel used to bring the women to London, for which I have no doubt you have paid for handsomely, in return for increasing your wealth by eventually putting those wretched young girls on the streets. But that monsieur is the least of your troubles."

The senior detective had the prisoner's undivided attention, but still the Frenchman showed no signs of co-operating in the slightest.

"You are going to hang monsieur for being complicit in the murder of a young man who worked for you by the name of Egbert Graham, an unfortunate lad who was throttled to death by your man, Sidney Froggatt when acting under your instructions and who as you know, is no longer with us."

"I have no idea what you are talking about," the restaurant owner said, still speaking in French.

"Please monsieur, I know you speak good English having conversed with you previously, when attending your restaurant with my wife, so there is no need to try to later plead ignorance of what is being said to you."

"Ah, now I remember, oui, you sat at the table near to the window."

Rayner nodded and then asked, "My only query is why you ordered the death of Mr. Graham."

"I didn't and I have no knowledge of anyone of that name, sir."

"Then let me refresh your memory."

Rayner then first read out the statement made by Louis Bastien, before reiterating the written record of Arthur Justin's statement. By the time he had finished, the smugness on Duboir's face had disappeared and the Frenchman looked pale.

"In addition to that evidence, it is only fair to tell you that, Ronald Polo, the gentleman who has been employed by you as a waiter and was present when those five young women arrived at St. Katharine's Dock, is in fact, Sergeant Jack Robinson, who works for me."

Duboir's head dropped, as though he'd just been hit by a coal merchant's shovel and he stared down at the table, unable to make any comment.

"Now monsieur, why did you order the death of Mr. Graham?" Rayner knew the answer but needed it to come from the prisoner's mouth.

"It appears Inspector that you hold all of the cards, I congratulate you, sir."

"Why did you have that young man killed, Mr. Duboir?"

The man shrugged his shoulders and quietly confessed, "Because of business and nothing else. He was threatening to expose our activities to people such as yourselves and if we didn't silence him, he would have done so."

"I see, then tell me, how many other young women have you got in this country, working as prostitutes for you."

The Frenchman sat for a while in silence, obviously thinking about the question, before admitting to being responsible for another ten young women, all working in Whitechapel and Smithfield.

"And all from Holland."

"No, some from Francaise."

At Rayner's request, the man then wrote down a number of addresses where the women could be found, but when the Chief Inspector asked about the details of the barge, La Angelina, Duboir refused to disclose any more information. It mattered not, as far as the senior detective was concerned. It wouldn't take much for a few enquiries to be made with the French Police and for the necessary arrests to be made. In any case, this particular prisoner was almost certainly going to the gallows.

After returning to the first floor, Richard Rayner directed Henry Bustle to bring the prisoner Sir Giles Lamfrey, from the cell block to his office and when the Knight of the Realm arrived, he found the Chief Inspector sitting behind his desk with Frederick Morgan also in attendance.

After inviting Sir Giles to take a seat, Rayner gave a detailed account of what had taken place, emphasising the fact that his son, Egbert Graham, had been murdered and those responsible would face justice.

"The man who actually killed your boy is no longer with us," he explained, "Having been killed by one of my men whilst trying to avoid arrest but the instigator of the murder will I have no doubt, go to the gallows for the atrocity that was committed. So, Sir Giles, you were perfectly correct in your assumption that your son did not commit suicide."

"Thank God, Mr. Rayner, you have no idea what a relief it is to hear you say that. I really do appreciate everything you have done on my behalf, and of course to remove the stigma that was attached to Egbert's name. I shall now go to my Maker with a clear conscience."

Those last few words surprised both the Chief Inspector and Frederick Morgan, considering what Lamfrey was about to be charged with, for which he would receive a term of imprisonment and not the noose, but there were more important things to address at that moment in time.

"I have fulfilled my part of our agreement, Sir Giles," Rayner pointed out, "And now, wish to know what exactly you are aware of concerning the murder of Raymond Carter on Tower Bridge."

"Yes, I see sir, well I shall uphold my part of our understanding," the prisoner expressed, "But first, I must request that you give me some guarantee that you will speak on my behalf when mitigating in order to avoid the noose sir."

Rayner quickly ascertained that he could not give such an undertaking, knowing that the man had committed crimes of deception to facilitate the larceny of monies belonging to the Women's Hospital and had administered a hallucinatory drug that no doubt had a bearing on the suicide of the young doctor, Tobias Corncrake. He inferred that he would submit a report to the judge at Lamfrey's trial, confirming any assistance the prisoner gave to the police relating to the apprehension of the culprits responsible for Mr. Carter's murder. However, it was highly unlikely he would hang for his misdemeanours, no matter how serious they were.

"But to go beyond that would require me to tell lies on oath to a court of law, and that would go against my own position and principles."

Sir Giles sat back in his chair, slightly deflated and considered further his position, as he stroked some fluff from his trousers.

"I am fairly confident however, that with all the contacts you are associated with in high places, you will be quite capable of procuring a lenient sentence," Rayner added.

"And I'm certain you have already been busy making a mental note of those high-ups you intend approaching my old mucker," Frederick Morgan commented.

Lamfrey knew that nothing on this earth would convince Richard Rayner to change his mind and in fairness the detective had honoured his part of their agreement, so decided to be a gentleman and do the same.

"Very well, gentleman, it appears I have no more cards to play, so I shall tell you all I know. I take it you have already met the chairman of the board of governors at the Women's, Sir Oswald Plumb and his lovely wife, Lady Margaret."

Rayner nodded, not really surprised by the mention of their names.

Sir Giles then continued to explain that Lady Margaret, was in fact, not such a lovely lady as she portrayed to be.

"In reality, the woman is a vixen, who rules the roost as they say. She has expensive tastes and poor old Ossie is subservient to her desires and whims."

Lamfrey carried on, describing how together, the Plumbs had been running a network of labour distribution for a few years, drawing commission from unskilled people for whom they found highly paid employment. The practice from which they maintained their coffers was legally fraudulent, but they were careful not to connect themselves with their practice, using individuals to make certain arrangements for those they recruited and collecting reward monies on a regular basis, and for as long as their subjects remained in employment.

"I was not aware that this man, Carter, was representing their interests but when learning about what happened during the construction of Tower Bridge, had a good idea that Sir Oswald and his wife would have been behind it."

"And you are suggesting that they would have murdered the man for whatever reason."

"No, not themselves personally, but they are quite capable of making the arrangements and using someone else to do their dirty work for them. The reason for the murder of that individual is for you to find out, but I do know they keep a ledger at their home that contains all the business transactions they have been involved in."

"How do you know that?" Morgan asked.

"Because I have seen it, when attending dinner one evening at their home. I came across it when alone in the library where they reside. It has a red leather cover and was resting behind a few medical texts I was interested in perusing through."

"How do you know that Raymond Carter was working for them?" Rayner enquired.

"I don't, as I have told you, I am assuming he did because of the nature of the fraud that was attempted during the construction of the bridge. But gentlemen, how many people in London do you know who are involved in such criminal misconduct."

"He has a point," Morgan quipped.

Rayner asked if Sir Giles had any idea of others who might be associated with Sir Oswald and Lady Margaret, a query that was met in the negative.

"Would you be prepared to make a written statement about what you have told us?" the Chief Inspector enquired.

"No, that I am afraid is beyond me. I do have my reputation to think about, although I appreciate it is somewhat in tatters at this moment in time."

"Very well, thank you for being so candid sir." Rayner nodded at Henry Bustle to take the prisoner back to the cell block.

"Can you tell me how much longer you intend keeping me here?" Sir Giles asked.

"Not long now, my old mucker," Morgan answered, "In fact, you are about to be charged with your crimes and will be leaving us very soon."

That was not what the man wished to hear, knowing that as soon as he had been formally charged he would be transported to Newgate Prison, where his immediate future would be devastatingly harsh.

After visiting a local magistrate and obtaining a search warrant, Richard Rayner expected to find only the butler and a small number of domestic staff present at the house in Cavendish Square. When asked if his master or mistress had arrived home yet, the butler told the Chief Inspector he would see if Sir Oswald was available, but before closing the door, the senior detective placed a foot inside and pushed his way past the servant, followed by Henry Bustle.

"Sir I must protest," the butler declared, nervously.

"There's no need my friend, I have a warrant that authorises my entry."

"Chief Inspector, to what do we owe the pleasure of your company." It was Sir Oswald speaking from the top of the staircase.

Rayner nodded at his Sergeant to search the library, in particular, the location where Lamfrey had said he had found the ledger.

"If I might speak with yourself sir, and your wife." the Chief Inspector spoke in an authoritarian voice.

"What is it you want, Inspector," Lady Plumb enquired, standing in the doorway of the downstairs drawing room, "And why has your man gone unaccompanied into our library?"

"Perhaps we could converse further in the drawing room, madam," Rayner suggested.

As soon as all three were seated, Henry Bustle entered the room grasping a red leather covered book under one arm. He smiled and nodded at Rayner, before handing the ledger to his Chief Inspector.

"Well done Henry," Rayner complimented, before turning over a few pages and quickly scrutinising some of the entries contained within it.

"Could you please tell me what this is all about, sir?" Sir Oswald demanded to know.

"It's quite simple sir, both you and Lady Margaret are under arrest for crimes of fraud and deception, and you will be taken to Scotland Yard for further questioning. You see, we are aware of the scheme you have been practicing for a number of years in relation to the manipulating of unskilled labour on the pretext that individuals were qualified to do certain specialised jobs of work."

Sir Oswald looked across at his wife, who remained silent and just sat there, staring down at the carpet.

He then returned his solemn gaze to Richard Rayner and suggested, "Then I suppose we had best be going, Inspector."

On the journey back to Scotland Yard no words were exchanged, which surprised Richard Rayner. He had also been a little confused by the absence of any argument or denials back at the house, in particular from Lady Margaret. After all, according to Sir Giles Lamfrey, she was a woman who frequently debased her husband, although at that time and in their current circumstances, there had been no sign of disrespect towards Sir Oswald.

The Chief Inspector decided to interview the woman first, away from the company of her husband. Together with Sergeant Bustle, they sat opposite the lady with Richard Rayner glancing down at the pages contained in the ledger.

"There appears to be two separate specimens of handwriting recording these payments received, Lady Margaret. I take it they belong to yourself and your husband."

"Yes," she answered, in a subdued manner.

"I also take it that you have no intention of denying the allegations made against you."

"What would be the point."

Rayner nodded, again surprised at the apathy now being shown by the woman.

"So, pray tell me, who else was in your employ to arrange for these unemployed souls to be recruited into your little schemes."

"No names, Inspector, you already have what you want."

"There is one name, Lady Margaret, I wish to discuss with you and your husband, that of Raymond Carter, the man who was found hanging from Tower Bridge after arranging for unskilled individuals to be employed for skilled labour during the construction of the bridge."

"I have never heard of the name."

"What is baffling me is the reason why you arranged and was complicit in the man's murder."

"I wasn't, I've told you, I never knew the man."

"You do realise you are facing a severe sentence of imprisonment, madam."

"Of course, but your threats mean nothing to me, sir."

"Very well, I shall speak with you later."

When Rayner spoke with Sir Oswald Plumb, he received responses similar to that given by Lady Margaret. He confessed to being instrumental in the scheme referred to by the Chief Inspector but denied knowing Raymond Carter.

When the two detectives exchanged their opinions in Richard Rayner's office, they both agreed that there was something bizarre about the way in which both Sir Oswald and Lady Margaret had been so willing to accept responsibility for the allegations put to them, with the exception of the murder of Raymond Carter, of course.

"There is more to this than we are being made aware of, Henry," the Chief Inspector suggested.

"I agree sir, but what? I suspect they are both hiding something between them..."

"And whatever that is, I do believe we shall find it is the same reason for Carter's murder. I think we should pay another visit to their home and speak with that butler of theirs. Perhaps he could throw some light on whatever we are missing."

Chapter Thirty Four

The very man they were calling to see, Sir Oswald and Lady Margaret's butler, Charles Rickinshaw, opened the door and looked inquisitively at the two Scotland Yard men.

"I take it sir, you already know where my master and mistress are at present," he remarked, with a hint of sarcasm.

"Yes we do, Charles, but I wish to have a word or two with you, if I may."

Rayner and Bustle were led into the library, where the butler remained standing facing the two detectives with a hint of suspicion in his eyes.

The senior detective reminded the young man that his Investigation was of the most serious nature, involving the crime of murder and that any attempt to obstruct such an Inquiry would be dealt with severely.

Those few words brought a look of anxiety to the butler's face, and he quickly confirmed, "I have no intention of obstructing anything sir."

Rayner then asked a number of questions, including, what kind of visitors to the house did Sir Oswald and Lady Margaret entertain; had there ever been individuals who gave the appearance of being working labourers, or had the butler ever heard of the name, Raymond Carter. But nothing useful was shared that would have helped to disclose whatever it was Richard Rayner believed was being kept from them by Charles Rickinshaw's employers and the senior detective was convinced the young servant was being truthful.

"Has Sir Oswald ever discussed any of his business dealings with you, Charles?" He then asked.

"No sir." It was the answer Rayner had been expecting and he now reached a stage whereby he was happy that nothing more would be gained from the conversation.

"Very well, thank you for your time."

"Will sir and madam be returning shortly sir," the butler asked.

"I cannot answer that at present, but I think it highly unlikely."

As the two men were making their way towards their official carriage, for some unexplainable reason, Richard Rayner happened to look back at the front of the house in time to notice something he deemed to be very odd. A curtain in one of the front upstairs bedroom windows moved, and for a fleeting second the Chief Inspector saw the face of a man, peering down at him.

Charles the butler was closing the door when Rayner returned and asked who that gentleman was in the upstairs bedroom.

The servant looked slightly agitated and admitted in a quiet voice, "I cannot say, sir."

"You cannot say, or you won't say?"

"I have my instructions, sir."

Rayner forced his way back inside the hallway, followed by Henry Bustle and both detectives raced up the open staircase on to the upper balcony. The Chief Inspector quickly calculated the location of the room from which he had seen the face and found the door to be locked. He nodded to his Sergeant who, without hesitation, kicked the obstruction open and once inside the room, they found themselves being confronted by a young, robustly built man with dark wavy hair covering his ears and sporting a bushy moustache. He was well dressed in a quilted lounge coat and was standing with both legs apart, grasping an iron bar.

"I do hope you are not intending to use that thing on us," Rayner calmly said, stopping short of approaching the aggressor, with Henry Bustle moving to his side in readiness to pounce.

"You are trespassing, get out of here, whoever you are," the man demanded, holding the iron bar high above his head, ready to strike at the first attempt of an assault.

Remaining calm and speaking in a quiet voice, Richard Rayner identified himself and his Sergeant, asking if the young man actually lived at the house.

"Get out," was the only answer given.

Then, leaving Henry Bustle standing close to the open doorway to prevent any attempt at escape by the young man, he slowly moved across towards a bed up against the wall on his left and sat on the edge.

"It really has been a tiring day young man, and we are in no mood for playing silly games. Unfortunately, Sir Oswald and Lady Margaret are in serious trouble and we have been trying to help them. I take it you are related to them."

The armed man said nothing, but Rayner could see his level of anxiety was beginning to rise, no matter how much he was attempting to keep the situation calm.

"I was thinking sir, perhaps you could help them by answering a few routine questions. I do believe I am addressing their son."

Suddenly and without warning, the man inadvertently dropped the iron bar that went crashing to the floor and with the speed of a striking Adder, Bustle flew across the room and clubbed him half senseless, before he could retrieve his weapon. With some help from Richard Rayner, the young man's arms were pinioned behind his back and his wrists secured with handcuffs.

The Chief Inspector then forced the man to sit on the edge of the bed beside him and remaining extremely placid, quietly asked if he was correct, that he was the son of Sir Oswald and Lady Margaret Plumb.

"I have no business with you," the man said.

"Perhaps not, but we have business with you, Mr. Plumb."

The prisoner looked away and Rayner spoke to Bustle.

"Search it."

Whilst the Sergeant was rummaging through cupboards and a wardrobe, Rayner continued speaking to the occupier of the room, trying to get the man to converse with him, but without much joy. Then Henry Bustle spoke the senior detective's name, producing a folder containing a number of photographs of individual men.

Looking at one in particular, the Chief Inspector explained that he thought the facial features looked very similar to that of a gentleman he had seen recently lying on a slab in the mortuary.

"Did you know Mr. Raymond Carter?" he quietly asked.

"Our friend's name is Jackson," Bustle said, "Jackson Plumb, whose name is written on the back of the folder sir."

"Ah, so you are the son of the couple who normally reside here."

Jackson Plumb just smirked.

"And it would appear from these photographs that they are individuals for whom your father and mother have solicited work."

"Photography is my hobby," the man said.

"I'm sure, and it looks like you are very good at it. Tell me, Jackson, why did you throttle Raymond Carter who was working for your father and then throw him off Tower Bridge with a noose around his neck." Rayner was taking the bull by the horns and watched to see the younger Plumb's reaction. Both he and Henry Bustle were taken aback when their prisoner began to openly weep.

Both detectives remained silent to allow the young man to recompose himself and before the Chief Inspector suggested that it would be beneficial in his effort to avoid the man's parents from meeting the hangman, if he told the whole truth about what involvement he played in the death of Raymond Carter. However, the young man remained reluctant to converse further and from his facial expression and the way he rocked to and fro on the edge of the bed, Rayner detected that Jackson Plumb might well have been retarded in some way.

As they escorted the gentleman back downstairs, intending to take him to Scotland Yard, the Chief Inspector stopped to congratulate the butler, Charles Rickinshaw, on his loyalty to his master and mistress.

"However, I must warn you that such behaviour could be viewed by others as being proof of your involvement in whatever criminal activities have taken place here."

"Am I to be arrested as well, sir?"

"No, not on this occasion but you should be aware of the difference between loyalty and stupidity."

When Sir Oswald was later told of his son's apprehension, he groaned and sighed, and groaned again. When the same news was shared with Lady Margaret, she went berserk and had to be subdued by Rayner and Bustle. Finally, when the woman restored herself to some level of normality, she quietly spoke of everything that had taken place, leading up to the death of Mr. Raymond Carter.

"Our son was born with a mental deformity," she explained, "Oh, he's not a violent man, but whereby the simplest of people could work out a small problem, Jackson would find it impossible. He also lacks in the ability to converse logically, hence the reason we have kept his existence so secretive."

"Are you telling me that throughout his life, you have kept your son locked up in that room at your house," Rayner queried.

"No, no, not all, he is allowed the freedom of the house and the grounds and occasionally accompanies us on various excursions, hence the reason we spend a great deal of our time in Switzerland, but we never introduce him socially to friends and business acquaintances."

She continued to explain that Raymond Carter was employed by herself and her husband and when those unskilled workers were discovered at Tower Bridge, they were naturally refused payment for what little labour they had performed.

"And yet, Carter still demanded we paid him the usual commission that would normally cover a month's work, which at first we refused until he became persistent."

"And you succumbed to his demands."

"Yes, but then a little later he called at the house, further threatening to tell the authorities what had been going on, unless we paid him the same amount again, as expenses incurred whilst he attempted to find more men willing to work. He became very aggressive when we refused and told him to leave but unfortunately, Jackson was present in the drawing room." She paused, feeling some emotion begin to overwhelm her.

"Please go on, Lady Margaret," Rayner prompted.

"He threatened me with a knife and our son reacted in a way we had never seen before. Jackson took the knife from him and they fought, until Jackson's strength overcome Carter and, well you know the rest."

"He strangled the man to death."

"We tried to stop him, but our son was like a mad man, unable to control his temper."

"Then, whose idea was it to throw him off Tower Bridge?"

"Both of us. We had this absurd idea of tying a noose around his neck and taking him to his place of work and trying to make it look like suicide, but of course, that was doomed from the very start."

Richard Rayner felt some pity for the woman and for her husband and had no doubt that if they had come forward and told the truth initially, their circumstances might have been very different, with the courts taking a more lenient view. But, because of their denials and lying, they would both be found guilty of being complicit in the murder of a man, who was just too greedy and who had tried to bully and blackmail them.

"Will we hang for this, Mr. Rayner?" the distraught woman enquired.

"No, I very much doubt that, but I shall not lie Lady Margaret, you and your husband will in all probability have to serve extensive terms of imprisonment for all that you have both done."

"And what of our son, sir?"

"In the circumstances, I believe the court will view his crime with leniency and I cannot see him facing the noose. After all madam, he was acting in self-defence."

"Thank you."

"Please do not thank me, it will be for a judge to decide whatever happens to the three of you, but for what it is worth, I do feel some sympathy and understanding towards you."

Jack Robinson was sitting up in his hospital bed with his wife Lizzie and young daughter at his side, when Richard Rayner and Frederick Morgan finally had the opportunity to visit their younger colleague. The Sergeant had his injured arm in a sling but looked fairly healthy and optimistic for an individual who had suffered a gunshot wound.

The Chief Inspector kissed Lizzie on both cheeks and taunted Robinson by telling him that when he returned to work, he would be forced to do an office job to keep him off the streets. When the injured man realised that the senior detective was only jesting, there was general laughter.

Morgan then presented him and his small family with three tickets to attend the Pratchett and Goodfellow Circus, when Robinson was fit and well again, which made their daughter's eyes light up.

"Finally, it appears that all our recent work has been successfully accomplished," the Chief Superintendent remarked, "So let's all drink to the next escapade awaiting us." He then produced from his person, four small shot glasses and a half bottle of Scotch whiskey he'd managed to smuggle into the hospital.

"How are your piles now, sir?" Robinson thoughtlessly enquired.

The look he received from the Welshman would have sunk a fleet of ships and he immediately followed up by quietly apologising.

"No matter, Robbo, the missus has finally persuaded me to go under the knife and I'm off to see the sawbones in the morning.

Rayner regarded that as excellent news but refrained from passing any comment. He just caught Jack Robinson's attention and surreptitiously winked at him.

Morgan then made mention of the murder of Raymond Carter, asking why it was that the couple had disappeared to Switzerland as soon as the Chief Inspector began to make enquiries with them.

"I initially thought, quite wrongly, that Margaret Plumb wanted to take her husband away to prevent him from finding out about her previous relationship with Sir Reginald Hammond, but it is now obvious she wanted to get their son,

Jackson, away from the home in case we discovered his existence. I will never understand why people regard their own children as an embarrassment.”

“Well, my old mucker, position and pride sometimes tends to corrupt their views on what life is really about, but it seems she still might have a future, and that son of theirs, but I cannot see the old man outliving his sentence in Highgate.”

Jack Robinson looked across at his wife and whispered, “What a complex and devious life, these aristocrats lead.”

“Well Robbo,” Morgan quipped, “You know what they say, when they have money, they always want more.”

“Yes sir, and that’s why I’m glad we are poor.”

Rayner just smiled in silence, proud to work with such colleagues as these two.

About the Author

John Plimmer was a high-profile Detective Superintendent with West Midlands Police during which time he investigated over thirty murders, all of which were detected. He studied Law and Philosophy at Birmingham University and has been a feature writer for both the Sunday Mercury and Evening Mail newspapers. Plimmer has also written numerous articles published in various magazines, and has been involved in script writing for some of television's most popular dramas.
He is a prolific novelist and to date has over seventy books published. Some of his works include 'Brickbats and Tutus' - the biography of Julie Felix, Britain's first black ballerina, and Backstreet Urchins – a humorous account of life in the Birmingham slums of post war Britain.
The eight book 'Dan Mitchell' series involves international espionage and murder, and his popular Victorian Detective Casebook series describes the adventures of Richard Rayner and Henry Bustle of Scotland Yard.

Other published books by the same author in the Victorian Detective's series
include:

The Victorian Case Review Detective
The Graveyard Murders
A Farthing for a Life
The Bullion Train Robbery
Rayner's Ripper
The Fourteenth Victim
The Pie Man
25 Augustus Street
Murder and Revolution
Life and Death – The Final Torment
The Seven Daughters of Diongenes
Fire & Brimstone
The Richter Claim
The Black Mamba
The Daisy Chain Murders
Morgan's Revenge – the sequel to The Daisy Chain Murders
The Warwickshire Assassin
The Secret of Annie Crockett
Bloody Retribution